THE VISIONS OF
RANSOM LAKE

Center Point
Large Print

Also by Marcia Lynn McClure and available from Center Point Large Print:

Dusty Britches
Weathered Too Young
The Windswept Flame

**This Large Print Book carries the
Seal of Approval of N.A.V.H.**

THE
VISIONS OF
RANSOM LAKE

Marcia Lynn McClure

CENTER POINT LARGE PRINT
THORNDIKE, MAINE

This Center Point Large Print edition
is published in the year 2017 by arrangement with
Distractions Ink.

The text of this Large Print edition is unabridged.
In other aspects, this book may vary
from the original edition.
Printed in the United States of America
on permanent paper.
Set in 16-point Times New Roman type.

ISBN: 978-1-68324-313-7

Library of Congress Cataloging-in-Publication Data

Names: McClure, Marcia Lynn, author.
Title: The visions of Ransom Lake / Marcia Lynn McClure.
Description: Center Point Large Print edition. | Thorndike, Maine :
Center Point Large Print, 2017.
Identifiers: LCCN 2016056405 | ISBN 9781683243137
    (hardcover : alk. paper)
Subjects: LCSH: Large type books.
Classification: LCC PS3613.C36 | DDC 813/.6—dc23
LC record available at https://lccn.loc.gov/2016056405

To Patsy,
My angel-friend . . .
For our beloved intrigue
with silver queens and old things.

THE VISIONS OF
RANSOM LAKE

CHAPTER ONE

"Oh, Vonnie, this is so exciting! Just think . . . we're out west! Really west like we've only read about. We're actually here!"

"Hush, Vaden. For pity's sake, hush! My head is pounding from your endless chatter," Yvonne Valmont sighed, placing a weary finger to her even wearier temple.

"But, Vonnie, just look at this land. At the space! Gaze on the beauty of that horizon," Vaden exclaimed, marveling at the beautiful, white, fluffy clouds drifting across the bluest of blue sky. "It's as if . . . as if our spirits can breathe out here! And when we get to Aunt Myra and Uncle Dan's little town . . . well, they're sure to have quaint little town socials and pumpkin patches and enormous red barns and quilting bees and cowboys and . . ." Vaden rambled as she gazed dreamily out the stagecoach window.

"And gunmen and bank robbers and wells instead of pumps and plumbing and bedbugs and horse manure in the middle of the street," Yvonne added with a prominent tone of sarcasm.

But Vaden Valmont was undaunted. Nothing or no one, not even her prim and proper, ever-apathetic older sister, Yvonne, could squelch her enthusiasm about the journey they were taking and the exciting life experience surely awaiting them. So she smiled and shook her head as her sister frowned in irritation and closed her eyes.

"Oh, Vonnie, you have no appreciation of nature's beauty, no sense of exploration or adventure, no dreams." Turning her attention once more to the landscape outside the stagecoach, Vaden sighed and added, "How can you enjoy life with such a dreary attitude toward existence?" The stage rattled on, and Vaden endeavored to keep her excitement to herself.

It was true Vaden cherished her sister, Yvonne—adored, admired, and loved her. But Vaden could never quite understand Yvonne's often rather pessimistic attitude toward the simple joys of living. It was Vaden's opinion Yvonne was far too concerned with propriety and far too incessantly worried about the serious concerns in life. She felt Yvonne spent much too much of her time laboring over her own appearance. It was true Yvonne was a profound beauty, and she labored diligently to present herself as such. However, Vaden thought it a waste of life to agonize over endeavoring to appear so flawless. She preferred to spend more time in studying other people, not having other people study her. People were interesting to Vaden, and this trip she and her sister were making west, to live new experiences and meet different people, seemed far beyond fascinating to her.

The new scents and the freshness of the unfamiliar dry air of the western United States sent Vaden's imagination whirling with excitement. As she watched the passing trees, weeds, and wildflowers from the stagecoach window, she thought again of how magnificent it was to travel far from home to a different place. The very idea of it was truly romantic! Yet as Yvonne squealed and angrily brushed a large black-and-yellow spider from her sleeve, Vaden sighed, disappointed at her sister's inability to simply enjoy the novelty of their adventure.

"My darlin's!" Myra Valmont sighed. She dramatically put a hand to her chest as she watched her two lovely nieces descending from the stagecoach. "My own girls! How . . . how lovely you've grown to be! I half-expected to see you two still in braids and stockin's."

Yvonne stepped down first. Gracefully descending the stagecoach steps, she hugged her aunt affectionately. "Vaden should still be dressed in braids and short skirts, Auntie Myra, but I'm quite grown up. Don't you think?" she asked. Yvonne did not intend to appear greatly conceited. It was simply her naive, sometimes tactless manner. She did, at times, have a playful aspect to her nature kith and kin to her sister's, in fact. However, in public she rarely displayed it.

Myra shook her head in delighted disbelief

as she took Yvonne's lovely face in her hands, marveling at the girl's beauty. Yvonne was tall and slender, nearly as tall as Myra. Her raven black hair was boosted high and impeccably styled, and her hat sat atop her head with just the perfect pitch and angle. Her eyes were the deepest of browns and her fair complexion flawlessly free from freckle or blemish of any sort.

"You're an angel," Myra agreed. "A livin' angel! I can already see the string of poor broken-hearted boys you'll leave behind you here, Vonnie." Yvonne's brown eyes sparkled with flattered delight.

"Auntie Myra! Auntie!" Vaden called as she stood perched in the stagecoach doorway.

Myra Valmont released Yvonne and looked up to see her younger niece exit excitedly from the conveyance in a solitary leap from coach to ground. The small, awkward stage steps had been completely ignored, replaced by one hurdle of youthful exuberance. Vaden rushed forward, throwing her arms tightly around her aunt's neck, and Myra laughed. "Dear Vaden. As cheerful and carefree as always. Now *you* haven't changed all that much, have you?"

"I take offense, Auntie," Vaden claimed, though still smiling and obviously elated. Her dark green eyes twinkled brightly as she continued, "You think Vonnie an angel, but in me you see no change?"

Myra shook her head. "Oh, I see that you've grown. I only meant you . . . your spirit is unchanged. And *that,* my other angel, is a heavenly thing." Myra marveled at how Vaden had changed, however. Her striking nut-brown hair was pulled up, but not nearly as perfectly and neatly as her sister's. Vaden's complexion was smooth and faultless too, but a bit darker than her sister's, and Myra had no doubt Yvonne took greater care to protect her porcelain skin from the sun. Vaden was smaller by several inches, and it emphasized her appearing younger and less poised. Myra could only smile at the girl. Secretly, she had always favored Vaden. Vaden's eyes flashed with a deep love of life, and Myra was completely invigorated by merely being in her company, tasting the joy exuded by her spirit.

"Let's get you two settled in. Your Uncle Danny is out just now, but when he gets back he'll be glad to see you here safe and sound. Oh, I've such plans, girls! And I know you'll like it out here. I know you will," Myra assured them.

Then the attention of all three was arrested by a wet, mucking sound. Yvonne looked down to see her freshly polished boots ankle-deep in a pile of soft, moist, brownish lumps. She sighed and said, "You see, Vaden, horse manure."

Vaden clamped one hand over her mouth to suppress the wild giggle begging release. Yvonne glared at her. Myra made no effort to hide her amusement and laughed out loud. The song of Myra's delightful laughter could cheer even the coldest of hearts, and Yvonne, proper and serious-minded though she tended to be, giggled at the humor of the situation as well.

Myra dabbed at the mirthful moisture in her eyes and sighed. "Oh, Yvonne, you do need to watch your step a bit more carefully hereabout. But you'll love it, you'll see."

Soon after, having changed to more comfortable day dresses, Vaden and Yvonne sipped tall glasses of refreshment as they sat at a small table inside the general mercantile. Their Uncle Dan and Aunt Myra owned the mercantile, and both girls smiled contentedly as they listened to their aunt's plans to add a dress shop in one of the back rooms.

"I know we can do it, girls," Myra assured them. "You two are excellent seamstresses. It comes from your mother's diligence, no doubt. And I'm a fair hand myself. There have been so many new people move into the county, and I just know we can tempt the ladyfolk around here. Oh, I've such ideas! And besides, your Uncle Danny's leg is givin' him so much trouble these days. We really do need the help in the store. There've been times lately when I can hardly keep up with the customers."

"Mother knew we would be a help to you, Aunt Myra. That's why she let us come," Yvonne reminded.

"I only wish we never had to go back," Vaden sighed. Standing, she strolled dreamily to the open door looking out onto the road. "I think I should have been born here."

Myra chuckled. "You may not think so for very long, Vaden. It's hard work that's needed out here."

"Hard work is good for people, Auntie. It keeps their bodies strong and their minds busy. It's what God intended. 'Idle hands,' you know," Vaden stated.

"Vaden would not see a gray cloud were she standing in the midst of a hurricane, Auntie," Yvonne said as she smiled at her sister. Yvonne secretly admired Vaden's positive manner. She worried about it too, for she feared one day there would be something to blacken Vaden's happy heart.

"That's why Vonnie and I love each other so dearly, Auntie. We balance each other. She helps me to keep my feet on the ground, and I help her to have an occasional glimpse of the sky," Vaden explained, teasingly wrinkling her nose at Yvonne.

Myra laughed and shook her head. "Oh, I knew you girls would do me good. It's goin' to be a wonderful year. I know I'll just wither up and die when you leave at the end of next summer."

"Then don't think of it now, Auntie. It's an entire twelve months off in the distance, and I . . ."

Vaden stopped midsentence, her attention suddenly arrested by an approaching buckboard—rather, by the person driving the fine-looking team pulling it. "Now, there's an intriguing-looking character," she mused aloud. Yvonne and Myra both rose and went to the door, their eyes following Vaden's gaze down the road.

"Character is exactly it," Myra confirmed. "Well, girls . . . there you have it. The county hermit," she announced, nodding in the direction of the approaching buckboard and its driver.

"Quit staring, Vaden! I swear, you have no manners," Yvonne scolded, trying to shift her own attention from the vision. But Vaden could not tear her gaze away and continued to stare curiously as the team pulled the buckboard closer to the store.

The man driving the horses sat tall in his seat. He was dressed in very worn blue jeans, a tattered-looking white shirt from which the sleeves had been completely torn away at the shoulder seams, and a hat far beyond having any resemblance of its original shape. His hair was sable-black, hanging well past his shoulders, and a dense black beard with auburn streaks now and again hung nearly to his chest. The deepest of irritated, questioning frowns furrowed his brow. His expression intimidated even the likes of Vaden, who found it rare to be unsettled by any human being.

Still, for all the stranger's menacing appearance, as his buckboard leveled with the doorway in which they stood, Vaden was further intrigued when Myra waved a friendly hand and called, "Good afternoon, Mr. Lake." The man reined in his team, rather unwillingly it seemed, and nodded toward Myra. "And what brings you to town today, Ransom? Will you be comin' into the mercantile later?" she inquired.

Vaden could not help herself. She continued to stare, mesmerized by the stranger. Yvonne's elbow was near to breaking one of her ribs with its firm nudging.

In response to Myra's question, the stranger simply shrugged his shoulders. His gaze fell to Yvonne, lingering only a moment before returning inquisitively to Myra.

"These are my nieces, Ransom. They've come to help us out for the year. This is Yvonne," Myra explained, pointing to her eldest niece, who nodded cordially. The man's responding nod was hardly conceivable. "And this is young Vaden."

The stranger's gaze then moved to Vaden, who thought her knees might fail her as the intensity of the odd, light gray tint of his eyes studied her. His fixed attention on her made her feel as if he were reading her thoughts, silently gathering every secret she hid within the deepest regions of her heart. It was almost as if the privacy of her mind

17

had been invaded somehow. It was very rattling to her senses.

Yet she managed a smile and stammered, "Hello." The stranger again offered a barely discernible nod in return. He slapped the lines at his team's back, looked to Myra, and touched the brim of his hat in a gesture of farewell.

The three women stood silent in the doorway watching the peculiar man until he turned his team at a nearby corner and was out of view.

"I hope he's the only one of those around, Auntie," Yvonne said, releasing the nervous breath she had been holding.

"That he is, darling. A sad, strange man. Keeps completely to himself. Hardly ever utters a word, and when he does you can hardly tell what he's saying through all that beard. He lives on a place up in the mountains, but he owns a farm about a mile east too. Hardly ever works it though. I think he prefers the seclusion the mountains give him," Myra explained.

Vaden still stared at the corner around which the stranger had disappeared. "Has he been that way his entire life, Auntie? Or does he have some deep, painful, recent tragedy that keeps him in hiding?"

"Who knows?" Sighing, Myra waved her hand, gesturing ignorance as to the answer. "I've no idea even how old he is. Could be twenty . . . could be a hundred. Like I said, I don't think anyone's ever seen him clean-shaven. He's lived here goin' on about nine or ten years though. He seems a nice enough man. He's always polite and one of the first to help whenever there's trouble. I remember when that twister went through a couple of years back. It tore up a farmhouse near his, and he let the young family that had lost their home live in the house on his land until they were able to rebuild. He did a lot of the work his own self too, as I recall."

"He gives me the utter willies," Yvonne muttered, returning to the interior of the store.

Vaden smiled. A mystery! Only one hour into arriving for their adventurous year and already a mystery at hand. Something inside of her leapt with anticipation. Her mind began to burn, visualizing potential circumstances. A criminal, perhaps? Hiding out in this small western town? The possibilities were endless in Vaden's imagination.

"You two girls must be completely tuckered out," Myra observed, interrupting Vaden's musing. "Why don't you both lie down and rest for awhile before dinner? Your uncle will be home any minute, and you'll feel more like visitin' after a nap. And besides, there's a social tomorrow night, and I don't want my gorgeous girls going with dark circles under their eyes."

"A nap? Auntie, really!" Vaden still gazed down the road where the stranger had disappeared around the corner. "We're no longer toddlers." Then, realizing of what else her aunt had informed them, she turned to her and excitedly asked, "A social? Will everyone be there?"

"I expect so." Myra smiled. She loved the look of excitement in Vaden's eyes.

"How fun! We'll get to meet everyone, Vonnie!" Vaden took hold of Yvonne's hands and spun about in a circle.

"Have mercy on me, Vaden! It's only a social." Yvonne smiled with delight, however, unable to hide her own enthusiasm.

"How can I possibly nap, Auntie?" Vaden squealed. "How can I possibly sleep with all of this going on?"

"All of what going on?" Myra chuckled, pleased at Vaden's exuberance.

"All of . . . all of . . . all of *this!*" Releasing her sister's hands, Vaden threw her arms out to her sides and twirled around merrily. "A quaint mercantile. Townsfolk. Mysterious hermits with no sleeves on their shirts. All of it! It's too exciting!"

"Well, maybe. But stage rides are tiresome all the same, sweet pea. I swear my bones ached for a week after my last visit out to see you and your folks."

Yvonne nodded in agreement. "Well, Vaden may think the dirt out on the street and the unkempt men in it are the most interesting things in the world . . . but I for one am weary. I think I will lie down, Aunt Myra. But be sure to wake me when Uncle Dan gets home."

"Of course, sweetie."

Vaden's shoulders drooped, her zest having once again been dampened by the lack of enthusiasm of others. Turning halfheartedly, she followed her sister as she walked to the hallway at the front of the mercantile, which led to the house. "I guess it would help me to perk up a bit," she muttered.

"As if you ever need more perking up, baby sister," Yvonne teased.

However, as Vaden lay on her bed staring up at the strong wooden beams of the ceiling, she could not keep her mind from returning to contemplation of the odd hermit-man who had ridden past the store. His name was Ransom Lake. She knew she would never forget so unusual a name. And there was something about him, something mysterious and fascinating. His eyes, for one thing. They were so unsettling! When his stormy gray gaze rested on her, it had felt to Vaden as if he looked directly into her soul for a moment. She nearly convinced herself that were she to meet him face-to-face, she would indeed see tiny gray storm clouds floating midst the rain color around his pupils. She was wildly curious about so many things concerning him. She wondered why a man would intentionally rip the sleeves from his shirt as it appeared he had done.

She wondered how a man could tolerate so much hair covering his head and face. She wondered why he was so reclusive. Did he hold some great secret cached away in the depths of his heart? Was he indeed a criminal hiding from the law to avoid stretching his neck from a rope?

She hoped desperately he would visit the store that evening. Then she could get a really good look at him. Oh, she told herself it would be hard not to stare, and she must be shrewd in her visual investigation of him. It would not do for him to sense any hint of her curiosity about him.

"Vonnie?" Vaden whispered then, rolling over on her side and looking across the room to where Yvonne lay sleeping on her own bed. "Vonnie? Are you awake? I can't sleep."

"For pity's sake, Vaden," Yvonne whined. "Let me rest. I know your mind is a whirlwind of excitement and questions . . . but I really do want to—"

"Isn't this all just too exciting? I can hardly keep still! Just think of the experiences we're bound to ave out here. Experiences that will help shape who we become and how we—"

"Vaden!" Yvonne almost snapped, turning to face her sister. "I am tired. Go for a walk or something if you can't let me rest. Go out into this dusty, spider-infested world and see the sights of the town. You're sure to find something to interest you."

"I'm sorry." Vaden knew she could be terribly over verbal most of the time, and she was not angry at Yvonne for being irritated with her. She rose from her bed, smoothing her skirt. "You're right. I'll leave you to rest. Goodness knows you'll need it if you're to remain patient with me for our first few days here."

"What are you doin' up, dear?" Myra asked as Vaden entered the mercantile. "I thought you were restin' with Yvonne."

"My body can't rest when my mind is running faster than the wind, Auntie," Vaden expressed with a dramatic, breathy whisper. "I'm just so entirely excited to be here. There's something in the very air, Auntie. My life will change somehow because of this visit. I can feel it in my heart. I can feel it in the depths of my very soul."

Myra smiled at Vaden, amused at her niece's theatrics. "Well, why don't you find something to do? A walk maybe."

"Ah, yes! A walk. Fresh air for the lungs and food for the mind!" Vaden sighed happily, leaving by way of the mercantile front door.

At her leisure, she meandered down the main thoroughfare of town. She passed a blacksmith's shop, a barber, a feed and seed store, and several other businesses, all very quaint and interesting in their simplicity. However, when she at last came to the corner around which the wagon carrying the mysterious Ransom Lake had disappeared,

23

something impish gained control of her will. She felt her body turn and start down the dusty road. As she walked along, the town fell farther and farther behind, and she didn't care, for the sights to be seen on the roadside were visions of fantasy to Vaden.

As she left the last building of town behind her, an enormous pumpkin patch, of such vast dimensions that she could not have begun to guess at the number of pumpkins, stretched nearly as far as she could see on either side of the road. Some of the pumpkins, already a stunning shade of orange, were peeking out from under large green leaves. She bit her lip, thinking a small child could easily become lost among the vines searching for just the perfect pumpkin to carve into a jack-o'-lantern on October 31. She would have to ask her Aunt Myra who owned the patch and if the owner sold the pumpkins. She had to own one, just the right one! She would search for it herself until she found her perfect pumpkin. What fun it would be, wading through the mounds of vine and pumpkin. Vaden felt awash with delight at such a beautiful sight as the simple pumpkin patch and at the idea harvest would soon be upon Myra and Dan's world. She thrilled at the thought of being witness to it.

Sighing with delight, she spoke aloud the words of a poem she'd once read, " 'And midst the blue of heaven's sky, the orange of sun's set drawing nigh, doves fair and white amid it fly, with plumming purples drifting by . . . a kiss is born of you and I.' " The verse had simply popped into her mind as verse often did when Vaden felt inspired.

Vaden loved to memorize and recite fragments of descriptive poetry. It was her opinion that particular phrases compounded the beauty of nature and romance, such wordings keeping the resplendence of loveliness fresh in one's mind. Closing her eyes for a moment, she inhaled deeply of the untainted country air, savoring its freshness and letting the beauty of Mother Earth lift her spirits to even loftier heights than before.

When at last she reached the final boundary of the immense patch of pumpkins, she recognized the leaves, vines, and large ripening ovals of a watermelon patch. Though this parcel of land was not as vast as the pumpkins had been, still it was tremendous. As the rather wicked inclination to taste the ripening fruit without asking rose foremost to her mind, Vaden reminded herself inwardly her mother would definitely consider it an act of thievery were she to snitch one of the lovely melons. Smiling, she remembered a time when she and Vonnie were children and sat at their Uncle Dan's knee mesmerized by the tales he would tell about "snitchin' watermelon" as a boy.

As Vaden walked on, admiring the wildflowers flourishing in the uncultivated areas along the road, she noticed wagon ruts to her right. It was obviously a well-traveled path, though not well-traveled enough to have created an actual and easily traversed road. Knowing full well she could not simply continue following after Ransom Lake (for she might actually meet up with him and have to offer an explanation of her presence), she turned down the wheel-rutted path and walked on.

To her profound delight, perhaps half a mile down the path, she came upon the most enchanting vision of a brook. There before her, winding its way along, perhaps twenty feet in width, and lined on either side by large cotton-woods and maples, was a clear, gurgling creek. A quaint and rickety-looking bridge arched over it nearby. She immediately ran to it, stepping onto its squeaking boards tentatively. The bridge's railing seemed sturdy enough, and she leaned on it, peering down into the clear water flowing beneath. There were water spiders, minnows, rocks, and moss, and in the silence of the secluded area, the ramble of the brook sounded like the music of heaven itself.

"This is it," Vaden whispered aloud. All her life, wherever the family had lived, she had needed her own place—a secret, tranquil vicinage of her own where she could escape and think or mourn or simply sit. At home she had found such refuge beneath an ancient lilac tree on the family's property. It was a difficult place to reach, for it required crawling on one's hands and knees through the dirt to reach the open space behind the tree. Its troublesome accessibility was one of the reasons she loved it so. No one, especially Yvonne, was willing to crawl into it to retrieve or bother her. Certainly this brook was more publicly approachable, but her heart loved it immediately, and it was fairly well hidden by the enormous trees along its banks.

Vaden watched a large maple leaf float gently through the air, landing quietly on the surface of the water. It traveled away from her as the water babbled on, and she smiled, knowing autumn was nearly upon this blessed part of the world. Oh, how she loved autumn! To Vaden Valmont, there was nothing so beautiful as the earth in autumn. Reds, yellows, oranges, greens, and even purples captured the leaves of trees, bushes, and vines. The air was crisp and cool and fresh, and apples and pears abounded. She inhaled deeply of the fresh country air and thought of what it must be like to watch harvest erupt in a small western town such as this. Certainly the aroma of baking apples with cinnamon and sugar or pumpkin laced with nutmeg would sweeten the air nearly every evening as women set their pies to cooling on windowsills. No doubt wagons laden heavy with pumpkins would ramble down the road through town when whoever owned the monstrous pumpkin patch began to harvest it. She envisioned a wagon overflowing with ripe, refreshing watermelon ambling awkwardly down the road, an ill-placed melon falling from the wagon and breaking open as it hit the ground. She smiled to herself as she thought of small boys dressed in tattered trousers and dusty shirts rushing to the ruined fruit to snatch up sections of it, dirty or not, and delightedly devouring it without any thought to the sticky juice dripping from their chins and elbows.

Sighing contentedly and glancing at the sun hanging low in the sky, Vaden let her feet carry her from the celestial view of the bridge and its brook and back toward town. She hated to leave the brook and the bridge, the watermelons ripe for snitching, and the marvelous fields of pumpkin. Still, as she turned the corner and saw her Uncle Dan standing on the porch of the mercantile looking down the street in her direction, her heart leapt, and she waved to him.

"Vaden!" he hollered as he hurried to meet her.

Vaden's smile only widened as she watched him lumber happily toward her, his charmingly bowed legs giving him a funny, awkward appearance. His hair was nearly white where it once was dark, and the wrinkles around his merry eyes were plentiful from many years of smiles and laughter.

"Uncle Dan!" she exclaimed as he reached her, at once taking her in his strong and merciless embrace.

He chuckled, his husky voice wonderfully

familiar. "Vaden! You've grown up, girl! Just take a look at ya." Dan held Vaden away from him for a moment as he studied her carefully. "Dang! You can't be that same little girl who used to sneak in on me when I was sleepin' at night and stick beans up my nose."

Vaden laughed and shook her head. "Uncle Dan, you know I was so small then."

"Yeah, I know. But it just weren't too comfortable a way to wake up—them hard ol' lima beans in my nose." They both laughed.

"It just always seemed to me when I was little that people's nostrils were made for more than breathing in and out of," Vaden explained, giggling at the memory of her Uncle Dan shouting as he sat up from a deep sleep and tried to pry the beans out of his nose.

"Oh, child," Dan Valmont sighed as he cupped her face in his roughened hand. His skin was like tough leather, and Vaden liked it that way. "How you've grown. Makes a man feel old, I'll tell ya."

"You'll never grow old, Uncle Dan. You're as handsome as you ever were, same as Daddy."

Dan chuckled and put his arm around Vaden's shoulder. "Let's get on home. Your Aunt Myra will tan our hides if we're late for dinner. She's got apple pie coolin' on the back porch."

Vaden smiled and sighed contentedly. "I've missed you."

"I've missed you too, sweet pea."

• • •

That night after dinner, Vaden and Yvonne sat in the parlor with their aunt and uncle. The day had cooled into a comfortable evening, and the early dusk breezes breathed through the kitchen.

"Aaaahhh," Dan sighed, patting his stomach dramatically. "That was the best pie ya ever done baked, Myra."

Myra smiled and shook her head at the girls. "He says that every time I make a pie."

"Well, I guess ya just get better and better at it, honey," he explained.

Vaden looked over at her sister, who sat busily working on her needlepoint. "It's coming out truly beautiful, Vonnie," she complimented.

"Oh, I don't know. I had to pick a patch out earlier today while you were off wherever you were off to," Vonnie explained, winking teasingly at her sister.

"Well, you're the one who told me to go for a walk, Vonnie," Vaden defended. "And I'm so glad you did. What a pumpkin patch just outside of town, Uncle Dan! Whoever in the world owns it?"

"I figured ya might have found that already, Vaden," Dan chuckled. "That monstrosity belongs to none other than Vaughn Wimber. How he keeps after it, I'll never know. But he's had it out there every year since . . . well, since we been here, ain't that right, Myra?"

"Goodness, yes! It's quite a sight when he starts in to harvestin' those fields." Myra added.

"I can imagine," Vaden agreed.

"What else did you find on your travels, Vaden?" Yvonne asked. "Any handsome young man that might do for a beau for your spinsterly sister? You didn't run into that frightening, hairy recluse man, did you?"

"No. On both accounts," Vaden sighed, disappointment obvious in her tone.

"What frightenin', hairy recluse?" Dan inquired.

"Oh, Ransom Lake rode through town just after the girls arrived today, Danny," Myra explained. "He gave Yvonne quite a fright . . . but I think our little Vaden found him somewhat of an interest."

"He's a good man, that Ransom Lake. I spoke with him just today, in fact. And you'll never believe it, Myra." Dan dropped his voice at his next utterance. "He's movin' into town for the winter."

"No!" Myra exclaimed in a whisper. Her brow wrinkled, and her eyes widened in disbelief.

"True as blue! He's bringin' down his stock and everything this year. Says he has his reasons and that he feels like he's neglected the farm here near town for too long."

"Glory be!" Myra whispered, shaking her head, still obviously astounded.

"Where does he usually stay in winter, Uncle Dan?" Yvonne asked. Vaden smiled, for she could see her sister had laid her needlework aside, indicating her attention was truly arrested by the conversation at hand.

"In the mountains. We usually don't see hide nor hair of the man from October to early May. Not that we can expect to see any more of him when he's here anyway. He's to himself. Likes it that way."

"Why?" Vaden asked simply.

Dan shrugged his shoulders. "Don't know. Could be he's afraid some little character of a girl will be shovin' lima beans up his nose when he's not lookin'." He laughed heartily as Vaden rolled her eyes and sighed, pleased by his memories of her.

"Well, now," Myra began, "you girls keep your mind off ol' Ransom Lake. I got other boys in mind for the two of you."

"Oh, help us all now," Dan mumbled, shaking his head.

"Quit that," Myra scolded, teasingly slapping the man on one thigh. Turning to the girls, she said, "I think any number of our young men hereabouts would make wonderful husbands for you two girls."

"Like who?" Dan asked, unconvinced.

"Like Nathaniel Wimber or Toby Bridges. And that nice Jerome Clayton. Now he's one that'll catch your eye, Yvonne."

"Yvonne and I have quite high expectations

when it comes to beaus, Aunt Myra," Vaden mentioned, smiling lovingly at her aunt.

"Yes. Incredibly high," Yvonne affirmed. "Lofty, in fact."

Myra chuckled and sat back in her chair, smiling as if she held some great secret. "Believe me, I wouldn't let just anybody come acourtin' my nieces."

"Are there nice girls here as well, Auntie?" Vaden asked.

"Yes. We have some very nice young ladies in town. A couple of real cats too. But for the most part, they're all darlin' girls. I'm certain you girls will find some friends hereabouts."

Vaden stared into the fire in the hearth, wondering what kind of friends she would find. All too quickly, however, her thoughts returned to their musing over the oddity of Ransom Lake. He intrigued her. She had seen him only once, but something about him kept bringing her thoughts back to him.

Even as she lay in bed that night looking out through the bedroom window at the bright, shining stars set in the darkened western sky, she thought of him. She wondered again what turned the eccentric Ransom Lake to the life of a hermit. What had squelched the bright star in his soul?

CHAPTER TWO

After a nourishing breakfast of griddlecakes and bacon the next morning, Myra set about teaching Yvonne and Vaden how to tend to the store. There were so many things to be explained—which customers were allowed credit, which weren't, where things were kept, how to work the cash register holding the money, and so forth. Numerous townsfolk came into the mercantile that morning as well. Vaden began to wonder how many of them were visiting just to gawk at Myra Valmont's nieces, for very few purchased any merchandise.

"Oh, some days I guess folks just want to visit, and others we sell a lot of things. Today I think folks are in the visitin' mood," Myra explained.

"I'll never remember everyone's names," Yvonne sighed. There had been so many people in and out of the store in such a very short time even the ever-positive Vaden felt a bit rattled.

"It'll be easier at the social tonight, Yvonne. Faces and names will come together easier then. They always do at get-togethers," Myra said.

"When will we ever find time to successfully stock a dress shop, Auntie?" Vaden asked, for she was indeed quite overwhelmed by all the new faces, new names, and new tasks at hand.

"We'll get to the dress shop eventually." Myra smiled at her niece with understanding. She knew Vaden only longed to be out exploring. She understood how madly Vaden pined for the outdoors and its beauty.

"Sable," Myra greeted as a woman of about her own age approached, accompanied by a handsome young man. "Jerome! How wonderful to see the two of you out today. This is Mrs. Sable Clayton and her son, Jerome, girls."

"How do you do?" Yvonne greeted, taking Mrs. Clayton's offered hand. "I'm Yvonne Valmont, and this is my sister, Vaden." Mrs. Clayton smiled and offered her hand then to Vaden, who shook it, smiling pleasantly.

"I'm Jerome Clayton," the young man informed them. He grinned at Vaden, tipping his hat in a friendly manner before turning and repeating the gesture to Yvonne. Vaden smiled at the charming-looking young man. His hair was blond and his eyes a deep brown. His grin was rather boyish and delightsome, and he was handsome, tall, and well formed. Obviously, he was polite as well. Vaden remembered her aunt mentioning this particular young man the night before, and she could see why she had felt inclined to do so.

"Myra has been so excited about your comin'," Mrs. Clayton confessed. "We thought she was gonna burst at the seams yesterday mornin' at the town meetin' when she announced you two were comin' to stay with her and Dan. It's nice to have some lovely new young ladies in town. This should please all the young bucks hereabouts, shouldn't it, Jerome?"

Jerome nodded in agreement, winking flirtatiously at Yvonne.

Yvonne blushed appropriately and humbly mumbled, "Thank you, Mrs. Clayton."

"Why?" Vaden blurted in forthright honesty. "Aren't there any other girls in town? I truly hope you didn't ask us here just to marry us off, Aunt Myra."

"Vaden!" Yvonne snapped, turning scarlet with embarrassment.

Myra and Mrs. Clayton only chuckled as Myra replied, "No. We didn't ask ya here to marry ya off, Vaden. But . . . if that's what should come of your visit . . . I'd only be too happy to have ya livin' nearby all the time."

Yvonne rolled her eyes, horrified at her sister's behavior as Myra and Mrs. Clayton continued to look amused.

Jerome, however, seemed to sense the unsettled emotions arising between the two sisters. "Well, on behalf of all us 'young bucks' in town . . . I'm just plain delighted to have two such lovely ladies to help beauty up the place."

Though his eyes were firmly set on Vaden, it was Yvonne who responded to his compliment. "Why, you're too charming, Mr. Clayton. If everyone in town is as nice and complimentary as you and your mother, we'll be spoiled rotten before our first day is done."

Jerome continued to stare at Vaden. She cleared her throat uncomfortably and looked to Mrs. Clayton. "May we help you with anything in the mercantile today, Mrs. Clayton? We're only just getting our feet wet, but Yvonne and I like to jump right into new responsibilities and challenges."

Mrs. Clayton opened her small handbag and withdrew a piece of paper. "As a matter of fact, Miss . . . Vaden, is it? There are a few things I've been intendin' to pick up the next time I was in." She handed the paper to Vaden, who smiled, relieved to have a task to remove her from beneath the unnerving stare of Jerome Clayton. He was quite handsome, and it always made Vaden uncomfortable when a handsome man noticed her.

"Leave it to me, Auntie," Vaden chirped, and she went about the store gathering the items on the list.

Though she busily accumulated the things Mrs. Clayton had listed, her attention was arrested immediately when Mrs. Clayton said to her aunt, "Have ya heard that Ransom Lake is moving into town for the winter?"

"Mercy, yes! Danny told me just last night, and I thought surely he had misunderstood. Ransom Lake never winters in town. He hides up there in them mountains, and I don't know why they don't find him just a solid chunk of ice every year come spring," Myra commented.

"It's true, I tell you. My Raymond saw him just this morning over at the blacksmith's. He was telling ol' Manfred Dennis that he'd be needin' some new brandin' irons done up 'cause he planned on bringin' his new heifers down with him, and he's changin' his brand."

Myra shook her head, clicking her tongue in disbelief. "I can't imagine what would've made that man do it. You know how secretive he's always been. Well, this will certainly set tongues to waggin'."

Vaden turned and smiled at her sister, who also smiled in amusement at the tongues already wagging. She was unsettled immediately, however, when her eyes fell to Jerome Clayton to see he still stared at her, grinning and seeming pleased at what he saw. In the next moment, Vaden felt a prickling at the back of her neck, and she involuntarily shuddered. Something in the young man's expression had changed. Hadn't it? She couldn't quite be sure what it was, but for a few moments Vaden felt truly uneasy in his presence. She inwardly told herself it was, as always, her dramatic imagination and returned her attention to the conversation at hand.

"How I'd like to know what's in that man's mind," Sable Clayton muttered. "What made him take to the hills like he did?"

"My guess is tragedy. Pain of some kind," Myra answered. "A man just doesn't live like that without somethin' sending him to it."

Vaden set the items she had gathered on the counter and turned to find a hush had fallen over the room. All eyes, including Jerome's, were turned toward the front entrance to the store. As Vaden herself looked up, her heart began to pound madly with excitement. There in the doorway stood none other than the mysterious Ransom Lake. He nodded slightly in greeting to the onlookers.

Amazingly, Myra found her composure at once. "Mr. Lake! What can I help ya with today?" Vaden knew by the crimson color rising to the face of each and every person in the mercantile, they all were wondering how much of their gossip Ransom Lake heard before they noticed he had entered the building.

The hermit seemed to sense the discomfort in the room and simply mumbled, "Boots," in a lowered voice.

Vaden's eyes fell to the well-worn boots the man wore. She blushed a deeper cherry hue when she looked up to find him staring defiantly at her.

"Well, of course, Ransom," Myra said. "I'm certain you've got a busy day ahead, so I'll just bring out a few pair for ya to look at." She went to a far corner of the room and began rummaging through a variety of footwear.

Vaden could not help but stare at the man. He stood no more than six feet from her, his eyes all the more disturbing. She noticed his long black hair was slightly graying at the temples, and for some odd reason, it appealed to her. It seemed to deepen the mystery prevailing in the very air around him.

"We hear you're planning to winter on your farm in town, Ransom," Jerome stated bluntly.

The hermit nodded.

"It'll be good to have ya here," Jerome added. "It's always helpful to have another man around when a hand is needed with winterin' cattle and such."

"That's a wonderful piece of property you've got out there, Mr. Lake," Mrs. Clayton remarked.

"Thank ya, ma'am," the man mumbled.

"Will any of these do, Ransom?" Myra asked, holding up a pair of large boots in each hand.

Ransom Lake's brow puckered in a thoughtful frown of consideration. "Do ya have any higher up?" he asked. "To just below my knee maybe?"

Vaden was thrilled by something about his voice. Something tantalizing. It was quite deep, and he seemed to mumble his words more than speak them. It was unusually masculine some-how, even if most folks may have considered it impolite. She could only continue to stare at the man, for he was incredibly intriguing! As she had noticed before, the sleeves to his shirt had been torn away at the shoulder seams, and his massively muscled and sun-bronzed arms were no less than astounding, impressive. She had never seen the like! Of course, most men wore sleeves, so their arms weren't publicly displayed as a rule. But she was positive most men's arms hidden beneath proper sleeving were not of the size and perfect formation this man's were. Glancing quickly at Jerome Clayton's sleeves, she was only more convinced of this fact. Ransom Lake was also taller than she had been able to surmise before, and his shoulders were definitely a pair of the broadest she'd ever seen.

"Oh, dear. I'm not sure, Ransom," Myra mumbled. "Why don't ya go ahead and try a pair of these on and I'll have Vaden take a look." Myra handed the pairs of boots she held to the man. He set them down on the floor, removing his own worn ones there in the middle of the store. "Vaden, would you please . . ." Myra began. "Vaden!" Vaden tore her curious gaze from Ransom Lake and looked to her aunt. "Did ya see any other boots that might serve Mr. Lake while you were rearrangin' the boxes this mornin'?"

"Yes," Vaden said quickly, excited somehow at the prospect of being able to help the man. "Yes. I think I did. I'll get them at once." She turned and looked up to the high rows of shelves nearby.

Mrs. Clayton cleared her throat uncomfortably, gathering her purchases and laying her payment on the counter. "Here ya are, Myra. We must be off now, Jerome." She left promptly, taking hold of Jerome's sleeve and pulling on it so he would follow her. Both of them were obviously uncomfortable in the presence of Ransom Lake.

Cowards, Vaden thought as she began to stretch up toward the higher shelves. It irritated her that people were such thoughtless cowards when faced with those they didn't know or understand.

"Oh, for pity's sake, Vaden! Use the stool!" Yvonne whined, having turned to see her unconventional sister scaling the tower of shelves in an effort to reach a particular box of boots placed very high up.

"Be careful, Vaden," Myra gasped. "You'll fall!"

Vaden secured her right foot on another shelf and reached up further, knowing full well her feet were anchored on shelving at least three or four feet from the floor. "I've got it now. Don't worry so, Auntie."

"Vaden Valmont! There is a man present. Get down from there at once! I swear. You have no vision whatsoever of propriety," Yvonne scolded in a loud whisper.

Vaden, realizing she had climbed dangerously high and that Yvonne was founded in some of her scolding, was determined, however, to obtain what she had set out to obtain. Therefore, unaware both her aunt and Ransom Lake stood directly beneath her, she stretched her arm high and began

42

tugging on a boot box with her fingers. "I've got it now. You worry too much, Yvonne. I've just about . . ."

In a last, strenuous effort to clutch a firm hold on the box, Vaden gasped as her other hand, which had anchored her by holding solidly to another shelf, slipped. Instantly, she felt herself falling down and backward. Though she landed with great force, the floor did not feel as hard as she had anticipated. This was, she realized in the very next moment, due to the fact her fall to the floor had indeed been cushioned. She felt strong hands at her waist as Ransom Lake pushed her off his own body and onto the floor beside him. Vaden had fallen from the shelving, knocking Ransom to the floor and landing on him instead. She gasped once more as he sat up in time for the box of heavy boots, tumbling from the high shelf, to hit him squarely on the head.

"I'm . . . I'm so sorry, Mr. Lake," Vaden stammered, horrified as she watched the man put a hand to the top of his head where the box had hit him. He then studied his fingers as if he expected to find blood there from a head wound. "I was only trying to help, and I . . . I didn't stop to think."

"You rarely do, Vaden," Yvonne muttered. Then, sighing, she added, "You could've been hurt and . . . oh, are you all right, Mr. Lake?"

Vaden watched as Ransom Lake stood, brushing

the dust from the seat of his pants before offering a hand to her. Vaden felt a shudder as the angry, intense gray of the man's eyes bored into her own. Feeling completely undignified, humiliated, and juvenile, Vaden took the offered hand. Instantly her senses went whirling, for his touch caused goose bumps to break over her like a rising fever. The man possessed profound physical strength. As he pulled Vaden to her feet, he either over-estimated the weight of the girl or underestimated his own muscle, for his powerful yank on her arm propelled Vaden up and forward with such force that instead of standing gracefully, she stumbled forward, bumping against him. At the same time, she tromped mercilessly on one of his stockinged feet with the heel of her shoe. The man let out a short groan and closed his eyes for a moment before the intensity of their tempestuousness glared at her once more.

"Oh, dear," Vaden heard Myra moan.

Vaden knew Ransom Lake must be in awe of her clumsiness, as well as furious for the damage done him by it. But without a word, he simply bent, picked up the boots that had spilled from their box upon hitting the floor, and pulled them onto his stockinged feet.

"They'll do," he muttered, looking to Myra.

"Are ya sure, Ransom? I mean, I don't want ya to feel obligated—" Myra explained.

"They're fine. How much?"

"Well, after what just happened . . . I don't feel I can accept—"

"How much?"

Vaden dropped her humiliated gaze to the floor as Ransom glanced at her again. Every inch of the surface of her body was crimson. The blush was so thorough it was almost painful.

Myra relented and accepted his payment for the boots. Then he picked up the overly well-worn boots he'd worn into the mercantile and tossed them in the trash barrel near the front door as he started to leave.

"Mr. Lake," Vaden called out. He looked to her again. "I'm truly sorry. It was so terribly clumsy of me and—"

"Yes, Ransom. Accept my apologies as well," Myra interrupted.

The unnerving gaze of the man lingered for a moment on Vaden. He looked from her feet to her head quickly, and Vaden fancied she could almost discern something like a grin beneath his heavy mustache and beard.

"None needed, Myra." With a nod in Yvonne's direction and a finger at the brim of his hat, he left the store.

"Good gravy on the taters, girl!" Myra exclaimed in a lowered voice a moment later. "What on earth possessed ya to—"

"Vaden . . . when will you learn to think before you act so unconventionally?" Yvonne interrupted.

"I was only trying to help," Vaden defended herself. "I'm sorry you both had to endure the humiliation of yet another of my thoughtless antics." Vaden brushed an embarrassed tear from her cheek as another followed. "I'm not you, Yvonne! I don't have your grace and beauty. And sometimes conventional propriety seems so ridiculous to me that I—"

"Now, girls," Myra soothed, "what's done is done. And besides . . . that's the first hint of a grin I've ever seen on that man's face."

Yvonne smiled at her sister and put a reassuring arm about her shoulders. "It *was* terribly funny, Vaden. And I'm sure Mr. Lake will think of it and smile to himself every time he sees you."

Vaden closed her eyes and sighed, further humiliated at the truth of Yvonne's assurance. "Thank you for that, Yvonne. I feel much better," she mumbled sarcastically.

"It's hard for Vaden to be cooped up, Aunt Myra." Yvonne smiled lovingly at her sister. She admired Vaden's spirit and love of life. "Why don't you take a little walk, Vaden? It always helps you to feel better."

"Yes, sweet pea. You go on ahead. It's almost lunch, and then Yvonne can take a little time for herself when you're back." Vaden sniffled, knowing full well she was simply irritating everyone and they were the ones in need of respite.

Without a word, she walked toward the front door. She paused, however. Looking back to see Myra and Yvonne already occupied with something else and not looking in her direction, she reached into the barrel near the front door and retrieved the boots Ransom Lake had discarded there. Her daddy had always said you could tell a lot from a man by studying his boots. Quickly she turned and dashed down the hallway at the front of the store to her room. Bolting the door, she set the boots on the floor, sitting herself down in front of them.

The leather had been good, strong leather at one time, she observed. Still was, in truth. She noticed the straps at the top of the boots used to help the wearer pull them on were nearly torn away from so many days of being tugged at. She took one boot and turned it over, studying the sole intently before turning the other boot over and comparing its sole. "He's left-handed," she muttered. The left boot was in much worse shape than the right. The toe was torn away, the sole was nearly worn through, and the heel was worn shorter. It had a blackened area at the ball of the foot, and Vaden surmised this was the boot used to kick out coals from fires. Then, hurriedly, she unlaced her own boots and slipped her tiny feet into the cavities of Ransom Lake's abandoned ones.

"Never judge a man 'til you've walked a mile in

his shoes," she whispered. Clunking around the room several times, she thought about the boots and their owner. These were boots owned by a driven and hard-working man, boots that had walked, ridden, climbed, waded, and run. But the left boot was uncomfortable on one side of her calf. Reaching down, she felt a sheath had been fashioned inside, and she withdrew a large pocketknife. She held the knife up to inspect it better and was intrigued to see an inscription along one side.

"Denver S. Lake," she read aloud. *"Leadville, Colorado."* She had heard of Leadville, the little town in Colorado that had grown into a rich silver bonanza. " 'Silver lines the clouds above. Reflects like rain, is rare as love,' " she recited. She had never liked the particular badly written line of poetry until that moment. Turning the knife over, she mused aloud, "Denver? Not Ransom." Then she gasped as she realized Ransom Lake was certain to remember he had left the knife in his old boots and would no doubt return looking for it. What if he already had? What if he had returned to find his old boots gone from the barrel in her uncle's store?

Removing the boots, she shoved them under her bed and put on her own once more. Then, clutching the knife securely in one hand, she dashed out into the mercantile to find it thankfully empty except for Yvonne and her aunt.

"I thought ya were out walking," Myra mumbled with a puzzled expression.

"I . . . I had to put something away," Vaden answered. "But I'm going now." Without pausing for further conversation, she hurriedly left the store, walking down the street in the direction she had seen Ransom Lake go. As if fate had intended it, he appeared suddenly, having just exited the blacksmith's establishment.

"Mr. Lake!" Vaden called, waving when he turned and looked at her. Immediately, she froze as the unnerving color of his eyes settled intently on her. How would she explain the knife being in her possession? She couldn't simply approach him saying, *I stole your boots from the trash barrel and found this within.* When she made no move to approach him, Ransom Lake strode determinedly toward her. So entirely determined did he seem that Vaden took two steps backward as he approached, for he was ever so intimidating.

"I-I . . ." she stammered as he came to stand before her, his stormy eyes glaring at her from beneath long, dark lashes. "I-I . . . found this in the trash barrel after you had gone." Slowly she held out her hand to him, opening it to reveal the pocketknife sitting on her trembling palm.

Ransom Lake looked down at the knife, his eyes returning to Vaden's and narrowing as he reached out and snatched it quickly from her hand. Vaden looked to the ground where her foot began to kick at a pebble. "I-I would also like to apologize for . . . for my fall and for injuring you. I truly am sorry."

The man made no audible sound to indicate he was accepting her apology, so she looked up to see him still glaring at her. "I said I am sorry, Mr. Lake."

Still he said nothing, only stood staring at her.

Vaden felt the hot blush of humiliation rising to her cheeks. How dare he stare at her so, making not the slightest gesture of offering any forgiveness? "Mr. Lake," Vaden began sternly, "I have apologized to you. A gentleman does not stand silent at such an offering. Even a nod would be more acceptable than your simply standing there glaring at me."

"I'm no gentleman, Miss Valmont," he mumbled. The deep, somehow sultry intonation of his voice as he spoke her name gave Vaden cause to pause as goose bumps enveloped her arms and legs. Vaden struggled to quickly regain her composure.

"Yes, you are," she stated. He frowned, obviously surprised at her arguing. "You can hide away in the mountains and grow all the hair you want to try to hide yourself from the world, Mr. Lake, but it doesn't fool me. You were not raised to be a heathen."

Then she gasped, horrified, as the man reached forward, taking her chin brutally in one hand. He bent toward her, and she felt the warmth of his breath on her face as he growled, "You don't know anything about how I was raised, girl. I am a heathen. A man cursed with afflictions and burdens that a child like you could never even imagine. If you're some overbearin' missionary-type with wild aspirations of savin' my soul . . . don't waste your time."

Reaching up, Vaden grasped the man's nose tightly between her thumb and index finger. "Let go of my face!" she demanded. Stunned at her own actions, she was determined not to let him know how horribly she was intimidated. The tumultuous gray eyes glaring at her widened in astonishment, but he did not release her. Pinching his nose tighter, Vaden repeated her demand. "Let go of my face, Mr. Lake."

"Let go of my nose, girl," he barked, but his grasp on her chin did not tighten. The fact he did not try to cause her further discomfort whispered to Vaden her instincts were right about this man. Her soul sensing this, she felt there was no further reason to provoke him, and she released him. An instant later, he dropped his hand from her chin.

Vaden cleared her throat, straightened her spine and, smoothing her skirts as she met Ransom Lake's steel glare, she repeated, "Again, I apologize for my clumsiness this afternoon in the store, Mr. Lake."

"Forgiven," he growled.

Vaden nodded, turned, and began walking away.

"Thank you," he called out, causing her to stop and turn toward him once more, "for the knife. It's important to me."

Suddenly, Vaden felt guilty for treating him so harshly. "You're welcome. I'm glad I could return it to you." Then she watched as Ransom Lake tucked the knife into his new boot before she turned away from him once more.

"That was a quick walk," Myra greeted as Vaden entered the mercantile only minutes after she had originally left. "But your cheeks are rosy once again, so it must have done the trick."

"*Quite* rosy," Yvonne commented somewhat suspiciously as she studied her sister for a moment with the curiosity of a cat.

"Yes. I suppose so. The . . . um . . . the breeze was very invigorating." Vaden tucked one fist firmly beneath her chin as she leaned on her elbows over the counter and smiled up at her sister and aunt. "Thank you for having us here, Auntie."

"Oh, sweet pea," Myra cooed affectionately, "thank you for coming."

"I'm home, girls! I'm home!" Vaden, Yvonne, and Myra turned to see Dan enter the store. "I'm home, and I'm ready for the social." he announced. Vaden giggled as her dear, bowlegged uncle began to perform something akin to a jig on the wood-planked floor beneath his feet. "I've been practicin' my dancin' all the day long, girls! Ain't I the purty boy?"

"For pity's sake, Danny! Settle yourself down. What if customers should come in?" Myra laughed.

"Then I'll show 'em how it's done!" Dan hollered as he swept Vaden into his arms and began dancing about the room with her. "It reaches my big ol' ugly ears that you've already captured one young man's heart in town, sweet pea!"

Vaden felt her heart leap in her chest. "I have? You mean he—"

"You bet ya! That slick feller Jerome Clayton has already got every young man for miles ready to beat down your door! I expect they'll be havin' to go through him first though." Dan stomped his feet even harder as he danced.

"Oh," Vaden muttered. And then she beat herself mentally for even allowing Ransom Lake's name to jump into her mind when her uncle had said what he did.

"Oh? Every female under the age of thirty and unmarried has been tryin' to catch that boy for near two years now, and all you can say is, 'Oh'?" Dan looked to Myra and shrugged his shoulders.

"Leave it to Vay not to realize a blessing when she sees it," Yvonne sighed, smiling at her sister.

"It's all right, darlin'. I understand. Not every man in the world can be as good-lookin' as me!"

Vaden smiled again then, and her uncle added, "Besides, ya gotta make sure a man's got the right nostrils for bean storage."

With that, Vaden was further amused and joined her uncle wholeheartedly in the happy romp around the room.

Yvonne looked the very image of perfection! As Vaden awkwardly climbed down from the wagon, she turned and watched Yvonne alight gracefully. Her sister's dark hair was perfectly piled, darling little ringlets cascading everywhere about her face, neck, and shoulders. Yvonne walked into the town hall with an air of grace and dignity only the finest women could master. Her dress of peacock blue was dazzling, and Vaden lagged behind her some distance, for she felt dowdy and plain in her sister's presence. She wished she had preceded her sister into the town hall so when Yvonne did enter, the crowd within gasping in awe, she could straighten her shoulders, showing her pride in her sister's beauty.

Vaden's own dress was scarlet and extremely becoming. It complemented her perfectly curved figure and caused her eyes to look all the more as if tiny, sun-glint diamonds had been sprinkled about in them. Vaden was completely unaware of the fact she outshone her sister's grace and beauty. Vaden's delight with life blessed her with modesty. It shone plainly in her already beautiful countenance, enhancing the loveliness of the young woman beyond description.

"I hate that I look better in scarlet than blue," Vaden mumbled to her aunt as they entered the hall. "See, Auntie. Everyone's staring at me wondering how a beautiful, tropical bird like Yvonne could have such a clumsy, ridiculous-looking sister. See how they stare?"

Myra took Vaden's lovely lace-gloved hand, patting the back of it tenderly and sighing. "Oh, sweet pea. Humility becomes the most beautiful of women all the more."

Almost immediately, Yvonne and Vaden found themselves nearly pounced upon by eight or ten bachelors of rather varied ages. Yvonne, immediately flattered, captivated them with her charms. Vaden almost deplored their attentions, knowing full well the group of young ladies standing nearby would only resent the Valmont girls attracting such attentions from the men.

As the group of admirers surrounding Yvonne began to introduce themselves to her, the group of young bucks around Vaden did the same.

"Toby Bridges, Miss Valmont," one almost attractive, dark-haired young man said, extending his hand to Vaden.

"Vaden Valmont. I'm so glad to meet you," Vaden replied, smiling politely.

"Nathaniel Wimber, Miss Vaden," another dark-haired young man offered.

"Mr. Wimber," Vaden acknowledged. She glanced at the group of young women to her right. Yes, they were irritated to say the least. One young, browned-haired girl in particular seemed to be glaring at her.

"And ya haven't forgotten me, have ya, Miss Vaden?"

Vaden looked up to see the flirtatious grin of Jerome Clayton affixed on her. Immediately, Vaden was unnerved. Somehow this particular young man unsettled her. But being polite was of the utmost importance at social gatherings, and Vaden knew it.

Therefore, she forced a friendly smile and politely offered, "Of course not, Mr. Clayton. How delightful to see you." Then, glancing at the on looking young ladies again, she added, "Would you excuse me please? I'd like to meet some of these ladies over here." Mustering every ounce of courage she could find within herself, Vaden walked away from the doting young men and toward the circle of gossiping young ladies. "Hello," she greeted. At first, she was met by only startled expressions. "I'm Vaden Valmont."

"Belva Tibbits," the brown-haired young woman still glaring at her responded. Quickly the girl smiled artificially and offered a gloved hand. Vaden inwardly hoped her feigned friendly smile to Jerome Clayton had looked more believable than did this girl's. Vaden took the offered hand to find it was as limp as a dead fish. This girl would be no friend. Vaden knew it at once.

"I'm Selma Wimber," a cute brunette said with a friendly smile. Her handshake was welcoming and firm. Vaden was hopeful.

"Raylin Wimber," another girl said. The other girls seemed kind as well. Only Belva Tibbits radiated negative emotion. Soon, Vaden found herself accepted by nearly all in the group and was involved in their conversation. They discussed their dresses, all the girls endlessly flattering one another. They discussed their hair and what challenges they had each endured in finding just the right pin-points in styling. And, much to Vaden's expectation, it wasn't long before the youthful, feminine conversation turned to another foreseen topic.

"Jerome Clayton walked me home from the mercantile this afternoon!" Selma exclaimed in a hushed and obviously excited voice.

"Oh, Selma! Really?" another young woman with auburn hair exclaimed softly.

"That's nothin'!" Belva sneered. "I heard Ransom Lake is winterin' in town this year."

"Ransom Lake never winters in town, Belva, and you know it." Raylin was obviously not inclined to believe Belva's announcement.

"I tell ya he is! I heard Mr. Clayton talking to Mr. Dennis this morning. He's movin' to town for the winter. I saw him ridin' toward his farm today." Belva beamed with an irritating air of superiority.

"I bet you're just breathin' heaven, aren't ya, Belva?" Selma turned to Vaden and explained, "Belva has had, uh . . . an interest in a peculiar hermit who has lived in the mountains for years. Personally, I'm scared to death of him."

"Oh, I think he's just not comfortable with people," Vaden blurted. She regretted voicing her opinion that very second, for every pair of female eyes around her arched in surprise.

"Is that so?" Belva's eyes narrowed daringly. "And how is it that you can come to town yesterday and presume to know more about one of our citizens than we do?"

"I-I . . . Mr. Lake came into the mercantile today. He seems nice enough . . . just wary of people. At least that's what it seemed to me." Vaden swallowed hard. Belva already had a way of intimidating her, and she didn't like the feeling.

"You mean . . . you've spoken with him?" Raylin asked, obviously astonished.

"Well . . . yes. I mean, he came into the mercantile today for some boots and—"

"I hardly think you can accurately judge the man's personality by a single conversation with him, Vaden." Belva was obviously irritated. Vaden decided the particular moment to confront this girl was not at the first town social she attended.

"You're right, I'm sure," Vaden surrendered,

smiling apologetically. But deep within her heart, she knew her discernment where Ransom Lake was concerned was accurate.

"Would ya do me the honor of the first dance, Miss Vaden?"

Vaden looked up to see Jerome Clayton's charming smile affixed to her yet again.

"Uh . . . certainly, Mr. Clayton," she accepted politely, placing her hand in the hand he offered to her. She smiled at the group of girls as she left, wondering how many more enemies she had made by being the first girl of the evening to dance with the handsome Jerome Clayton. She would much rather have stayed in the company of the girls. Although her mind hesitated uncertainly when he asked her to dance, Vaden was too polite, too sensitive to the feelings of others, and too kindhearted to refuse him.

"Belva's a pill," was the first thing Jerome said to her as they began to dance. "Ya don't want to rub her the wrong way. But both the Wimber girls are nice. And Julianna Havens and Laurie Cox are sweet too. I see you're makin' friends fast enough."

"Trying," Vaden admitted.

"And apparently you've even softened the likes of Ransom Lake."

Vaden looked up at Jerome astonished. "What do you mean?"

"I saw you talkin' to him this afternoon.

Actually, ya looked pretty put off. But I imagine he can be an exasperatin' man to deal with."

"He bought a new pair of boots. You remember he came in when you were just leaving. Anyway, he accidentally threw a valuable-looking pocket-knife away in our trash barrel. I was returning it to him." Vaden wondered why she felt so guilty. Why did she feel she had to explain her speaking with Ransom Lake to Jerome Clayton?

"That was thoughtful of ya." Jerome smiled again. His smile was charming. Surely Vaden's discomfort toward the man was caused simply by the fact he was handsome and attentive toward her.

"Well, it was the least I could do, especially after the incident when I . . ." Jerome raised his eyebrows, waiting for her to continue. "Well, your mother certainly seems like a wonderful woman. My Aunt Myra speaks very highly of her."

"She is a wonderful woman. And I'm sure you'll find I'm an all right boy . . . even if ya have already picked me out as a flirt." Jerome chuckled and winked at her.

Vaden returned his friendly smile, though out of politeness rather than sincerity, and admitted, "Well, it just unnerves me terribly to have people stare at me. I'm sure you can understand that."

"I ask your forgiveness then, Miss Vaden, for starin' at ya. It's just that you are the most beautiful

60

girl I've ever seen." Jerome continued to smile.

Vaden raised an unconvinced eyebrow. Unlike Yvonne, Vaden did not esteem overbearing flattery as a rule, especially when it was handed out on the occasion of only the second meeting between people. She distrusted a man who would say such things so soon. "You really sprinkle the sugar on thick, Mr. Clayton."

"I think most women like the sugar thick," he whispered.

"Most do." Then giggling, she smiled sincerely at the young man. She had to admit most women did prefer such flattery. Vaden resigned herself to the fact perhaps Jerome Clayton wasn't so different from other young men after all. Perhaps it was just the fact he was new to her, interested in her. Perhaps these were the things making her hesitant and suspicious of him. Still, lingering in the back of her mind was the vision of the odd, bearded hermit from the mountains.

Invariably, all through the evening, Vaden found herself glancing at the entrance to the town hall. Her instincts knew Ransom Lake would not arrive. Still, she hoped he would, if for no other reason than she held a secret wish to simply hear the intriguing tone of his voice once more. But he did not arrive, and Vaden spent the evening dancing with every young man in town, Jerome Clayton most often. He was quite attentive and charming, and Vaden did finally allow herself to inwardly admit he made the evening a pleasant experience for her. The other young women there, with the exception of Belva Tibbits, were also very friendly. Vaden enjoyed talking with them and was all the more glad she and Yvonne had been allowed to stay with their Aunt Myra and Uncle Dan for a time.

"Isn't it grand to be the belles of the ball, Vaden?" Yvonne sighed contentedly as they lay in their beds late that night. "I simply want to wallow in the prideful knowledge that every young man there was purely mesmerized by our presence."

"Vonnie!" Vaden could not abide her sister's vanity at times. Yet at the same time, she felt on Yvonne's part it was warranted.

"Oh, I know, Vaden. You'd have rather been off mucking around in a creek or climbing trees to look in filthy birds' nests." Yvonne turned on her side facing Vaden and propped her elbow on her pillow. "I know the streak of romantic desire is thicker than pudding in you too, Vaden. How can you not be profoundly flattered at all the attention we received tonight?"

"Because . . . because my idea of romance is different than yours, Vonnie." Vaden sat up in her bed and smiled at her sister. Then she looked out the window at the bright, beckoning glimmer of the stars. "You like to have attention—to be flattered and fought over. And I suppose all women do, even me. But I want so much more. I want someone to love me, just me. To be *so* in love with me that I can't even imagine the enormity, the depth of it. And I want to love one man with all my heart, with everything that I am. I want a man I can laugh with . . . a man who will hold me in his arms when I need to cry, someone who needs me as much as I need him. Just me. I want a man whose kiss is so passionate and so perfect that I feel as if I might die from the ecstasy of it! I want to marry him and have his children grow inside me . . . watch them mature into adults who reflect his strength and uniqueness." Vaden looked back to Yvonne staring at her, entirely absorbed in what her sister had whispered in the quiet of the night. "I know it's what you want too, Yvonne," Vaden added. "The difference is . . . I guess the difference is . . . I can't enjoy the attentions of other young men because my heart is always searching for . . . for him."

"You mean for this faultless lover you dream of?" Yvonne asked. Vaden nodded. "But, Vaden . . . you expect so much in your dreams. No one is perfect, Vay. I'm afraid you'll be disappointed. I'm afraid you'll let life pass you by. You need to live more for the moment and not look so much to what you hope the future will bring to you."

"I know, Vonnie. I know. But . . . but it's me. My heart whispers it to me. There *is* such a man for me, Vonnie. Oh, no one is perfect . . . I realize that. I'm not saying I want the man to be perfect. I just want him to be perfect for me. And I know he exists, whether I find him now or in ten years or in twenty. He's there, somewhere. I know he is."

"You must think me so shallow . . . so heartless, Vay. But I'm not. Truly," Yvonne sighed.

"I know you're not," Vaden assured her sister. "Just as you watch me stumble into ridiculous situation after ridiculous situation, put up ever patiently with my spontaneous whims of adventure, and still you know my soul . . . I know yours. I know it must be wonderful to be the most beautiful woman in the room and have every man in it at your beckon call. Yet I know that you want the same things I want out of life—a husband who was begotten only for you, who will father children with you, and together they will all bring you boundless joy and fulfillment. I do know that, Vonnie."

Yvonne smiled at Vaden. "How I love you, little sister."

"And I love you, big sister."

Yvonne closed her eyes for a moment and inhaled deeply. "Someone's burning cedar in their hearth tonight. Isn't it a heavenly fragrance?"

Vaden closed her eyes and lay down on her bed. "Heavenly!" she sighed. She imagined a fireplace in a cozy house. She imagined sitting before it watching the fire burn and crackle, wrapped securely in strong, capable, masculine arms. "I wonder why he tears away his sleeves," she whispered aloud a moment before sleep overtook her.

CHAPTER THREE

"Well, I have to say it," Dan stated one morning at breakfast. "I just have to say I don't know what we did for fun before you girls arrived."

"I'll second that," Myra agreed. "You girls make the days brighter and the nights warmer. And what a swarm of young people we've had 'round since you two moved in! I swear, I think Jerome Clayton is plumb gone on you, Vaden. And every other bachelor in the state must be camping out across the street waitin' for Vonnie to come out of the mercantile so they can catch a glimpse of her!"

Yvonne smiled. "Everyone in town has been very friendly and accepting."

"Everyone except Belva Tibbits," Vaden corrected.

"Belva Tibbits don't count," Dan chuckled. "Her nose is too long, and her eyes are too far apart."

"Now, Daniel," Myra scolded, trying in vain to suppress a smile.

"She's only jealous because Jerome Clayton is Vaden's beau," Yvonne stated.

"Jerome Clayton is not my beau, Yvonne. And you know it!" Vaden felt overly defensive. For the past two weeks, she had been mercilessly teased by her Uncle Dan and Yvonne. Jerome Clayton appeared at least once a day in the mercantile, claiming to have just stopped in for a visit with Dan. He stared at Vaden all through church on Sundays too, and though Vaden knew he was every girl's ambition, she could not commit herself to the idea of being too involved with him. At times his consistent and obvious attentions caused her unbearable discomfort. He was too attentive, and often the expression in his eyes sent a nervous shiver down her spine. Perhaps, she had mused over and over, it was merely because she wasn't used to such intent attention from a particular young man. Everyone adored Jerome Clayton and sang his praises at every turn. However, Vaden felt differently. Somehow, she wasn't sure she trusted him. Furthermore, ever in the back of her mind lingered the image of Ransom Lake, and she secreted a profound curiosity about him—a need to know him. Ever he was in Vaden's thoughts—quiet, alone, and tragic. Her mind never lingered on Jerome Clayton that way—never.

Suddenly, at the sound of Dan's jolly voice again, Vaden once more returned her attention to the conversation going on around her.

"It seems we've got young folks under foot here and there every free minute of the day. I just can't believe it's been two weeks since you girls got here. How time does fly," Dan said, continuing to chew his toast.

Vaden and Yvonne had made several friends among the girls in town since their arrival. And they did have prospective suitors buzzing around like bees to honey. Yet this only served to remind Vaden that Ransom Lake hadn't shown his face anywhere near the town citizenship since the day he'd been in the store to buy boots. Often, when she had free time or Yvonne and Myra sent her out on a walk, she would sit in the largest maple tree on the creek bank near the old bridge or on the bridge itself. She'd let her bare toes skim across the water's top and watch the road she knew led from town to Ransom Lake's farm, hoping to catch a glimpse of the strange man who kept to himself. But she hadn't seen him and had almost given up hope of ever seeing him again.

"Vaughn Wimber says he's gonna start his punkin harvest next couple or three weeks, Vaden. I knew you'd be lookin' forward to that." Dan winked affectionately at his niece as she looked up and smiled. "Maybe you and Yvonne could go out and choose a few of the biggest and best to buy for us to use or sell in the mercantile."

"I'd love it, and you know it," Vaden admitted, returning her attention to the conversation.

"I thought ya might."

As quickly as her attention had been arrested, it was lost. She thought of having finally met, and distinguished in her mind, the two Wimber families in town. One was the Vaughn Wimber family. Vaughn owned the pumpkin patch. He and his wife, Sue Ellen, were Nathaniel's parents. They had two younger daughters as well who had been in the mercantile several times. Raylin and Selma's parents were Kent Wimber, Vaughn's brother, and his wife, Margaret. This family had three young children as well as a new baby. Though Vaughn Wimber owned the massive pumpkin patch outside of town and Vaden admired him for it, it was Selma and Raylin's family Vaden favored.

"Well, I gotta get goin', Myra," Dan said, folding his napkin and placing it on the table next to his plate. "I told ol' Ransom Lake I'd deliver those supplies he ordered today."

Everyone jumped as Vaden's fork fell from her hand, clanking loudly as it hit the edge of her plate and tumbled to the floor.

"Why don't you take Vaden with you, Uncle Dan? She's been a bit edgy lately and needs to get out," Yvonne suggested, winking at her sister.

"Could ya do without her for a couple of hours, Myra?" Dan grinned at Vaden. He knew Vaden desperately preferred the out-of-doors to being inside.

"Of course. I know she'll come back all rosy-cheeked and ready to work like the dickens afterward. Right, sweet pea?" Myra grinned, for she too knew how much Vaden needed fresh air to motivate her.

"I promise!" Vaden squealed.

Vaden could hardly believe her Uncle Dan was actually taking her to see Ransom Lake. Of course, he wasn't actually taking her to see the man, but she would see him, and that was all that mattered.

"You take after your daddy, Vaden," Dan commented as he and Vaden rode along in the wagon. "And after me. I hate bein' cooped up in the house all the durn time. Gets me fidgety and irritable. You've been workin' hard since ya been here, and I knew ya needed to get out."

Vaden reached over and linked her arm through her uncle's. "Look at the beauty of that patch, Uncle Dan." The pumpkin patch was on either side of them now, and the beautiful squash seemed to glow orange from beneath the leaves. "Doesn't it just give you all the more reason to appreciate God's creations?"

"That it does, sweet pea. That it does."

They rode in silence then, for they were alike. Both enjoyed the beauty of nature, the autumn scents in the air, the cool, crisp breezes. Before Vaden knew it, Uncle Dan was reining the team in before a small, white, cozy-looking farmhouse. A large black dog barked and ran to the wagon, wagging its tail and panting happily.

"Hey there, Ragamuffin. How ya doin' today?" Dan climbed down out of the wagon and scratched the dog's belly. As Vaden climbed from the wagon, she too crouched down to pet the dog.

"He certainly seems happy," she said as the dog licked her hand.

"Mornin', Dan." Looking under the wagon, Vaden saw a pair of familiar-looking boots approaching from the direction of the house. The sound of Ransom Lake's voice as he uttered a greeting sent a thrill traveling through her.

"I've got your supplies together, Ransom. Ya sure are stockin' up thorough for winter. It looks about like what ya take when ya winter in the mountains. You are plannin' to stay out here all winter, aren't ya?" Vaden looked up at her uncle as he spoke but remained crouched down petting the dog. For some reason, she was uncertain as to whether she wanted to face Ransom Lake again.

"I am winterin' here. Just like to be prepared," Ransom Lake replied. When he walked in front of the team and came to stand before her uncle, Vaden noticed his eyes narrowed with a frown when he glanced down and saw her. Instantly, she was startled, for he wore only his boots, trousers, and suspenders—no shirt! Vaden was unsure if she could keep her composure under such a circumstance. It was obviously no fault of Ransom Lake's that he should appear in such a state of undress. He would have had no reason to think anyone other than her uncle would deliver his supplies. Still, it was the first time Vaden had had a view of a man's bare anatomy.

"Good morning, Mr. Lake," she managed to sputter at last, standing and offering her hand. The man continued to frown, making no move to accept and shake her extended hand. He simply nodded and looked back to her uncle.

"Ya missed quite a town social a couple weeks back, Ransom," Dan said as he walked to the wagon and lifted out a sack of flour. "Dancin', pies, pretty girls—just about everything a man could want." Dan handed the sack of flour to Ransom Lake, who hefted it onto his shoulder, walked to the house, and set it down on the front porch. " 'Course, I know ya don't go in much for social gatherin's . . . but still, the pies were good."

Vaden again found herself staring shamelessly at Ransom Lake as he worked to help her uncle unload the wagon. Actually, her staring had nothing to do with the fact she had never before seen a man in such a state of undress. Granted, his chest and stomach, his entire torso, was a fascinating mass of perfectly sculpted muscles, but Vaden was more intrigued with his manner. He seemed self-conscious and yet, at the same time, indifferent.

"Wimber gonna harvest those pumpkins soon?" Ransom Lake inquired of Dan.

" 'Bout two or three weeks, so he tells me," Uncle Dan answered. "I hope we'll see ya out at the Halloween social, Ransom. It's Halloween night out by the old oak west of town."

Ransom Lake didn't answer. He simply hefted the sack of sugar Dan handed him onto his shoulder and carried it to the porch. When he returned, he paused and said, "Don't think folks want the likes of me roamin' around at the socials."

"They're simply scared of you because you make them feel ignorant." The statement was past Vaden's lips and into the autumn air before she could stop. She winced as she looked at the man, afraid he might literally bite off her head.

As the turbulent gray of his eyes pierced the softness of Vaden's, Dan chuckled. "She's got it right there, boy."

"Ignorant?" the man questioned. "Explain that to me, girl."

Vaden clasped her hands together to try to still their trembling as she spoke. "You're obviously a man who wants no one and needs nothing from others to survive. Most people aren't like that, so independent and self-sufficient. They all know you don't need them or want them, and they feel less confident in your presence is all. And you do look a bit intimidating. I know you look as you do intentionally . . . to disguise yourself from the world for whatever reasons you have. But they probably think you do it on purpose to look frightening and to try to emphasize your superiority."

Ransom Lake scowled deeply as he reached into

the wagon and withdrew a bucket of lard. "Your niece is a very presumptuous girl, Dan. Is the other one this bad?" he asked.

"The other one is the picture of Missy Proper Polly. This one's honest and says what she thinks. But I'll warn ya, Ransom . . . don't take your eyes off of her or you're liable to find beans up your nose." Uncle Dan looked at Vaden all too aware of her humiliation and chuckled merrily.

Vaden closed her eyes and wished she could melt into the ground so it could absorb her into oblivion. She couldn't believe her uncle had said what he did! It had started out to be a compliment, she knew. But, oh, what an ending!

"Don't know nothin' about beans, but I do know somethin' about boots conkin' ya on the head," Ransom Lake said. Vaden opened her eyes to see him staring at her with the possibility of a grin hiding beneath the abundant facial hair he wore. She wanted to feel his hair at that moment, to know whether it was soft or coarse.

Dan chuckled quietly and placed the back of one hand tenderly against Vaden's scarlet-warmed cheek. Vaden cast her eyes to the ground again, for Ransom Lake continued to stare at her with his unsettling eyes.

"What's the winter gonna bring this year anyhow, Ransom?" Dan asked. Vaden almost forgave him for teasing her, for she knew he was taking the attention from her blush.

Ransom Lake paused in unloading his supplies from the wagon. He leaned against it for a moment and folded his muscular arms across his impressive chest. "I'm thinkin' it's gonna be bad. Birds already leavin'. Heard some wild geese overhead only this mornin'." Vaden looked at him as a pleased smile spread across her face. That morning she too had noticed the quiet, barely audible call of the wild geese. She had looked up, shading her eyes from the sun, and caught a glimpse of the flock as they flew high above her and over town. "Skunks and squirrels already diggin' in, and the mountain got a siftin' of snow last night."

Dan turned and looked to the mountains standing majestic in the distance. "Shore 'nough," he mumbled.

"It'll wait 'til late November, I'm thinkin'," Ransom continued. "Then it's gonna bury us in snow and ice this year."

"My bones are achin' already," Dan sighed.

"I've got some late apples that're ready for pickin', Dan. Why don't ya go on and fill up a couple of bushel baskets and I'll unload the rest of this."

"If ya don't mind . . . I think we'll do just that, Ransom. Thank ya kindly." A smile spread like melted butter across Dan's face. Vaden's smile increased, for she well knew her uncle's delight in eating apple dumplings and pies.

"I left a couple of baskets out under the closest tree last night. Just fill those up and take them." Ransom nodded at Dan and lifted another sack of flour out of the wagon.

"We'll do it!" Uncle Dan clapped his hands together and rubbed them back and forth with delighted anticipation. "Come on, Vaden. You and me ain't picked apples together in years!"

Vaden started to follow her uncle toward the nearby orchards and then paused and looked back at Ransom Lake when he called out, "You be careful, girl. Don't go climbin' up higher than ya can handle."

Vaden clenched her teeth together. With great indignation, she turned and walked toward the orchard with her uncle.

A good twenty minutes had passed when Dan finally said, "I think we 'bout got these full, sweet pea. You come on down from there now, and we'll head home."

"Okay, Uncle Dan," Vaden answered from her perch high in the upper branches of a tree. "Let me just get this big juicy one on this branch up here. It's just calling to my mouth!" Carefully, she began to shinny up a nearby limb, pausing to reach for the large ripe apple growing at its tip.

"Vaden, your Aunt Myra will skin me alive if ya come home all banged up. Now come on down from there." Vaden heard her uncle's instruction, but the apple was just at her fingertips. Just an inch more and it would be hers. Finding a sturdy knot on the limb, she pressed her boot firmly against it and raised herself slightly.

"I've just about . . . just about . . . there! Got it!" she squealed triumphantly as she took hold of the apple and pulled hard. It snapped from any lingering attachment to its mother tree. "See there, Uncle Dan? Now there's an apple worth stretching for!" She held the apple out for him to see. A moment of dizziness seized her when she looked down and realized she was much higher than she thought.

"Well now . . . this doesn't surprise me one\ lick. Nope. Not one." Vaden looked across the orchard to see Ransom Lake approaching. He came to stand beside her uncle, both men gawking up at her. "I just knew I'd come out here to find that child stuck up a tree, Dan."

"She ain't stuck. Are ya, darlin'? She just likes the best out of life, just like her ol' Uncle Dan. Ain't that right, sweet pea?" Uncle Dan chuckled.

"That's right. I am *not* stuck, Mr. Lake," Vaden said. Unbuttoning several buttons at the front of her shirtwaist, she protectively placed the apple inside and began her descent. She was miffed at Ransom Lake's assumption she had yet again gotten herself into another precarious position. When she reached a limb that wasn't quite so far from the ground but still well above the men's

77

heads, she sat down and locked her knees firmly around it. Throwing herself backwards, she turned a somersault and landed smartly in a crouching position at Ransom Lake's feet. Standing with an air of victory, she pulled the apple from its place at her bosom. Biting into it fiercely, she held it in her teeth as she rebuttoned her shirtwaist, all the while meeting the impressed expression in Ransom Lake's eyes. She pulled the apple from her mouth and continued to chew, savoring its sweetness. "That's a good apple you've grown, Mr. Lake."

"And that's a fine petticoat you're wearin' there, girl," he mumbled, something of a smile apparent beneath his mustache and beard.

Vaden's eyes widened with indignation. When Dan's amused chuckle burst from his lips and into the spicy autumn air, however, Vaden sighed and smiled. Ransom Lake possessed a good sense of humor. Vaden was not surprised, for she had expected as much, but it was delightful to actually see him demonstrate it, no matter how inappro-priate his remark.

"Now, we want to see ya out at the Halloween gatherin', Ransom," Dan boomed as he helped Vaden into the wagon after the apples were loaded. "There'll be fun and purty girls and pies aboundin'."

"I don't go in much for social gatherin's, Dan. Ya know that." Ransom Lake's stormy eyes met

Vaden's for a moment before he looked back to her uncle.

"Nonsense, man! Everyone goes in for pies!" Dan chuckled.

Ransom Lake looked at Vaden and shook his head, as if to acknowledge it was a losing battle to argue with her uncle.

"Thank you for the apples, Mr. Lake," Vaden said.

He nodded. Dan slapped the lines, and the wagon lurched forward. "Ya come on into the mercantile soon, Ransom. We'll have some pie together," Dan called over his shoulder. As the wagon pulled away, Dan commented, "I think ol' Ransom Lake is taken with ya, sweet pea."

"I think I cause him to be taken with insanity," Vaden responded. "Oh, why do I act so . . . so irrationally, Uncle Dan? I can't believe—sitting here with you, still eating this delicious apple—I can't believe I cherry dropped from that tree limb!"

Dan chuckled. "Well . . . your pride was at stake, child. Ya had to defend your honor. And I'll tell ya right now, ya done a fine job of it. A fine job! We just won't say anything to your Aunt Myra or Yvonne 'bout it, now will we?"

Vaden rolled her eyes, imagining what the consequences would be if either of the two females at home found out. "Aunt Myra might never let me out again. And Yvonne . . . Yvonne would lecture me for six months on propriety and social graces and things unbecoming a young lady."

"I figure that would be the least ya could expect, sweet pea." Uncle Dan chuckled again. Vaden looked at him and was delighted in the complete mirth obvious in his eyes as they joined his mouth in laughter. "Never seen Ransom's eyes so wide before as they were when ya dropped at his feet today."

Ransom Lake's eyes *had* widened. He was a bit surprised. Vaden smiled at the thought. As the wagon approached the turn leading to Vaden's beloved babbling brook and quaint rickety old bridge, she asked her uncle if she might walk the rest of the way into town. She hadn't been to the creek in several days and longed to hear its relaxing murmur and watch the leaves fall to the ground from her perch in the arms of the giant maple.

Dan agreed, ever unable to deny Vaden anything. Soon she was perched high in the branches of the maple, gazing into the bright autumn sky.

Vaden rested her head against a strong limb and closed her eyes. She listened, inhaling deeply, as she savored the air and its blessed fragrance. She savored the aroma of tree bark and the slight scent of the leaves falling quietly to the ground. The comforting perfumes of autumn reached her senses when the breezes brought the sweet fragrance of over ripened apples and pears, the smell of the grasses in the meadow nearby, the scent of burning cedar and applewood. Scents and smells were cherished by Vaden Valmont, for they created divine memories and would often spark sentimental reminiscences at the most unexpected times. Filling her lungs with the heavenly scents of fall once more, she listened intently—listened to the trickling, splashing sounds of the creek below, to the breezes as they danced about in the leaves of the maple and the grasses of the meadow, to the comforting lowing of cattle in the distance, and to the call of mourning doves somewhere nearby.

" 'I long to taste the honeyed breeze and touch the rubied apple's flavor—to speak with soft conversing leaves, the songs of sky's white clouds to savor.' " Vaden whispered the verse quietly to herself, pausing often to ensure its adherence to the softness of her mood and the stillness of the moment.

What reprieve nature gave her! What a lift to the soul it did provide! She opened her eyes and looked about. Off in the distance she saw a herd of cattle grazing and caught the vision of the massive pumpkin patch so close to being harvested. For the first time, she realized it was Ransom Lake's roof and orchards she could see peeking up from beyond the distant hill. She had often wondered as she sat in her tree if it were indeed Ransom Lake's house that was visible. Now that she knew it was, she could come and sit in her tree and gaze at his house whenever she was able to get away.

"Oh, my!" Vaden suddenly exclaimed out loud. She knew she must get home. Aunt Myra would be needing her help. She had dallied long enough. She climbed out of the tree. Picking up a large maple leaf, she gently rolled each point toward the center, forming a cup. She removed two apple seeds from the apple she'd just been eating, placing them tenderly in the leaf's center. Then she knelt beside the creek and carefully placed the leaf on the water's surface. As she watched it float away downstream toward Ransom Lake's property, she whispered, "Grow another apple for me, Ransom Lake—one as good as I know your soul to be." She watched the leaf for several moments before turning and dashing toward the road that led to home.

It was speaking to him again—the vision in his mind. Even though Ransom Lake dreaded the change it might bring, he followed the instructions of his sixth sense and walked to the creek that passed behind his house. He stood at the bank for a moment. It was no more than a few seconds when something in the water captured his attention. He bent down and retrieved the large maple leaf floating toward him. Two apple seeds lay on it, and he knew they were of his fruit. He had known before he saw the leaf floating in the water.

As Vaden walked past Mr. Wimber's pumpkin patch, she heard him call out, "Hello there, Miss Vaden."

She smiled, waved to him, and replied, "Hello, Mr. Wimber! Are they nearly ready?"

"Just about."

Vaden saw as Jerome Clayton approached from the other side of the road then. She smiled politely, but somewhat uncertainly.

"Hey there, Miss Vaden. Can I walk a ways with ya?" he asked.

Vaden wondered what his reaction would be if she told him truthfully she would rather walk alone.

"Why certainly, Mr. Clayton," she answered, sounding delighted, though all delight within her was squelched at that moment. Her thoughts wanted to linger on the mysterious man who hid himself away from the world, not on Jerome Clayton.

"Where ya been this mornin'?" Jerome pried. No doubt he had already been in the mercantile. Vaden could tell he was irritated at not knowing for sure where she had been, though she guessed he had an idea.

"Oh, I went with Uncle Dan to deliver some

supplies. I asked him to let me out of the wagon so I could enjoy this heavenly day awhile longer." She smiled at Jerome, hoping he would accept her explanation and not pry further. She was relieved for a moment when he nodded, but her nerves gave a sensitive jump as he spoke again.

"Been out to ol' Ransom Lake's farm, huh? Is he still alive out there?" As she had suspected, he did know where she had been. There was no point in trying to hide it any longer.

"Yes. Quite alive and well. Very well," she added nervously, remembering the vision of him in only trousers and suspenders. "He gave us a couple bushels of apples, and I'm sure Aunt Myra will have Yvonne and me canning them this afternoon."

"Oh," Jerome muttered as a frown puckered his brow. "I was hopin' ya could go for a walk with me later today."

"Oh, I'd love to, Mr. Clayton . . . but I promised Aunt Myra I'd help her this afternoon. After all, I've already been out and about while poor Yvonne has been stuck inside." Vaden sighed inwardly, for she didn't feel like enduring a walk with Jerome that day. Actually, she never felt like enduring a walk with Jerome, but he was so persistent that propriety demanded she be polite in accepting him once in a while.

"Ya like bein' outside, don't you, Miss Vaden?" Jerome commented. His smile was understanding and charming, and Vaden felt guilty for not wanting to walk with him.

"I do. The outdoors breathes life into me," she confessed.

They talked lightly as they walked toward the mercantile. When they reached it, Jerome tipped his hat to Vaden. She smiled at him before entering the store and thanked him for escorting her home.

"He's plumb gone on ya, sweet pea!" Myra exclaimed as Vaden entered the store.

"I think you've got him captured completely," Yvonne affirmed.

"What if I don't want to have him captured completely?" Vaden sighed.

Yvonne laughed. "Don't be ridiculous, Vay! Now, where have you been? Uncle Dan's been home for half an hour!"

Vaden glanced to her uncle for support. He smiled and shrugged his shoulders as he winked at her.

"I'm glad you're finally back. Them Wimber children have been waitin' on you near to an hour, Vaden," Myra lovingly scolded. "Child! You've gotten mud all over your skirt again, dear. Ya must be more careful. But, then again . . . you're the one havin' to scrub out the stain."

"I'm sorry, Auntie. I just . . . I just . . ." Vaden began to defend herself.

"I know, sweetie. I know." Myra smiled lovingly

at her niece. "Now, what about these little stinkers? They've been waitin' on ya."

"But I told them a story only two days ago, Auntie," Vaden reminded. The Wimber children, and there were so many being there were two Wimber families in town, had discovered Vaden's unique talent for storytelling several days after she and Yvonne arrived. Sue Ellen Wimber had asked Vaden and Yvonne to keep an eye on her young ones and their cousins while she and her sister-in-law, Margaret, went out to visit old Mrs. Tilits, who lived a ways out of town and was ailing. It wasn't long before Yvonne's nerves were completely frayed, and Vaden was left to tend to the children alone. So she told them a story— the story of Snow White. They adored it, sitting in silent memorization as she dramatically acted out the tale to them. There were five younger Wimber children, and the smiling, anxious faces of the two boys and three girls beamed at Vaden as she approached them.

"I just told you a story two days ago," Vaden stated as she placed her hands on her hips and frowned down at them.

"Oh, please, Miss Vaden! Just a short one. Please!" they pleaded.

Vaden smiled and relented. "Just one short one. Just one." The children squealed with delighted, sitting down where they stood, in the center of the mercantile, awaiting their story. "Very well, we begin. Now this," Vaden began, dropping her voice to a near whisper, "is the story of Rapunzel." She rolled the *r* off the tip of her tongue theatrically as she reached up, pulling the pin from her hair to let it cascade down her back and around her shoulders.

Dan and Myra both smiled, and Yvonne, who stood behind the counter, sighed and rolled her eyes in exasperation. "It wouldn't be so bad if she charged them a penny apiece," Yvonne murmured.

"Hush, sweet thing. Let the children enjoy the tale," Myra said.

"For you see, Rapunzel had long flaxen hair that shone like gold in the sunlight. She was kept prisoner in a high, high, way up high tower—a tower that had only one window through which the gentle breezes and yellow sunlight could enter. And that one window was Rapunzel's only view of the world. 'Twas a wicked and ugly old crone who kept her locked in the tower so that her profound and glorious beauty could never be seen, for you see, the crone was ever so jealous of the great loveliness possessed by R-r-r-r-r-apunzel."

Sometime later, when heavy sighs escaped their lungs and clapping made their hands ache, the happy children rose, tears apparent in their eyes at hearing the tale of the blinded prince and how his sight was restored by the loving tears of his beloved Rapunzel.

"Thank ya so much, Miss Vaden," one of the smallest Wimber girls sighed, tenderly taking hold of Vaden's hand.

"You're welcome, Violet," Vaden said with a smile. Then, bending to speak into the girl's ear, she whispered, "But wait a few days to return or my auntie will have my hide for not getting my chores done."

Violet smiled, her eyes sparkling with admiration as she looked up at Vaden. "I think ya look just like R-r-r-apunzel, Miss Vaden," the child sighed.

Vaden smiled, flattered at the child's adoration. "Even though her hair was as gold as the morning sun and mine is as dark as night?"

Violet Wimber nodded. "It reminds me of chocolates on Christmas morning."

Vaden was enchanted. She bent and sweetly kissed the child on one cheek. She affectionately watched the children as they left, waving and calling out their goodbyes to her.

Turning, she was prepared for the disapproving expression she would find on Yvonne's face.

"Oh, come now, Vonnie. Let them be children! Remember how wonderful it was to be a child? To believe in princesses and princes, magic, and true love?" Vaden asked.

"I only remember wanting to grow up so I could dress like a princess, Vaden," Yvonne sighed. "Now, while you've been out wallowing in the mud . . . I've been telling Jerome Clayton to come back every fifteen minutes for the past two hours!" When Vaden sighed with disappointment, Yvonne could hold her tongue no longer. "What is wrong with you, Vaden? He's adorable! He's kind and courteous and polite and—"

"And average," Vaden finished.

"He's far from average," Yvonne contradicted. "Any girl in this town would love to have his attentions . . . which he seems to be directing at you and which you almost rudely choose to ignore!"

"Yvonne . . . you know how I—"

"Hello, Mr. Clayton. Again," Yvonne interrupted, winking at her sister.

Drawing in a deep breath, Vaden turned to face the handsome young man as he entered the mercantile.

"Hello, ladies. I forgot what time it was ya told me to be here this evenin', Mrs. Valmont," Jerome stated to Vaden's aunt. "For supper, I mean." He smiled at Vaden. "I forgot to tell ya, Miss Vaden, your aunt invited me for supper tonight, and I just wanted to let ya know how much I'm lookin' forward to it."

"Why . . . how wonderful," Vaden said through gritted teeth. "I guess we'll have our time to talk after all."

"Yes. One way or the other," Jerome said pointedly.

"We'll expect ya at five thirty sharp," Myra answered. She looked like a child who had just been caught stealing cookies. "Is that all right, Jerome?"

"That's wonderful, ma'am," Jerome nodded. He tipped his hat and said his goodbye.

When he had gone, Vaden turned to Yvonne, disappointment all too blatant on her face.

"I meant to tell you, Vaden. Really! But he just walked in so soon after you finished your story and—" Yvonne began.

"I know. I know. I suppose I should resign myself to him," Vaden sighed.

"Don't make it sound like an execution, Vaden."

"But he's not . . . he's not . . ."

"Him," Yvonne finished for her. "Who is he, Vaden? You act as if you've already unearthed him. And knowing you, that's probably literal."

Vaden wanted to confess to her sister—to shout, *He's Ransom Lake! Can't you understand that?* But she knew she dared not, for Yvonne would not understand. Yvonne did not see Ransom Lake as Vaden did. Her eyes were blurred by his shaggy appearance and lack of social graces.

And so she endured supper with Jerome. Rather, she tried to enjoy it. He was forever staring at her, flashing his charming smile in her direction, inquiring about aspects of her life and family back east. Yvonne was delighted, and Vaden knew it was because she had hopes this charming, good-looking young man would have a settling effect on her sister's wild-hare ways.

But Vaden knew. She knew herself, and she could never settle for Jerome Clayton. And that is what it would be, were she to further encourage his attentions. Settling, settling for far, far less than she wanted, needed, would accept.

"You'll have to take Vaden out to Vaughn's pumpkin patch when he harvests, Jerome. I'm certain she would love to meander through the vines," Myra suggested. Vaden sighed heavily, though she forced a smile at Jerome.

"It's quite a sight to see, Miss Vaden. Wagons and wagons full of pumpkins. Yep, I'll be sure and take ya 'round when the time comes." Jerome winked at Vaden and continued with his meal. Vaden found it nearly impossible to stomach eating her own. Myra was a wonderful cook, but the company was affecting Vaden's appetite.

"Ol' Ransom Lake seems to be farin' well," Dan stated. "I don't wonder if havin' people so close might bother him. He seems to take to Vaden though. I suppose it's because she's so honest in what she says to him."

Every mouth at the table stopped chewing, and every fork or spoon paused in midair as all eyes turned to Vaden. She felt her cheeks begin to heat, and though she loved her Uncle Dan dearly, she could have pinched him hard for bringing up the subject.

"Just exactly what did you say to him today that was so honest, Vay?' Yvonne asked, the snap in her voice all too apparent.

"Nothing. I . . . I . . ." Vaden stammered as she looked to her Uncle Dan for salvation.

"She plumb blurted out why it is that all the townsfolk avoid him so. Ya know . . . why nobody seems to feel comfortable 'round the man," Dan answered for her.

"And, uh, just what reason is that, Vaden, dear?" Myra asked, though it was obvious she was uncomfortable speaking about another man in front of their guest.

"People are intimidated by him. Frightened at his unconventional ways. That's all," Vaden admitted. She looked at Jerome, whose smile had faded and whose eyes were narrow as they studied her intently. Again, the hair at the back of her neck prickled as she looked at this man. Something just didn't set right in her estimation of his character. However, he grinned at her a moment later.

"I figure ya got that one square on the head, Miss Vaden," he said in a low voice. "Looks to me like readin' people is another one of your many lovely attributes."

Vaden somewhat resented his syrupy compliment, but she forced a friendly smile and said, "Thank you, Mr. Clayton, but you are far too flattering to me."

"No one could ever be too flattering to you, Miss Vaden," he responded, winking at her. Vaden could not help the blush that rose to her cheeks. It was embarrassing to have him so obviously flirting with her in front of her family. She knew she would never hear the end of it, one way or the other, from any of them.

Later that night, Vaden folded the small square of muslin protecting two tiny apple seeds and placed it under her bed in one of the large, well-worn boots she hid there. As she did this, Vaden further knew she could never love Jerome. At least, she could not naturally fall in love with him. It would be an actual effort to love him as everyone thought she should or might. And though love alone was enough for some women, it was not for Vaden Valmont. She needed to be *in* love. She needed to have someone be in love with her. Still, as she lay in bed, she wondered if she were doomed to be joined forever to a man she merely tolerated. She knew the man she truly wanted was out of reach—too distant from life and wanting it that way.

Then everything, all the thoughts and emotions bursting about in her mind, could stay silent no longer, and as she pulled her quilt up around her neck, she whispered, "Vonnie? Promise you won't speak of this to anyone?"

Immediately, Yvonne was alert and sitting up in bed. She knew all too well whenever Vaden spoke that particular phrase, the information she was about to divulge was worth listening to. Furthermore, as she swore, "I promise," she knew Vaden was confident in her sister's loyalties. Yvonne Valmont would never repeat whatever it was her sister was about to confide in her.

"Today," Vaden began in a whisper, "today when Uncle Dan and I went out to deliver those things to Ransom Lake . . ."

"Yes? What?" Yvonne anxiously prodded.

Suddenly Vaden sat up and blurted out, "Oh, my goodness, Vonnie! He came out of the house in nothing but his boots and trousers!"

"Do you mean to tell me he appeared before you with only his undershirt covering his torso?" Yvonne was indeed stunned.

"No, Vonnie! He wore only his boots and trousers. There was nothing covering his . . . his . . . chest!" Vaden confessed. Yvonne gasped in horror. Vaden continued, trying to lessen the shock. "Well, he did have his suspenders on, but they were hanging about his hips and legs, so I don't suppose you could actually count them as being worn . . . because, of course, they weren't being worn. They were just hanging there."

"Vaden! Do you mean to tell me that you've . . . that you've witnessed . . ."

"Yes, Vonnie. I have. I've seen a man bare from the waist up. And let me tell you this. It is very unsettling—very unsettling, indeed!"

"Well, do you mean good unsettling or bad unsettling? Really, Vaden, try to be more specific." Yvonne's eyes were as large as supper plates, and Vaden had a moment of delight in the fact she had a knowledge her sister did not.

"Oh, good unsettling, definitely. But . . . I do think that it would depend on whose bare torso one was viewing. The torso of Ransom Lake was rather . . . sculpted, I suppose. So obviously solid and defined. I never quite imagined one to look as it did. I'm certain if you were to push at it with your index finger, it would be as solid as stone."

"Vaden!" Yvonne exclaimed in a whisper, dramatically covering her ears with her hands. "Don't speak of such things!"

"And I'm quite certain that were Jerome Clayton to parade around in such a state . . . well, I'm quite certain . . . quite certain the view would not be nearly as . . . nearly as favorable," Vaden added.

Yvonne sighed and lay back down in her bed, her hand to her forehead. "I'm sure you're completely and utterly corrupted now, Vay. I'm just glad it wasn't me who was forced to witness such an indecent display."

"You, my dear sister, are lying." Vaden blew out her candle, snuggling down into her warm bed.

"One too many sacks of flour, Dan," Ransom Lake announced in his provocative, deep, mumbling voice as he entered the mercantile early

95

the next morning. Vaden's heart immediately began to pound as he carried the sack of flour into the mercantile and set it on the floor against the counter. This time it was Vaden's elbow jabbing Yvonne's ribs as she noticed her sister curiously staring at Ransom Lake, as if trying to imagine what he would look like bare from the waist up.

"Well, honesty is a lost virtue these days, Ransom," Dan said, taking Ransom's hand and shaking it firmly. "I thank ya, boy."

Ransom glanced quickly to Vaden, but then his eyes went to Yvonne, lingering on her face for a moment before he leaned on the counter and spoke to Dan. "I hear ya got young Jerome Clayton payin' worship over here near to five times a day."

"It's them nieces of mine," Dan chuckled.

Vaden went crimson, knowing full well both men were aware of the discomfort caused her.

"Ain't never seen a man so gone on a filly before as that boy is on my Vaden."

"Well, it may be ya oughta remind the boy of the bean story ya mentioned yesterday before he's too far gone." Ransom turned to Vaden, an unfamiliar smile taking form on his mouth. "So what is the whole bean thing about anyhow, Dan?"

"Oh! Uncle Dan," Vaden sighed, her cheeks blushing cranberry. She turned and began frantically dusting the shelves behind the counter.

"You told him about the lima beans, Vay?" Yvonne whispered softly.

"I did no such thing!" Vaden whispered in return, grateful that the men's conversation had turned to other subjects. "Uncle Dan mentioned it."

Vaden tried to look busy as she eavesdropped on her uncle's conversation with Ransom Lake. They talked about men-type things, like the new brand Ransom had registered that morning and the horses old man Tilits used to raise before he died—things men liked to discuss—but Vaden found it interesting if for no other reason than to her senses. The sound of Ransom Lake's voice was like a soothing breeze across the brook.

"Well, hey there, Mr. Valmont," Jerome greeted as he entered the mercantile. Vaden sighed heavily and rolled her eyes when she heard Jerome's voice and felt Yvonne tug at her sleeve. Slowly she turned around, forcing a smile as Jerome's face immediately lit up at the sight of her. "And to you too, Ransom. But especially to you two ladies, Miss Yvonne, Miss Vaden."

"Hello, Mr. Clayton," Yvonne gleefully greeted. "And what brings you in so early this morning?"

Vaden wanted to turn and run as Ransom Lake's attention turned to her, his eyebrows raised in obvious mirth at the situation.

"Oh, just thought I'd stop in and thank ya all again for the wonderful supper and company last evenin'," he answered.

Vaden battled the guilt that welled up within her. After all, Jerome was a handsome, charming, polite, and perfectly proper young man. But standing there in the same room with the bearded, rather unkempt-looking Ransom Lake, she still preferred the unobtainable to the majority choice.

"You're welcome, Mr. Clayton," Vaden blurted out when Yvonne's elbow met mercilessly with her rib.

"Well, I'll be headin' back and let ya all visit," Ransom Lake said as he shook Dan's hand. "Thanks again, Dan." He turned to leave but paused. Turning back to the girls and reaching into his shirt, he withdrew a large, golden, perfectly ripened apple. Striding to the counter, he held it out to Yvonne. "I brought this in for ya, Miss Valmont. Your sister got the best one for herself yesterday. I thought ya might enjoy one as well, since I'm sure your Aunt Myra has the rest set aside for what she will."

Vaden watched, hot with jealousy, as Yvonne tentatively reached out and took the piece of fruit. Vaden also knew Yvonne was most likely dumbfounded Ransom Lake had produced it from within his sleeveless shirt.

"Why . . . thank you, Mr. Lake," Yvonne said, and the smile on her face was nothing but sincere delight. Vaden tried to breathe calmly, tried to force into silence the jealous screech rising in her throat.

Ransom Lake tipped his hat to Yvonne and then turned to leave. "Oh," he said and stopped as if he had remembered something. Vaden's heart beat wildly as his attention turned to her. He said, "And look here what I found for you, Miss Vaden." He reached into his shirt again and withdrew a golden, perfectly formed pear. "I thought ya might like this, bein' as how ya like to have the best piece of fruit from the highest branch in the tree. I had to climb a ways up to get it, but," he lowered his voice, and Vaden fancied the gray storm in his eyes almost softened as he looked at her, "I'm sure my petticoats weren't nearly as well ironed as yours when I dropped off that pear tree limb." Turning from her, he patted the countertop in front of Dan and said, "Thanks again, Dan. We'll be seein' you, Jerome." He strode out of the store, leaving Vaden's heart pounding madly and Yvonne's eyes as wide as platters as she looked at her sister.

"Petticoats?" Yvonne whispered.

Vaden had no desire to explain the remark to her sister, and although she was jittery inside to near exploding at the attention from Ransom Lake, she dove headlong into a conversation with Jerome in order to deter her sister's inquisitiveness.

"We were glad to have you last night, Mr. Clayton," Vaden said, cupping the pear tightly between her hands.

"I-I hope ya all will have me over again

sometime," Jerome stammered. He seemed uncertain what to think as he stood staring at Vaden.

"Certainly! Auntie loves to show off her good cooking." Vaden was walking on air. Not even the ever-present question of what to do about Jerome Clayton could dampen her mood.

Jerome soon left the store, and Dan went into the back to check some stock. Vaden sighed heavily and bit into the sweet, juicy pear.

"Vaden Valmont!" Yvonne exclaimed. "Aren't you going to wash that piece of fruit first? After all, think of where it has been!"

"I know," Vaden sighed. "Isn't it just too delightful?"

"Vaden!" Yvonne scolded. "You're . . . you're . . ."

"Oh, come on, Yvonne. Go ahead. Bite into that apple Ransom Lake carried here in his shirt . . . probably against his bare—"

"Stop it, Vay! You're horrid!" Then a twinkle sparked in Yvonne's eyes, and a mischievous smile donned her face. With Vaden enjoying the sweet taste of Ransom Lake's crop, Yvonne furiously bit into her apple.

Late that night, two seeds from a golden pear and its stem joined the contents of the boot hidden under Vaden's bed.

CHAPTER FOUR

If it hadn't been for the beauty of the season swirling about her, the next several days would have seemed unbearably mundane for Vaden. Fortunately, the autumn flavor in the air, the cool evenings, and the majesty of nature's colorful fall wardrobe sustained her delight with life. Oh, how the trees did inspire, their leaves of all colors raining down at each gentle breeze. Vaughn Wimber's pumpkin patch began to fulfill its promise of bounty as the vines began to wither, accentuating the bright orange of the eagerly anticipated squash. And then, on that crisp first day of October, Vaden sensed something rather different in the air—something rather ominous in character.

That day, Vaden went about her work in the mercantile comfortably enough. All the while, however, an impressive, quiet nagging at the back of her mind gave her thoughts a quantity of distraction. She found herself jittery and easily startled.

Jerome Clayton was in and spent nearly half an hour following Vaden around the store while she busily labored over her chores. Strangely, she was almost glad to have him there for a while. He seemed to divert the odd whispers of foreboding in her bosom. When he had gone, a strong sense of insecurity began to wash over Vaden as the day further progressed.

Suddenly, just after lunch, there was excitement in the day when Vaden turned and looked up from the counter to see Ransom Lake enter the store.

"It's Mr. Male Anatomy himself," Yvonne quietly whispered to Vaden, who jabbed her sister in the ribcage with her elbow.

"Good afternoon, Mr. Lake," Vaden nervously greeted. Every inch of her body was tingling with elation.

He simply nodded and continued to stand just inside the doorway, looking about the room as if he himself were wondering why he had stepped into the building.

"Can we help you find something today, Mr. Lake?" Yvonne asked.

Frowning, Ransom Lake only looked at her, his turbulent gray eyes glaring intently.

Vaden was irritated that the man stared so at Yvonne. She did not like his attention being settled on her sister. Soon enough, however, Ransom Lake's stormy gaze moved to Vaden. He turned and looked back out the door and then back to Vaden, who stood just before the counter and parallel with the open door of the mercantile.

Ransom Lake again briefly looked back. When he finally addressed the two young women, there was an air of confusion in his voice. "I . . . I, uh . . . only came in to see if your uncle is here. I . . . I, uh . . . wanted to speak with him about . . . somethin'."

"He's gone down to Mrs. Tilits's with Aunt Myra. She's feeling poorly, and with the changes in the weather—" Yvonne started to explain.

"What's the matter, Mr. Lake?" Vaden interrupted. She looked beyond him for a moment to see a group of small boys playing in the street in front of the store. "You seem a bit—"

In the very next instant, Ransom Lake glanced back out the mercantile door once more before quickly lunging forward and roughly taking Vaden's shoulders between his powerful hands.

"Move, girl!" he shouted a split second before Yvonne screamed as the repeat of a rifle split the calm quiet. Unable to comprehend immediately what had transpired, Vaden could only watch, dazed and helpless, as she saw the face of Ransom Lake wince before he fell forward, his masculine weight knocking her back against the counter. His head hit the corner of the counter with inordinate force as his body crumpled to the floor.

Instantly, a great commotion erupted outside, but Vaden cared nothing for the goings-on in the street. Falling to her knees, she gasped when she saw the bright red, moist stain saturating the back of Ransom Lake's shirt. Even as she struggled to roll the heavy man to his back, she knew that his head hitting the counter could have caused an even worse injury. Every fiber of her body ached with pain for him as she'd heard the force with which his head collided with the counter. The blood was already matting his hair. She tried to brush it aside to inspect the wound. A large cut was apparent, but she wondered if the impact had damaged him worse inside his head where she could not see.

"Don't stand there with your mouth gaping open, Yvonne!" Vaden shouted to her sister, who stood staring at her in horror. "Run get the doctor!"

"But . . . but there's gunfire out there, Vaden!" Yvonne was rattled. She stood nervously wringing her hands.

"Go! Look at all the people in the street! Do you think they'd be out there if it weren't safe now? Hurry up!" Yvonne dashed from the store. Vaden felt tears escape her eyes and begin to travel down her cheeks. She dabbed at Mr. Lake's wounded head with her apron.

"What happened in here?" a man asked as he burst into the store. It was Pete Davis, who owned a farm just west of town. His gaze was immediately drawn to the man lying on the floor. "I saw Miss Valmont in the street and—"

"Someone has shot Mr. Lake!" Vaden cried out. "Help me! I don't know what to do."

Mr. Davis hunkered down beside the girl and looked at Ransom Lake. "Well, he's breathing.

Those kids oughta be shot themselves for playin' with guns."

"What do you mean?" Vaden asked.

"Well, looks like a couple of young boys was playin' with a rifle 'cross the street in the alley. It must've gone off before they knowed what hit 'em. Though they're denyin' it like sin."

"It would've hit *me*," Vaden whispered. "I was standing there against the counter. Suddenly, Mr. Lake moved toward me and told me to move. The bullet hit him instead of me."

"Well, child, I don't mean to sound heartless . . . but a tough old bear like Ransom Lake will survive it a lot easier than you would've."

"Mr. Davis!" Vaden exclaimed, wiping the tears from her face with the back of her hand. "How can you say that?"

"Because it's true. I'm more worried about that cut on his head. Did he hit himself fallin' or what? The bullet wound ain't deep in him. But it ain't a good sign that he's still out cold."

Again, Vaden looked down to the wounded man who lay before her. She shook her head as the tears increased. "No," she whispered out loud. It couldn't be! Surely it couldn't be her fault that he was hurt. Taking one of his large hands in her own, she stroked the back of it gently. "He'll be fine. He'll be fine. It was as if . . . as if he knew it was going to happen," she mumbled to herself as she replayed the incident in her mind. Yes, it was just as if he knew. He had acted so confused and uncertain when he first entered the store. And he kept looking back out the door as if expecting to see something there. A cold shiver quickly traveled through her as she stared down at the unconscious man—at the closed, still eyes hiding the stormy gray her heart so adored.

"The bullet wound is not my concern, Dan," Doctor Sullivan said. Vaden stood in the doorway of the spare bedroom in the Valmont home intently listening. "He obviously has a severe head injury, else he'd be conscious by now. As I said before, I don't want to move him. And with so many in the county down with illness . . . I can't be here. You're certain your girls don't mind tending to Ransom until he wakes up or . . . or . . ." Dr. Sullivan looked to Vaden's frightened eyes. "Until he wakes up?"

"Of course they don't mind, John. We'll all help the boy. I just can't believe this. Shot and wounded in my own store." Dan wore an unfamiliar frown across his weathered face. He and Myra had understandably been horrified when they arrived home to find Yvonne and Vaden both in tears and Ransom Lake, shot and unconscious, in their spare room. Dan looked at Vaden then and, nodding, reaffirmed, "He's a good man to step in front of ya like that, sweet pea."

Vaden's voice was lost in her emotions. She

only nodded and wiped a tear that had traveled to her chin.

"Come to bed, Vay," Yvonne said quietly from the doorway late that evening. Vaden continued to sit in the chair at Ransom Lake's bedside, staring down at him.

"It's my fault, Vonnie," Vaden replied softly.

"No. It's not." Yvonne quietly glided into the room, reached down, and affectionately hugged her sister. "It's the fault of those silly children who were playing with a weapon. And I'm sure Mr. Lake will be fine. He'll be up and about in no time, and you can resume your endless curiosities about him. Now, come along to bed. You need your rest. You don't want him waking up and seeing you all baggy-eyed and pale, now do you?"

Vaden smiled at her sister and shook her head. "Is there never any other concern to you than your appearance?"

"Never," Yvonne giggled.

And so Vaden did take to her bed. However, she awoke every hour or so all through the night, tiptoeing quietly into the spare room to check on Ransom Lake. To make sure he did not have fever. To make sure he was there—that he was there and still alive.

Vaden was fidgety the next morning as she tended the mercantile. She wanted only to be with Ransom Lake, to sit next to him in case he should wake and need something. She was preoccupied when customers entered and needed help. When Jerome Clayton came in, however, she was so irritated that the emotion replaced her constant concern for a moment. He set a small box on the counter and greeted, "How are ya doin' today, Miss Vaden?"

"How am I doing? Didn't you hear? It's my fault," she whispered with emotion, putting a hand to her bosom to stop her heart's ache.

"What? Ya mean what happened to Ransom Lake?" Jerome grabbed Vaden's shoulders with his hands and looked steadily into her eyes. She shivered at his touch—not a pleasant shiver like she experienced whenever Ransom Lake appeared. Rather it was a disagreeable experience. "It was no fault of yours, Miss Vaden. None of it. Accidents happen, and this was just that . . . an accident." Vaden shook her head in disagreement. "How is he, anyway?" Jerome asked.

"He's still unconscious. The doctor says he can't tell how badly he may be hurt from striking his head on the counter. I just feel so responsible, Mr. Clayton. The bullet would've hit me. He protected me, and if he's terribly wounded . . . I'll . . . I'll just . . ."

Suddenly Jerome pulled Vaden into his arms, embracing her tenderly as tears escaped her eyes. He stroked her hair softly and spoke quietly as he said, "Now, this wasn't your fault, Vaden.

Not at all. He'll be fine. He's as tough as horse meat." Vaden pushed away immediately, wiping at her tears.

"Look here," Jerome began as he reached for the small box he'd set on the countertop. "Look what I brung you. This oughta cheer ya up right nice." Handing her the box, he smiled and waited for her to open it. Vaden didn't feel much like receiving a gift and having to thank anyone graciously for it. She opened the small box to find it filled with pieces of molasses taffy. "My mama pulled taffy yesterday, and I thought ya might like to try some. The sweetness will cheer ya a bit," Jerome said.

Vaden smiled, for it was a thoughtful gift. "Thank you, Mr. Clayton. And thank your mother. I'm certain this will help to take my mind off the fact that Mr. Lake is lying in our spare room near to death and all because of me." She brushed another tear from her eye.

"Now, you call me Jerome, first of all, Miss Vaden. And quit blaming yourself for—"

"Well, you *should* feel very thankful that he wasn't killed on your behalf," Belva Tibbits snapped as she entered the mercantile, obviously having overheard the last bits of conversation. Raylin was with her and immediately went to Vaden's defense.

"Really, Belva. Ya know it was no fault of Vaden's." Raylin smiled reassuringly at Vaden.

"Besides, Doctor Sullivan said the bullet might have been fatal for Vaden if it had hit her. Mr. Lake will be all right. I'm certain of it." Vaden smiled at Raylin in thanks for her encouragement.

"I certainly hope so. I wouldn't want to be the one to walk around with his death on my head for the rest of my life," Belva mumbled as she glared hatefully at Vaden.

"Belva," Jerome began. Vaden looked to him and could tell he was angry. The whites of his eyes were reddened, and his hands clutched into fists at his sides. "First of all, the bullet wouldn't have killed Vaden. She's . . . she's too strong a woman for that. And anyway, I, for one, think it would be an honor to take a bullet for her. I certainly wouldn't think the same of the likes of you," he growled.

Belva gasped indignantly, glared once more at Vaden, and said, "I won't stand here and be insulted! I'll just tell mother she can come into the mercantile and fill her own list." She turned to leave, snapping at Raylin. "Come along, Raylin. I've been utterly insulted in this establishment, and I won't stay another moment."

"You did the insulting, Belva. Go on home by yourself," Raylin told her.

Belva's bosom rose and fell dramatically with her angry breathing, and, shooting another hateful look at Vaden, she took her leave.

"She twists my patience sometimes, I'll tell you

that for sure," Jerome muttered, sighing with relief himself.

"You two are dear friends to defend me so. But she is right. If he hadn't been trying to—" Vaden began.

"Hello, all," Yvonne greeted upon entering from the back room. She took one look at her younger sister and sighed sympathetically. "Vay, why don't you go on back and sit down for a spell? I'll watch the store now."

Vaden did feel the need to escape, so she thanked Yvonne for offering and turned to leave.

"Thank you for standing up for me, Raylin. And you too, Mr. Clayton."

"Jerome," he corrected.

Vaden forced a friendly smile. "And do thank your mother for the taffy. I'm sure it'll make me feel all the better," she lied.

Vaden went directly to the room where Ransom Lake slept. She sat down promptly in the chair next to the bed and began wringing her hands.

"Oh, please wake up. Open those stormy eyes of yours and comfort me with knowing you're all right," she whispered. She covered her mouth with one hand as she tried to extinguish the sobs wanting release. After a moment, she drew in a deep breath and tried to calm herself once more. "You'll be fine," she whispered, taking the man's large hand in her own. "You'll be fine."

She raised his hand, studying it for a moment.

She caressed the calluses formed by hard labor on his palms and thought of their picking a certain, and very beloved, golden pear from an upper tree branch. This was his left hand, and she knew he had picked the pear with it. She lifted his hand to her face, laying her cheek on its back as she thought of the way he had held the lines to his team that first day she had seen him. She studied the small gold band on his little finger. It was simple, just a small band of gold. Being the curious cat Vaden was, it suddenly piqued her interest. Ransom Lake, for all other outward appearances, did not seem the type of man for jewelry. A split second of anxiety coursed through her veins as she thought it might be a wedding band. Perhaps he had been or, worse yet, was married! That thought quickly eliminated itself, for it would have been on his ring finger were that the case. At least it seemed a logical assumption to Vaden.

Then, looking about to make certain no one else had entered the room, she tugged at the ring on Ransom Lake's finger, finding it a difficult task to remove the band. After a moment of tugging and twisting—during which she watched his face closely, should he choose that particular moment to awaken—the ring slipped off. Vaden laid the small band in the palm of her hand to study it. It was definitely a woman's ring, she determined, for it was small and reminded her of her own mother's wedding band. As she looked inside the small golden loop, she could see the remnants of an inscription. But, try as she might, she could not make out all the letters, though she did discern what seemed to be a name.

"D-A-R-L-I-N . . . Darlin?" she whispered to herself. Could it have been *Darling?* she wondered. She looked at the expressionless features of the man lying before her. "Darling?" she whispered again. Could Ransom Lake's hermithood have been sparked by the loss of a wife? It bothered her to think of Ransom Lake's having been married to another woman, to think of him loving another woman, holding her in his arms, giving her his heart. But it would be a possible explanation for his cringing from society as he appeared to be doing.

Gently, she returned the ring to his finger and then bent until her lips were close to his ear. She could smell the lingering aroma of lye soap on his skin. No doubt Myra had bathed his neck and arms when the doctor had been attending to him.

Quietly, she whispered, "Who is the Darling who owned the ring, Ransom Lake?" He remained motionless. "Who is the Darling? Are you married? Were you married? Is the Darling your wife?"

Vaden startled violently when from the lips of the sleeping man broke the word, "No." It was only a breath, but very distinct.

Placing a calming hand to her bosom to try and

steady her breathing again, she asked, "Mr. Lake? Are you conscious? Are you awake?"

There came no answer, and the man remained unmoved. His eyelids did not flinch; his breathing remained as steady as it had been before. Vaden shook her head. Had he heard all she had said to him? Was his mind alert though he remained unconscious outwardly? Vaden sat beside him for a long while, waiting for something, anything—any sign that he would be well.

When Myra called for her to come join her in the mercantile, Vaden first went to the wardrobe where her aunt had asked her to hang Mr. Lake's trousers and shirt after they had been laundered. She had noticed a loose button at the collar when he had first been lying on the bed, his blood soaking the cloth of the shirt at the shoulder. How odd she should notice a loose button at that particular moment. Quickly she pulled the button from the shirt and dropped it into her apron pocket. The least she could do was sew the button back on the shirt properly, she thought. But as the day wore into night, Vaden found herself finally tucking the button from Ransom Lake's shirt into the boot under her bed.

"I'm a thief, Vonnie," she confessed to her sleeping sister as they lay in their beds in the dark of the night. She wondered about the ring and the woman who had worn it. Who was she? What had she meant to Ransom Lake? Her mind hurt from the wondering, but eventually she was able to sleep until morning.

Vaden wrung the water from the cloth and into the basin. As she moved to place the cloth on Ransom Lake's forehead, she paused, thinking to herself that, although he was not conscious, it might be soothing to his body were she to gently wipe his face and neck with the cloth. After having done so, she realized it could have done little good for him because so much of his face was covered with his heavy beard.

Yvonne came into the room and asked, "How is he? Still unconscious? It's been two days. How much longer does Doctor Sullivan think it will be?"

Vaden shrugged her shoulders. "I don't know." She studied the man's face for a moment. "I wonder what he looks like under all those whiskers," she whispered to her sister.

She had been wondering that same thing since the day she had first seen him. But now, with him before her for two days, unmoving and seemingly unaware of what was going on around him, Vaden's curiosity was enormous. She'd had hours to stare at him, study him, imagine what he might look like, and it was voraciously eating at her.

"Probably worse," Yvonne answered quietly. "I swear, I sit here anticipating his eyes just popping open and that odd color of them stopping my heart cold. His gaze is so . . . so . . ."

"Mesmerizing," Vaden stated.

"Terrifying is more like it."

"But . . . I do wonder, Vonnie. What does he really look like? It's impossible to tell through that forest of facial hair." Vaden tried to bury the thought springing forcefully to her mind. But it was too intriguing, too easy to do with Ransom Lake in his present state. Quickly she stood up and went to the dressing table nearby. "Hurry, Vonnie. Boil some water for me, and get a couple of extra towels."

"Vaden," Yvonne warned. "You're not actually planning to—"

"How do we ever expect the man to recover unless he's completely comfortable?" Vaden asked as she gathered her uncle's spare shaving soap and mug, brush, and razor from the table.

"Vaden! You can't! You can't just—"

"Hurry, Vonnie, before he wakes up. Aren't you just the least bit curious too?"

Yvonne drew in a deep breath and released it slowly. "You take the punishment, Vaden. I'll not be on the receiving end of his wrath when he wakes up."

"I will," Vaden promised. "I will. It will be worth anything he throws at me."

Some thirty minutes later, the two sisters sat, astounded as they stared down at the freshly shaven and astonishingly handsome face of Ransom Lake.

"Oh, my . . . oh, my!" breathed Yvonne. "You never would've known that he looked so . . . so . . . that he looked like that!"

"I knew he would," Vaden admitted as she meticulously studied him.

He was far and away more attractive than even she had imagined, however. His jaw was strong and square, a slight cleft in his chin. His cheekbones showed strength, and the set of his lips was perfect. He was, without a hint of doubt, the most physically attractive man she had ever imagined. A delightful warmth washed over her, and she felt rather breathless as she gazed at him. Ransom Lake was magnificent! She began to sighed, awed by the perfect, rugged beauty of the man. She trembled, fearful of his suddenly opening his eyes, for she was sure the fully revealed magnificence of his face combined with the intensity of his uniquely colored eyes would melt her into oblivion. She reached out, smoothing the hair from his forehead. "All he needs now is a barber's trim."

Yvonne shook her head emphatically. "No, Vaden. He'll probably devour us as it is! No."

Vaden smiled as she twisted a long ebony strand of his hair about her index finger. "It would be too awkward anyway," she conceded. She immediately released the strand of his hair when a frown suddenly puckered his handsome brow.

"Oh, my!" Yvonne gasped. "He's waking up!"

But Vaden shook her head. "No, he's just . . . Yvonne. Look."

Vaden watched as a single tear escaped from the corner of his right eye and traveled slowly down his temple.

The crimson of the blood seemed to stain every vision in Ransom Lake's mind. "Not again," the unconscious man's soul pled with his memory. But it came. The all too familiar vision, accompanied by the soul-wrenching emotional pain, played itself out again in the mind of Ransom Lake as he lay unconscious. The smell was there—the smell of wounded flesh, of blood, of death, of fire, and of guilt. He tried to shout in anguish, but no sound could escape his throat.

"Is he in pain, do you think?" Yvonne asked.

Something in Vaden's young heart whispered to her then, and she answered, "Not from the wound, I think." She reached out and caught his tear on her finger, placing it gently on her own cheek where her own tears had all too recently been. "Do you think," she asked Yvonne, "do you think he's like Sleeping Beauty, Vonnie? Only a prince instead of a princess? Do you think he'd wake up and fall in love with me if I kissed him?"

Yvonne moaned and rolled her eyes in exasperation. "Really, Vaden. You do beat anything else in the world." And standing up, having tired of her sister's infatuation with the unconscious man before her, she left the room.

Vaden giggled. It was ever so fun to try to provoke a reaction from Yvonne. She enjoyed it immensely. Yvonne did have such difficulty most of the time trying to discern whether Vaden was in earnest or jest. As another solitary tear escaped Ransom Lake's eye, Vaden's smile faded. She reached out, smoothing the frown from his strong brow gently with her fingertips, and the thought struck her again—only not as an irritant directed at Yvonne this time.

"Would you, I wonder?" she whispered softly. "Would it wake you, Ransom Lake?" Then simply being in the room alone with the man wove a spell of emotional intrigue over her. " 'Tis Heaven's sweet when lips are meet, a nectar most divine,' " she whispered to herself, studying the heaven-formed features of the man who lay before her. " 'Two hearts inspire a passion's fire, resplendent kiss . . . is thine.' "

Taking a deep breath in searching for her courage, Vaden bent and placed a gentle yet lingering kiss on the quiet lips of Ransom Lake. His lips were unexpectedly soft. She had expected them to be rough somehow. And though there seemed to be nothing conscious about him, Vaden perceived an enchantingly peculiar warmth permeate her being at the wonderful sensation of her lips pressed to his. An excited flutter caused her to shiver suddenly, and she broke from him, studying his unflinching features for a moment. He exhibited no reaction of any sort, and she sighed, somehow relieved. No doubt the man would be furious when he awoke to find himself shaven. It would have been all the worse were he to have awakened to find himself the unwilling recipient of such a gesture. With a heavy sigh and a warmth in her heart and on her lips the like she had never experienced, Vaden whispered, "'Resplendent kiss . . . is thine,'" and left the man to his rest.

"Is he still sleeping?" Myra asked as Vaden entered the mercantile.

"I'm afraid so," Vaden answered, suddenly blushing at the realization of what she had just done. She scolded herself for taking such a liberty as to kiss an unconscious man—to be so forthright in initiating the kissing of a man at all, for that matter. Yet she smiled too as the feel of his lips lingered in her mind. What a delightful secret she held!

"Well, the Wimber children are here for a story as ya can see, sweet pea." Myra pointed to the group of children sitting quietly in one corner. "You go on ahead and give them a tale. I'm runnin' out to the shed to fetch your uncle, so mind the store while you're at it, all right?"

As the minutes passed and Vaden wove her tale of heroes and princesses, the children were enthralled, as always. Vaden loved to see the expressions that crossed their young faces during a storytelling. She'd always held a secreted pride in her uncanny ability to weave a wondrous tale. She smiled, delighted by their now enraptured expressions as she continued with her story.

" 'Try to spin, my dear,' " she whispered. " 'Try,' the evil fairy whispered to the princess. 'Spin. Spin the wheel, love.' " Vaden cackled in an old crone's voice and giggled a moment when the children's eyes all widened in horrified anticipation. "And then . . . the princess did, ever so lightly, touch the spindle of the spinning wheel, pricking her lovely finger. 'Ouch,' the princess cried. 'Oh, help me, old woman! I've pricked my finger and suddenly . . . suddenly I feel . . .' The old woman laughed evilly as the princess crumpled to the floor in a sleep so deep as to resemble death." Vaden put her hand to her forehead and swooned gracefully to the floor. "The good fairies came at once to the lovely princess's side and tenderly laid her on a bed of purple velvets and ivory laces." Vaden unpinned her hair, letting it lay about her as she stretched out on the floor before the children. She closed her eyes for dramatic effect, crossing her hands over her bosom. "Then the good fairies flittered hither and yon, putting the entire kingdom to sleep so that all would be near, familiar faces who loved the young princess, should a handsome prince ever find her and break the spell she was under. And so she slept—the lovely princess on her bed of purple velvets and ivory laces. She slept as years and years floated past like the sands in an hourglass. Roses bloomed 'round the bed, beautiful white and fragrant roses. And the dust dared not settle on one so lovely as the princess who was sleeping for eternity." Vaden sighed heavily and paused, peering through the slit of one barely opened eye at the emotionally over-wrought faces of the children as they waited.

"And . . . and she slept always?" Violet asked.

"She slept for years and years. Decades and eons until early one autumn day, a day just like this, a dashing prince—the like that had never walked the earth before . . . handsome and strong was he—she slept until that lovely autumn day when the prince of her dreams was riding by the old castle and curiosity led him into it. He searched each room, seeming driven by some force only his heart could understand." Vaden's eyes remained closed, her hands motionless at her bosom. "Then, in the very last room to which the prince's heart led him . . . he saw her—the most beautiful woman he had ever imagined, lying on a delicate bed of purple velvets and ivory laces. 'What magic is this?' the handsome prince muttered to himself. 'What fairies pure

have kept such a creature hidden from the world?'
Then . . . he went to stand beside her bed, and
in a moment, he dropped to his knees, overcome
with sudden and absolute love and passion for
the beautiful princess before him."

"What's passion, Miss Vaden?" Violet innocently inquired.

"Um . . . passion is . . . well, it's like love,"
Vaden stammered, not wanting to explain the
deep meaning of the word. " 'Forgive me, beauty
who lies before me,' the prince whispered softly
to the sleeping beauty. 'Forgive my indiscretion
. . . but I must taste of your berry-red lips. I must
. . . for my soul has searched for you always,
and I love you.' " Vaden smiled when she heard
the girls giggle with delight. "And then," she
continued in a near whisper as she lay on the
mercantile floor. The children leaned forward on
their hands and knees, their eyes wide with anticipation. "And then, he bent and kissed her ever so
sweetly as she lay before him, ever lovely on her
bed of purple velvets and ivory laces." Vaden
placed her own fingertips to her lips, kissing
them briefly before letting her hand float gracefully into the air. "And as the handsome prince,
dark-haired and brave, gazed into the face of his
beautiful, nameless love, her eyelashes fluttered
a moment before she opened them to see before
her her own true beloved as he appeared that
very—" Vaden gasped and pulled herself imme-

diately into a sitting position, for as she had opened her own eyes in telling the tale of the sleeping beauty, she had found that none other than the handsome, dark-haired, and brave Ransom Lake stood looming over her, glaring down furiously.

"Mr. Lake!" Vaden exclaimed in a whisper, for his eyes were as gray and tumultuous as thunderclouds.

"Miss Vaden," he growled. "Would ya be able to explain to me how I came to wake up in your aunt's house to find myself completely shaved of my beard?"

Vaden struggled to her feet and stood to face him. But her mouth only gaped open, silent with guilt. He had obviously found his clothes in the wardrobe, for he stood before her dressed in his trousers, his shirt hanging open, and Vaden was glad he had not chosen to storm out to confront her in only his trousers.

"Let me ask ya another way then," he continued when she did not answer. His chest rose and fell heavily, and Vaden knew he was wrathful as he fairly bellowed, "Why in thunderation did ya take it on yourself to shave away my whiskers?"

"I-I . . . thought it might make you feel more comfortable," Vaden stammered.

"Missy, I think I'm a good enough judge of what makes me comfortable and what doesn't!" he informed her, raising the volume of his voice dramatically.

"I'm . . . I'm sorry, Mr. Lake," Vaden apologized, smiling reassuringly at the children as the entire group suddenly stood and exited the store like the building itself was aflame. "Truly . . . I was only trying to help you to rest more comfortably. Are you . . . are you feeling yourself again? You look just as hearty as ever. The color has returned to your face and—"

"Yes. I'm feelin' hearty, as ya put it. But I'm afraid I've seen one too many of your antics, Miss Vaden. Ya shaved me to see what I looked like under my whiskers. It was your curiosity gettin' the better of ya that finds me this way, pure and simple. And I'll take a minute to remind ya it was curiosity that killed the kitty, miss."

"I simply wanted to refresh you, Mr. Lake—a feat of impossibility with such an accumulation of whiskers," Vaden argued in defense of herself. "Therefore, and I've said my apologies . . . I'm sorry if it has disturbed you. And besides . . . you are a handsome enough man, Mr. Lake. I can't for the life of me understand why you've been hiding under that mess of a hairy thicket for so long."

"Handsome?" he muttered as if he could not believe what she had said. "You've heard the old sayin', Miss Vaden: never to judge a book by its cover." He glared resentfully at her. "I assume it's been Doc Sullivan that's been tendin' to me. Tell him I'm up and about and fine, and I've gone home." Then he turned, storming furiously out of the store.

Vaden stood where she was for a moment, trying to calm her nerves and pinning her hair. Several thoughts battled within the confines of her head—the first being Ransom Lake was far too attractive! How unkind of the heavens to put such a handsome, astoundingly attractive man on the earth to make the hearts of women beat wildly. Beneath the mass of beard and mustache had been hidden an utter, classic work of art. It just wasn't fair to send a girl's heart to racing so.

The second thought that rushed back and forth in her brain was it was horrid to have him so angry with her. But, after all, what had she expected? She knew he would be furious, but at the time she and Yvonne had shaved him and found themselves gazing down at perfection in masculinity, that particular concern had not mattered to her in the least. Now, however, she felt differently. She had vexed Ransom Lake too often already, and she knew this was something he viewed as unforgivable.

Third, she had been lying on the floor, her hair strewn everywhere, her eyes closed and telling a fairy tale to small children—yet another mortifying fact! What he must have thought when he entered the mercantile to find her in such a state.

With a heavy sigh of humiliation and discouragement, Vaden forced herself to finish a few chores in the store.

"He's up? You mean to tell me he just up and walked out of here like nobody's business?" Yvonne squealed, having returned with Myra and Dan to hear Vaden's announcement that Ransom Lake was gone.

"I-I think he's had enough of folks being in his business," Vaden pointedly answered to her sister.

Yvonne's eyes widened in understanding and she mouthed, *I told you so.*

"Well, I'm sure he was plumb irritated to be down in the first place." Dan just shook his head as if the whole incident were quite trivial.

"Dan. The man is wounded," Myra scolded.

"He wouldn't have left if he didn't have the mind and strength to." All three women looked to Dan in disbelief at his lightheartedness toward the issue at hand. "Girls, all three of ya . . . Ransom Lake's a tough ol' bird. I'm sure he just wanted to get on home."

Myra's mouth gaped open, and she shook her head. "Men," was all she said.

"Was he quite infuriated?" Yvonne asked sometime later when Dan and Myra had gone out on an errand.

"Does the wrath of Zeus himself mean anything to you?" Vaden replied. "He was furious! I swear, if I were a man, I think he would've beat me to a pulp."

"I knew it! I knew it! You should've let him be, Vaden."

"No," Vaden sighed, smiling. The twinkle in her eyes was as bright as the sun itself. "It was worth it. If he never speaks to me again, I think it was worth it. He's heaven embodied, Yvonne. Admit it to me."

Yvonne fought a smile, but her mouth won over her will, and the grin spread across her face mischievously. "It was worth it. Anyway, he'll still talk to me."

"Ha, ha," Vaden sneered.

Later that same eventful day, Myra sent Vaden on an errand to deliver a shipment of hair tonic that had arrived at the mercantile. Mr. Polowsky, the barber, had ordered it from Myra some weeks before, and Myra knew he would be in a hurry to receive it.

"Run it over for me, Vaden, please. He's probably simply desperate for it by now," Myra explained, handing three large bottles of the stuff to her niece.

Still greatly unsettled from being reprimanded so harshly by Ransom Lake, Vaden rather nervously walked toward the barber's building. She felt as if everyone she passed was aware of her vile deed against Ransom Lake, though she knew no one could possibly know of it.

"Good afternoon, Mr. Polowsky," Vaden greeted

as she entered the building. She noticed a customer sat tilted back in the barber's chair nearest the door, a steaming towel covering his face. Mr. Polowsky was busily snipping away at a young Wimber boy's hair. The boy squirmed almost constantly, and Vaden could clearly see the frustration on the barber's face. "Your shipment came in on the stage today, and Aunt Myra sent me over."

The man clearly had his hands full, so Vaden began looking about for a place to set the heavy bottles. "Just there, Miss Vaden," Mr. Polowsky directed, motioning to a nearby shelf. "Just set them down, and tell your aunt thank ya for me."

"There," Vaden sighed, depositing the bottles on the indicated shelf. The small redheaded boy in the chair began to bounce up and down, annoying Mr. Polowsky further. "You sit still for Mr. Polowsky, Ronald, or I won't finish the story I started for you today next time." The young boy nodded at Vaden and smiled. "You've certainly got your hands full today," Vaden called to Mr. Polowsky as she took several steps backward toward the door, still watching the irate barber battling with the boy. "I wouldn't want to be in your shoes, that's for—oh!" Vaden felt her foot catch on something behind her. Before she could even attempt to regain her balance, she was helplessly tumbling backward. She tripped again, this time on the barber's chair closest to the door, and landed solidly in the lap of the man who sat there.

"Ooof!" the man breathed as Vaden's tender seat landed squarely in his lap.

"Oh!" Vaden gasped, reflexively reaching out and taking hold of the man's arm in order to stop herself from toppling completely backward and onto the floor. "Forgive me. I . . ." she apologized. When the warmed towel fell from the man's face as he sat erect, she gasped as she found herself gazing once again into the tempestuous eyes of Ransom Lake.

The disturbingly attractive man scowled angrily at her, drew in a deep, calming breath, took hold of her arms, and roughly pushed her from his lap. He was astounding to look at! Vaden could only stand staring at him as he removed himself from the chair and stood before her. "You will be the death of me yet, girl," he growled. Vaden's eyes widened, for she was simply awestruck by his appearance. His hair had been cut to a neat and smart length, and it only served to emphasize his already inconceivably appealing appearance.

"You . . . you cut your hair," she mumbled.

Ransom Lake's eyebrows rose from a frown to their normal position. He said, "You've taken my beard from me, ya little Delilah. I figure I may as well go the whole way as Samson did. And, like I said, you'll be the death of me. I'm startin' to believe that. Ya didn't even have the consideration to take proper care of my face after ya stole my whiskers. My face hasn't seen the sun in near to ten years, and now it's sore as a mule's behind from razor burn." Turning to Mr. Polowsky, he mumbled, "Thank ya, Dale." Taking his hat from the hat rack near the door, he looked to Vaden once more, disapprovingly shaking his head before storming off.

After watching Ransom Lake walk a ways down the street, every person he passed understandably gawking at him, Vaden turned to find Mr. Polowsky staring at her with raised eyebrows.

"He needed a shave," she stated. "Don't you agree?"

Mr. Polowsky only shook his head as if he hadn't heard her correctly and returned to his redheaded task at hand. With a heavy sigh, Vaden left Mr. Polowsky's shop and started home. No sooner had she passed the next building, however, when she was bombarded with the attention of Belva, Selma, and Raylin.

"Did ya see that?" Raylin squealed, taking hold of Vaden's arm. "Did ya see that dream of a man that just went walkin' on by down the road?"

"Yes. I saw him," Vaden answered bluntly, for it only at that moment came to her realization that in having shaved Ransom Lake for her own curious purposes, she had exposed his superb grandeur of physical feature to all the world. Now every woman for miles around would be pining away after him. She scolded herself inwardly for giving into the temptation and shaving his face. Before she had done it, he had been hers. Yes, Belva too had been intrigued by him, but for the most part people had kept their distance from Ransom Lake. Now it would be different, painfully different.

"I knew he'd be handsome under all that mess," Belva whispered.

"But did ya see that? Sakes alive! He's . . . he's . . . unbelievable!" Selma sighed.

"I shaved him," Vaden blurted out. She couldn't stand their not knowing. Her pitiful ego had to divulge the information. It had to let the other girls know she had been the first to lay eyes on his astounding appearance.

"What do ya mean by that?" Belva spat.

"While he was unconscious in my uncle's house, I thought . . . I thought he might be more comfortable after a shave." Vaden returned Belva's glare, though she could not match the hatred in it.

"What's goin' on, ladies?" Jerome asked as he and Nathaniel approached.

"You have got to see Ransom Lake, Nate," Raylin squealed. "Ya won't believe it! He's all shaven, short hair, and walkin' around town like it's nobody's business."

"It is nobody's business," Belva spat. "Ya all treat him like some freak at a circus, worst of all you, Vaden Valmont. I've no doubt he thinks you're the biggest nosy-rosy busybody in town. Imagine! Takin' such familiarities with a man, a convalescin' man at that. You had better think twice about this girl, Jerome. Hard tellin' what she'll try to pull on you."

"What in tarnation are ya goin' on about, Belva?" Jerome asked, obviously irritated.

"I'm going home," Vaden choked as tears rose to her eyes. "I'm just going home."

"Miss Vaden?" Jerome reached out and smoothed Vaden's forehead, moving a stray strand of her hair away from her eyes. "What's goin' on?"

"Let Belva tell you. She thinks she knows everything. I'm certain the story will be much more exciting and degrading to me in her words." With that, she turned and fled toward the mercantile.

It did not take long for the gossip to begin about the newly revealed Ransom Lake. By the very next morning, townsfolk were coming into the store in droves to quiz Vaden and Yvonne, Dan and Myra, and whoever else may have seen the shaven hermit.

"They say he's better lookin' than some of them Greek gods were supposed to have been," Sue Ellen Wimber told her sister-in-law as they stood chatting with Myra in the store.

"I've seen him! He's . . . it's unimaginable why

a man that looks like that would hide away like he's been doin'!" another woman said.

"Oh, he's plain as mud," Jerome Clayton argued as he and some other young men entered the store.

"You're just afraid of a little competition, old man," Nathaniel teased his friend.

"Ransom Lake ain't no competition, boys," Jerome assured him. "Miss Vaden, you were the first to see him. Is he as all-fired good-lookin' as everyone says he is?"

Vaden cleared her throat. Every set of eyes in the store was intent upon her as the people of the town waited for her answer. Jerome's eyes narrowed, and Vaden knew he was irritated about the whole matter.

"He's extraordinarily handsome," she stated. Then as the hot blush began to rise to her cheeks, she added, "Excuse me," as she walked through the crowd of people, out the front door, and into the street.

Yvonne was quickly at her heels, knowing well the signs of her sister being upset. "Vaden? What's wrong?" she asked.

Vaden paused and turned to face her sister. Yvonne was disturbed when she saw tears brimming in Vaden's eyes. "Nobody cares that he was shot right there in the mercantile only a couple of days ago, Vonnie! All they care about is what he looks like, and . . . and . . . they're going to hound him, and his privacy will be completely destroyed because of me! I'll be surprised if he doesn't grind me into the ground with the heel of his boot."

As understanding enveloped Yvonne, she smiled affectionately at her sister. "I'm sure Mr. Lake will not blame you for that. I had no idea you were so completely in love with him, Vay. Why didn't you tell me how desperate you were toward him?"

Vaden's indignant expression answered Yvonne's question even before her voice did. "I am not in love with him! And anyway, I'm entirely certain you wouldn't have understood why I found myself in this . . . this . . . obsessive curiosity where the indecorous town hermit is concerned."

Yvonne guiltily cast her eyes to the ground for a moment before putting a comforting arm about her sister's shoulders. "Forgive me. I've been totally insensitive as of late. Forgive me, darling."

"That was quite a blunt answer you gave in there," Jerome stated, coming out of the store and approaching the girls.

"A forthright answer to a forthright question," Vaden explained rather sharply. She had no desire to deal with Jerome at that particular moment.

"Well, let me just tell ya this." Jerome took hold of Vaden's arm rather roughly as he continued commandingly. "An old goat like Ransom Lake ain't no competition to me."

"How dare you speak to me in such a tone, Jerome Clayton?" Vaden snatched her arm from his grasp, rubbing its sudden soreness and glaring up at him.

"Don't you handle my sister like that!" Yvonne scolded.

Jerome seemed to ignore her and continued to glare at Vaden as his chest rose and fell heavily with withheld anger. "He's probably twice your age, probably hidin' from the law or some woman he done wrong."

"I knew it," Vaden said calmly, looking at him with complete distaste. "You're like everyone else around here—judge, jury, and executioner. I knew you weren't any different from all the other old gossips in town." She despised Jerome Clayton at that moment. How dare he speak so of Ransom Lake? How dare he?

"I'm sorry, Miss Vaden," Jerome apologized, his manner softening. He did seem sincerely remorseful in that moment, but Vaden was wary of him all the same. "It's just that . . . well, I'm so dang hanged up on ya and—"

"Then act like a gentleman and prove it to her," Yvonne scolded.

"You're right, Miss Yvonne. Of course, you're right," he conceded. "I'm so sorry, Miss Vaden. I—"

"Let the ladies have their walk, boy." Vaden looked up to see Ransom Lake approaching from across the street. Her heart began to pound fiercely as he nodded in greeting to Yvonne and then to her. Goosebumps broke over every inch of her flesh; she was as thoroughly overcome by his incurably handsome appearance as she had been the first time she had seen him unshaven and awake.

"Your daddy's team is for sale, I hear," Ransom Lake said to Jerome. "I'd like to take a look at them if I could. Why don't ya come on into the mercantile with me and tell me about them?"

Jerome looked to Vaden, irritated. Then, nodding, he followed Ransom into the mercantile. Yvonne and Vaden watched in silence as the men entered the mercantile. Vaden wondered if Ransom Lake had intentionally coaxed Jerome away from irritating her further.

"I hope those cackling hens in there don't make complete idiots of the women of the world and swoon right at his feet," Yvonne whispered as Vaden clutched her hand.

As she and Yvonne stood outside the mercantile watching what was taking place within, Vaden's heart pounded madly. She prayed the women in the store would not rudely stare at him.

All seemed well save the fact Jerome kept glancing out the window at Vaden. She started to heave a relieved sigh, but someone bumped her shoulder. She turned to see Belva, Raylin, and Selma headed for the mercantile, Nathaniel and Toby Bridges at their heels.

"Well, let's have a good look at Mr. Ransom

Lake, shall we?" Belva snipped pointedly as she glared at Vaden.

"Oh, Vonnie," Vaden breathed as she watched in horror. Yvonne gripped her hand tighter, and Vaden knew she too was watching with great trepidation.

Yvonne and Vaden couldn't hear what was being said. It was plain enough, however, what course the conversation in the store was taking. Belva boldly walked up behind Ransom Lake, tapping him on the shoulder. Ransom Lake turned and shook the girl's outstretched hand. At the same moment, Jerome stared at Vaden through the window with obvious disapproval.

"I-I can't watch!" she cried out and turned and fled.

"Vay! Wait! Don't run off!" Yvonne called. But Vaden knew all too well what this meant—what the town's sudden acceptance of, and interest in, Ransom Lake meant. Whatever small amount of his attention she had been able to capture thus far would fall by the wayside in the wake of the newfound acceptance he would have. Angrily wiping at her tears, she ran down the center street of town, turning off at the road to the pumpkin patch. She didn't even stop to wave to Mr. Wimber when he called out. At last she reached her haven.

Climbing quickly up into the secluded branches of her favorite maple, she sobbed bitterly for some time. He'd made it plain enough the day before. Ransom Lake had told her exactly how he felt about having his face shaved without his consent. And then, she'd managed to find herself squarely in his lap at the barbershop! Vaden buried her face in her hands. She had been nothing but an anvil tied about his neck—an irritating cat walking between his feet as he was trying to get somewhere. And now, now he would have all the attention, all the help, and all the friends he wanted, even if he didn't want them. Vaden sobbed bitterly. Ransom Lake was completely lost to her now. There would never be another moment when he would walk into the mercantile causing everyone to evacuate in discomfort. More likely they would flock to it like ants to spilt sugar!

An hour passed—a long, excruciating hour during which Vaden accepted the fact it had all been a silly schoolgirl's dream. Why had she allowed herself to become so enamored with the man? Why hadn't she listened to her sister? To her aunt? Jerome Clayton was a fine young man, they all assured her over and over again, a young man of many divine qualities. And it seemed to be true. He seemed safe, she mused. And safe avoided heartache. Oh, Vaden had been one to champion love against all odds, but that day in her maple as she reflected over and over again on the triumphant expression on Belva Tibbits's face, she realized Jerome Clayton was reality—a nice, safe reality—while Ransom Lake was only a dream—a beautiful, dangerous, and unobtainable dream. Dreams were for little girls, and she was growing up. It was a harsh, unwanted, unfriendly truth.

Letting the last of many maple leaves she'd picked float gently down through the air and into the brook, Vaden inhaled deeply and brushed the last tear from her cheek. Her soul had been searched and, in being searched so long and so ardently, had lost the certainty of life. Slowly she climbed down from her perch in the maple and started back toward home.

CHAPTER FIVE

"Ya've just been too darn quiet as of late, sweet pea," Dan stated. He sat beside Vaden on her bed one evening a week or so after Ransom Lake raised himself from the Valmont's guest chamber and walked out of Vaden's grasp. "Your auntie and I . . . well, we just worry. Look at them cheeks of yours, girl, usually all rosy and full of life. They're nearly pale now. And the spark to your eyes is dwindlin' more and more every day."

"I-I've just been a bit downhearted is all, Uncle Dan," Vaden explained. Forcing a smile, she looked at her uncle's concerned face and assured, "I'll be fine soon enough. I promise."

"Well . . . all right then. I'll let ya be for now. I know Jerome will be here any minute to take ya for a ride." Dan paused and drew in a deep breath as if he'd meant to say something more. He must have reconsidered, however, for he kissed her affectionately on the cheek and left.

As Vaden looked at her reflection in the mirror, she too noticed the pallid complexion looking back at her. Pinching her cheeks mercilessly, she forced a smile and said, "Jerome Clayton will be here any minute, Vaden Valmont. And each time you agree to go riding with him or for a walk or let Aunt Myra invite him for dinner . . . each time you're coming closer to reality."

Closing her eyes for a moment, she let her mind conjure up an image of Ransom Lake the way he'd looked only that morning when she had seen him coming out of the blacksmith's shop. He'd seemed completely oblivious to everyone looking at him when he passed them by. One by one, he'd sauntered past people, completely unaware and completely irresistible. Her heart endured a deep pang of misery, of unhealable sorrow, as she thought of him. Several times during the week she had seen him in passing, even once while she had been walking back from her maple near the brook. Each time he'd nodded to her politely, not smiling, however, and not speaking one solitary word to her.

Worst of all, she had willingly allowed Jerome Clayton to begin courting her now. And instead of helping her to move on and try to accept that Ransom Lake would never love her, it only served to drive the blade of disappointment and heartbreak further into her soul. She had thought that giving herself the opportunity to know Jerome better, to find things to like about him, would help her to accept the inevitability of having to put Ransom Lake out of her mind. But it hadn't helped. It had instead made things worse, for every time she forced herself to be pleasant to Jerome, to laugh at his wit, to admit his attractiveness, it was as if someone had plunged a dagger into some part of her heart. Yet it seemed the truth of life. Yvonne assured her Jerome was a wonderful boy. Everyone assured her he was. And she knew everyone approved of him. But yet . . . something in her couldn't accept him. And she was certain this was because everything in her loved the mysterious, the deliciously handsome Ransom Lake.

"Ya don't quite look yourself tonight, Miss Vaden," Jerome remarked as he helped her into the buggy.

"Oh, just a bit tired today, I suppose," she sighed, buttoning the top button of her coat, for it was a rather chilly night. At that moment, as if fate meant to drive the dagger of despair deeper into her heart, Ransom Lake stepped in front of the mare that was hitched to the buggy.

"How ya doin' this evenin', Jerome? Miss Vaden?" he asked in his masculine, mumbling manner.

"Just fine, Ransom. And you?" Jerome greeted, standing up and reaching across Vaden to shake Ransom Lake's outstretched hand. She didn't look at him at first, afraid she might burst into tears at the sight of the tantalizing storm color of his eyes. But when he addressed her directly, she knew she must face him.

"You two out for an evenin' ride then, Miss

Vaden?" he mumbled. Her hand had been resting on the rim of the buggy. When she felt the worn leather of Ransom Lake's glove cover her hand, she startled, looking directly into his hypnotic gaze.

"Yes . . . yes. It's a nice evening for it. Don't you think, Mr. Lake?" she stammered. Oh, how handsome he was! How enticing! Vaden was unsettled as she felt the moisture in her mouth increase as she continued to look at him.

"I'm just in to talk to your Uncle Dan a minute, so ya have fun now," he said, stepping back from the buggy as Jerome slapped the lines at the horse's back.

"Good evenin' to ya then, Ransom," Jerome called.

Vaden closed her eyes as the buggy lurched forward and away from her heart's one desire. Over an hour later, Jerome pulled the mare in front of the mercantile and offered Vaden his hand to assist her down. As he walked her to the porch and paused before the closed doors, she realized it was the first time since they'd left Ransom Lake standing there that she fully heard what Jerome was saying. All evening, though Jerome was at her side, ever flattering, ever attentive, her thoughts had been of nothing else but the vision of Ransom Lake standing next to the buggy and so near to her, his eyes intent on hers in a manner of thinly masked disapproval.

"I'm sorry, Mr. Clayton. I-I know I haven't been good company tonight," she apologized as Jerome took her hand in his, squeezing it tightly. "I've just . . . just had some things on my mind and—"

"It's all right, Miss Vaden," he accepted. "I think ya just need . . ."And in the next moment, before Vaden could move to avoid it, she felt the moist warmth of Jerome's kiss on her lips. She wanted to pull away from him, slap his face, but she knew she had led him to this. She had accepted his courting, encouraged him even as of late. What else could she expect? When his kiss lingered, threatening to become more than a tender bidding goodnight, she stepped back from him.

"Goodnight, Mr. Clayton," she whispered. "I do thank you for your company this evening."

Jerome's eyes were narrowed, his expression serious. "I love you, Vaden Valmont. I'm a good man, and I'll make a good—" he began.

"You are a good man, Mr. Clayton," Vaden interrupted, though her compliment was not in earnest. She did not want to hear his confession, his assurance that he would be a good companion for her throughout life. "I . . . just be patient with me, please. Be patient." He seemed satisfied with her response for the moment and smiled, nodding a goodnight as he turned and descended the porch steps.

Vaden watched Jerome disappear down the

street and into the night. A heavy sigh escaped her lungs, and a horrible sense of guilt and disappointment churned in her stomach. She had allowed him to kiss her goodnight, and his kiss had meant nothing to her. It had no effect on her, save it caused her to want him to leave. She closed her eyes, trying to call up a vision, the sensation of what it might feel like to be in the arms of Ransom Lake had he been the one to have briefly kissed her. She knew with everything that made her Vaden Valmont that had the kiss been from Ransom Lake, however brief, she knew severe exhilaration and delight would have overwhelmed her. Further, she knew such bliss could never be achieved from kisses forced by Jerome Clayton.

She thought her imagination's creation had come to life for a moment when she heard Ransom Lake's voice near. But when she again heard his voice say, "Miss Vaden," she opened her eyes and turned to find him actually standing at the foot of the porch steps glaring up at her.

"Mr. Lake," Vaden exclaimed, blushing, for she suddenly feared he could read her thoughts somehow.

A frown furrowed his brow as he shook his head slowly. "I thought better of ya than that."

"What do you mean?" Vaden asked, folding her arms across her chest.

"He's a worm."

"Who?" she asked, for her most recent thoughts had been of Ransom Lake, not Jerome Clayton.

"Jerome Clayton, girl! Who do ya think I mean?" He seemed overly vexed but not uncharacteristically so.

"He's a very nice young man, Mr. Lake. Everyone speaks well of him. I don't understand why you—"

"He's a worm," he repeated. "Why would ya let him kiss you like that?"

Vaden's mouth gaped open slightly as the horrid heat of a guilty blush rose to her cheeks. "What do you mean, Mr. Lake?"

Observably irritated, Ransom stomped up the porch steps, coming to stand before Vaden. "Why would ya let a little worm like that kiss you, girl? He certainly don't know how to do a proper job of it," he growled.

Vaden was completely flustered and speechless. She was horrified in the knowledge he had witnessed her exchange with Jerome. Yet Ransom Lake held no great desire for her, so what right did he have to scold her so? She wanted to scream at him—to shout, *You don't want me, so who else is there?* Instead she said, "I don't think this is any of your business! He's a very nice young man, and I hold him in high esteem." She wondered why she was so vehemently defending Jerome when she herself was in doubt of his sincerity of character at times.

"Exactly. So why are ya lettin' him slobber all over ya like a parched camel?" Ransom Lake's eyes narrowed as he glared at her.

Vaden felt the heat that preceded stinging tears well up in her throat.

"He hardly slobbered all over me, Mr. Lake," she defended. "And I still don't see what business this is of yours."

"You'd think the boy would at least try to do a proper job of it since ya let him kiss ya. But he's too wormy to even come close to it. I expected more from you, little girl." He turned and started to leave, but the tone of hurt in Vaden's next utterance seemed to stall him.

"And who do you think you are, Ransom Lake? I suppose you think you could do a *proper* job of it!" Her voice cracked with restrained emotion as she spoke.

She watched as he turned toward her, glaring, his broad chest rising and falling with his exasperated breathing. His eyes narrowed once more. He leaned forward until Vaden could feel his breath on her face as he spoke. "You bet them neatly ironed petticoats of yours I could, sweet pea," he growled. Then, without any further warning, Ransom Lake took hold of her mittened hand and pulled her down the steps after him.

"What are you doing? Let go of me!" she protested as she tried to pull her hand free of his grasp. But Ransom Lake led her forcefully to the side of the house and out of the light of the lantern on the porch.

"First thing I'd do is get ya out of the light so every danged neighbor for fifty miles around can't peep at us. Can't kiss ya proper when you're worried about who might see." Rather roughly, Ransom Lake turned Vaden to face him, pushing her back against the building. "Then I gotta back ya up against a wall so ya can't turn away from me." He took her hands, stripping them of her mittens and tucking the woolen warmers tightly into her coat pockets. He whisked her cap from her head, tucking it safely into his own trouser pocket.

Vaden gasped and tried to grab at his hands as he then quickly unbuttoned her coat.

"What are you—" she gasped.

"Be quiet," he growled. "I gotta get rid of some of this so ya know it's me warming ya up and not—"

"What?" Vaden gasped. "I can't believe you would say something like that!"

"Yes, ya can. You know me well enough by now, Vaden." And with that, Ransom Lake's utterance of her name so informally, Vaden Valmont was undone. Not that she really wanted to elude him anyway, but now, after hearing and seeing his mouth say her name so familiarly, she was dazed for a moment. She could only stare into those unusual gray eyes as he continued.

"Now," he began in a whisper—as he moved closer to her, she could no longer see the warmth of his breath turning to fog before her—he said, "I'll show ya the difference between that wormy Jerome Clayton and the likes of Ransom Lake."

Vaden shook her head ever so slightly. She already knew the difference—the profound and obvious difference. She closed her eyes for just a moment as one of his powerful hands caressed her cheek. As his roughened thumb traveled lightly over her soft lips, she looked away from him shyly.

He did not force her to look back at him, but as he traced the outline of her lips with his thumb once more, he said in a lowered voice, "I'd bet my life that your pretty little mouth tastes sweeter than sugar."

She looked up to him quickly, breathless and unable to believe what her ears had heard him say. He was so handsome, so fatally and lethally attractive. Surely she was simply daydreaming.

"Hasn't that wild curiosity of yours ever wondered . . . haven't ya tried to imagine what my kiss tastes like, Vaden?" he whispered.

"No," she tried to state emphatically. "No. Never." Then her curiosity even at that moment rose to an uncontrollable height, and she asked, "But . . . what do you mean *tastes* like? I don't . . ." she stammered, finding it difficult to control her breathing.

Ransom Lake chuckled, and a triumphant grin spread across his face. "Well, that right there proves the boy didn't kiss ya proper."

"You're just trying to—" she stammered in a whisper.

She gasped into silence as she felt Ransom's hand move beneath her coat and rest at her waist for a moment before sliding to her back and pulling her body against his. Again his free hand caressed her cheek. He put his thumb under her chin, pushing her face up and forcing her eyes to find his. His hand moved, his thumb caressing her throat as it encircled her neck. Even for his bulky clothing, his body was warm against hers, the muscles in his chest and arms solid as he held her to him.

"He didn't even hold ya proper . . . didn't let his hand feel the softness of your face like he should have before he . . . you didn't enjoy that kiss at all did ya, Vaden?" he mumbled.

The deep intonation of his voice seemed to echo throughout Vaden's head, and she struggled to keep from collapsing at his feet.

"Why are you teasing me like this?" she breathed in a frustrated whisper. She was trembling, uncontrollably so. Being in Ransom Lake's arms, the feel of his body pressed to hers, it was exhilarating!

"I'm not teasing you. I'm teaching you, teaching ya that ya don't go lettin' every wormy boy in town enjoy your kiss."

She looked up, and his gaze seized hers.

"What . . . what makes you different than anybody else?" she managed to ask, though her voice was nearly lost to the bliss of being held by him, to the pleasure of his touch.

He grinned somewhat triumphantly then, and her insides began to quiver uncontrollably, for it was definitely her final undoing. "I think ya know what makes me different from the likes of Jerome Clayton, now don't ya?"

Vaden couldn't answer. She couldn't even nod an acknowledgment to him. She could only close her eyes as his head, his handsome, roughly shaven face, and his tempting mouth moved closer to hers. It was too torturous, and she was certain he could hear her heart pounding madly. She opened her eyes and tried to look past him to the stars in the skies, the leaves falling softly to the ground from a nearby tree, to anything that might help her not to faint in his arms.

When he spoke next, she felt the warmth of his breath on her lips. The wondrous sensation caused excessive moisture to drench her eager mouth.

"There's more to a kiss than my lips on yours, Vaden," he whispered. Her skin prickled with goose bumps as his lips brushed hers teasingly. "There's the feel of my arms around ya so ya know it's me holding ya here." The tip of his nose brushed her forehead as his lips placed a soft kiss on her own nose. "There's the feel of my whiskers rough on your cheek and around your mouth so ya recognize I'm a man and not some wormy boy."

His hand left her neck and traveled down her right arm to where her own hand anxiously clutched the fabric of her skirt in its fist. Tugging at her hand, he coaxed it to release its nervous grip on her clothing and directed it to his face, where her open palm rested for an instant before he pushed her hand up, her fingers being lost in the softness of his hair for a time before they came to rest along his masculine and well-defined jaw. "If ya leave your hand on my face just here, you'll be able to feel it there too when I kiss you."

Then, though Vaden was certain she would awaken at any moment to find the dream vanished, Ransom Lake, the man she was beginning to realize she had been born to love, kissed her lips softly and somewhat hesitantly at first, tenderly, teasingly, and without demand. Brushing her cheek with his own then, he whispered, "Don't hold your breath, girl. You'll faint dead away. There's nothin' to be afraid of from me."

"I'm . . . I'm not a child, and I'm not afraid of you, Mr. Lake," Vaden corrected him, barely able to find the breath to do so.

"Oh, I know you're not a child, Vaden. I do know that."

The piercing gaze of his gray eyes held hers

for a long moment with the miracle of their fascinating storms. Then both arms belonging to Ransom Lake embraced her, pulling her securely against his perfectly constructed and powerful body. His mouth took hers at once, moist, demanding, and thorough, and she was weakened in his arms, afraid her knees would give way beneath her. She didn't feel the chilled breeze on her face, and she was unaware of standing in a small mud puddle, the water finding its way into her boots. There was nothing else in the world at that moment, nothing but Ransom Lake— nothing but the feel of being in his arms, the taste of his heated mouth as it instructed her responses, leading her instincts in returning the exchange. And he instructed well, led well, kissed fantastically, as if he himself had invented that particular act of physical affection. It was the first thoroughly impassioned kiss Vaden had ever experienced, and she knew in that instant she would never desire such a kiss from any other man. She was certain no other man could ever create such a kiss. It could only be from him, this man who held her in his arms at that dream-borne moment. She would never want, never allow, another kiss from any man save it were Ransom Lake.

Abruptly he ended their embrace, took her face firmly between his powerful hands, and kissed her fiercely one last time before releasing her completely. Vaden leaned back against the wall, afraid she might crumple to the ground in her weakened condition.

"That's how he should've kissed ya, Miss Vaden," Ransom Lake stated in a lowered voice. "That's what your first kiss from a man should've felt like. And believe me when I tell ya, child . . . that ain't nothin' compared to what would've taken place between us if we were any more familiar with each other. If Jerome Clayton can kiss ya like *that* . . . then I guess I'm wrong about him. But I doubt it." He retrieved her cap from its place in his pocket and plopped it promptly on her head.

Vaden touched her lips with her fingertips, still able to sense the taste and feel of Ransom Lake's kiss there as she watched him walk away through the dark and moonlight. She could do no more than simply stand where she was for several minutes, uncertain what to do. She looked about her to see if anyone may have witnessed the kiss. Then she ran her fingers through her hair as she struggled to regain her senses.

She had never imagined! Not in her wildest, most romantic of dreams had she imagined that kissing the mysterious man would be such a completely euphoric experience.

"I can't believe it," Vaden whispered out loud to herself. Finally, as the astonished confusion of it all began to wear off, she sighed and let her body relax against the building's outer wall. She smiled, completely enraptured by the memory of being held by Ransom Lake, kissed by his capable mouth. Closing her eyes, she let the cool breeze brush lightly across her face, tickling her nose now and again.

Ransom Lake had kissed her! The same Ransom Lake who had occupied her dreams, thoughts, and curiosities for weeks—the same physically gorgeous, flawlessly attractive Ransom Lake who had every female heart in town aflutter. He had kissed *her!* She squealed with delight as she turned and dashed back onto the front porch and to the door. She would simply have to tell Yvonne, that very next instant! But, pausing before she opened the door and walked into the fire warmth of the house, she remembered what had happened only moments before Ransom Lake had kissed her.

Jerome. The thought of Jerome Clayton dampened her excitement more than a little. She knew Yvonne approved of Jerome's attentions toward her, seeing him as a suitable beau for her younger sister. He was polite, well mannered, and safe. Yes, Vaden thought, that's why Yvonne approved of Jerome. He was safe in her eyes. No doubt he would provide well for his wife, whoever she turned out to be. He would never indulge in liquor or other devastating vices. He would never hide his past or become a hermit. And, she thought determinedly, he would never—rather Jerome could never—kiss her the way Ransom Lake had. Jerome would never be able to send her thoughts, feelings, and spirit soaring into delicious oblivion with a simple kiss. And Vaden needed to soar! Maybe Ransom Lake wasn't safe, but he was magnificent, unique, provocative, and captivating.

Vaden breathed a disheartened sigh. Yes, Ransom Lake was everything—everything her soul could ever dream of. And he was completely out of reach. He would never want her with any kind of permanency—a short, ridiculous girl who was forever causing him discomfort in some form, whether it was boots hitting him on the head, waking to find his beard gone, or finding her in his lap in the barber's establishment. Vaden knew Ransom Lake could never be hers. But to settle for Jerome? She couldn't do it. She couldn't! Not as long as Ransom Lake breathed the air of the earth. And even if by some unthinkable tragedy his wonderful, his heaven-scented breath would stop, even then Jerome would not do for Vaden. She knew it. She had changed a bit suddenly, and she knew the time had come. Because of one heavenly kiss from the man of her dreams, she knew she must tell Jerome—soon. She must tell him his pursuance of her was in vain.

"How was your evening, sweet pea?" Myra asked as Vaden entered the house. At the sound of her aunt's voice, her thoughts instantly scattered.

"Um . . . fine. Fine, disappointing, and wonderful all at the same time, Auntie."

Myra quirked a puzzled eyebrow.

Vaden simply went to where her aunt sat on the sofa in the parlor and hugged her tightly around the neck. "I know it's not exactly what you wanted to hear, Auntie. But that's the truth of it."

Myra smiled at her niece and kissed her lightly on the cheek. "Well, it's late now. Yvonne's in bed nearly thirty minutes already. You run along." Vaden smiled, giggling as well as she stood and noticed her Uncle Dan sound asleep in his nearby rocker, a book open and lying on his chest as he snored quietly.

Vaden entered her room to find it dark. She heard Yvonne's quiet breathing, soft and regular, indicating she slept soundly. Quietly she removed her dress, corset, stockings, and such, replacing them with her soft nightdress. She stubbed her toe on her bed leg and gasped trying to stay quiet. But Yvonne lifted her head and sat up.

"You're home then. Was it a nice evening with Jerome?" Yvonne asked in a whisper.

"The evening itself did have one bright spot. The evening with Jerome was barely tolerable," Vaden whispered as she slipped beneath her covers.

Yvonne sighed heavily. "Don't tell me you were rude to him, Vay. How do you ever expect to catch him completely when—"

"I don't *want* to catch him, Vonnie!" Vaden snapped. "I don't want Jerome! Don't you see that? Why is everyone so intent on me capturing Jerome Clayton? I'm sick of it. I'm sick to death of it!"

"He's a good man, Vaden. Why don't you—" Yvonne began.

"Yvonne," Vaden interrupted, springing from her bed and going to sit on Yvonne's," he kissed me tonight. You have no idea what I felt. It was like—"

"Jerome kissed you? Tonight?" Yvonne gasped.

Even in the dark, Vaden could see the whites of Yvonne's eyes as they widened in astonishment.

"Well Jerome kissed me too, but—"

"What do you mean Jerome kissed you too?" Yvonne was aghast, and Vaden knew it.

"Yes, Jerome kissed me, out there on the front porch—a kiss I'm certain most girls in this town covet. And yet . . . and yet I felt like I wanted nothing more in the world but to escape it! To rinse my lips under the pump." Vaden sighed with discouragement.

"What do you mean Jerome kissed you too, Vay? Are you trying to tell me that someone else . . ." Yvonne asked, her words trailing off in a whisper and then vanishing in the quiet of the room. It was obvious by the expression on her face that her disapproval battled with insatiable

159

curiosity—like a cattle rancher and sheep farmer arguing over grazing lands.

"Ransom Lake kissed me tonight, Yvonne. Ransom Lake!" Vaden confessed as the excitement, the all-encompassing, total exhilaration of his kiss, returned anew to her memory and senses. She ran her hands over her forearms, reveling in the feel of the goose bumps the memory raised.

Yvonne gasped, her hand covering her mouth in disbelief. "Vaden! Do you mean to tell me that you have kissed two men in one night?" Yvonne buried her face in her hands and began to mumble. "Where did I go wrong? I've never taught you to . . . two men . . . kissing you in one night! Two men alone is bad enough, Vay," she scolded, looking up again, "but two in one night?"

"You forget, Yvonne. I didn't want the kiss from—"

"I knew it! I knew that hermit was no good. Imagine! Forcing his—"

"It was Jerome's kiss I didn't want, Yvonne," Vaden interrupted. Then, throwing her head back for a moment, she sighed with heavy frustration. "Yvonne, I don't want Jerome. I want Ransom Lake. I love Ransom Lake. Can't you see that? Can't you see it? I've loved him from the first day we came here! You even told me you thought I did. And I feel him—"

"Vaden! You feel him? Whatever do you mean by that? What a thing to say to me! I can't believe

160

you, Vaden. You shouldn't be touching him, kissing him, let alone feeling him! Sometimes I can't believe you." Yvonne was horrified.

Vaden shook her head in frustration. "I swear, Vonnie, you are the hardest person to talk to. Don't you understand plain speaking? I *feel* him. Here," she whispered, putting a hand to her bosom, her voice pleading for understanding from her sister. "I feel him in my heart, in my mind, in my stomach, in my arms! He's become the food for my soul, Yvonne. Can't you at least imagine what it would feel like to love someone like that? Or is it that you're just too aware of propriety, of assured financial stability . . . of what looks proper to the world . . . are you too worried about those things to understand what I'm feeling?"

Yvonne was silent for a moment. Then she spoke quietly. "It's impossible, Vaden. No one can have exactly what they expect from love, from marriage, from life. You set your dreams, your ambitions, your heart too high. I fear you'll simply plummet when you realize one morning that Ransom Lake will never love you. He's not capable of it. But Jerome—"

"No. He may not love me, Yvonne. And I know that. But he's capable of loving someone far more thoroughly and honestly than Jerome Clayton is," Vaden said.

Yvonne sighed. "Every unmarried woman in this town, Vay . . . every one of them . . . and I suspect there are some married ones who would think of leaving their husbands if the opportunity to possess Ransom Lake came along. Every woman is mesmerized by him, Vaden. You can't possibly be certain he favors you."

"He doesn't favor me, Yvonne," Vaden admitted sternly. "I know that, but I love him. I don't love him simply because he's so astoundingly handsome or because he's so mysterious. I love him because I know who he is. I've seen something in him that every other woman in this town is too shallow to see. And obviously, Yvonne . . . that includes you."

As Vaden stood and returned to her bed, Yvonne whispered, "I only love you, Vay. I know if you have your heart broken . . . it would break so much harder than anyone else's would. I . . . I just don't want to watch you—"

"It's already breaking, Yvonne. Just the knowledge I will never be to Ransom Lake what he is to me . . . that knowledge in itself is tearing my heart into shreds." Vaden climbed into her own bed and pulled the covers up around her neck.

There was silence for some time, and Vaden thought her sister had gone back to sleep. But then Yvonne's voice broke the darkness, and Vaden was surprised when she said, "I've never been kissed by a man. Not a man I consider to be a man, anyway. Oh, there was Charles Rogers on my sixteenth birthday, but he was only eighteen.

And then, of course, you know about William Acron. And even though he was nearly twenty-two . . . he wasn't a man. Do you know what I'm trying to say?"

Vaden was still angry and hurt by her sister's apparently insensitive manner of the previous conversation, but she had no desire to stay so. "I do know," she answered.

"He's a man. Ransom Lake is as much my ideal of a man as he is yours, Vaden. I will admit that to you. And . . . and . . ." Yvonne was stammering, seeming as if she could not find the courage to finish her thinking.

"I will admit to you, Vonnie, that he did treat me somewhat as if he were dealing with a child at first. He began lecturing me on how Jerome's kiss was not a kiss worth wasting time on. You see, Jerome kissed me first on the porch when we were saying goodnight. Then, out of the autumn darkness, Ransom Lake appeared, and he scolded me for letting Jerome kiss me. He said Jerome couldn't do a proper job of it. Then Ransom Lake whisked me to the side of the house, removed my mittens and hat, and kissed me. I do not exaggerate to you when I say that it was like nothing I could ever have imagined, Vonnie. If I should die tonight, I could not have wished for a more profoundly perfect thing to have experienced in my life."

"Was it wonderful simply because he's older

than Jerome, do you think?" Yvonne asked boldly.

"No. It's because he's a man with skills of affection and an unconscious desire to weaken a woman's knees when she's in his arms. He's a man of hard work, of hidden pain. Ransom Lake is a man of passion. I only wish I were the object of his passion."

Yvonne was silent after Vaden's answer.

And then Vaden turned in her bed and said, "I can by no means settle for Jerome Clayton, Yvonne. It would be a sinful dishonesty to my soul and to Jerome. I will never be the same again. For, even now as I lay here in the dark, I long to be held by Ransom Lake, held in the power of his arms, and feel his kiss to my lips again. And my heart hurts for I know it is never to be again. Goodnight, Vonnie."

"Goodnight, sweet Vaden. You teach me more than you will ever know. And I'm ashamed to be so shallow a woman. When I listen to you, I'm ashamed to be me."

"Be glad you are you, Vonnie, for I would never wish this sort of torturous heartache on even my worst enemy." Wiping soft tears on her pillow, Vaden was silent, knowing the conversation with her sister was ended. "Well, maybe my worst enemy," she whispered to herself.

CHAPTER SIX

Vaden tried to breathe calmly as Ransom Lake stood at the far counter several days later. As she watched him studying the merchandise, she whispered, "He's so handsome, Vonnie." She paused, fascinated by watching him. "You know how in summer we used to pass Mrs. Kingston's peach tree over on Delilah Avenue? Do you remember that?" Vaden asked. Yvonne nodded, and Vaden continued in a whisper, "Remember how sweet and fresh and moist those peaches were? How we'd look up at that tree and our mouths would just water and water for a taste of just one bite of a sweet, beautiful, delicious peach? That's how I feel now. I watch Ransom Lake while he's just standing there—doing nothing . . . nothing at all—and I have to swallow constantly because my mouth longs to have him kiss me again. So much worse than it ever longed for those peaches on a hot summer day, Yvonne."

"Shh!" Yvonne scolded in a whisper, hitting her sister squarely in the ribs with her elbow. "He'll hear you! And quit staring. For pity's sake, Vaden."

But she could not tear her gaze from the man. She was completely intrigued by him—every movement of his body, every gesture of his hand, every expression on his dream-borne face.

"Are ya findin' everything all right, Ransom?" Myra asked as she entered the store from the back room.

"Mmm hmm," he mumbled.

"We've some new books that have just come in. If you'd like to take a look—" Myra began.

"Thanks. But not today," he rather shortly interrupted. Then, much to the horror of all three women present, he suddenly turned, glaring angrily in Vaden's direction. "Confound it, girl," he growled as he strode across the room toward her. "I can feel your eyes burning holes in the back of my head! Isn't it enough ya stripped me of my beard, forced me to have my hair whacked off, trip me up everywhere I go?"

"I . . . I'm sorry about those things," Vaden apologized, utterly astonished and entirely unprepared for his outburst. "I've already told you that, Mr. Lake. Time and again."

"Maybe. But every dang time I come in here, you're starin' holes in me! Would ya like me to strip down buck naked so ya can have a real good, thorough look?" he nearly shouted.

"Ransom!" Myra scolded.

Vaden dropped her guilty gaze to the floor and blushed bitterly. "I'm sorry," she apologized softly. "It's just that . . . just that . . ."

"I know, I know," he sighed. "I'm the town odd

man. You're no different than anybody else I suppose."

"Yes, I am!" she spat at him suddenly as tears filled her bright eyes. "I am different! I'm different because I find you positively fascinating. You're a puzzle to me. A soul in torture who . . . a mystery. I feel as if . . . as if . . . everyone else simply . . ." As his eyes widened, Vaden realized she'd revealed too much. "I'm sorry," she repeated, wiping a tear from her cheek and fleeing to the other room.

"She's just young, Ransom," she heard Myra remark, causing her to feel all the more humiliated.

Running to her room and closing the door firmly behind her, she burst into unrestrained sobbing. Going to her nightstand, she removed her most beloved book of poetry from the drawer, opening it and removing the long lock of ebony hair she had hidden inside—the lock of Ransom Lake's hair she'd found clinging to her skirt after she'd returned home from delivering Mr. Polowsky's hair tonic. It must've been on Ransom Lake's lap when she'd accidentally found herself sitting there. She'd known at once that it was his, for it was at the least eight inches long and the exact color of his hair. At the mere touch of it, her fingers began to tingle, and she wiped at her tears with her apron. Why was she so fatally drawn to Ransom Lake? It was so much more than the fact he was so lethally handsome. Her soul craved his company, his approval. Her body was experiencing a strange and longing loneliness she felt could only be appeased by being held safely in his powerful arms. She ached for his kiss again, to be the cause of a smile spreading across his face, to be able to smooth the perpetual frown from his brow, to ease the pain caused by whatever tormented him. Shaking her head as the tears increased, she whispered, "No! No!" She wouldn't let her mind admit what her heart was telling it. She wouldn't dwell on what she knew she was feeling for the strange and lonely man—the love, the need for his love.

"Vaden?" Myra's voice called from the other side of her door. "Vaden? Mr. Lake is asking to apologize to ya, dear. Do come out."

Looking about the room frantically, her attention was arrested by the window. By the time Myra grew impatient enough to open the door herself, the room was empty, the curtains billowing in the breeze that breathed through the room from the open window.

Vaden let her feet carry her through the alley and out into the street. Because she was trying to hide her tears by hanging her head, she did not see her Aunt Myra and Ransom Lake standing on the front porch of the mercantile. She didn't see her Aunt Myra point to her or hear Mr. Lake apologize to her aunt for upsetting her young niece.

Once she had crossed the street to the road leading to her quiet spot and to Ransom Lake's house, she hiked up her skirt and petticoats and began running down the familiar route, intent on reaching her tall maple and the brook.

The mid-October air was cool and crisp, and Vaden wished she had taken a shawl with her for she was not sure she could comfortably endure the chill for very long without it. As she reached the massive pumpkin patch belonging to Vaughn Wimber, her pace slowed to a walk again, for there were a number of men harvesting the large orange orbs and placing them into the backs of several wagons. Vaden's heart landed disappointedly in the pit of her stomach, for even though she had been looking forward to the pumpkin harvest, it seemed sad somehow to know the patch would soon be empty, the fruit having been severed from the withering vines, with only the leaves remaining to fade and die away. Quickly she wiped the tears from her cheeks with her apron as Mr. Wimber approached her.

"Well, hey there, Miss Vaden! Ya comin' on over to pick out your pumpkins today? Your Uncle Dan said he'd send ya over . . . but I thought he said this evenin'," the pumpkin farmer called as he came to stand before her.

"I-I thought I'd just come a bit early and look around," Vaden stammered.

"Well, go at it! If ya do find a few, just let

me know and I'll hold 'em back for ya, okay?"

Vaden nodded and smiled. The man was pleasant enough, and Vaden could see the resemblance to his niece Violet Wimber in his smile and eyes. As she looked about, searching for a starting point, he added, "Now right over yonder there's some big ones! Nice and orange . . . no green left nowhere. But be careful," he cautioned, pointing in an eastern direction. "Somethin' went on over there, and there's five or six big ol' boys that went rotten. Mice or somethin', I suspect. It's pretty slick and messy, so watch your step."

"Thank you, Mr. Wimber," Vaden called as she started in the direction he pointed. Maybe it would lift her spirits a bit to wander through the pumpkin patch. Maybe it would take her mind off that man Ransom Lake. At least for a little while.

Vaden lingered carefully while inspecting the pumpkins. Even for her damp mood, she was delighted, for never had she imagined there would be so many hiding hither and thither beneath the leaves. She rolled several over, inspecting their undersides and shapes, but had not yet come upon one she favored when she heard a voice that startled her.

"Girl, if you ain't the hardest child to track down."

Spinning around, she saw Ransom Lake approaching, haphazardly stepping over the large orange mounds that were between him and Vaden.

She was entirely unnerved and hiked up her petticoats and skirt, preparing to bolt again.

"Now, hold off there, miss," he instructed, increasing the speed of his approach and shaking a warning index finger at her. "I just run all the way down here to apologize, so don't ya go runnin' off again."

Vaden dropped her skirt and stood waiting for him to reach her. Her heart was pounding frantically, and she doubted whether she could stay still to hear him out, for she was all the more humiliated he should find her wandering through a pumpkin patch after the embarrassing display back at the store.

In another moment, he stood before her, his breath somewhat quickened from his pursuit of her. "Now listen here, girl," he began. "I'm sorry I nipped at ya like I did. Ya don't deserve that, and well I know it." Again he held an index finger out, pointing at her as if he were scolding a child. "But it's been awful rough on me lately the way people have suddenly started lookin' at me like I was walkin' around town stark naked. I'm not used to public attention, and it makes me uncomfortable. And to tell ya the full truth of it, girl . . . you're the worst of the lot. Every time I come into the store, ya gawk at me like you've never seen me before. Not that it's any worse today than it was before we had our moment the other night . . . but—"

"I do not gawk at you, Mr. Lake," Vaden interrupted to defend herself. Her cheeks were vermilion at his mentioning their intimacy.

"Yes, ya do," he corrected her. "But that doesn't give me the right to bite your head off like I did. I've come out here to apologize to ya and—"

As he took another step toward her, his proximity disturbed Vaden all the more, and she took one step back away from him. As she did, however, her foot met with the slick, rotting remains of a large pumpkin that had split open and poured its innards onto the soft ground. Her foot slipped, and she began to topple backward. She took another step backward to try to keep from falling. Instinctively, her flailing arms reached forward for support. The support her hands found was the front of Ransom Lake's shirt. Vaden's tight grasp on the shirt as the weight of her body began to fall unbalanced the man, and he too began to fall forward, unable to get a hold of his own footing because of the slick pumpkin remains beneath him.

Vaden felt herself hit the ground hard, knowing instantly by the cold, moist sensation soaking her back that she had landed exactly in the space saturated with rotting, orange slime. The incredible weight of Ransom Lake's body, coming down solidly on top of her own in the next instant, completely knocked the breath out of her. Matters worsened when Ransom Lake, instead of raising himself from her immediately, let his body remain on hers as he lifted his hands off the ground at her sides for a moment, inspecting the smelly muck covering his palms.

"What kind of mess have ya pulled me into this time, girl?" he grumbled. His expression and voice only too clearly showed his exasperation, and Vaden, still struggling for breath, tried to push him to one side. "Now hold on there," he instructed. "Let's take a minute. I don't want to end up face down in this . . ."

His words were lost as Vaden managed to squirm from beneath him, his own body landing squarely in the slop that hers had lain in only moments before. Vaden sat up, feeling the back of her head and trying to pull the pumpkin seeds from her hair. Ransom Lake raised himself to his knees and inspected the stringy, seedy mess covering his entire front side.

When his head slowly turned toward Vaden, she immediately began to defend herself, assuming he was about to scold her much more harshly than he had in the store. "This was not my fault. You frightened me," she began in her own defense.

"I frightened you?" he repeated. "How do ya figure that?" His voice was stern but lacking the intonation of fury she had expected.

"You . . . I thought you were going to . . ." she stammered, unsure herself what she had expected.

"Paddle your behind?" he finished. "Wash your

173

mouth out with soap? Well then, ya weren't listenin' to what I was sayin', were ya? I came out here to apologize to ya. Remember?"

Vaden looked away from him for a moment, still picking seeds from her hair.

"I followed ya out here to apologize, and ya end up pullin' me into a . . . a . . . a puddle of rotten pumpkins!" He sighed, shook his head, and raised himself to his feet.

Vaden continued to sit amid the muck, feeling it must be her penance for acting so cowardly back at the mercantile. She glanced up, completely startled when she heard a very odd, very unfamiliar sound erupt from Ransom Lake's lungs.

Vaden looked to see him standing before her, his shirt and trousers dripping with pumpkin mush, laughing boisterously, as if the situation were the first humorous thing he'd seen in his entire life. The pure joy of amusement evident in his gray eyes and smile was wonderful, and Vaden could not help but smile with him. He was all the more handsome when a relaxed, amused expression owned his face, even than he was with the nearly perpetual frown he usually wore.

He bent over, laughing so hard he put his hands on his knees as he sighed to try to stop the laughter. "Look at you!" he gasped. "Just sittin' there. Sittin' there as if sittin' in a mess of rotten squash was the most natural thing in the world.

And look at me." He laughed for a moment before he was able to get his breath again, and Vaden began to laugh with him, for the sound of his laughter was instantly contagious. Then, drawing in a deep breath and exhaling a long sigh, he wiped the moisture from his eyes and held a slimy orange covered hand out to her. "Come along, girl. We'll run on down to the creek and rinse off a bit before ya go home."

Vaden was uncertain how to react. Ransom Lake, standing before her, his hand outstretched in an offering for her to take it? He wiggled his fingers and nodded, indicating she should take the hand offered her. So, tentatively, she reached up, placing her own hand in his. Immediately she was pulled with such a great strength that she nearly fell headlong into him again before she was stable on her own feet once more.

"Here now," he began, turning from her but still holding her hand as he led her through the pumpkin patch, "we'll go out the other way here instead of back to the road. The creek is closer that way, and anyhow, we won't have to go trampin' through all the pumpkin pickers."

I'm holding hands with Ransom Lake, Vaden thought. And the thought, though perhaps a little dramatic, astounded her. His hand, one of the same that had held her, caressed her so perfectly, was warm and strong, and led her with confidence. It was a little disheartening when they reached the edge of the patch and he dropped her hand casually. A chuckle still rose in his throat every now and again as Vaden followed him in silence toward the brook. When they reached the cold, refreshing water, she gasped when he led her to exactly the spot that she favored. She watched as he hunkered down beside the stream beneath her maple and began vigorously rubbing his hands together in the water. Ransom Lake looked up at her, smiling, and Vaden felt as if she might faint at the pure splendor of his smile.

"Go on," he instructed, nodding his head toward the water. "Rinse that sticky stuff off." Vaden knelt on the brook's bank, not worried about the soil that might stain her skirt, for the backside was already orange forever from the pumpkin.

As she slipped her hands into the water, frigid with autumn, she looked to Ransom Lake when he stood and began unbuttoning his shirt. Quickly she looked back to the water and began rubbing her hands together all the more furiously as out of the corner of her eye she saw his shirt land in a pile on the ground next to her.

Chuckling, he offered, "Here's your chance, Miss Vaden Valmont. A few of them curiosities that have been bouncin' around in that head of yours are about to be satisfied." Then he hunkered down next to her, picked up the shirt, and doused it with water. "First of all," he began as he wrung the article of clothing out, "I tear the sleeves off my shirts 'cause they bother me—always gettin' caught on somethin' while you're workin' if ya don't roll them up. And if ya do roll them up, they're always comin' unrolled and givin' ya irritation." Still Vaden did not look at him, although she inwardly gasped at his knowing she had considered the reason for his sleevelessness for some time. "Next," he continued as he took the wet shirt and used it to rinse the pumpkin mess from his chest and stomach, "I don't wear flannels because they itch me. I always hated them, and now that I'm grown up, nobody can force me to wear them . . . so I don't."

"That's very interesting, Mr. Lake," Vaden commented sarcastically. "But I have no idea why you think you need to explain to me the reason for—"

"Next," he interrupted, "and I'm not goin' to show ya my underdrawers, Miss Vaden . . . 'cause a man has to have some privacy . . ."

Vaden gasped audibly and stood up, staring at him, her mouth gaping open in stunned horror at his impropriety in conversation.

But Ransom Lake stood too, reached out, and unexpectedly took her hand, placing it palm down on his stomach.

"Like I was sayin' . . . next," and he slid her hand upward over his chest to his shoulder before letting it go, Vaden snatching it away quickly, "*that's* how it feels to touch me." He quirked an eyebrow and lowered his voice. "I mean, it's a different touch than the one the other night. This is how it feels to touch my bare skin." Then, taking hold of her wrist tightly, he pulled her body against his abruptly. She couldn't breathe as he held her firmly against him with one arm. "Kind of interestin', don't ya think?" he mumbled, a sly grin spreading across his magnificent features.

Vaden looked away, her breathing rapid both from the embarrassment of his actions toward her and the ecstatic thrill running through her at the feel of his skin on her palm. "How dare you!" she scolded as she felt the blush rise to her cheeks.

"Oh, don't go twistin' yourself into knots over what's proper and what's not, girl," he told her as he released her and again doused his shirt in the brook. He wrung it tightly and threw it over his shoulder as he grinned at her. "Now, I'd go ahead and walk ya on back to town, Miss Vaden, but the way I'm dressed . . . or I guess ya might say the way I'm undressed on account of you . . ." He paused to chuckle at Vaden's astonished expression. "I don't think folks would understand. And all I need is more things to keep the tongues in town waggin' about me."

"You are completely uncouth . . . a . . . an utter brute!" Vaden exclaimed.

"Well then, talkin' like that—and I'm not sayin'

you're wrong about it—but I can only guess you've joined the ranks of everyone else in town," he muttered, his amused grin fading.

"You know I interpret that as an insult, Mr. Lake," Vaden scolded. "I just mean that, even though you see me as a child . . . someone who is forever and always tripping you up in one way or another, it doesn't mean I don't hold to certain standards, certain ideas of propriety and respect."

"But ya have been wonderin' about those things. Don't deny it, girl, 'cause I know different." He smiled slightly again, the anger at her accusation gone. "Now, run on home and get that curious little mind of yours thinkin' of something else that'll give ya reason to stare at me with that strange intensity in your eyes next time I'm in the mercantile. Maybe ya could set higher goals to speculate about." He dropped his voice and leaned toward her saying, "Maybe now ya should start wonderin' what it feels like to kiss a man when he's only half dressed or what it will feel like when I touch your skin." When Vaden's eyes again widened in horrified astonishment, he chuckled and shook his head as he defended the statement. "I think ya took my meanin' way too seriously, girl." He laughed again. "I mean to say . . . the only skin women ever have showin' is from the neck up and the wrist down. And, uh," he lowered his voice again, "seems to me—now ya tell me if I'm rememberin' this wrong—but it does seem to me that I already know what those parts of ya feel like."

"Oh!" Vaden gasped. She felt the blush burning on her cheeks. "Oh!" She was speechless. However, could she respond to him when his flirting was of such a profoundly unspeakable caliber?

He grinned at her once more, studying her for a moment from head to toe. Then, nodding at her, he said, "Good day, Miss Vaden. I'll see ya at the Halloween social. You've convinced me it might be fun after all. Especially if there's a pumpkin rottin' anywhere in your path." Chuckling, he turned and began walking toward his home.

Walking back toward town, Vaden could not keep herself from smiling as she thought back on the conversation she'd had with Ransom Lake on the banks of the brook. Oh, she had acted aghast, and most of her astonishment had been sincere, but his teasing her had sent her heart and mind soaring with delight, for it was obvious indeed she had captured some meager amount of his attentions. How else could he have possibly known all the things she had been wondering about him? How could he have known she had wondered about the sleeves to his shirts, about the feel of his skin? How could he have known unless he had noticed her, taken some paltry measure of interest in her?

• • •

That night, Vaden carefully placed several pumpkin seeds into the boot still hidden under her bed. She had picked them up off the ground at the brook bank once Ransom Lake had started home following their incident in the pumpkin patch. Just as she slid the boot back into its hiding place, Yvonne entered their room, yawning as she climbed into her own bed.

"Well, Vay," she began. "You were gone for quite awhile this afternoon. Have you anything to confess to me? Any great adventure?"

Yvonne's sarcasm irritated Vaden, so she dramatically went to the bedroom door and closed it tightly. Then she walked to Yvonne, plopped herself down on the foot of Yvonne's bed, and announced calmly, "I've touched the bare skin of a man's chest."

Yvonne gasped, her hands flying to her mouth as it dropped open. Then she began swooning from side to side as if she might faint as she continued to struggle to catch her breath. "Don't tease me so, Vay! You nearly stopped my heart!"

"But I'm not teasing, Vonnie. I have done it. I've touched a man's bare—"

"Don't say it again! Vay! What are you talking about? Whenever would you have had the chance to—"

"Today. Ransom Lake sought me out. He

truly sought me out, Vonnie," Vaden whispered delightedly. "He found me in the pumpkin patch and was apologizing to me. I fell into a pile of rotten pumpkins, and he fell with me, so we both were covered in seeds and stringy squash."

"Are you telling me that . . . that you and Ransom Lake . . . Vaden! Most people at least choose hay to roll around in if they're going to act so irrationally . . . so immorally!" Yvonne was pale, and Vaden felt guilty suddenly for worrying her.

"No, no, no, Vonnie. It was purely an accident. I slipped and, trying to avoid the fall, pulled him down with me."

"How then, if this all was so innocent, did you end up touching his . . . his . . ."

"Chest," Vaden finished. "He helped me up, and we walked to the stream to wash our hands . . . only his shirt was soaking with pumpkin so he removed it to—"

"He removed his shirt in your presence?" Vaden now feared Yvonne might truly lose consciousness. She was paler than ever.

"It was soaked in sticky squash innards, Vonnie. He used the shirt to wash off his chest."

"Did he not wear his flannels beneath? Are you telling me the man doesn't wear flannels?"

"No, he doesn't. He says they itch him. Anyway, it was amazing, Vonnie. He said he knew I had been wondering how he . . . felt . . . so he took my hand and ran it over his stomach and—"

Yvonne clamped her hands over her ears. "Don't speak it, Vay! Don't speak it!"

Vaden did not speak it, for she felt worried at shocking her sister so. Yvonne closed her eyes for a moment and then opened them again and dropped her hands from her ears. Then an odd glow captured the depths of Yvonne's eyes, and she took hold of Vaden's shoulders. "How did he feel, Vay? Tell me at once! How did he feel? Was it horrid? Was it—"

Vaden smiled. Yvonne was as curious as she was. She imagined every woman was and that sisters were blessed to have each other to share their experience and knowledge with. "He felt . . . well . . . his skin was soft. As soft as mine. But his stomach or rather the muscles beneath the skin of his stomach and chest were as solid granite, Yvonne."

"Was he warm or cold?"

"Warm. Very warm."

"Was it a pleasant experience or a horrid one?"

"Well, I suppose it would've been marvelously pleasant had I not been so completely unnerved. But, Vonnie, it unsettled me so. However, something deep within me tells my soul that had any other man appeared so scantily clad before me

. . . the effect on me would have been quite different."

Yvonne nodded emphatically. "Well! I would be worried all the more if it hadn't. But, Vay . . . you cannot make a habit of touching men! Especially bare ones."

Vaden smiled, amused at her sister. Yvonne was as curious as she was, and Vaden knew it. Yet Yvonne was ever the perfect example of a proper lady. "Oh, but Vonnie," Vaden whispered, "Ransom Lake is no ordinary man. He's more like . . . Adonis."

"Help us all, Vaden Valmont!" Yvonne scolded. "You've got the likes of Jerome Clayton chasing madly after you, and you're obsessed with this . . . hermit man."

Vaden sighed and rolled her eyes in exasperation.

Yvonne sighed as well and then smiled softly. "I will admit, Vay . . . Ransom Lake puts even a handsome man like Jerome to shame." Taking Vaden's shoulders once more, she added, "But you mustn't be touching him in such a manner again, Vay. Do you understand?"

"I know. I know." Vaden admitted the knowledge because she did know the impropriety of it from her sister's point of view.

Yvonne sighed and smiled, convinced her sister understood the seriousness of the situation. "Off to sleep with you, baby sister. Though I doubt it will come easily to you now."

Yvonne was right. Vaden could not go to sleep for long hours, for the vision of Ransom Lake smothered in pumpkin and smiling down at her kept itself vivid in her mind until the wee hours of the morning.

CHAPTER SEVEN

As Yvonne and Vaden sat in the back seat of the buggy on the way to the harvest and Halloween social in town, Vaden found it difficult not to fly from the conveyance and run headlong toward their destination.

"Oh! Why is he going so slow, Vonnie?" she whispered with irritation to her sister. "Doesn't he know this mare can go twice this fast and not be winded?"

Yvonne smiled and shook her head. "I'm certain everyone will still be there when we arrive, Vay. It's still a quarter of an hour before the party begins."

"But we should be there early . . . to . . . to help with things," Vaden stammered, though she knew she could not fool Yvonne. Yvonne knew full well why Vaden was so anxious to arrive at the social.

"You're going to break Jerome's heart tonight if you ignore him completely, Vay," Yvonne whispered.

"I won't ignore him completely," Vaden assured her sister. However, the mention of Jerome dampened her spirits enough that she no longer felt the need to complain about Uncle Dan's relaxed attitude toward arriving at the social.

When at long last the Valmonts did arrive at the

large oak just west of town, Vaden's heart soared for a moment before sinking as she noticed that Ransom Lake had indeed decided to attend. There he stood, not far from the large oak's trunk, completely surrounded by the ladies of the town, young and old. To make matters worse, Jerome was upon her instantly, offering a gallant hand to help her down from the buggy.

"Ya look more divine than the stars in heaven tonight, Miss Vaden," he flattered.

She forced a smile. "Thank you, Mr. Clayton. But you flatter far too dramatically."

Jerome smiled and winked at her, offering her his arm. As Vaden walked with him toward the platform that had been raised for the purpose of dancing, she looked to where Ransom Lake stood surrounded by female admirers. His eyes held hers for a moment, and he nodded a greeting. Vaden nodded in return, praying inwardly for him to simply break free of his admirers and approach her. *Please,* she pled with him inwardly. *Please come to me, Ransom Lake.* But then Belva Tibbits tugged on his sleeve, and he looked to her and away from Vaden.

"Well," Jerome sighed and Vaden looked up to him, feeling guilty, for she was certain he had caught her staring at Ransom Lake. "Ol' Ransom Lake has certainly taken the town by storm since he rid himself of his whiskers, hasn't he?"

Vaden frowned, slightly disturbed at the barely

discernible twinge of resentment in Jerome's voice. She looked at him, but his face showed no sign of what she had felt in his voice.

"I know you're just as fascinated by him as the next girl, Miss Vaden. But don't worry." He covered her hand with his own and patted it warmly. "I'm patient. I know it's just the mystery of it all that catches your attention. I can wait until it's passed."

Vaden shook her head, unable to be certain she had understood him correctly. "I am not infatuated with Ransom Lake, Mr. Clayton." The statement was true enough, for Vaden knew her love for Ransom Lake went far and away beyond mere infatuation. "And I think you should understand that—"

"Sshhh," Jerome whispered, putting an index finger to his lips. "I know. I know. You're going to say you're not like the other girls in town. That he doesn't cause ya to act as they do. I know. I know you're different. That's why I've chosen you. And, Vaden . . . I do think it's time ya started callin' me by my first given name. Don't you?"

Something about the conversation was making her very uncomfortable. Jerome's implications where she and he were concerned were far too serious. Furthermore, she hadn't liked his using her first name and was determined he understand that she would not use his. "But, Mr. Clayton, I think a formal address between us is more—"

"Let's dance," he interrupted, helping her to step up to the platform. He smiled benignly, and Vaden felt relieved. She had been reading too much into the conversation. She obviously had a tendency to do this often, for even though she and Ransom Lake had shared at least two intimate conversations or moments, he seemed almost indifferent to her as he assisted Belva Tibbits onto the platform and led her in a dance very near to where she danced with Jerome.

As the night wore on, Vaden was hurt and dismayed when the situation did not change. Not once did Ransom Lake ask her for a dance, though he seemed to dance with nearly every other female on the premises—several of whom spitefully mentioned the fact of it to Vaden. To make matters worse, Jerome was entirely too attentive to her, almost possessive, and she began to resent him for it. She was all too relieved each time one of the other young men would ask for a dance. It became a chore, the social—a chore in Vaden's eyes instead of a party. A grand and glorious disappointment.

And then, late in the event, nearly at its intended ending time, Vaden broke free of Jerome's attentions long enough to stand before the enormous bonfire alone for a moment. She looked up into the dark night sky watching the sparking bits of wood that would break free and fly into the blackness above, lighting it for only a moment.

The burning wood smelled comforting and warm, and Vaden hugged herself, sighing wistfully.

"'And so burns the cedar, warm . . . with spice. Lending fragrance to the air and . . .'" she began to recite to herself. She happened to glance to one side and caught sight of Ransom Lake standing nearby, Belva Tibbits attached to his arm. He was looking directly at Vaden, a mischievous glint to his mesmerizing gray eyes. As Belva babbled on about something Vaden could not discern above the crackling of the fire, Ransom Lake continued to stare at her. She looked away for a moment, unnerved by his intense scrutiny of her, only to look back to find him still staring at her. A sly grin slightly curved the corners of his mouth as he held out a hand toward her, motioned with his fingers for her to move toward him, and then proceeded to place his hand at his stomach, running it up and over his chest in exactly the manner he had directed her hand to do only a week earlier.

Vaden's mouth dropped open in an indignant gasp. Ransom Lake's smile broadened at her reaction. At that moment, Belva tugged on his shirtsleeve, once again gaining his attention. Vaden wondered why it was he even owned a nice shirt with sleeves to wear to such a function, for it had twice taken his attention from her. Vaden looked away from Ransom Lake. Through the flames of the fire, she could see Jerome talking with Nathaniel, Toby, Frank Hodges, and Randy Lange. Though Vaden had been to several gatherings at which Nathaniel and Toby were in attendance and was familiar with them, she was not very familiar with Frank and Randy, though she knew they were about Jerome's age and two of his friends. Jerome paused in his conversation, looking about. Vaden could only surmise that he searched the darkness for her.

"I'm going home, Vonnie," Vaden informed her sister after pulling Yvonne aside from the table overflowing with good things to eat.

"What?" Yvonne asked, utterly perplexed. "You can't go home now, and why would you want to anyway?"

"I'm going, Vonnie. Just tell Uncle Dan and Aunt Myra for me, will you?"

Yvonne frowned, for it was entirely unlike her sister to want to leave any kind of social gathering. And to want to leave one at which Ransom Lake was in attendance was completely unthinkable.

"I'll come with you then, Vay. Are you sure you're feeling all right?"

"Yes. I'm fine. And you stay here. I'm just . . . just tired. I want to go. Stay here, Vonnie. It would upset me too much if you were to give up your fun for me." Vaden hugged her sister and turned toward home.

It was a beautiful night for walking. The sky was

clear, the air crisp, and the stars bright overhead. She smiled as she passed Vaughn Wimber's house, which had a grinning, impressively carved jack-o'-lantern donning every window. What a harvest he had! She admired him for working so hard at growing pumpkins.

The air was thickly scented with the mingling aromas of applewood and cedar burning to make houses warm and cozy. The chill delightfully nipped at her cheeks and nose, and Vaden managed a somewhat halfhearted smile for the wonder of October.

Then her thoughts turned to less pleasant venues as she thought again of Ransom Lake's nearly ignoring her at the social, of his instant and irritating popularity there, of Jerome Clayton and his possessive attentions toward her. Her evening had been a dismal experience, and in one way or the other, each of the men in her thoughts had contributed to it.

So deep in thought was Vaden Valmont as she walked along the deserted street on Halloween night that it wasn't until the smothering wool blanket was covering her head, something else binding her arms to her sides, and someone lifting her into a wagon that she even realized there had been anyone else near to her. She tried to scream out, but something was tied around the blanket at her mouth, and she could only struggle. She heard laughter—the laughter of Halloween pranksters. But not of children intent on tipping over outhouses. This cruel laughter was the laughter of young men. And her fear rose to immensity as she felt the wagon lurch forward.

"We need to bury someone, Miss Vaden Valmont," a man's voice, altered intentionally, whispered in her ear. "We got to appease the spirits, ya see. Offer up someone. Ya ever been buried before?" it asked. "Well, sweet thing . . . there's a first time for everything they say, now don't they?" Again there was the laughter of evil mischief, and Vaden struggled with all of her might.

"Where's that little sister of yours, Miss Valmont?"

Yvonne turned to see none other than Ransom Lake standing before her inquiring about Vaden. She thought of how utterly thrilled Vaden would be to know the man had asked after her.

"She's gone home, Mr. Lake. She said she was tired," Yvonne answered, smiling at him. Her smile faded, however, when his face immediately puckered into a frown.

"On Halloween night? Doesn't she realize the tricksters are out in full force about this time?" he asked.

"Tricksters?"

"There isn't a county in this good country where the boys and young men of the town don't pull pranks all night long on Halloween, miss.

I'm not sure it's all that safe that she's gone home alone."

"She'll be fine, Mr. Lake," Yvonne assured him, though now she too was ill at ease. "It's Vaden, after all."

Ransom Lake nodded, still seemingly unconvinced. Closing his eyes for a moment, he seemed less so. "Well, guess I'll run on home now. Ya tell your sister I missed her this evenin', Miss Valmont. Shoot, I didn't get conked on the head, sat down on, shaved, or covered in squash. I feel pretty unfulfilled."

Yvonne giggled even though Ransom Lake's frown deepened as he gave her a nod of departure.

On his ride home, Ransom Lake closed his eyes and shook his head several times at the pain inside it. The feeling was there—the sensation of despair, of ominous evil lurking somewhere. He felt the fear in his heart. At least he thought he did, but there was no picture in his mind, nothing to guide him. For the first time in his life, Ransom Lake found himself intentionally searching for the visions in his mind, but nothing came to him—only the frustration of the uncertainty. He shook his head and tried to ignore the feeling in his chest. He tried to convince himself all the way back to his place that all was well.

When he arrived home, Ransom removed his

shirt, tossing it onto a nearby chair. He went to the kitchen and got himself a glass of refreshing water. Suddenly he dropped the glass, and it shattered as it hit the floor. The mad pounding of his heart increased as the all too familiar feeling of deep anxiety possessed him. Rushing to the door, he pulled on his boots, pausing for a moment to close his eyes and search for a vision. But still none came—no scenic premonition to help him pinpoint the fear he felt, someone else's fear. Nothing to help him ease his panic. And he remembered again the thing he could never forget—the first time he'd felt the horrid panic rise within him, beckoning his soul in a direction it must go. He'd sworn that never again would he brush it off as he'd done the first time. Though he'd sensed something earlier on his way home, there had been nothing to confirm it, only the beginnings of the sense of panic. But now he felt it wholly!

Rushing out into the cool late of the night, he took only the time needed to bridle his horse. The feeling of panic, of impending doom, caused his hands to tremble violently as he mounted the animal's bare back and dug his heels into the horse's flesh to signal a gallop. He was being pushed out into the night, and he knew where he was being sent. It frightened him, for since she'd arrived in town, his visions had begun to center on only her. He had no doubt it was her need prompting his soul now.

• • •

"Why . . . Ransom," Myra stammered as she opened the door to find Ransom Lake standing before her only half dressed. He nodded, not waiting for an invitation to enter, and walked into the house past Myra and directly to where Yvonne sat on the sofa in front of the fire.

"She's not home," he stated rather than inquired.

"No. No," Yvonne sputtered. She didn't know whether to avert her eyes or look at him while answering him. He wore no shirt and no flannels either. He stood before her bare from the waist up, and she realized why Vaden had been so overwhelmed at touching him.

"We're beginning to worry, Ransom," Myra admitted. "In fact, Danny has gone out to look for her. It's cold out and so late, and I know she didn't take a proper coat. Ransom? Ransom? What's the matter?"

Ransom Lake stared into the fire as it popped and crackled in the hearth. Closing his eyes, he waited, for he felt it approaching his mind—the insufferable sense of fear, the horror and panic of being closed in. It was sucking the air from his own lungs. There was more in that instant, and then he knew where to go.

"It's bad. I've got to get to her now," he mumbled to Myra as he rushed from the house.

"Ya mean you know where she is?" the woman

called to him from the front porch as she watched him mount his horse.

"I have my suspicions," he mumbled before riding away at a gallop.

The tears streamed down Vaden's temples as she tried to calm her breathing. She could not sob, for it would surely smother her, her mouth being gagged as it was. The blanket had been removed from her head and body, but now a cloth bound her mouth, and ropes held her arms to her sides and her feet together firmly. She had to breathe calmly through her nose. If she continued crying, her nose would swell and she would not be able to breathe, she reminded herself again. So her mind prayed for release, for safety. She tried not to think of the fact she couldn't move, couldn't speak. She wondered over and over why the young men had chosen her! She wasn't even sure if she knew her tormenters. In the darkness and with all the scuffling, she hadn't been able to see their faces. What had she done to provoke such actions from them? She heard them laughing and heard something hit the lid of the coffin.

"We're buryin' ya now, Miss Vaden. Don't mind it too much. You'll just run out of air and go to sleep. It won't hurt none." And then she recognized it was Frank Hodges's voice speaking to her. She knew him! One of her own peers, a supposed friend, was doing this to her? She heard him laugh as another thud sounded on the wood over her.

Then she did begin to panic. She tried to thrash, to loosen the ropes that bound her arms and her feet. She cried then, unable to stop the tears and sobbing rising from her of the fear and panic attacking her mind and body.

"Settle down in there!" Frank shouted. "It'll only make it worse for ya." She stopped thrashing when she heard him say, "Who? Who's comin'?"

Trying to remain silent, Vaden listened and felt hope rising within her as she heard the drumming of an approaching horse.

"What are you doin' here?" one of the other men shouted.

She heard a scuffle and shouting, and then a voice she thought she was dreaming growled, "I oughta tear your throats open for this." She held her breath, unable to believe what she had heard. Who she had heard! There were more scuffling sounds and shouting, and then she began to cry as she heard someone prying the lid off the pine coffin. When the lid lifted and the moon and starlight shone in, breaking the darkness of impending death, Vaden closed her eyes, offering a thankful prayer. There, looking down at her, stood none other than her cherished Ransom Lake.

"What kind of fools would . . ." he mumbled angrily, profound concern apparent in his fiery eyes as he reached into the coffin and pulled

Vaden from it. Embracing her momentarily, he let her feet drop to the ground. "They oughta have their hearts torn out for this," he continued to mutter as he removed the piece of linen from her mouth, drew the knife from his boot, and cut away the ropes binding her. As the ropes fell from her body, she collapsed against him. He didn't hesitate but gathered her into his powerful arms, carrying her toward the nearby wagon.

Vaden glanced about to see Frank Hodges, Toby Bridges, and Randy Lange lying about on the ground, each bleeding from their nose and mouth and doubled over, clutching at their midsection. Her own supposed friends had done this to her. It was unthinkable! How could they?

"You get up there and drive that team, boy!" Ransom commanded, looking to Nathaniel Wimber, whose face was indeed bloodied and bruised, though he still stood. "Now, boy! Unless ya want another dose of angry Ransom Lake!"

Clutching his stomach, Nathaniel struggled onto the seat of the wagon as Ransom lifted Vaden into the wagon bed, climbing in behind her. He whistled to his horse, and the animal approached, allowing its master to secure its reins to the wagon. Her rescuer settled against the sideboard, pulling Vaden into his arms and against the security of his warm body. "Get a move on, boy!" he shouted. "I think ya know where to go, now don't ya?"

Nathaniel paused, looking back at his friends. "What about—" he began.

"I don't care if the coyotes tear them to bloodied shreds, boy! And if ya don't want to join them in hell, ya get this team movin' toward Dan Valmont's place now!"

Nathaniel clicked his tongue, and the team lurched forward. Vaden had begun to tremble excessively, her nerves and emotions completely out of control. Ransom wrapped her tightly in his arms and spoke soothingly, "It's all right now, girl. It's all right."

His warm breath in her hair and the sympathy in his low voice caused her to tremble all the more, and she sobbed. It took her several moments before she realized her cheek was flush with the bareness of his chest. His skin was soft and warm, but she pushed herself from his embrace all the same. It was all too improper, even for Vaden. The thought went through her mind quickly that Yvonne would've dropped dead on the spot at knowing her sister had allowed a man's body to touch her own.

But when the tantalizingly attractive Ransom Lake reached out and wiped the tears from her cheeks with the back of his hand, Vaden Valmont cared nothing for propriety and threw herself into the comfort of his arms once more.

"They meant to . . . to . . ." she stuttered.

"They meant to frighten ya is all. But there's

nothin' funny about a prank like that," he spoke quietly. His voice was so deep, so soothing that in a moment, Vaden began to cease her trembling.

"All the same . . . I thought they meant to—"

"We only meant it as a joke, Miss Vaden," Nathaniel defended. Vaden's arms slid around Ransom's waist for comfort. She pulled herself tighter against him, trying to drown out the sound of Nathaniel's voice. But her anger, anxiety, and residual fear only heightened as he added, "Looks to me like you're the one who's needin' a lesson or two, Ransom Lake. Forcin' that poor girl against you like that. You're nothin' but a dirty old man."

"You can shut your mouth or be signin' your own death certificate, boy," Ransom growled. Nathaniel spoke not another word, only continued to drive the team.

As the wagon rolled on, the noise of it rumbling along the road to town heightened as the terrain became rougher and rougher. The loud rumble of the wagon wheels on the hard earth, the sideboards rattling, all of it added to Vaden's anxiety. At least, she thought, Nathaniel wouldn't be attempting to speak to her, for the noise was profound. Even if he did attempt it, she was comforted to know she would not be able to hear him.

Vaden began to feel warmer, within and without. It was an inebriating sensation being held by

Ransom Lake. His strong hands stroked her hair comfortingly as he held her, and the horrid fears and anxieties she had experienced at the hands of the young men were lessened for a time. She marveled again at the warmth of him. And it testified to her of how the temperature had dropped.

"I'm sorry," she spoke to him. "To drag you out in the cold like this. I—"

"What? Don't you be apologizin' for anything," he scolded. "This is none of it your fault, girl."

"I shouldn't have left the social, shouldn't have been so foolish. And then . . . then . . . I was so scared. I know it's silly of me. Stupid to let a prank affect me so . . ." she began, tears still streaming down her face.

"None of this was your fault. And anybody would've been scared near to death at havin' this done to them." Ransom Lake took her face between his powerful hands and glared into her eyes. Vaden's own eyes widened, for the anger apparent in his gray eyes was almost frightening. "It's over now. Ya put it out of your mind."

"I can't," she cried. "I can't. I keep thinking about—"

"Then think about somethin' else," he told her calmly.

"I-I couldn't move! I couldn't breathe! All I could smell was that pine box and the dirt and—"

"I know," he comforted. "Sssshh."

Then, because of the state of lingering panic and fear in Vaden's mind, because of the interminable need she felt to receive comfort from him, to feel security somehow, she did stop crying, and her attention at that moment was completely arrested by his mouth.

"Ssshhh," he whispered again as he held her face in his hands.

Before Vaden could stop herself, her fevered, tormented mind had instructed her body to act, and it did. She reached up, pulling his hands from her face and freeing it from his grasp. Raising her face to his, she kissed him directly on the same enticing mouth that had tried to verbally silence her fears a moment before. She did not kiss him long, nor passionately, but indeed longer and betraying more of her own desire than she intended. She had closed her eyes in that moment of the kiss, letting the warmth and strength of him push aside the horrid thoughts of what she had endured before he had come for her. She opened her eyes to see him frowning at her; his expres-sion otherwise was one of surprise. Humiliated suddenly at her brazen act, Vaden fought for an explanation.

"I-I . . ." she stammered. "Thank you. Thank you for coming for me. I-I only wanted to thank you."

He continued to frown at her as if he did not believe her reason for kissing him was merely a thank you for his chivalry. He said nothing— uttered not one word—only persisted in staring at her in his unnerving manner. As the heated blush of her ever-increasing humiliation began to burn throughout her body, Vaden attempted to push herself free of him. But each time her palms would push fiercely against his powerful chest, his strong arms would only tighten about her body. Finally, as tears flooded her cheeks once more with her frustration, he abruptly released her, and she scooted away from him to the other side of the wagon bed. She looked at him for a moment as he stretched his arms out, resting them on the side of the wagon sideboard he sat against. His eyes still studied her incessantly, the frown still puckering his brow. Vaden looked away to what lay behind the wagon, and when the terror of the incident only renewed itself, for she could still smell the sickly sweet aroma of pine, she turned and looked at the team of horses pulling the wagon toward home.

The air was more than chilled now. It was cold, and Vaden, without a proper coat, was beginning to shiver. Drawing her knees to her chest, she hugged them against her body tightly and looked once more to where Ransom Lake sat across the way, ever staring with his stormy, disturbing eyes. She looked away from him again and glanced at Nathaniel, who drove the wagon on determinedly.

But when she could still feel the heat of Ransom Lake's gaze on her, she looked to him once more and said curtly, "Aren't you cold? Why didn't you wear a coat? A shirt, at least?" Her voice was too brusque, and she knew it. But he was making her uncomfortable now. The heaven-sent man who had saved her from further anguish and pain was the cause of her irritation now.

"Didn't have time to dress for the weather," he answered loudly, yet still in his mumbled, low, almost slurred manner. "And aren't ya glad I didn't waste the time on it?"

Vaden sighed and looked away, ashamed that she would talk so rudely to him.

"And besides," he continued, his voice taking on the provocative intonation that always sent Vaden's innards to taking flight, "it's not like it's anything of me ya haven't seen before, now is it?"

Instinctively Vaden glanced to Nathaniel, who only continued to drive the team, seemingly having not heard Ransom Lake's rather personal statement.

"That sounded terrible! The way you offered that remark!" Vaden scolded him.

Ransom scowled and tipped his head to her. "What? What did ya say, girl?"

Again Vaden looked to Nathaniel to ensure that his attention was straightforward and he was not listening over his shoulder. "I said that sounded terrible! The way you—"

"What?" Ransom Lake interrupted, cupping a hand to his ear.

Vaden exhaled with exasperation. Then, moving forward until she was on her hands and knees in the wagon bed and closer once more to the man so that he might hear her, she repeated, "I said that sounded terrible! What if he had heard you?"

"What? Heard me say that out by the creek the other day, I took off my shirt and you—" Ransom Lake was silenced immediately as Vaden lunged forward and put her hand over his mouth.

"What are ya doin' back there, Ransom Lake? That's Jerome Clayton's girl ya got back there, and I don't think he—" Nathaniel began as he started to look over his shoulder.

In one swift movement, Ransom Lake's powerful arms left their resting place on the wagon board, pushed Vaden's hand from his mouth, and took hold of her wrist tightly, rendering her unable to move back to the other side of the wagon. "Keep your eyes on home, boy," he growled. "Unless ya want me to break your neck and leave ya out here to the coyotes."

Nathaniel was silent as Vaden tried to pull her wrist free of Ransom Lake's grasp. But as she attempted to pry his fingers from her wrist, his other hand took hold of her free wrist as well, and he held both tightly as he frowned at her. "What're ya tryin' to get away from me for, girl?" he asked in a lowered voice.

Vaden dropped her head as she began to sob once more. Her strength was gone. Her will to defend herself from great harm or simple teasing was gone from her. She felt weak and tired and insecure. When Ransom Lake's hands released her wrists, his strong arms encircling her body and pulling her once again onto his lap and against the warmth of him, Vaden simply collapsed. Letting her arms encircle his waist for a moment, she inhaled deeply of the scent of his skin as her tears bathed his chest. Her hands slid up the length of his back to his shoulders, where they rested as she returned his comforting embrace.

After she had cried out the anguish in her heart, she lifted her head from him, wiping her tears with the backs of her hands and asked, "How did you know where they had taken me? Did you simply guess at it? I've seen no one else out this way since we started for home. How did you know where to look?"

Ransom sighed heavily and let his hands travel to her waist, holding her firmly as he sat her between his legs. He drew his knees up on either side of her and rested his forearms on them. Vaden watched, intrigued as his jaw visibly clenched and unclenched several times as if he were fighting not to say something.

"I just . . . I just knew," he mumbled, looking away from her.

"What do you mean? How could you just know?" she asked.

"I guessed at it," he nearly snapped, glaring at her. "I-I just figured it's where boys might go to . . . to . . . play pranks." He took Vaden's shoulders and turned her so her back leaned against his chest, her legs stretched out on the wagon bed before her. She sensed he didn't want her to look at him. She wondered what he was hiding. "Now, them draggin' ya out here and actin' like they were gonna to bury ya . . . that's all they did, right?"

"What do you mean is that all they did?" Vaden snapped, wishing she could turn and look at him again. "I think it's a horrid enough thing, and I—"

"I mean . . . your shirtwaist . . . the collar on this side and shoulder," he said. She shivered with pleasure as she felt his fingers fumbling with the torn fabric, which exposed her shoulder and camisole strap. "They didn't try to—"

"No," Vaden interrupted. His meaning was all too clear and justified she knew. But she hadn't wanted him to have to speak of it further. "It was torn when they removed the blanket they'd put over my head. I tried to run, naturally."

"Naturally," he repeated in agreement.

Vaden's body tensed as she felt his warm, strong hand cup her bare shoulder for a lingering moment.

"I-I tried to run, and . . . and my shirtwaist was torn when one of them grabbed it to stop me." Vaden tried to calm her breathing and her emotions.

It was too much, too torturous a night! To be terrorized, to fear for her life, and in the next moment to find herself in the arms of the man she loved—it was too much! As she felt the warmth of Ransom Lake's breath on the flesh of her neck where her collar was torn away, her tears moistened her cheeks again. She thought of the moment when they had stood on the banks of the brook and he seemed to have read her mind, knowing full well she had wondered why he tore the sleeves from his shirts, how the smooth contours of his chest would feel beneath her palm. She remembered his telling her to go home so her curiosity could get busy on other things of wonderment. *How it feels for me to touch your skin,* he had said. As her body broke into an involuntary shiver, goose bumps covering every inch of her, she realized he had answered that curiosity himself, for she trembled uncontrollably as his hand squeezed her shoulder for a moment before his fingers slipped caressively beneath the strap of her camisole for an instant. Then he straightened out one of his legs, turning her body so her legs lay across it, her back against his other leg still bent and supporting his own forearm. This action, whether for reasons of his own discomfort or his concern for hers, placed her shoulder, exposed because of the tear in her clothing, under and against his own arm still resting on his knee.

"You're cold," he mumbled in the low, sultry voice that was Vaden's undoing every time. His arm left his knee then and encircled her shoulders, pulling her tightly against the warmth of his body. "I guess I should've taken the time to bring a coat," he whispered. "You're shakin' like a leaf."

Vaden could only shake her head as he let his other arm embrace her as well. She couldn't speak a word, forced into silence by the magnitude of the realization she was being held, protected, comforted by Ransom Lake. She adored the sensation of her bare shoulder tucked warmly under his arm. She relished the idea of being restrained in his arms, possessed by his will. For those seemingly brief moments between his finding her and their arriving home when she would have to face the memories of the cruelty to her, she rejoiced in the things, the ways, the hint of affections that were given her of Ransom Lake.

Her head nestled firmly against his chest, and she reveled in the low, rhythmic sound of his heart as it beat to give him life. It was a strong, powerful rhythm given to a strong, powerful man, and she fancied for a moment the rhythm therein increased suddenly. Looking up, she found his puzzled frown had returned, and he once again intently studied her.

Why do you look at me that way? she thought to herself.

As if to have read her mind, he whispered, "It would be mighty easy for a man to take advantage of this situation, girl."

"How could a man take advantage of this situation?" she asked, though she knew—she hoped she knew—what he intimated.

"Don't play the fool with me, Vaden. I know your mind. You know full well what I mean," he chuckled.

Vaden was delighted to delirium at his addressing her so personally. "Well then . . . if it would be so easy," she paused, unable to believe she was going to say the words she intended, "why don't you?"

Immediately his eyebrows rose from their intensity of a frown to that of astonishment. He chuckled shortly and shook his head. "Did they hit ya over the head when they drug ya off?" he asked.

"No. But I want you to—" Her words were cut short when his fingers pressed against her lips and he hushed her. *I want you to kiss me,* she finished in her thoughts.

"Now don't be sayin' things you'll regret later, Vaden," he mumbled.

She smiled slightly when she noticed the way

his eyes lingered on her mouth as she pushed his fingers away.

"You're just upset over the things that went on and . . ." His words were lost, and Vaden felt her heart soar as, continuing to stare at her mouth, he moistened his own lips with the tip of his tongue.

Ransom Lake had lived a solitary life for no one knew how many years. But Vaden Valmont had guessed long ago that the years had been many. She knew enough of men to know a man of Ransom Lake's strength, health, age, and years of loneliness must own some yearning, some need of a woman's soft affections. The mesmerized expression in his storm-filled eyes told her she was correct in her estimation of him. So she placed her own fingers gently to her lips, kissing them softly before she reached out to tenderly place them on the lips of Ransom Lake. His lips were warm, and as her fingers lingered, caressing them, Vaden began to doubt for a moment that he could be weakened. But an instant before she would've pulled her hand away from him, he took it firmly in his and closed his eyes for a moment as he kissed the delicate tips of her fingers. Then, guiding her hand under his arm and around to rest on his back, he bent, cradling her securely with both arms and kissing her fiercely.

From the first touch of his lips to hers, Vaden imagined the bonfire that had burned so ferociously and hot at the Halloween social that

212

evening was holed up within her. This kiss was different from the kiss she'd received from Ransom Lake while standing in a mud puddle some weeks earlier. This kiss revealed his absolute masculinity, his intense virility. It was insistent, demanding reciprocation, and Vaden responded willingly, for she knew how desperately the powerful love she secreted for him needed this physical attention. She also knew of the needs, both emotional and physical, that Ransom Lake had been deprived of or of which he had deprived himself.

The short whiskers of his roughly shaven face scratched at the tender flesh around Vaden's mouth as this likeness of perfect masculinity, Ransom Lake, worked a kiss of a magnitude to be entirely thorough and passionate. She did not worry for this discomfort nor for the discomfort of nearly having the breath squeezed from her lungs so tightly did he hold her against his powerful body. For in those wholly shared moments of impassioned kisses, Vaden Valmont knew Ransom Lake was her own. Even as her mind and senses whirled with the bliss of his intimate attentions, she knew it would end and that he would again be lost to her. But for those glorious moments in time, for the enraptured duration of their kiss, Ransom Lake was hers. Vaden sensed that, though the chance would be merely an instant, she controlled the powerful, independent man. She alone held the reins to his mind, his desire, and his will in that instant. She let her hand rest at his jaw as he had instructed her to do on the previous occasion of his kissing her. The fire that blazed within her burned feverish in her heart as she could indeed feel the intensity of his determination to draw from her the essence that would quench his desire. As her hand caressed his jaw, her thumb rested for a moment in the slight cleft of his chin, and she marveled at his mastery of manipulating her emotions.

Suddenly, he broke from her. As she gasped for breath, for she truly had not realized how much his consummate kiss had deprived her of it, he held her tightly to him, whispering in her ear over and over, "I'm sorry, Vaden. I'm sorry. I'm so sorry." Then he took her chin in his hand and looked remorsefully into her eyes. "I would never do anything to hurt you. You've been my sweet, loyal . . . friend." He stumbled over the words as if he were trying to find them as he went.

Vaden's heart, which only moments before had been soaring in the heavens of love, began to fracture once again. With his admission to her that he valued her as his friend only, all the pain she felt at knowing he could never love her as she did him, all the pain inflicted her by the cruel men that night, all of this pain fused together, and

Vaden Valmont knew she would never thereafter be the identical person she had been. In an instant, the naïveté of youth was stripped from her soul, and she knew true, painful heartache and disappointment—true fear. Vaden Valmont had changed.

As the wagon stopped before her uncle's house, Myra and Yvonne dashed out of the door and into the street. Ransom Lake lifted Vaden, whose heart was now heavy with hurt, cruel treatment, and loss, down from the wagon. As Myra took her lovingly into her arms, Vaden felt nothing. Nothing but the lack of her own caring.

"Land's sake, child! What happened?" Myra gasped at viewing her niece in such an obviously traumatized state.

"We only meant it as a prank, Mrs. Valmont. I swear it," Nathaniel began to explain. His efforts in defending himself were in vain when Ransom Lake reached up with one powerful hand, took hold of the young man's shirt, and, pulling him from the wagon, threw him to the ground.

Ransom Lake moved quickly to Vaden, took her face in his hands, and spoke to her directly as his stormy-colored eyes pierced her own.

"Let this go, Miss Vaden. All of it! Don't linger on it. It will only destroy your spirit if ya don't let it go." Then he untied his horse from the wagon and walked to where Nathaniel still lay on the ground, trying to regain his breath.

"Ya tell your folks about this, boy. You do it . . . 'cause if I have to come to your house to tell them, I don't know if I'll be able to keep from beatin' ya into your own grave! Do ya hear me?" Nathaniel only glared at Ransom Lake. Yvonne and Myra gasped as Ransom Lake's boot met Nathaniel's midsection with brutal force. "You hear me now, don't ya, boy?" he asked.

Nathaniel doubled over, clutching his stomach, and nodded.

"What happened, Ransom?" Myra asked the man standing before her, angry still and yet ready to take his leave.

"They had her nailed up in a coffin out by the grove of elms east of town, Myra," he explained bluntly. "They had her mouth gagged, her arms bound to her sides, and her feet tied . . . all the while she was lyin' in a pine box with them tellin' her they were gonna bury her alive."

Myra gasped and shook her head, horror at the thought piercing her heart. "Vaden! Honey! Are you all right?"

"They threw a blanket over my head when I was walking home. Then they took me out there . . . tied me up," Vaden stated bluntly, her voice void of emotion.

"They should be whipped near to death, Myra. Jailed up in the least. But I suppose all they'll get is a good talkin' to," Ransom Lake mumbled. He swallowed hard and dropped his head for a moment before straightening his shoulders and looking directly at Myra. "There's . . . there's somethin' else I think ya should know, Myra. Where I'm concerned, I mean. Concernin' my own behavior tonight. I suppose that really I don't have any right to be beatin' this boy around after what I myself have done where your niece is concerned."

Vaden looked to her aunt.

Myra's frown deepened. "What are ya tryin' to say, Ransom?" she asked. She was tentative in her question, as if she feared the answer.

"Well, I . . . Myra, I . . ." he stammered.

"It's obvious, Auntie!" Yvonne interrupted. "He's feeling bad about not being properly dressed, can't you see?" Vaden glanced at her sister. "Isn't that it, Vaden?" Yvonne prodded.

Vaden wondered why Yvonne would defend Ransom Lake so.

"Yes. He did have his arms around me on the way home, Auntie," Vaden confirmed. "It was so terribly cold. He only meant to keep me warm."

Ransom Lake looked at her, a frown of disbelief puckering his brow. "But, Myra, I . . ." he stammered, unable to find his words, for the emotion of surprise seemingly stifled his thoughts.

"For pity's sake, Ransom Lake!" Myra exclaimed, throwing her arms around the man and hugging him gratefully. "Do ya honestly think that would worry us at a time like this?"

"Myra, I—" he began, but Vaden stepped between him and her aunt and met his confused gaze.

"Thank you, Mr. Lake, for . . . for coming for me this evening." And having thanked Ransom Lake for the last time she intended, she turned and entered the house, a worried Yvonne following closely at her heels.

"Thank ya, Ransom," Myra whispered. "Thank ya so much. How did ya know? When ya came here . . . how did ya know?"

Vaden paused just inside the house and listened, for she too still wondered at how the man knew where to look for her.

"I guessed who might be up to no good tonight and where they might be at it," he mumbled as he mounted his horse.

For one instant, Vaden nearly turned to rush to him, to plead with him to stay with her, to hold her safely in his arms again. But now even the zealous Vaden Valmont wouldn't dare to do that, for she had changed in that one late hour. She had changed. Vaden Valmont would never see the world as sweetly rosy and wonderful again. Tragedy, violence, cruelty, and severe, unhealable heartache had irreversibly wounded her this night.

CHAPTER EIGHT

Vaden stood at her bedroom window, staring out but looking at nothing. She didn't think of the beauty of the white, frosty flakes of snow floating through the air during the soft flurry occurring outside. She didn't evoke a line of lovely poetry from her memory to recite in their honor. She didn't think of their beauty because she didn't see their beauty. She didn't see anything as she stared silently out. She didn't see the Wimber children run past on their way into the mercantile to ask if their beloved Miss Vaden could tell a story. She didn't hear their disappointed groans as Myra sent them away with a, "She's not herself today children." She didn't care if the trees had lost their leaves, their branches flocked in glistening frost. She didn't care whether her Aunt Myra had made a heavenly apple pie for dessert. She didn't care if Yvonne thought her ignorant, didn't care if her Uncle Dan wore a perpetual frown of worry on his face on her behalf. She didn't care that Jerome Clayton dropped into the mercantile four different times that day to ask Yvonne how Vaden was faring. And although she heard Ransom Lake's voice drifting down the hall from her aunt's parlor as even he inquired about her well-being, she was too stunned, still too unbelieving of what had happened three nights before, too filled with heartbreak to sneak into the hall and have a peek at he who was such a wondrous attraction.

For there was an inner struggle to face a new day, to breathe, to find the radiant love of life again battling within Vaden Valmont. The horrors that could be in the world had touched her—damaged her emotions and mind. That people could think to be so cruel to another person and then to find humor, amusement, in someone's terror was beyond comprehension to her. Vaden, who had always seen the shiny side of the coin, who had always seen the beauty in the world and the good in people, now found herself struggling to find any beauty, any good. Vaden, who had believed that true and destined love could be hers, had been shown that it could not. She hadn't spoken a word to anyone for three days. She'd said yes and no when it was absolutely necessary but no other verbal indications. Her smile had faded, and the sparkle of delight in life had dulled and was gone from her beautiful eyes.

"Ransom Lake is here to inquire about you, Vay," Yvonne whispered as she entered the room. "Surely you'll come out for him."

Vaden only continued to stare out the window, for not only was she facing heartbreak where Ransom Lake was concerned but it seemed the only emotion left to her, felt by her, was humiliation. And she felt it deeply each time she thought of her attempt at capturing the man for her own that night in the wagon bed. How could she ever face him again? What he must think of her!

Yvonne sighed and began wringing her hands mercilessly. She worried desperately for her sister. She even blamed herself, feeling that somehow her constant nagging at Vaden to see reality in the world had caused this to happen to her precious sister—to squelch that delighted joy in life Vaden possessed and spread to everyone who knew her. "Come on, Vay. We could hurry and get you dressed. I mean, he did rescue you from . . . oh, Vay, won't you even come out to see Mr. Lake?"

The single spark of happiness, of joy, in Vaden's heart did glimmer at the thought of him. In fact, it began to burn with a renewed brightness, but as Vaden reminisced again of the humiliation she now felt at having been found by Ransom Lake in such a state as she had been, having acted as she had, she buried the glow and only spoke softly to Yvonne. "Tell him . . . tell him I thank him. I thank him more than he can ever know." She was silent again as she unlatched the window and opened it. Perhaps the cold, crisp air of November, of approaching winter, would clear her mind of the horrid memories and the battle raging within her.

"Oh, Vay," Yvonne sighed. But she knew it was futile to try further, so she left the room.

Vaden closed her eyes and inhaled deeply of the cool air entering her room through the open window. She felt the snowflakes alight on her cheeks, nose, lips, and eyelashes and tried to enjoy the feel of their moisture as they melted against the warmth of her skin. She inhaled deeply again, struggling with everything she was to find a scent of loveliness on the air—something to fill her lungs and chase away the smell of pine and dirt, to drive from her mind the feel of a dirty handkerchief at her mouth, of the ropes that had bound her arms and feet rendering her helpless— something to gladden her broken heart.

And then, as if by magic, a tear escaped her softly closed eyes as a faint scent of a thing beloved and familiar did tickle her senses. It was the scent of shaving soap, of leather gloves, of horsehair and saddles, mingled with the fragrance of freshly baked bread. Myra had been baking bread, and Vaden had been breathing the comforting aroma for some time. But now it seemed stronger, closer somehow, and she opened her eyes to behold the enchanting vision of Ransom Lake standing before her. He stood just outside her window looking in at her, his expression plain and indiscernible, a loaf of Myra's freshly baked bread wrapped securely in a cloth and tucked beneath his arm.

He put a fist to his mouth as he coughed several times before he frowned and barked firmly, "Snap out of it, girl."

Vaden parted her lips to try to say something,

but no sound could be forced from her throat, for she did not know what to say to him. He coughed again, reached through the window, and took her chin determinedly in his gloved hand.

"Don't let it beat ya down. Don't let one bad thing in life beat the warmth of your heart into the dirt. You'll lose it forever if ya don't buck up now. I know the fact of that." Ransom Lake tugged at Vaden's chin in his hand, and she leaned out the window toward him. The house's foundation being only a foot or less from the ground put her gaze nearly level with his, and the warmth of his breath on her face caused Vaden's heart to begin racing with excitement once more. His face was so near to hers as he stared intently into her eyes that were she to move less than one more inch forward, she might have accidentally been blessed with a taste of his lips, and it thrilled her. She scolded herself inwardly for even thinking of it, for she knew now the consequences of acting so boldly.

"Rein in, girl. Don't let it get the better of ya. Next time I'm out this way, I want that spark for life back in your eyes. Ya hear me?" Then he released her, coughed twice more, and, as quickly as he had appeared before her, was walking away down the alley.

Vaden watched him walk away through the flurry of snowflakes, and the glow of love left in her did not fade away but rather stayed, warming her bosom some. She knew it was the feeling of love for the man Ransom Lake that had kept her from completely losing herself. Even if he would never love her, she did love him, and she had been his friend at least. He had said so himself. And that was something. She put her hand out the window then and caught several flakes of snow n her palm.

"They are charming bits of loveliness," she mumbled to herself. Her attention was arrested by a small boy running down the street. He twisted and turned as he went, his face turned upward, his mouth open wide and tongue hanging out as he tried to catch the frozen particles of moisture in his mouth. At watching the child's carefree joy, the corners of Vaden's mouth turned up slightly for the first time in days.

Myra radiated her joy from every pore as Vaden, fully dressed and feature of face relaxed from frowning, sat down to supper with the rest of the family that evening.

"Are you . . . are you feeling better, sweet pea?" she asked.

Vaden smiled and said, "I will. I know I will, Auntie."

Myra sighed with relief.

There was no reference made to anything too important during supper, and Vaden knew the family was being sensitive to her tender emotions. Dan discussed trivial things about the stock and neighbors, and Myra complained about the condition of her bread, its imperfections caused from having the oven too hot or too cool.

Then, just after dinner as the family was retiring to the parlor, there came a loud knock at the door. Yvonne responded to it and returned momentarily with a small wooden box in hand.

"This was on the front porch," Yvonne announced as she entered the parlor. "It's got a paper here with your name printed on it, Vaden. Rather sloppily if I do say so. Perhaps one of your little fairy tale lovers has left it."

Vaden reached out, taking the small box from Yvonne. Removing the envelope from its place on top of the box, she placed it on her lap and opened the envelope that simply had *Miss Vaden Valmont* written on it.

"To Vaden," she read from the small piece of paper within. "That's all it says," she added, looking at the back of the paper just in case.

"What is it?" Myra asked, now curious as well and coming to stand beside her niece.

Vaden opened the box, and there, beneath a layer of white linen, lay several tan-colored objects that resembled some sort of cookie.

"Pralines!" Myra exclaimed. "Oh, they are *so* delicious! And I know of only one person in town who makes those. Sable Clayton!"

Vaden felt her heart immediately sink. "You mean you think . . . you think . . . Jerome Clayton left these for me?" she asked in disappointment.

"Well," Myra explained, sensing her niece's rather odd disappointment, "Sable sells them too. I suppose someone could've purchased them and left them for ya."

"My, my, my, little sister," Yvonne teased lovingly. "Your first secret admirer."

Vaden did smile then, for whether or not she desired attention from Jerome, it was a romantic gesture. Picking up a piece of confection, she tasted for the first time the brown sugary, pecan blended flavor of the praline. "Mmmmm!" she sighed. "That is the best thing I've ever in my life eaten! Try this, Vonnie."

Yvonne sighed and nodded. Carefully she broke off a small piece of the candy and placed it daintily on her tongue. "I've not tasted anything like that!" she admitted quite sincerely.

Vaden passed the small box around until Dan had taken two and Myra, scolding her husband for being greedy, had taken one. Then, when Myra had given the box back to Vaden, Vaden scowled as she noticed a piece of straw protruding from beneath the linen on which the candy sat. Carefully, so as not to damage the confection, she pulled back the linen and saw a rock nestled in a handful of straw.

"That's odd," she murmured as she looked at it. "Why would the box be weighted with a rock?"

"Perhaps he, whoever 'he' is, feared a wind

would come up and blow the thing off the porch," Yvonne offered.

But as Vaden lifted the linen and candy completely out of the box, she saw another note lying next to the rock. Carefully she drew out the second piece of paper and opened it, reading to herself.

"For pity's sake, Vay, what does it say?" Yvonne whined.

"It says, *Hard, cold, and unfeeling to look at. But look inside. I'd like to see the smile that this will bring to your pretty face, for nothing on earth can match the beauty of your smile.*" Vaden, still too traumatized to be over flattered, frowned, though Myra and Yvonne both giggled with delight. "How can you look inside a rock?"

Myra shrugged, as did Yvonne.

But Dan's eyes seemed to twinkle, and he said, "Turn it over, sweet pea. Look inside." Vaden smiled at him, for it occurred to her this secret admirer could very well be her sweet, dear Uncle Dan. She took the rock from its nest of straw, and an odd thrill ran through her body as she touched it. Then, turning it over, she drew in a quick breath as her eyes beheld the inside of the rock, which was hollow somewhat yet with inner walls covered in beautiful amethyst crystal.

"Would ya look at that," Myra exclaimed in a whisper.

"I've never seen such a thing before," Yvonne added.

"It's a geode," Dan stated, holding out his hand. Vaden smiled and placed the lovely piece of nature in his palm. "Them crystals form inside some kinds of rocks. It's deceivin', ain't it?"

Vaden knowingly smiled at her Uncle Dan and whispered, "Thank you, Uncle Dan."

Dan shook his head as he handed the stone back to Vaden. "I didn't have nothin' whatsoever to do with this, darlin'. No matter what you're thinkin'."

Vaden smiled all the same, and the love she felt for her uncle helped in healing her heart some-what. It was good and wonderful to be loved by family and friends. Especially certain friends, she thought.

Within three or four days, Vaden was something akin to what she once had been. She could laugh again, though not as heartily. She could see |beauty in life, though not as much of it. Little by little, a much more grown-up Vaden was finding frag-ments of herself again.

Jerome, who had been excessively concerned about her well-being, came to see her often. The fact was that Vaden's emotions were not as passionate as they once were, thus allowing her to be more tolerant of his still undesired atten-tions. She finally found the patience to pity him in seeing his side of the situation.

"Will ya come for a walk with me this evenin', Miss Vaden?" Jerome inquired on that particular afternoon. "It would do ya good to get some fresh air."

"Oh, I think I've had enough fresh air for a while. But I thank you for asking, Mr. Clayton. And I appreciate your concern." Vaden reached out, squeezing Jerome's hand reassuringly when his expression showed disappointment. "I'm sure I'll feel like a walk very soon."

Jerome smiled, encouraged. "Well, soon then. Soon. I've been miserable without ya, Miss Vaden. After what happened and you were so . . . so . . . not yourself. I found myself dreamin' of that beautiful smile of yours."

Vaden quickly looked to him, but she could not discern whether there was hidden meaning in his remark about her smile.

Then he lowered his voice and spoke, "Forgive me, Miss Vaden. But I've been so angry, so enraged, about what my friends . . . those men did to ya."

Vaden shook her head and turned from him, not wanting to be further reminded of the experience. "It's in the past. The near past perhaps, but the past all the same, Mr. Clayton. Let's not speak of it."

"Please. Let me finish. Let me say my piece, Miss Vaden." He was so stern and blunt that she did indeed nod and wait for him to speak. "I was so angry with them that it took me until yesterday to think on what happened afterward. What happened when Ransom Lake found ya. I've heard he wasn't even hardly dressed. And that he was forcing ya to—"

"Nathaniel Wimber abducted me from the street, Mr. Clayton!" Vaden exclaimed, suddenly very vexed. "Nathaniel, Toby, Frank, and Randy! People I thought were my friends . . . tore my shirtwaist handling me so brutally, tied me up, and forced me into a pine box and nailed it shut! And you stand before me questioning Ransom Lake's behavior? Ransom Lake stopped it! He stopped their cruelty to me and brought me safely home. Do you think it matters a whit to me, my aunt and uncle, or anyone else who could imagine what I had gone through . . . do you think it matters to anyone else that he didn't pause to dress for the occasion?" Vaden calmed herself as another thought struck her. "What else did Nathaniel tell you, Mr. Clayton? What other slanderous things did that troublemaker tell you? My clothing was torn away at the shoulder, Mr. Clayton. I was without a proper coat for protection from the cold that night. Ransom Lake did nothing more than keep me warm— nothing more than protect me from the people that had hurt me!"

"You're very protective of him, Vaden," Jerome stated. Vaden was irritated at his use of her given name. "Nathaniel said that you and he were—"

"Were what?" Vaden exclaimed. "What? I may be very protective of Ransom Lake—protective of the man who delivered me from those idiots you call friends—but you're unusually protective of Nathaniel. Do you agree with what he involved himself in? Do you think what they did to me was amusing? Do you wish they would've invited you along so you too could've enjoyed my terror?"

Jerome sighed, and his face softened somewhat. Shaking his head, he said, "No. No, of course not. They were wrong. And you're right. There's no reason to accuse Ransom Lake of any wrong doin'."

Vaden untied her apron and slammed it down on the countertop. "You're right, Mr. Clayton. I do need some fresh air. A walk would be very nice. A walk by myself!" After going to the back room, snatching up a wrap, and telling Yvonne she was going out, Vaden left by way of the mercantile front door, leaving Jerome looking guilty and discouraged.

It was thus that Vaden found herself perched high in the branches of her favorite maple. The dear tree was nearly barren of leaves now, and it made for a broader view of the landscape. The late afternoon air hinted of the frigid evening to come, perhaps even snow. Vaden sighed heavily as she gazed out across the land at Ransom Lake's rooftop. It was some time before she realized no smoke rose from the chimney. Odd, she thought, for it was very chilly out, and, no doubt, he would've built his evening fire by now. Something cold traced Vaden's spine as the realization penetrated her mind and an oppressive feeling of uneasiness washed over her. Climbing down from the tree, she started toward the road and was relieved to see Vaughn Wimber driving his wagon in the direction of Ransom Lake's home.

"Mr. Wimber!" she called out, walking to him when the wagon stopped. He nodded in greeting. "Good evening, Mr. Wimber. Would you perchance be going to visit Mr. Lake?"

"Miss Vaden, I want ya to know that we're so sorry about Nathaniel's behavior the other night," the man apologized very sincerely. "We just can't believe that our boy would do such a thing and—"

"It's forgotten," Vaden lied. She had no time to accept apologies. She felt in her soul something was not right where Ransom Lake was concerned. "Are you indeed going to visit Mr. Lake?" she asked again.

"Well, yes." Vaughn Wimber looked puzzled. "I'm going out there this minute with my own apologies for his trouble as well. Would ya like to come along? I'll only be a minute, and then I'll drop ya back home."

"That would be fine. Just fine. Thank you, Mr.

Wimber," she sighed, climbing onto the wagon seat beside him. Glancing back to the bed of the wagon, she let her mind linger only an instant on those wonderful moments she'd spent at that very spot in Ransom Lake's arms. Then she looked ahead. No more looking back. She tried to sit still as they rode slowly toward his house.

Vaden's heart began to pound wildly as it always did whenever she was anticipating a meeting with Ransom Lake. As the house came into view and the wagon approached it, she feared Vaughn Wimber might actually hear the mad beating of her heart.

Vaughn pulled the team to a halt just before the house and helped Vaden down from the wagon. Then he followed her as she rushed to the front door and knocked firmly.

As they stood together before the door, Vaughn muttered, "It sure is dark in there. And where's his dog?"

Vaden began to panic and kicked the door three times with her foot. They waited, and Vaughn sighed and said, "There. Here he comes," as they heard a scuffling from the other side. The door opened slowly, and Vaughn greeted, "Afternoon, Ransom. I've come to offer our family's apologies." Ransom Lake stood before them wrapped in a blanket and coughing violently, his cheeks blazing red and his eyes only open narrow slits. Vaughn Wimber stepped in front of Vaden, pushing his way past Ransom Lake and into the house. "How long ya been sick like this, Ransom?" he asked.

Vaden was horrified to find Ransom Lake in such a weakened condition. She followed Vaughn into the house and looked around, noting the cold, dark, and cluttered state of the room.

"Just got me a bit of the 'under the weather,'" Ransom Lake forced out, his voice raspy and fevered.

"Ya got more than a bit of it." Vaughn put a rough hand to the man's face. "Yer plum burnin' up! How long's this been goin' on?"

"It'll pass," Ransom Lake stated. Again he coughed. Vaden could hear it came from deep within his chest.

"It was the bitter cold on Halloween that finds you this way," Vaden remarked as a familiar pang of guilt dug at her heart.

"Just a bitty cough, girl. Nothin' to take too serious," Ransom argued.

Vaden knew better. Immediately, she practically pounced on the man, holding one palm to his forehead while the other hand fumbled with his grasp on the blanket at his chest. "Let this go!" she demanded, and more out of surprise than anything else, Ransom relaxed his grip on the blanket. Vaden put an ear to the man's sculpted and overly warm chest and listened intently. "Go for my Aunt Myra, Mr. Wimber. Doctor

Sullivan is gone to visit his daughter for the holiday, and Mr. Lake's lungs are rattling something terrible. Have her bring some broth and . . . well, she'll know what else. Tell her he's got fever, rattling lungs, chills. She'll know what to do."

"Well, I . . . I can't just leave ya here alone with the man, Miss Vaden." Vaughn Wimber was obviously unconvinced he should leave.

"I've been in far worse predicaments, Mr. Wimber," Vaden reminded him, though not cruelly. "It's plain he's worsening and not getting any better. It could be pneumonia! My Aunt Myra will know what to do. Hurry!"

With a nod of determination and something of guilt, he left quickly. Vaden stripped off her wrap and let it fall to a heap on the floor. Quickly she built a fire in the hearth. The room needed warming.

"Let's get some water boiling." She went to the stove in the next room and began stoking a fire there. "The steam will help you breathe better. I can't believe you haven't been into town for help. Actually, I can. Men. They think they're impervious to disease and illness and . . ." She stopped talking when she heard his weakened body fall to the floor in a heap not far from where she had dropped her wrap.

"I think I'm sick, Natalie," Ransom Lake moaned.

"Natalie?" Vaden whispered curiously as she

235

tried to pull him to his feet. His heavy body was terribly weak and awkward. With great difficulty, she helped him toward a chair near the fireplace. She placed the blanket around his shoulders once more. Instead of sitting, however, he laid down on the floor.

"I'm hot," he breathed, throwing the blanket aside. "It's so hot in here."

"You're feverish," Vaden explained, going to the pump and wetting a cloth beneath its cold running water. She returned to the ailing man and, folding the cloth, placed it on his forehead. "This will help cool your body," she explained soothingly. She sat down near his head and was surprised when he raised himself long enough to scoot his body up, depositing his head in her lap.

"I guess I should've taken the time to grab a coat the other night," he said, his speech more mumbly than usual. "At least you're not taken ill."

Realizing he was coherent enough to know who she was and that his calling her by another name must have been purely an accident, she asked, "Who's Natalie?" She felt at that moment, serious as his illness was, that she must know about the woman in his past—the woman who perhaps sent him into seclusion—the woman who may once have worn the ring Ransom Lake now wore on his smallest finger.

"Natalie?" he repeated, startled.

"Natalie. You called me Natalie before." Vaden watched him closely. He seemed unsettled by her question.

Suddenly, his body was wracked with the violence of his coughing. He inhaled deeply and continued to let his head rest on Vaden's lap.

"So," Vaden prodded, undaunted, yet feeling fairly guilty for pushing him to answer when he was clearly so ill.

"So, what?" Ransom Lake mumbled. "I don't feel like talking right now, girl. Can't ya see that?"

"Just tell me who Natalie is, and I'll let you be." Ransom Lake glared up at her, and she glared back. What was he hiding? What had he been hiding for so long? She had to know. She had to know about this Natalie.

After glaring at her for several more moments, he finally said, "Natalie was . . . was Natalie. And that's all of it."

"But that's no—" Vaden began.

"That's all of it, girl," he growled at her. "Now close that curious mouth of yours and help me heal . . . or leave me in peace."

"Is Natalie the reason you . . ." she began. But when his glare intensified, she knew she was wrong to push him. Ransom Lake held his secrets cached deeply in his soul. He would not share them, and she was a fool, an idiot, to suppose that if he did, he would choose an imbecilic young girl like her. So she was silent. She picked up the cloth from his forehead and turned it over, placing the other side to his skin. Then, as he closed his eyes and seemed to rest for a moment, she stared into the blaze in the hearth.

It seemed hours to Vaden, the minutes of sitting there waiting for help, sitting there with the ill, stricken, silent man. And in those moments of silence and intense worry, she stared into the flames and thought of the tragedy of not being able to win over the man she loved so desperately. It was sad, grievously lamentable, that she would love him so completely as she did and yet know he would never be hers. She thought again, however, that though he was unattainable, she had owned at least a part of him for a moment, for she still knew that during those intimate kisses they shared in the wagon bed, he had been hers. His manner, his soul, or something surreal had spoken to her mind in those moments, assuring her he knew it was Vaden Valmont he held in his arms—Vaden Valmont had caused him to lose his senses for a brief time. It was Vaden he meant to kiss, not some long-ago lost love he still pined for. Vaden knew it was she and she alone he meant to administer his affections to in those beloved, dreamlike moments. And if nothing else, if Ransom Lake should wake in the morning healed and decide he never again wanted to lay eyes on the bothersome being Vaden Valmont, still she would always have the memory of the moments he had been hers.

Half an hour passed, and still Mr. Wimber had not returned with Myra. Vaden tried to move her legs a bit as they still supported the weight of the man's head and were beginning to tingle with discomfort. She removed the cloth from Ransom Lake's forehead, knowing it would do no good to him now, being it was nearly as hot as his body.

As she gazed down at him, listening to his raspy breath, the breath he seemed to struggle for, she thought of Jerome Clayton. Was she doomed to belong to him? Everyone knew he cared for her. Everyone, including Vaden, knew he appeared the ideal young man—tall, handsome, charming, courteous, proper. Certainly Jerome Clayton would never remove his shirt in front of a young woman. And Vaden, though she had never spoken it aloud, thought and wondered how a woman could find attraction to a man when there was no excitement, no surprise, no delight, in one who did not enjoy to some extent teasing a girl.

Still, Ransom Lake could not be hers, and Jerome Clayton already was, according even to his own admission. With Jerome, there would be stability, a home, a husband, and, she guessed, a kind father to their children. At the thought of having Jerome Clayton father her children, Vaden actually grimaced. Just one mere kiss from Jerome had sent her body into repulsed shivers.

She could not imagine having to endure more physical attention from him. Still, her own mother, though deeply in love with her father, had told Vaden it was not always perfect between a man and a woman, that often other aspects of relationships outweighed the lack of physical attraction.

Was this to be her lot in life? No. Certainly the heavens intended a better companion for her, for no matter what his appearances, no matter how admired he was by everyone else, Vaden did not feel comfortable in Jerome's presence. It wasn't so much that she didn't like him. After all, he was pushy and rather possessive but likable enough. It was something else, something she just couldn't quite identify. She felt almost, well, unsafe when she was with him. Surely no one could expect her to settle for him when she felt so averse to him. She couldn't expect herself to settle for him.

Looking down into the perpetual frown on Ransom Lake's face, Vaden tried to smooth the wrinkles from his forehead with her fingertips. At just touching him thus, the flesh on Vaden's arms rippled with goose bumps, and she doubted more fully that she could endure a relationship with a man who did not affect her so. She caressed one of Ransom Lake's fevered cheeks with the back of her hand, letting the fingers of her other hand slip into the softness of his hair. She let her thumb trace the outline of his lips gently, and he stirred for a moment, turning himself on his side so that his face was nearly flush with her stomach. This position was not as comfortable for Vaden, for it occurred to her then this might not appear quite decent when her aunt walked into the room. So, placing one palm against his chest and the other on his forehead, she attempted to gently squirm from beneath him. But the fevered man groaned in protest, a scowl returning to his features, and one powerful hand pushed Vaden's hand from his chest.

"Mr. Lake, I . . . I have to move. My legs have fallen asleep under your weight. I'll . . . here," she said, reaching for the blanket he had discarded earlier. "Here." Lifting his head from her lap, she bunched up the blanket and tucked it beneath his head as she moved herself from under him and stood up. Almost immediately, however, the man began to shiver uncontrollably, his visible flesh prickling with tiny bumps. Going to the sofa nearby, Vaden retrieved another blanket and placed it over his feverish body just as the front door opened and her aunt, Mr. Wimber, and Yvonne stepped into the house.

"He's very ill, Auntie," Vaden blurted out, relieved she had removed herself from the man soon enough.

Myra dropped to her knees beside the man and placed a tender, maternal hand on his forehead.

"He's burnin' up," she mumbled. "Vaughn, run get that kettle on the stove and fetch a bucket of water from the pump. Hurry." Vaughn Wimber wasted no time in doing as Myra instructed. "Help me get him onto his back, girls."

Yvonne's eyes widened when, as the three women worked together to turn the man, the blanket covering his body slipped away. Had the situation not been so dire, Vaden might have laughed at the expression on her sister's face. Myra picked up the cloth Vaden had used to cool Ransom's head. When Mr. Wimber returned with the water, Myra combined enough of the boiling water from the kettle with the cold water in the bucket to create just the right tepid temperature necessary.

"Vaughn, go on out and get some more firewood. We need to keep it warm in here." As Mr. Wimber left, Myra continued, "Yvonne, soak this cloth in the water and bathe his head, arms, neck, and chest. It will help to soothe the fever." Yvonne's eyes widened in horror, but she did as her aunt instructed. "He's pale, Vaden. Find somethin' to put under his feet."

Vaden looked about frantically and then saw that her aunt had removed the blanket from beneath Ransom Lake's head. Quickly, she bunched it into a bundle and placed it under his feet. She looked to him when she heard him groan once more and begin coughing.

"That cough is deep in him," Myra mumbled as she pressed a hand firmly on his chest to feel his heartbeat and lungs. "He's worse off than I already feared we'd find him."

Vaden felt the trepidation begin to increase in her bosom. *What if,* she began to think, but the sound of Ransom Lake's voice interrupted her thoughts.

"What are ya doin'?" he nearly shouted. "I'm fine. Let me be!"

"You're very ill, Ransom," Myra told him firmly. "Lay still and—"

"There ya are," he mumbled, his voice softening as he looked up at Yvonne. She was so startled she dropped the cloth she'd been using to bathe his fevered skin. "Help me up," he ordered, reaching out to wrap one arm about Yvonne's waist. Taking hold of her arm, he tried to pull himself up. Yvonne's eyes widened, and her mouth dropped open in astonishment. "Help me up! How do ya ever expect to find yourself helpless in my arms if I can't even get up there to kiss ya, precious?"

It was Vaden who gasped next as Ransom Lake managed to pull himself to his knees, his fevered gaze intent on her sister.

"He's out of his head, Yvonne. Ignore what he's sayin' to you. Ransom's a good man, and don't ya go thinking badly of him," Myra instructed her niece as she put her own arms around Ransom

Lake's chest and pulled him away from Yvonne. "Help me get him to the sofa, Vaden. He needs to be sittin' up." Vaden paused for only a moment, preoccupied by her sister's all too pleased blush, delighted expression, and unfaltering stare at Ransom Lake. "Vaden!" Myra commanded. Vaden quickly took one of Ransom Lake's heavy arms and placed it about her own shoulders, helping him to stand.

"Where'd she go?" Ransom Lake mumbled. "That girl sets my mouth to waterin'." Even for the gravity of such a situation, Vaden knew the sharp sting of jealousy as it erupted in her stomach.

By the time Vaughn Wimber had returned, Ransom Lake was resting peacefully on the sofa in a sitting position. As Vaden helped the others endeavor to help the man heal, the thought struck her that perhaps Ransom Lake was no different than any other man on earth. Perhaps the only reason Vaden had captured any of his attention at all was because he felt Yvonne was too out of his reach.

"No. No," she whispered to herself aloud. He was feverish. After all, hadn't he called her by the wrong name only a short time before? Vaden tried to dispel her anxiety by comforting herself with this knowledge.

It was a long and fearful night for Vaden. Myra had sent Vaughn Wimber home hours before, and now Yvonne rested peacefully in a nearby chair. Myra rested on the sofa next to Ransom Lake. His fever had broken about an hour earlier, and Myra assured Vaden he would be fine. Still, she wanted to wait until morning after he awakened before leaving him alone. Vaden had learned a great deal during those long hours when her aunt had tended Ransom Lake. She knew the knowledge she had gained that night pertaining to helping someone overcome illness would serve her well in years to come.

Glancing at Yvonne, she thought to herself maybe the experience would help her in tending her own children one day—the children she would never have with Ransom Lake. Would they be the children she might share with Jerome Clayton? Her stomach churned at the very thought of Jerome Clayton, and a sort of anxious fear engulfed her fatigued mind. Again she wondered what it was that pushed her away from accepting Jerome as the nice, well-mannered, desirable man everyone else thought him to be.

"I feel like a pile of horse . . . manure, run over by every wagon wheel in the county." The low, raspy mumble caused Vaden to turn in her seat at Ransom Lake's feet, overjoyed to hear his low, mumbly voice again. He pulled himself into a sitting position on the sofa, leaning on his knees with his elbows as he buried his scowling face in his hands. He frowned, his eyes opening to only narrow slits as he looked inquisitively and rather grouchily at Vaden. "What did ya do to me this time, girl?" he asked.

"Nothing!" Vaden spat, irritated and turning away from him. How horrid that he would assume because he felt so bad, she had once again been the cause of it. His low chuckle stopped the tears from escaping her eyes not a moment too soon. When she felt the warmth of his capable hand slip beneath her hair and clutch the back of her neck, she turned to look at him again. "I'm gonna swallow my pride and thank ya for comin' with Vaughn last night. I felt pretty bad."

"Well, I'm relieved to see you feeling better, Ransom," Myra chirped, stretching and standing up from the sofa.

"Much better. I thank ya, Myra," the man responded, dropping his hand from Vaden's neck and looking up to her aunt. "And you too, Miss Valmont," he added, nodding a thank you at Yvonne, who could not meet his gaze for her blush was crimson.

"Well, there's no doubt in my mind ya caught that nasty sickness the night ya brought Vaden home, Ransom. And I want to remind ya how grateful we are to ya for that," Myra said, smiling.

"My pleasure, Myra. I'm indebted to ya for this." He offered a hand and firmly shook the one Myra offered in return.

"We've left ya some muffins for breakfast. If ya get to feelin' badly again, ya drive over to the house, ya hear me?" Myra instructed.

"Yes, ma'am," he chuckled.

"Come along now, girls. We've done our nursin' well, and we need to be getting' on home. I don't think you ever dropped off for a rest, Vaden child. Ya must be done in."

"I'm fine, Auntie." Vaden stood and reached for her wrap, which was hanging on a nearby coat rack. She didn't think she could turn and look at Ransom Lake and still leave him. His pale coloring, weakened state, and still raspy breathing frightened her. Coupled with the fact she felt a need to run to him and prove she was as good and desirable a woman as Yvonne, she couldn't look at him.

"Thank ya, ladies," he mumbled as the women started toward the front door.

"Now you stay sittin', boy," Vaden heard Myra scolding. "There's no need to see us out." Still Vaden didn't turn to look at Ransom Lake but only continued to follow Yvonne and Myra as they walked to the door. "Let us know if ya need anything, Ransom," Myra added. " 'Bye now. And you take care."

"You're welcome to take the wagon home, Myra. I don't feel right lettin' you three walk and—" Ransom began.

"The fresh air will do us good. Now, you put

yourself to bed. Do ya hear?" With that, Myra left the house.

"You have a nice day, Miss Valmont," Ransom called after Yvonne, who turned, blushed, smiled, and nodded.

Vaden couldn't wait to escape Ransom Lake's house. She felt panic, sorrow, fear, and heartbreak all over again. But as she started out the door after Yvonne, she was stopped as she felt the back of her skirt catch on something. Turning to see what was stopping her so she might free herself, she saw at once that one fold of her skirt was indeed caught—caught tightly in Ransom Lake's grasp. Knowing it was unavoidable now, she raised her eyes from her skirt to find him looking at her.

There was no smile to his features nor a frown as he said, "I guess we're even now, huh? An eye for an eye, so to speak."

"I think your deed was much more that of deliverer than ours, Mr. Lake," she managed to say bluntly. Quickly he released his hold on her skirts and took her hand. Vaden glanced out the door to see her aunt and Yvonne were already to the road and had turned toward home.

"It depends on your point of view, I suppose," Ransom Lake mumbled, and Vaden looked back at him. He smiled slightly and added, "Natalie is my older sister's name, Vaden."

"Oh," Vaden said nonchalantly, though she sighed with relief. "Well, that's interesting to know, Mr. Lake." Ransom Lake's smile broadened, and Vaden's heart warmed, knowing that, whatever the reason, she was the cause of the smile across his divinely featured face.

"Thank you again," he added with a friendly wink.

"Thank *you* again," Vaden answered, pulling her hand from his nerve-stirring grasp. As Vaden hurried to catch up with her aunt and sister, Yvonne turned and flashed one of her dazzling smiles in her direction.

"You were right to send for Auntie, Vay. She knew just what to do." Vaden was disturbed by her sister's beauty at that particular moment. Never before had she been truly envious of it. Vaden had always, though perhaps feeling it a greater challenge to use her less obvious feminine wiles to attract attention, been confident in herself. Never before had she let Yvonne's beauty intimidate her. Until now. With what had transpired between Yvonne and Ransom Lake while he had been feverish, Vaden was beginning to wonder more and more if perhaps Ransom Lake's serious interest had always been directed toward her sister.

"I knew she would," Vaden answered finally.

"That Ransom Lake," Myra sighed. "I don't know how he's avoided death this long as solitary as he keeps himself. I'll be honest, and not just to pat myself on the back for knowin' what to do, but if we hadn't have helped him through the night . . . well, things may have been much, much worse." Myra put a comforting arm about Vaden's shoulders. "What's that scowl cuttin' your brow for, sweet pea?"

Vaden rubbed at her temples for a moment and then said, "Oh, I'm just very tired, Auntie. Truly."

"Well, I think the poor soul should be invited for Thanksgiving dinner." Yvonne looked completely guiltless in her reasoning when Vaden quickly looked up at her. "After all, he's so . . . so alone. Don't you think so, Vaden?" Yvonne winked, and Vaden felt guilty for having thought badly of her sister for even a moment. It was obvious Yvonne knew it would please Vaden to have Ransom Lake in for Thanksgiving.

"It's a wonderful idea!" Myra exclaimed. "I'll come over with your Uncle Dan tomorrow to check on Ransom, and we'll invite him then." Myra frowned for a moment and mused, "Oh, dear. What if someone has already asked him?"

"Then we'll invite him for Christmas!" Yvonne chirped.

Vaden nodded her agreement. Her eyes wandered to her left as the road they trod passed by the turnoff to her favorite tree by the brook.

"Vaden," Yvonne began that night after the sisters had turned down the lamp and snuggled comfortably beneath their covers. "Vaden, I couldn't bring myself to confess this before . . . because I was astounded about it on Halloween night when he brought you home . . . and everything was so traumatic that I didn't say anything. But now I have to say it, Vaden. I had no idea!"

"No idea about what?" Vaden asked, though she already knew to what her sister referred.

"Well, I mean . . . when you told me that you'd . . . you know . . . that you'd seen Ransom Lake . . . improperly attired . . . well, I just had no idea he looked so . . . so . . ."

"Indescribable?" Vaden snapped.

Yvonne giggled slightly. "Yes! Yes, that's it exactly!"

"Did you think I made the story up then, Vonnie?" Vaden snapped.

"Oh, no! No! Of course not, Vay! I believed you. It's just that . . . well, I always thought somehow I'd be horrified to retching the first time I saw such a thing. But . . . but I wasn't. In fact, I would say the experience went beyond interesting. He's marvelously sculpted, Vay."

"I know."

"And soft-skinned. You know, I expected him to feel more like . . . I don't know . . . a fish maybe. All slimy and scaly."

"Now that's utterly ridiculous, Yvonne! You're only being dramatic now, and I refuse to listen to it!" Turning from her sister, Vaden held the blanket tightly around her shoulders.

"What's wrong, Vay?" Yvonne asked, genuinely

concerned. "You've been testy all day. Is it simply fatigue? Or is something else bothering you?"

"Nothing is bothering me, Yvonne. I'm simply too tired to talk." Vaden felt guilty lying to her sister, for she knew Yvonne would understand if she were to explain her concerns. But instead she simply mumbled, "Goodnight."

"And to think, Vay . . . he risked his health to rescue you from the clutches of evil that night. It's terribly tender, isn't it?" Yvonne sighed.

Vaden feigned sleep then. It didn't even occur to her that somehow the tables had turned. Vaden Valmont had begun to lose her ability to dream, to have her heart take flight over fanciful thoughts, while her sister, ever straitlaced and proper before, was talking in the language of fairy tales.

CHAPTER NINE

Ransom Lake recovered. He had accepted Myra's invitation for Thanksgiving dinner too. Thanksgiving was moving closer and closer, and Vaden still battled her emotions—her uncertainties—her prospects. Or rather, prospect. Jerome, as always, was overly attentive and charming. In the past three weeks following the incident of Halloween night, he had been more the perfect gentleman and friend than ever. And because he was so, coupled with the fact Ransom Lake had not shown his face in town since that time, Vaden had neglected to tell Jerome she could never settle for him. Inwardly her dreams battled with reality, and reality, for once, was getting the better of her. Jerome was an attractive, attentive, well-mannered man. He would, no doubt, work hard to make her happy, to build a family with her, and make a life for them all. And the truth of it was Jerome was reality.

Jerome came into the store every day, often bearing some small gift for her as a token of his affections. Vaden had taken several evening walks with him as well. She'd even relented to his continuing request and began calling him by his given name. Never, however, did she allow him to kiss her again in any fashion.

It began to seem to Vaden she would need to accept Jerome as her lot in life—that she would have to accept Ransom Lake had been allowed to touch her young existence only so she could learn that along with joy and wonderful things, heartache and sorrow were also part of living. She still struggled with the humiliation, the terror, and the tormenting memory of the devastating Halloween night. She struggled with the horrid residual memories of panic—and then with the blissful memories of Ransom Lake's kiss savored in the back of a wagon. All of these things created a great and unsettled turmoil within Vaden. She often felt as if her thoughts and her actions would never be wholly her own again.

It was two days before Thanksgiving, a cool, autumn Monday morning, when Ransom Lake did at last enter the mercantile. Yvonne and Vaden were straightening the store, and Myra was at the counter when he entered.

"Well, good mornin', ladies—Florence Nightingales of the county," he greeted with a smile and in his low, mumbly manner.

Vaden felt her heart leap into her throat but tried to turn slowly to greet him.

"Good morning, Mr. Lake," Yvonne welcomed exuberantly.

"Miss Valmont. Miss Vaden," Ransom greeted, nodding his head at first to one girl and then the other.

"You about ready for my world-famous pumpkin pies, Ransom?" Myra asked.

Ransom Lake smiled, nodding his head. "I sure am, Myra. I just hope I can get here on Thursday is all."

"What do you mean?" Vaden erupted, for it alarmed her he would even imply he wouldn't be with them for Thanksgiving when she'd looked forward to it so.

"There's a storm comin'," he answered, still looking to Myra. "A heavy one. I think we'll all be pretty snowed in nice and tight by Thursday morning."

"But you'll still come, won't you?" Yvonne asked. "You can't miss Thanksgiving, Mr. Lake."

"Oh, I suppose I'll make it somehow," he teased, winking at Yvonne.

Vaden was so upset by his attention to her sister that she turned from him and began slamming boxes into a stack.

"Oh, dear. Vaden, maybe ya should tell Mrs. Wimber ya can't watch the children while she goes visitin' dear Mrs. Tilits. I don't want ya gettin' stranded out there and not bein' able to get home to—" Myra began. Vaden had assured Mrs. Wimber she would tend the children while she went visiting the day before Thanksgiving.

"I'll be fine, Auntie. Mrs. Wimber never stays too late," Vaden said, turning to look at her aunt and Ransom Lake. "You know that." Then, unable to tolerate the three pairs of eyes boring down inquisitively on her for the brusqueness of her remark, Vaden walked toward the front door, announcing, "I'm to meet Jerome at nine, Auntie. I'll be back soon."

Without waiting for a reply or permission, she left, walked down the street, and turned onto the pumpkin patch road. Tears were immediately on her cheeks, and she brushed at them angrily as she walked. *Why?* she wondered. Why were her emotions so close to the surface all the time? Why did she read sarcasm and unfriendliness into everything everyone said to her? Why couldn't she just accept Jerome Clayton for what he was and forget Ransom Lake for what he was? Ransom Lake would never belong to her, it was obvious. In fact, it wouldn't surprise anyone if he ended up belonging to her beautiful and accomplished sister.

She thought maybe she should send a telegram to her father and mother asking for the money to buy a stage ticket home. She felt unable to sort out and deal with everything bottled up inside her. She wanted to scream, to sob more bitterly than ever she had. What was happening to her? What was happening to her life? The events of the past few months, especially these past few weeks, had scarred Vaden—changed her. She now had trouble assuring herself of what she wanted or needed in life, of what she loved and lived for. Things were harder now. Thinking was hard. Going about her daily tasks was hard—a different kind of hard than before. For now, instead of wanting to leave her chores to go out into the fresh air, hoping to bump into her cherished Ransom Lake, she only wanted to leave her chores to hide in her room away from questions and away from a decision where Jerome Clayton was concerned. She did not love Jerome. She knew it. Yet would she ever love anyone again? Ransom Lake had captured her love, her heart, and her spirit. Vaden considered Jerome only because she was unsure her heart would ever again be completely free. Oh, she knew well enough she would continue to live, that some things in life would bring her joy. But she doubted her joy could ever be any semblance of what it would've been with Ransom Lake in her life.

"You don't ever run off to meet Jerome, girl. He always comes lookin' for you."

Vaden startled at the sound of Ransom Lake's voice, and she quickly brushed the tears from her cheeks before turning to face him.

"Mr. Lake," she greeted awkwardly. It was obvious he had followed her, but the knowledge made her uncomfortable somehow instead of elated. "I thought you had business in the store."

"I do. But your sister said ya must be upset and sent me to fetch ya," he stated, grinning slightly.

"Why would she send you?" Vaden asked, though she immediately wished she hadn't, for she feared he might actually know the answer. Ransom shrugged his shoulders. "And how would you know whether I meet Jerome or not?" she asked, irritated that he would be so assuming.

"I do know. I know ya never seek him out. He always finds you. Am I wrong?" He was certain, as if he could read her mind.

His eyes were beautiful, too captivating, and she answered, "No."

"Then why did ya say ya were goin' to meet him?" he asked. The mischievous expression on his face revealed he already suspected she had done it for his benefit.

"Because . . . because I knew my aunt wouldn't stop me if she thought that's where I was bound. They . . . they think he's a nice young man. A gentleman. A perfect catch."

"You're not yourself anymore, Miss Vaden," he stated then, his face gone serious. "You've lost your way. Is it because of Halloween, or is it somethin' else?"

Vaden looked at him. He knew her so well. She knew there was no trying to weasel out of telling him the truth. "I . . . I'm not sure. Maybe I'm just growing up." Self-conscious, she folded her arms across her chest.

"Don't try feedin' me that. You're plenty grown up." She looked at him as he looked away for a minute, rubbing at his whiskery chin with a roughened hand before mumbling, "And I suppose I had more to do with that than was proper." He quickly turned to her, however, and, shaking an index finger in her direction, lectured, "But don't ya go doin' anything stupid, girl. Who ya choose to spend your life with is important. It's not somethin' ya go jumpin' into just because a nice boy comes along and everyone else thinks he's good for ya. I don't think he's good for ya—if my opinion means anything."

Suddenly, Vaden was angry with him. "Who are you to tell me what or who is good for me? You act as if you know me so well. As if you . . . what am I supposed to do, Ransom Lake? Wait until your long-lost brother shows up? Am I? Do you think you're so much better than every other man that . . ." Vaden stopped her scolding, for the color had completely drained from Ransom Lake's perfect face. It was visible by his expression that his jaw was tightly clenched, and his eyes even seemed to cloud over for a moment.

"What do ya mean by that, girl? My long-lost brother?!" he growled.

"I-I mean . . . you seem to think you're the only worthy male in this town. And I meant to say that . . . I know you're unavailable, so what do you expect us young women to do? Wait until you find an interest in one of us? Which we know won't happen, so I was simply—"

"Mockin' me?"

"Yes, sir." Vaden felt horrible inside. Obviously she'd touched on something very sensitive with Ransom Lake. He looked at her for a moment as if he didn't know what to say or do.

"I . . . I have to get some things from your aunt. You're right. It's none of my business. Forgive me, Miss Vaden." He turned from her and began walking away.

"Mr. Lake!" she called to him, hitching up her skirts and taking out after him. His stride was long and quick-paced, and she nearly had to run to keep up with him. "I'm sorry, Mr. Lake. I'm sorry. You came out here to try to cheer me, and I only upset you in return."

"I'm not upset," he spat.

"Please. I can't stand for you to be angry with me. I'm sorry. Please. I was only upset and—"

He stopped abruptly, turned, and took hold of her shoulders tightly as he glared down at her. "You and I are thrown into each other's paths far too often. Until one or the other of us gets control of who we are again, neither one of us will be content. Isn't that right?" He frightened her at that moment. He had far too great an insight into what she felt, but she wondered at his estimation of himself.

"I don't see how that applies to you, sir," she ventured.

"I belong alone, girl. I was happy that way. Life

was easier. I've lost sight of that, and I'm tryin' to find the middle ground of the two."

"And . . . and I trip you up. Is that what you mean?" Vaden offered as the tears filled her eyes once more.

"Yes. But not the way you're thinkin'."

Hanging her head then, for the humiliation was heavy in her heart and mind, she whispered her apology. "I'm sorry, Mr. Lake. For my behavior in the wagon that night. I . . . I'm truly sorry. I know how unbecoming . . . how completely improper it was, and I want you to know that I scold myself inwardly for it every day."

"What?" he asked. "What are ya talkin' about? I swear, you could send a man to drinkin' tryin' to understand ya sometimes."

"I acted so terribly. I . . . I tried to . . ."

"Seduce me?" he finished, and Vaden winced at the truth of his words. "You're trying to apologize for temptin' me." With that, the color returned to his face, along with the smile. Unexpectedly he took her in his arms then, embracing her firmly against his body as he chuckled. "You're a funny kid, Vaden Valmont. Has that been what's worried ya all this time?" Not wanting him to know it was only a small part of her worries, she nodded, letting her arms go around his waist. "Well, I'll tell ya what, little friend. I'll try to seduce you sometime, and then we'll be even. Okay?" Vaden looked up at him, shocked he would tease about such a thing and hurt once more at his deeming her merely his friend. "For pity's sake, girl. Don't let a little thing like that bother ya. Besides, that moment between you and me was my fault, not yours." When she did not answer, he released her and mumbled, "If it bothers ya that much . . . I'll swear never to do anything like that again. Cross my heart and hope to—"

Vaden reached up, clamping a hand over his mouth to stop the words of such a vow. "Don't even speak something like that!" she scolded, for it unnerved her to have him mention death.

"Somethin' like what? Somethin' like hope to die? Or somethin' like I'll never again do to ya what I did in the wagon?" A friendly grin spread across his face once more, and she realized he was only teasing her. "Come on. Your Aunt Myra will think I'm up to no good out here with ya."

Taking her hand, he began to pull her back toward the mercantile. How Vaden wished her aunt had reason to think Ransom Lake was up to no good with her. But it was not to be. She sensed that it never would be again.

As the wind howled outside the Wimber home, Vaden tried to calm her rising anxiety at Mrs. Wimber's not having returned. The hour was later than Vaden had expected to have stayed tending the children, and it gave her cause for concern. The storm was turning violent. She had visions of not only having to tend the children through the night but of missing Thanksgiving Day and the most coveted guest joining her family for dinner.

"Violet! Put your brother down, honey. You can't be dragging him around like that," Vaden softly scolded. Violet had been carrying the baby back and forth across the room for nearly half an hour. Vaden was worried the small girl might be getting more tired and weak than she realized. How she wished Selma and Raylin had not gone to their uncle's house for the night. Then they could have tended to their young brothers and sister.

"Tell us a story then, Miss Vaden. Please," Violet begged.

Vaden had not felt like telling stories for some time. Yet Violet's sweet, delighted voice convinced her at last, and she nodded her head amidst the pleadings of the children. "Very well."

Vaden glanced at the clock sitting on the mantel and noted Mrs. Wimber was nearly two hours late. Through the window she could see the snow falling and hear the wind. She was starting to worry once more that perhaps the children's mother would not be able to get home. Ransom Lake obviously had been correct in predicting the storm, and it was becoming severe. She did not want to be snowed in with the Wimber children for days and days on end. So with the anxiety over the storm building within her, yet the hope she would be able to get home, Vaden began to bewitch the children with her talent for story-telling.

"This is the story of Cinderella," she began. "Cinderella was a beautiful young woman. She had been loved oh so dearly by her cherished parents. Tragically, her mother died when Cinderella was very young, and her father, feeling his treasured daughter needed a feminine heart to care for her, married a widow with two young daughters of her own."

Vaden wove her tale, dramatically as always, trying to keep the children's minds, and her own, from the howling wind and blowing snow. As the tale wore on, so did the night.

"And Cinderella, in fleeing so quickly as to not be set upon by the castle guards, tripped. One of her beautiful dancing slippers—princesses *always* wear slippers instead of shoes—one of her beautiful dancing slippers fell from her foot and was abandoned on the castle steps." Vaden dramatically kicked off one of her boots, watching it land with a thud in the middle of the floor. "And there it lay as Cinderella fled, for the guards were so close behind her she had not one extra moment to spare in trying to reach back and retrieve her lovely slipper."

Vaden continued the tale, telling of the anguished prince, who searched and searched in vain for the fair maiden whose dainty foot would fit the slipper, thus revealing his one true love.

"But . . . why didn't the prince just look for her face, Miss Vaden?" Violet inquired. "Why didn't he just know who she was when he saw her?"

Vaden smiled and went to the fire, where she carefully dirtied her fingertips with soot from the hearth. "Because, you see, Violet," she began as she dabbed at her face with her soiled fingertips, "Cinderella's beauty, her feature of face, was hidden beneath the ashes and soot that gathered on her while she was cleaning the fireplaces in the house. So when the prince came to her stepmother's house to try the slipper on every maiden there, he did not recognize her. And her stepmother told the prince that their servant girl had not attended the ball."

Just then the door to the Wimber home was forced open, and in stumbled Mrs. Wimber, covered with snow from head to toe. Her face was red and chapped from the wind.

"Mama!" went up the general cheering among the children.

"It's the fury of perdition out there, Vaden! I don't know how Mr. Lake will ever get ya home in this. I've told him the two of ya should shelter here, but he says your Aunt Myra was very adamant ya be home tonight safe and sound," Mrs. Wimber explained between gasps and kissing the warm cheeks of her happy children.

"What do you mean Mr. Lake will get me

home?" Vaden asked, confused. "I thought Uncle Dan would . . ." At that very moment, Ransom Lake stepped from the furious storm without into the warm room within, closing the door firmly behind him.

"Your uncle's bad leg is actin' up, Miss Vaden, and he asked me to see Mrs. Wimber back and you safely home." He was so handsome, his presence so dominating!

"But . . . but she can't go yet, Mr. Lake," Violet argued, going to stand before him and tugging on his pant leg. "She hasn't finished Cinderella."

Vaden stepped forward, intent on explaining to the child why she must go at once, but she paused when she saw Ransom Lake smile and hunker down so he was more at the child's level. "Well, then, miss . . . I guess I'll just have to have a glass of water in the kitchen before I drag Miss Vaden away from ya." He smiled and gently squeezed the girl's cheek between his thumb and forefinger.

"Quickly though, girl," he ordered then, standing and scowling at Vaden. "This storm is comin' in quick." Then, as Mrs. Wimber smiled at her children and motioned for Ransom Lake to follow her into the kitchen, Vaden thought she might die of humiliation when he tripped over her boot that lay in the middle of the room. "Just a moment, Mrs. Wimber," he said, stooping and picking up her boot.

"Oh, no! It's just part of the . . ." Vaden stopped

when he raised his gloved palm in her direction, indicating she should be silent.

"Cinderella is it, Miss Wimber?" he asked Violet.

"Yes! Cinderella. And the prince has only just this minute tried the slipper on the awful stepsisters and is makin' ready to leave!" the child offered excitedly. "Ya see . . . he can't recognize his beloved Cinderella because she has soot all over her lovely face. See?"

Vaden wanted to shrink down and slip through the cracks in the floor, for at that moment as Ransom Lake looked at her, raised his eyebrows, and chuckled, she remembered the soot with which she had dusted her face.

"I do see, Miss Violet," he mumbled.

Vaden became even more uncomfortable and a little angry when Mrs. Wimber also was unable to suppress her laughter.

"But this prince was smart, ya see, Miss Wimber," the man continued, and Vaden's eyes widened as he approached her, holding her boot tightly in one hand. "Ya see, this prince could recognize Cinderella with his heart. He didn't need to see her face. And so he paused in takin' his leave." Vaden's heart began to beat frantically as he drew closer to her. She shook her head slightly, unable to believe he was involving himself in her tale. "He looked at the small girl in the corner, covered in soot and ashes. And his heart spoke to him, telling him this was she—the one who had stolen his heart at the dance.”

“Ball. It was a ball, Mr. Lake,” Violet corrected in a whisper before giggling delightedly at what was transpiring.

“Forgive me. Stolen his heart at the ball. The prince approached the lovely Cinderella, extendin’ his hand to her, hopin’ she would reveal herself in placin’ her own hand in his.” Vaden was instantly mesmerized, for he was astoundingly good at telling the tale.

“Take his hand, Miss Vaden,” Violet prodded. “It’s in the story.” Vaden only then realized Ransom Lake did indeed hold out his hand in her direction. Tentatively she took his hand, and immediately his touch, even with the glove covering it, sent her body tingling.

Ransom Lake continued, “The prince gazed into the beautiful emerald of Cinderella’s eyes and said, ‘Pray, try the shoe’—”

“It’s called a slipper, Mr. Lake,” Violet interrupted. “Princesses always wear slippers. Not shoes.”

“Thank ya, Miss Violet,” he whispered aside to the small girl. Vaden couldn’t help but smile, so charmed was she by his thoughtful attention to the children. “The prince gazed into the beautiful emerald of Cinderella’s eyes and said, ‘Pray, try the slipper, fair maiden. If not for your own ambitions . . . pray, try it for love of your prince.'" Then, much to Vaden's horror, he knelt on one knee at her feet, reached beneath her petticoats, and drew from beneath them her stockinged foot. "As the prince slipped the shoe—excuse me, slipper—easily onto Cinderella's tiny foot, she said . . ." he prodded, nodding with raised eyebrows.

"Oh! Um," Vaden stammered, completely undone by his holding her foot and directing it into her boot. "Um . . . Cinderella said . . . she said . . . 'Thank you, your highness' . . . um . . ."

"Yes." Ransom Lake chuckled and stood, again taking Vaden's hand in his own. "Cinderella said, 'Thank you, your highness.'" He paused for a moment, and his eyes narrowed, his smile fading as he mumbled, "'Thank you for seein' beneath soot on my face and lovin' my soul.'"

His words seemed pointed, but Vaden was certain she imagined his inferences toward her own willingness to look past the outward appearances of the hermit from the mountains to find the wonderful spirit of Ransom Lake beneath. Yes. She must've imagined it.

"What next?" Freddy Wimber asked curiously. "What next?"

Ransom Lake smiled at Vaden then, dropped her hand, turned to the coat rack, and retrieved her coat from it. He helped her to put it on and buttoned the collar button.

"What next, ya ask, boy?" the man chuckled.

"Well, next the prince bid everyone in the room a good day, swept Cinderella into his arms, and carried her off to his castle, where they lived happily ever after."

Vaden smiled and giggled delightedly as Ransom Lake actually lifted her into his own powerful arms, effortlessly as if she were no more than a child.

"And he kissed her too. Didn't he kiss her, Mr. Lake?" Violet's wide eyes sparkled with the anticipated answer to her question.

"Now you let Mr. Lake take Miss Vaden on home, Violet. It's bad weather we're havin' out there, and they need to be off," Mrs. Wimber explained to her disappointed daughter. "Thank ya again, Vaden. I'm so sorry about this. You tell your Aunt Myra we'll watch the weather better next time."

"I will, Mrs. Wimber, and it was my pleasure to stay with the children," Vaden said, still blissful at being held in Ransom Lake's powerful arms. Propriety dictated Vaden should try to free herself from his hold on her. Yet as she struggled, he only chuckled and secured her more firmly.

"I'll get the door, Mr. Lake," Freddy offered, opening the door wide. Vaden could see the horse and cutter waiting outside. Ransom carried her down the steps, setting her gently on the cutter's blanket-covered seat.

"'Bye, Miss Vaden!" Violet called from the

door. "Thank ya for bringin' my mama home, Mr. Lake!"

The child waved happily to the man, who tipped his hat to her. It was only Violet who stood at the door now. Suddenly, Ransom Lake leaned forward, whispering something to Violet that caused her to giggle with delight and nod her head emphatically.

"What did you say to her, Mr. Lake?" Vaden asked as he turned back to her and stood unmoving for a moment on her side of the cutter.

"I just told her the prince did kiss Cinderella." His hand was at her chin in an instant, his lips pressing to hers before she even realized he had moved. The kiss was sweet and quick, far from the kiss Vaden would have most chosen to receive from him, but obviously enough to satisfy the yearnings of Miss Violet Wimber to see the story ended properly. He tipped his hat once more to Violet before climbing over Vaden and seating himself next to her on the seat. Vaden waved to Violet and then to her mother, who appeared at the door, waving quickly before closing it to the violent elements of nature.

"I had no idea you were so skilled with children," Vaden commented, raising her voice a bit to be heard over the wind.

Ransom smiled and chuckled a moment. "Oh, I used to be able to weave quite a yarn myself, girl."

"Thank you for bringing Mrs. Wimber home so I wasn't left there all night with the children. She still must feed the baby most of the time, and I was becoming worried." She turned to him, concerned. "Is Uncle Dan all right?"

"The cold has caused the achin' in his leg and back to pain him. I was over tellin' your aunt that I wasn't sure I'd make it over tomorrow with all this comin' in . . . and . . . I knew she didn't want ya stuck out here all night." He frowned, however, and added, "But I'm not sure we shouldn't have stayed back there ourselves. It's nasty out here."

Vaden wrapped her scarf securely about her head, tucking it into her coat below her chin. "You're quite a good actor as well, Mr. Lake. What other talents do you secret?"

"None. Doesn't take talent to tell a tale or kiss a girl." Vaden raised her eyebrows, dubbing him vastly mistaken on both counts.

Ransom pulled up for a moment just as an enormous, frigid gust of wind cut through Vaden's coat to her body. He shaded his eyes from the snow and, standing up in the cutter, looked back. "I truly think we should've stayed back there. This is becomin' worrisome."

"But we can't be more than three miles from home." Then Vaden noticed she couldn't see a thing through the snow. No trees, nor the road ahead. No visible landmarks.

"Less. But this is bad. We could get lost out here and . . ." he began. Then, sitting back down, he slapped the lines and turned off the well-defined road they had been on.

"What are you doing?" Vaden asked. "Why don't you just turn around if you're uncertain?"

"Because . . . I think we'd get lost. Look at the road. In a matter of minutes we won't be able to see it with the snow driftin' so badly in the wind. And at this very minute . . . this place . . . I still know where we are." Taking Vaden's arm, he directed her to sit on the floor of the cutter at his feet. "Get down here. It'll keep that wind off of ya, and you'll be warmer."

She did as instructed and sat on the floor of the cutter, huddling up against one of his legs for warmth. She was astounded at how fast the temperature was dropping, how the moonlight seemed to have disappeared completely from the sky. The powerful man struggled with guiding the horse, and she could feel the taut muscles in the thigh and calf of his leg as he drove. But she knew she would be safe. No one would perish while under Ransom Lake's care. That she knew.

At last, Vaden heard his voice soothe the horse as he pulled her up before a large, dark structure, looming before them in the night.

"Come on," he said, taking her arm once more and pulling her to her feet. Vaden realized her feet were numb with cold. Quickly Ransom

Lake walked with her to the lightless building, kicked open a door, and pushed her inside.

"Wait here," he commanded. Turning, he ventured back out into the storm.

"Where would I go?" she muttered to herself as she tried to see through the darkness and further into the building. He returned almost immediately, much to Vaden's relief, leading the mare into the building.

"There you go, ol' girl," he said soothingly, patting the animal on the neck and leading her further back into the darkness. Again Vaden waited for him to return, completely uncertain as to what other action she might take. When he returned, he took her hand and led her deeper into the darkness of their shelter.

"This old house is on my property," he explained as he led her into a room and stopped before a large fireplace. Vaden was silent. The only noise escaping her body was the violent chattering of her teeth as she watched him go about building a fire, using a set of flints he pulled from a box on the mantel. In a few moments, smoke began to rise from a tiny bundle of sticks in the hearth. She watched as he carefully blew on the small bit of smoke. Soon an orange spark erupted among the kindling. He added some larger bits of wood as the room began to be illuminated by the light and warmth of the fire. He stood up and looked about the room. Picking up a dusty chair, he broke it into pieces and added it to the small fire. Vaden watched as it blazed brighter and warmer.

"I've gotta go out back and root up some better wood." He walked away toward the back of the house. Vaden stepped closer to the warmth of the fire, removing her mittens and rubbing her hands together vigorously to help send away the stinging numbness in her fingers.

"This wood should burn nice. It's dried out from sittin' out there for so long," he said as he returned, his arms laden with large pieces of wood. He dropped it carelessly to one side of the hearth and added some of the old, dry logs to the fire. They did indeed burn quickly and warm. Vaden removed her scarf and coat, tossing them onto another nearby chair.

"Well, I guess you're telling me we'll be here for awhile," Vaden said as Ransom Lake came to stand next to her, removing his own gloves, hat, and coat.

"At least the night," he answered, putting one fist to his mouth and blowing warm air through it, then the other.

"All night?" she inquired. Surely he could not possibly mean for her to spend the entire night alone with him!

The handsome man looked at her, a puzzled expression on his brow. "Yes, all night. Would ya rather get lost in that blizzard and freeze to death?" He looked back to the fire and then around the room. "It's holdin' up surprisingly well," he mumbled.

"The house?" Vaden asked to assure herself of his subject of comment.

"Yeah. It hasn't been lived in for so long, but it doesn't look any worse for the wear, except for the dust and creatures that have moved in." At his mention of living things perhaps lurking about, she unconsciously took a step sideways and closer to him. He chuckled. "Nothin' dangerous has taken up residence in here, I'm sure."

But Vaden's legs began to prickle and itch all the same as she noticed various large cobwebs donning every corner of everything.

"Ya warmin' up all right, girl?" he asked in his delightfully mumbly manner.

"Yes. Fine," she assured him. She glanced to him then, and her eyes could not tear themselves from his fine good looks and tousled hair. He was truly magnificent, and she smiled slightly at the thought that struck her.

"What?" he asked, noticing her smile.

"Nothing," she lied, looking away.

"No, what? Tell me."

"I was just thinking what Yvonne would say about this situation," she admitted to him.

Ransom Lake smiled. "Your sister is a strict one when it comes to etiquette and manners, isn't she?"

"Yes. It's a good quality in her." Vaden's smile faded as another thought entered her mind, and as was often the case, she blurted out her mental secrets before she could stop. "You fancy her, don't you, Mr. Lake? Yvonne, I mean."

"What do ya mean by fancy?" He still continued to gaze into the fire and periodically blow into his fists.

"I mean . . . you favor Yvonne. It's all right to admit it to me. You're always telling me we're friends, after all, and I've seen the way you look at her."

"We are friends," he confirmed, looking to her, eyebrows raised in perplexion. "And, yes, your sister is a fine woman to look at."

Vaden's teeth immediately began to clench.

"But . . . I don't favor her over anyone else. I don't intend to pursue her, if that's what you're gettin' at, little Miss Vaden, the curious cat." Since she still stared into the fire, unwilling to look at him, he put a hand to her shoulder, arresting her attention and causing her to finally look over at him. "Whatever would put such a thought into that connivin' little mind of yours?"

"My mind is not conniving. Just . . . observant is all," she said.

"No, tell me. Somethin' had to spark such a thought. Tell me," he prodded, turning to confront her face-to-face.

"The night you were ill, you . . . you on two

occasions did or said something to indicate that you . . ." she stammered.

"For the love of Pete, girl! You're holding somethin' against me that I said when my head was hotter than that fire before ya? Chances are I didn't know my foot from my hind end. And besides," he continued, "would there be somethin' wrong about me takin' an interest in your sister?"

"So you do favor her."

"No," he chuckled, smiling and shaking his head. "No. I just want ya to tell me why ya even brought the thing up."

Vaden scolded herself violently for slipping up and letting him have an insight into her worry over where he might choose to next place his affections. But, trying to stay calm and dispassionate in appearance, she said, "Oh, I was just wondering about it."

"Why? Are ya afraid I'll end up with Belva Tibbits?" He chuckled and turned from her, looking back into the fire.

Vaden just shook her head and sighed, irritated with herself. "Are you . . . are you planning on ending up with someone?" Vaden wanted to leave the house, to run from him! All the feelings she had tried to secret away in herself over the past few weeks, every dream and hope she held where he was concerned, were burning brighter than ever in her heart.

Ransom Lake smiled and turned to her with an

inquisitive glint in his stormy eyes. "Why? Are you interested in the job?"

Vaden gasped, looked at him, and shook her head vigorously. "Oh! No, no, no!" she assured him. "It's just a natural question, considering the stir you've caused in town among the young women and all."

"What stir?" he asked.

"Don't play the dumb bunny with me, Mr. Lake. You know full well what I mean." She shook her head, irritated he would take her for such a fool. "I'll admit to you now it's the reason I left the Halloween social early that night. I was sick to death of being badgered and taunted by the other girls because . . ." She broke off, thinking it might be far worse to confess that particular example.

"What? Finish what ya were sayin'," he demanded, his voice going low and even more mumbly.

"Nothing. It was a bad example. I'll think of another one. I—"

"No. Tell me what ya were gonna say, Vaden."

She looked at him, surprised at his use of her given name and the commanding tone in his voice.

"I mean . . . it was silly of me to feel slighted anyway. So it was a bad example. It was no fault of yours. It was petty of me to react so—" Vaden's mind was trying to sort out an escape from the conversation.

"What're ya talkin' about?" he unexpectedly interrupted her.

"You know," Vaden stammered. "About my feeling slighted because you chose not to dance with me at the social. Actually you chose to nearly completely ignore me altogether. That's why I decided to walk home early. Because I was feeling sorry for myself—as a result of the other girls taunting me about it . . . not that you slighted me."

"Do ya mean ya felt snubbed? Do ya mean to tell me ya left the social because I didn't ask ya for a dance?" he asked. His expression was that of disbelief mingled with tremendous guilt.

"Well, no." She had to find a way out of the muddy mess she'd slipped into. Something within her told her he would be very upset to know she had left because of him. "I know you already think me silly, clumsy, and juvenile, no matter how you persist in saying otherwise . . . and I don't blame you a bit for it, for my own actions that very horrid night paint a pretty clear picture of me. But it was just too irritating to take the taunting of the other girls for any longer, and I was tired of it. So I left. There you have it. Enough said. I'm so thankful you are handy with a set of flints, Mr. Lake. The fire is so warming."

Ransom Lake stood staring at her, looking dumbfounded as if a startling revelation had just plunged a dagger into his mind. "I'm sorry,

Vaden," he mumbled, and a sort of pain glazed the gray of his eyes.

"For what, Mr. Lake? It was none of it your fault." She felt the need to tie up the other loose end to the story. So she babbled on as every nerve began to twitch frantically within her body. "And I've already admitted to what you said. I . . . in the wagon . . . I did want you to . . . I tried to . . . my goal was to . . . that is what you mean isn't it, Mr. Lake? The fact you knew it would upset me to be slighted by you? And my completely barbaric behavior in the wagon on the way home. How I wish you could just forget it. And those are the reasons that . . . what other reasons could you possibly have for apologizing to me?"

Still he was silent.

Vaden knew how her confession could be misunderstood by him. Quickly she tried to correct her meaning. "You're not at all responsible for what happened to cause me to fall into the hands of those men, you know. It was entirely my own fault—my own ignorance and carelessness that found me in that horrid position. I suppose one could view the reason I left the social . . . one could aptly refer to it as pouting. Yvonne would surely call it that. She is ever and always accusing me of it. And I do admit to being guilty of something like it at times. Mr. Lake? Are you hearing me?" Vaden was uncomfortable as his gray eyes met hers intensely.

"Why would they be teasin' ya about *me* not askin' ya for a dance?" he asked plainly.

Vaden began to fiddle with the long lock of hair at her temple. "Whatever do you mean by asking that?" Then she looked at him, studying his eyes and general countenance. Could it truly be that he was unaware of his effect on the general female population? "Are you seriously ignorant as to the reason?" she asked plainly in return.

"Yes," he stated.

"They're all desperately attracted to you." Vaden looked from him and into the flames in the hearth. She would be honest with him. She would simply tell him bluntly, for it did indeed seem as if he were still completely unaware of the infatuation every female in town held for him. "You were the 'buck of the ball,' so to speak, Mr. Lake. All the girls in town were simply swooning as you passed because each and every one was holding her breath in hopes the mysterious Ransom Lake would beg a dance of her."

He chuckled quietly. "You are quite the prankster yourself, aren't ya, girl?"

Vaden looked to him again, but he smiled and turned from her. "You are truly innocent of it all, aren't you?" she questioned. "I thought— especially after your antics that first evening you kissed me—I thought you were all too clearly aware of the effect you've had on all the women in this town."

He chuckled again, but when he looked at her, his smile faded. She could only guess he had seen the sincerity on her face at last. "My antics, as ya call them, have nothin' to do with the women in this town. Antics?"

Avoiding the issue of the previous affectionate liaisons between herself and Ransom Lake, Vaden rushed boldly ahead in her explanation of the events of Halloween. "Belva Tibbits was the worst! I swear she had aspirations of being the first you chose to ki . . ." She stopped, for she knew she had already said too much.

"You're tellin' me the truth, aren't ya?" he whispered as a deep frown furrowed his brow.

Vaden nodded, dropping her guilty gaze to the floor.

"You say they were teasin' ya. How? What were they sayin'?"

She smiled, shook her head, and waved one hand in front of her face in a gesture of trivial subject matter. "Oh, nothing really. Certainly nothing to justify my stomping off like a coward."

"What did they say?" he demanded sternly. "Tell me."

Vaden looked about for a means of escape, but their isolation provided none whatsoever. There was no reason she should not answer his question. "Just things. Mean things females say to irritate other females. Women are more catty than you can imagine, Mr. Lake."

"What? Give me an example," he urged harshly.

"I don't remember," Vaden stalled. "Things like . . . Belva said a man like you wouldn't be caught dead dancing with me because . . . because . . ."

"Because?" he prodded.

"Because I'm the kind of girl men want to go fishing with—not sit out under a tree and spark with," she mumbled. "I'm unconventional, you see," she rambled on quickly. "I do like to run through the meadow rather than sit quietly under a parasol. And, yes," she stated firmly, "I'd rather go fishing and wading in the brook as opposed to waiting perfectly docile beneath a tree, my feet tucked properly beneath my skirts as I read on for hours and hours without flinching!" Vaden continued to stare into the fire even though she felt the piercing gaze of Ransom Lake drilling into her. "I suppose that's why those horrid, intoxicated men chose me to torment— because I'm a good sport most of the time."

Ransom Lake rubbed his temples for a moment. Vaden finally looked up as he spoke. "You're tellin' me that because I supposedly snubbed ya at the dance, every female there started in badgerin' ya about it, and so ya left? Then on your way home, you were taken by those idiots, and because I didn't heed my . . . so basically you're sayin' the whole affair was my fault, includin' what I did to ya on the way home."

"Oh, no!" Vaden exclaimed, taking hold of one of his solid arms. She looked up at him, her soul pleading silently with him as she explained, "It was my own pouty, weak fault that I found myself in that situation. Yvonne's always telling me I don't think before I act, and she's right. And you did nothing to me on the way home. It was me. I acted so . . . so . . ." She shook her head and put a hand to her suddenly throbbing forehead. "Oh . . . how did we get to this point? I only wanted to explain why I thought you . . . to apologize to you for my behavior in the wagon . . . to thank you for coming for me that night. For coming for me this night. How did it all come to this?"

The powerful man at Vaden's side shook his head and returned his gaze to the fire. "Well, I can't make heads or tails of half of what you're tellin' me, girl. I do think you're exaggeratin' a bit about my popularity, and if it helps your ego any, I think I oughta tell ya the reason I didn't ask ya for a dance is 'cause . . . every time I had a chance, you were out dancin' with Jerome Clayton."

Vaden's heart landed with a dramatic thud in the pit of her stomach. He would've asked her, if only she had been able to keep Jerome at bay long enough. She could've had the chance to be held in his arms just as every other girl had that night. But she felt the triumph rise within her at the knowledge she had been held by Ransom Lake—held by him and kissed by him in a manner the other girls in town were still dreaming of.

"And now I'll say it again," he continued, "and I want ya to take this to heart. I'm sorry. I'm truly sorry for what happened. All of it. And I see now it was more my fault than I even thought."

Vaden was disturbed by the look of deep guilt and remorse on his face. Somehow he felt responsible, and he wasn't. "You're not responsible, Mr. Lake. Do you see it now? Not for what happened on Halloween. Not for any of what happened on Halloween. The other girls are only too right where I'm concerned. My pointless babble has left you feeling guilty somehow, and I'm sorry. It would be better maybe if I were to just stop talking altogether," she mumbled, turning to let the conversation die before the fire.

"You're wrong. You're wrong, and I'm tired." He continued to face the fire and sighed heavily.

"I'm never wrong about anything!" Vaden nearly shouted. "Everything I told you was true. They did tease me! It did make me angry! I did try to . . . wanted you to . . . I caused what happened on the way home Halloween night. All of it. Every bit of it was my fault. You've only gotten to where you blame yourself for anything bad that happens because . . . because I don't know why. But you do it. And it's insane."

He sighed and whispered, "You seem to think ya know me quite well."

"I do," she said, turning to face him again. "I know you better than anyone else in town. And that's a fact."

He chuckled and shook his head, amused at her assurance of herself. Vaden felt hope begin to burn within her—perhaps the same feeling someone might feel rising within her bosom in anticipation of witnessing a miracle. As he turned his gray eyes upon her, she knew—she knew something profound was about to happen to her at the hand of Ransom Lake.

"You make a man feel almost . . . forgiven," he mumbled.

"Forgiven for what, Mr. Lake?" Vaden asked. She could no longer keep silent the question plaguing her mind since the moment she had first seen him. She sensed he meant to confess something to her, to confide his great secret. Immediately, his face turned ashen, and he looked away as moisture brimmed in his storm-colored eyes. "Tell me! Tell me what it is that causes such a tumultuous guilt in you. Please."

He tipped his head back for a moment, gazing up at the shadows from the fire dancing oddly on the ceiling. Vaden waited. Her heart pounded madly as she sensed the moment had arrived.

Ransom Lake was about to reveal his terrible secret to her. She would know. No one else. No one had cared to ask him before.

"Well, I suppose if there's anybody in the world I think deserves to know the truth about me . . . it's you, Vaden. Ya tried to befriend me long before ya saw what I looked like underneath all that mess of hair." He picked up the poker lying on the floor near the hearth and, hunkering down before the fire, used it to kick around a log inside. Vaden's body still quivered from the sound of his voice uttering her name. "It's been drivin' ya plumb out of your mind not knowin' why I took to the hills like I did, hasn't it?" He glanced at her, and she guiltily looked away. "You've been wonderin' since the first day ya saw me in the street—wonderin' what it was that made me so . . . solitary." He sat down solidly on the floor, still gazing into the fire. "Well, I think I'm inclined to tell ya on this cold winter's evenin' when there aren't any ears around but yours. You were the first to see my face, Vaden. Ya may as well be the first to see the black mire of my soul."

Vaden held her breath for a moment and tried to settle the frantic palpitating of her heart. She'd waited so long, wondered so many things! But she was silent, too afraid to speak for fear he would change his mind.

CHAPTER TEN

"I was sixteen when my daddy decided to move the family out west. He had a sister, my Aunt Shandra, who lived out here with her husband. They had built themselves a nice little house on some land my daddy bought for them as a weddin' gift. Anyway, I was sixteen that summer when we started out here. There was me and my mamma and daddy, my older sister by a year, Natalie, my younger brothers, Scott and Gavin— they were about twelve and ten—and my baby sister, Serena. Aunt Shandra and Uncle Garth, her husband, had traveled out to Georgia to help us on the way. They had their little baby girl, Sally, with them too. My older brother, Denver, was already grown up and livin' out in Leadville. So he wasn't with us.

"We hooked up with a wagon train goin' our way right outside of Georgia, and there was this girl that belonged to one of the families. Her name was Caroline. She was fifteen. She took a likin' to me for some reason and about drove me insane chasin' after me and flirtin' all the time. I didn't have a breath of peace. Anyway, everything went real well on the trip—no disasters with weather or the teams takin' sick. Everyone was healthy and strong.

"Then early one mornin' we were breakin' camp about two days by wagon from this very town. Caroline was already pesterin' me—stealin' my hat and running off, trying to get me to chase her and such. I was pretty near to turnin' her over my knee and whackin' her fanny, and it wasn't even seven in the mornin'."

He paused and seemed to be reflecting. Vaden was silent, intent on his story.

"Ya know, lookin' back, it all seems like a whole lot a nothin' now to be irritated with her about. Anyhow, Daddy told me to help hitch up the team, and I didn't want to do it because Caroline was stickin' to me like flies to a cowpie. So I argued with him and asked him to give me another job, somethin' away from camp that would get her out of my hair. He told me again to hitch up the team, and I was mad. 'No,' I told him. 'I'm not gonna do it.' And with him yellin' at me to get back to my chores, I stormed off, leavin' my daddy mad at me and Caroline feelin' put off. But I'd been hitchin' up the team every mornin' for weeks, and my disposition was bent outta joint over tryin' to avoid that poor Caroline twenty-four hours   a day. So I stomped off, tellin' myself I was a man. I wasn't a boy to be bossed around, and I didn't need to put up with someone I didn't want to. Off I went, just walkin' further and further away—at least a mile, as I figure now.

"Then, I heard an ear-splittin' noise . . . an explosion. I turned to see a big black cloud of smoke risin' in the air from the direction I had come. I felt it at the same moment. Even before I reached the camp, I knew what had happened. It was like a vision in my mind. I turned, and I ran as fast as I could back to the camp. When I got there, whoever had done it was already gone. It wasn't Indians. I found out soon after a group of outlaws had escaped from prison and had been robbin' and killin' in the area. I'm sure that's who did it, though I don't have proof to show anyone."

He paused again, and Vaden could see the fire reflecting in the moisture in his eyes.

"Everyone there was dead. Everyone. Not one livin' soul was left. Believe me, I know, because I checked every one of them over good before I buried them. I buried twenty-nine bodies that day and the next. Twenty-nine people. Some of them had been shot through the head or heart. Some of them had their throats slashed open, and some had been beaten to death. A couple of the children . . . some had been hung from a nearby tree."

Vaden winced and covered her mouth to try to stop the wrenching in her stomach.

"I won't go into more detail than that. I'll just tell ya that I buried my whole family except for one brother that day. And I've spent the last ten years wishin' I'd died along with them. Knowin' if I'd hitched up the team like my father told me to, we mighta been out of there before . . ." Ransom Lake looked at her, his eyes narrowing. "I think that's the quietest you've ever been at one stretch in all the time I've known ya, girl."

"They would've tracked you. Whoever it was would've tracked the wagon train," Vaden told him firmly, breaking her unusually long silence. "And it would've been unnecessary—wasteful and unbearable—for you to have been killed too. That would've left your brother, Denver, all alone in the world."

Ransom Lake looked back to the fire. He winced in pain. "He is all alone in the world. He . . . he doesn't know I wasn't killed."

"What?" Vaden exclaimed in horror. She couldn't believe what she was hearing. "You mean you never told him you . . ."

He shook his head. "No. I'm a coward, and I call myself one, 'cause I couldn't face him. I couldn't face him, tell him the family was gone, wiped out because of me. I sent him a telegram when I finally reached town and pretended I was someone else who had happened upon the massacre."

"But . . . but it had nothing whatsoever to do with you! You were a boy! There's nothing you could've done to . . . your family would've wanted you to be saved. Your brother . . . you have to let him know—"

"No!" he shouted angrily, rising to his feet. "No.

Let him think I'm dead. It's less painful to him than the truth would be."

Vaden clenched her teeth to keep from arguing with him. Now was not the time, and she knew it. "How . . . how did you survive? I mean, how did you come to own your land? Buy your food and pay for your shelter?"

He shrugged his shoulders. "I knew where my father had hidden his money and deeds to the land—under a board in the wagon. He had put all his money and deeds in a strong box and hidden them there. My mother's wedding ring was in there as well." He paused and glanced at the gold band on his smallest finger. "I had possession of the rights to this land, and my daddy was very wealthy. He had thousands and thousands and thousands of dollars hidden in that box in the wagon. The thieves didn't find it. I did. I say this land because I own the land this very house sits on. It's only a mile and a half out from my farm. This was my Uncle Garth and Aunt Shandra's house. It's just as they left it ten years ago. I came to town with the deeds, and since I looked like a full-grown man even though I was only sixteen . . . nobody knew the difference. They just all assumed my Uncle Garth had sold me the property."

Vaden hugged herself tightly, and a chill traveled through her body as she looked around her. But still the horror of what the man standing before her had endured was the focus of her attention. "How horrible for you," Vaden whispered, wiping a tear from her cheek. What pain he must have endured. What horrible visions must there be in his memory.

Ransom Lake turned on her again, raising his voice as he spoke. "What do ya mean? I'm the one still alive! Still breathin'! I wasn't tortured and mutilated!"

"It's not your fault." Vaden was not offended by his outburst. She knew for the past ten years Ransom Lake had blamed himself for the atrocities befallen his family and friends. "If you had been there . . . you would've been killed too, and what would that have accomplished?"

"I should've died too! If for no other reason than I was disobedient!"

"Why? So your family could've watched you suffer as well? So your name . . . your bloodline would be forever extinguished from the face of the earth? So the people who murdered your family would have yet one more murder on their heads come judgment day? Or is it for purely selfish reasons? Because, since you did live, you've had guilt." Vaden was on her feet facing him now as her mouth poured out her heart's feelings. "Oh, I don't mean guilt over the fact you were disobedient to your father or because you weren't there when it happened. I mean the guilt you're feeling because you know you have so much to offer other people . . . to offer the world. And instead of helping others, instead of bringing joy to others, you've chosen to hide away for years, selfishly keeping to yourself!"

"I've helped people plenty, Vaden! Whenever tragedy hits I—"

"Yes, tragedy! You do help then! More than most men would, and I'll not deny the wonderful deeds you do. But what about daily? What about the other hearts secretly aching like yours is? What do you do then? I mean . . . it's a selfish act in itself you've kept yourself hidden behind that pelt of hair for so many years. Just imagine the women who would've had their day brightened, their hearts filled with delight, at simply laying eyes on a man as handsome as you!"

Ransom grinned a bit, the anger seeming to rinse off him immediately as he chuckled quietly. "Oh, Vaden. Leave it to you to come up with somethin' like that as a method of doin' good in the world." The gloom and oppression hanging heavy in the room a moment before lifted. Smiling, he walked to her, taking her shoulders between his hands and saying, "I know there's reason to what ya say, girl. But . . . it's worn on me for ten long years. It's not just gonna go away because I told ya about it. But I know ya mean well. You're a good kid, ya know that?"

Vaden closed her eyes and wrenched herself from his grasp, turning to look into the flames of the fire. Her heart still ached from the pain of his story and was added upon by his condescending compliment.

"I am a woman, Mr. Lake—not an infant goat!" She was hurt. It hurt her deeply every time he brought to light that he saw her as a child.

"Now come on. I didn't mean it like that," he explained.

"Why is it that Yvonne being nineteen, only one year my senior . . . why is it because she's beautiful, elegant, soft-spoken . . . why is it she's considered a mature woman to be sought after by every eligible bachelor in the state? But because I'm short, plain, speak my mind . . . why is it I'm viewed as a child? Yvonne knows how to portray something she isn't entirely made of. I'm truly myself! At all times and in all places. Why is it everyone still treats me as a child? Everyone except Jerome Clayton."

Ransom Lake said nothing for a moment. She assumed he was still thinking of his painful memories. But then he did speak.

"It's the spark in ya, that light shinin' in your eyes like the brightness of the sun. It's one reason I was so mad when I realized what those boys had done to ya on Halloween. A life can be robbed of that spark—of that love for livin'. If anybody knows that, it's me. I was afraid they'd stolen your innocence that night, that you'd never be the sweet thing always gettin' herself into a fix and puttin' her foot directly into her mouth. But ya pulled through it." Vaden turned to see his eyes narrow as he approached her and once again took her by the shoulders. "You bucked up—kept your wits and your love of life about ya. I'm not blind! I know it scared ya. It made ya recognize ugly things ya hadn't before. And I suppose you'll never be quite the same now. But you were the one talkin' about makin' people feel happy, puttin' joy in their souls. Well, I figure that's how folks feel when you're around. Comfortable. Not like they've gotta treat ya different, but like they're your friend. And speakin' of Jerome Clayton, it's why I got so mad at ya for sparkin' with the boy. He's not worthy of ya. He doesn't appreciate ya or know how to make a life for a girl like you. I was mad at you for even considerin' on him. I'm irritated that ya still do."

"Is that why you chose to be so cruel to me that night? That first night you . . . in the alley? Are you trying to tell me that the reason you . . . you . . ."

"Kissed you?"

"Yes. Thank you." Vaden was uncomfortable. The thoughts of Ransom Lake's tragic life were pushed aside for a moment as his intense gaze made her uneasy. "Are you trying to tell me the reason you . . . did that is because you . . ." She was uncharacteristically tongue-tied for a moment. The hypnotic quality of his stormy eyes as they gazed at her in the firelight caused her to stumble in her words. "It was cruel," she finished.

"Cruel? How?" he asked in a whisper.

She couldn't possibly tell him the truth—that because of his kiss she knew she would never be able to kiss another man and not pine away for Ransom Lake. That his kiss had only served to seal her love more deeply.

"Because . . . because . . ." she stammered, "because you knew . . . you knew when you did it, I could never . . . I could never be content with a man like Jerome Clayton."

"A boy like Jerome Clayton," he corrected her. He smiled at her, dropped his hands from her shoulders, and said, "We're too tired to be discussin' such things, girl. You look worn out. I think I've taxed your mind and emotions enough this wicked night. Why don't ya just lie down on that old sofa over there? It's dusty, I know. But it'll do."

Vaden turned from him and closed her eyes, squeezing a tear from each one and letting the droplets of emotion sit on her cheeks as she opened them again and looked into the fire.

"I'll warm up here for a minute more, thank you," she mumbled.

"One more thing," he added. "What I've confided in ya tonight . . . it can't go beyond this room. Do ya understand?"

Vaden shook her head and wiped at the tears. "Why don't you just give me a good paddling and send me to bed without my dinner, Mr. Lake?" The sarcasm and hurt in her voice were heavy.

"You're one to be pointin' the finger at self-pity!" he nearly shouted unexpectedly. "There isn't one man in town who thinks you're a baby, Vaden."

Vaden turned to face him, surprised at his outburst.

"So quit tryin' to coax me into givin' way to my weaknesses where you're concerned and kissin' ya again." He cleared his throat and looked back toward the fire. "Now, settle your little fanny down on that sofa."

Vaden stood aghast at his remark. "I . . . what do you mean by . . . coax you into . . . I can't believe you would even say such a thing! I've apologized for that! And you should forget about it. I can't believe you would say—"

"Oh, yes, ya can. You know me better than anyone, or so you professed to me just a minute ago. It doesn't shock ya one bit." He moved to her again, taking her forcefully into his arms and pulling her body against the strength of his own. "Why don't ya just tell me the truth about it all? Rid your conscience of what you've been tryin' to say to me tonight in the lonely seclusion of this house."

She was helpless in his arms. So surprised had

she been to find herself there she was unable to react at first. And now, now it was such ecstasy to be there, bound tightly in his powerful arms, the warmth of his body heating her own and the smell of his skin, his hair, and his breath filling her lungs and taunting her senses, she was stunned into silence—paralyzed with delight.

"Scold me for it if ya must, but spit it out, girl. You're angry with me for goin' about it the way I did that first night I kissed ya. That's it, isn't it?" he whispered as he dusted the long-forgotten soot from her cheeks with the back of his hand. "Maybe angry at me too, for bein' weak that night Nathaniel was drivin' us home. But you . . . you provoked me." He paused for a moment, his eyes narrowing. "More than that, girl, of your own admission, ya willfully tempted me into takin' advantage of ya like I did."

"I-I . . ." she stammered, unable to defend herself, for he spoke no more than the absolute truth, and she knew it.

"I'm not blamin' you, Vaden. I'm not even telling ya that ya did anything wrong. You were frightened, sorrowful, and I was there, probably seemin' to you the knight in shinin' armor. But I was weak . . . in an uncertain state of mind myself."

Vaden closed her eyes, humiliated and unable to look at him as he continued.

"And I want ya to understand that I am sorry.

I'm sorry I failed you that night. That I let myself—"

"Stop it. Just stop it," Vaden pled in a whisper, shaking her head. "None of it was your fault. None of it. I . . . I was angry with you in a manner. Hurt because you slighted me so obviously at the social that night." But he wasn't listening. He seemed lost in his own thoughts, his own guilt. And when he spoke, his words puzzled Vaden.

"The night I caught Jerome Clayton slobberin' all over ya, maybe I wasn't so tender and patient with ya. But remember, I'm way out of practice. And in the wagon . . . well, I am a man, Vaden. How did ya expect I would react?"

"I have no idea what you mean," Vaden forced out in a whisper. She had to get away from him. It was too much, too wonderful to be in his arms, the fire warming them, the scent of the wood burning.

He lowered his voice when he spoke next, and the provocative intonation of it was Vaden's undoing. In Ransom Lake's arms, nothing else mattered in the world.

"Ya want to be treated like a woman, is that it? And ya don't think I treat ya like one, do ya?" Still holding her tightly against his body with one arm, he raised a hand to her face, cupping her cheek against his palm while his thumb traced the soft outline of her lips. "Well, maybe you're right. And I'll confess there's a reason for that. But there isn't anybody here now, is there? Nobody to gossip, nobody to get jealous, nobody to scold me."

Vaden closed her eyes for a moment, trying to believe what was happening. But she opened them again almost immediately to find his storm-filled eyes intent upon her.

"Do ya want me to kiss ya, Vaden? I mean kiss ya the way I didn't on those other occasions? There are so many different ways to kiss a woman. The way I kissed ya the first time, that was a teaching kiss—a kiss to prove somethin'. The way I kissed ya the second time, now that—and I'll say it to ya plain—was a kiss from a man who had been tempted physically by a girl he . . ."

Vaden opened her mouth to speak, to try to deter him, but no sound escaped her lips.

"Those other occasions were different. Forced somehow, I guess. I couldn't possibly have done a good job of it either time before, but look at me now—the fire burnin' warm, nobody around for miles. So . . . you just give me the chance, Vaden Valmont, and I'll kiss you like I didn't have time to before."

Vaden closed her eyes once more, digging deep within herself for something to cling to, something to anchor her to reality. She had to refuse him. To save herself, her heart, she must refuse him, remove herself from his embrace. But there was nothing—only Ransom Lake standing before her, the vision and feel of her love for him permeating her heart, mind, and soul. The desire was too strong. She wanted nothing else in that moment but to feel his lips on hers again. To taste his divinely perfect kiss.

"You can trust me, ya know, sweet thing. I'm no rounder," he said.

Then, before she could stop herself, she heard a barely audible, "I know it," escape her mouth. She prayed he hadn't been teasing her, hadn't been tormenting her just to make a fool of her—to prove her a child. But this was Ransom Lake, and he was not capable of rendering such a cruel gesture to her. As he pulled her even tighter against his body, her hands rested gently on his solid, muscular chest, and she could only stare into the warm storm in his eyes as he grinned triumphantly for a moment before his face went solemn as it moved down toward hers. But an instant before his lips would've touched hers, Vaden turned from him and tried to push herself away.

"Vaden?" he asked quietly.

"I'm . . . I'm not good at it," she confessed, ashamed somehow of her innocence and inexperience.

He took her chin in his hand and turned her face to his once more, an amused grin warming his features. "Vaden . . . you're good at everything. I wouldn't be tryin' this on you again if ya hadn't a boiled my blood the very first time."

"But you're . . . you're Ransom Lake," she told him, as if he weren't aware of the fact.

"Yes, I am," was all he whispered before he suddenly took her lips to his before she could shy away again.

His first kisses were like honeyed confection, sweet and tender, but after a few moments she felt his hand caress the back of her bodice as it traveled from her waist, over her back, finally entangling itself in the softness of her hair. He tugged ever so gently on her hair, and she tipped her head back slightly, gasping as she felt his kiss leave her lips and travel to her neck. He placed several long, soft kisses on her throat. The impassioned turbulence in his eyes captured her bliss-filled ones a moment before his kiss to her mouth was hers again, full, demanding, and enrapturing every fiber of her being.

Vaden understood in that moment there was nothing to be gained from experience when it came to returning a man's kiss. She knew either a woman loved a man, and for that reason her soul and body knew how to kiss him, or she didn't, and her soul, mind, and body had no cause to want to kiss him. However, Vaden knew with everything she was, with all her femininity, Ransom Lake was a man whose kiss went far beyond that of the average man. Ransom Lake was unusually proficient at it—the way his arms held her, the way his chest rose and fell with his breathing, the way he toyed with her mouth one moment and exhausted it with overwhelming and demanding passion the next. Vaden perceived she was made to fit his kiss perfectly—to return it the way he would most enjoy and relish.

Suddenly, however, he pushed her away gently, taking several steps backward as he ran his fingers through his hair, an expression of confusion on his face.

"What am I doin'?" he mumbled, a look akin to panic puckering the brow of his handsome face. Vaden felt self-conscious and somehow ashamed. "Your Uncle Dan would kill me. What am I doin'?" Then he lunged forward, taking her face between his hands as he nearly shouted, "What are ya doin' to me?"

"Nothing!" Vaden forced the defense from her lungs as tears escaped her eyes. "I-I haven't done anything."

His fingers went to her lips, caressing them with unusual softness as his hands shook anxiously. Taking her chin firmly in his trembling hand, he pulled her face to his once more, ravaging her mouth with a final, moist, intensely passionate kiss. When he ended it, slowly, tenderly, his trembling had ceased, and he smiled at Vaden understandingly.

"I've never tasted anything as satisfyingly delicious as you, Vaden. Not in my whole life. I think you're my favorite flavor." Then he turned from her, retrieved another log from the nearby pile, and tossed it into the hearth. "Now you go on over there and cuddle up on that sofa . . . alone. We'll get ya home first thing in the mornin'. And . . . uh . . . this . . . this business between me and you . . . I know you'll understand when I say that . . . it's just the moment here. The situation nearly demanded that I . . . the loneliness of the night and atmosphere."

She wanted to scream, *No! I don't understand! I love you, and you must at least care for me, else you wouldn't have told me your secrets. Why can't it happen every day, every minute?* But she nodded and muttered, "Yes."

She sat for long minutes that turned into an hour, simply staring into the flames of the fire as the wind moaned outside, causing anxiety to settle into her mind. Ransom Lake continued to sit on the floor before the hearth, toying with the poker every now and again, causing sparks to rise and crackle from the burning logs.

"I've learned a lot tonight, haven't I, Mr. Lake?" Vaden said softly as she finally stretched out on the sofa, pulling to her shoulders a dusty, heavy quilt folded in half long ago and laid on the back of it. He sat down on the floor before her, resting his back against the sofa. "I've grown up quickly tonight. I've learned the elements of heaven and earth can endanger a person's life. I've learned there are things people have witnessed, have experienced . . . things only nightmares are made of. Things that eat their hearts away and leave their minds scarred and tormented. Things that can never be forgotten or put aside."

"It's a lot to realize in such a short time. But that's usually how such things go. They blindside ya. Ya don't expect them or see them comin'," Ransom Lake added. He put down the poker he still had in hand, turned, and looked at her. "And what else have ya learned, Vaden?" His gray eyes narrowed, his features soft, his chest rising and falling slowly with his calm breathing.

She smiled at him, though she was beginning to feel sleepy. "I've learned I was right about you, Mr. Lake."

"Ya were?"

"You are an angel in disguises. Disguises both physical and of character."

He smiled and shook his head. "Ya think you're pretty smart, don't ya?"

"I am. I am very smart, Mr. Lake" she answered, returning the warmth of his smile in her own. She would not call him by his given name, for she sensed it would be her complete undoing. She sensed she would lose her ability to resist throwing herself at his feet and begging for his love. She smiled mischievously at him then and whispered,

"I'm so smart I've figured out that you're twenty-six years old. I think you look twenty-six."

He chuckled and shook his head, amused at her again. "Is that good or bad?"

"You figure it out," she giggled softly. Her eyelids were feeling heavy and hard to keep open. Even though the dream-borne vision of Ransom Lake was only inches away from her, an apparition of reality before her very tired eyes, she was giving into the warmth of the room and the need for rest. Her anxiety about the storm was gone, for the security he radiated was strong and reassuring. Just before her eyes closed completely and she drifted off to sleep, Ransom Lake pressed his thumb to his lips, placing the same thumb to her own lips for a moment.

"Goodnight, Sleepin' Beauty," he whispered.

"Cinderella," she corrected, and she heard him chuckling as she drifted into a light, uncomfortable sleep.

She dreamt visions, horrid visions that might have tainted the memory of Ransom Lake. She could smell the death at the wagon train when the young man had returned to find his family slaughtered. She could smell the dirt as the young man dug shallow graves, hear the sound of the shovel cutting the earth as he worked. She could feel the grief, the overwhelming, unendurable grief piercing his heart every minute for days, weeks, and years to come. And the pain of the grief was suffocating. It burned in her throat as she watched the visions in her mind. It hurt her limbs and body.

Vaden awoke with a start, her muscles aching from the tension in her body. She couldn't move for a moment, paralyzed with the grief and horror of her dreams. When finally she could move, she looked to see Ransom Lake standing before the hearth once more. Her intuition told her he hadn't slept as she had—hadn't dozed for even a moment. He stood staring into the fire, blazing warm and orange. His feet were planted firmly apart, and his massive, muscular arms were folded across his chest. He had removed his shirt, and it lay haphazardly over the arm of a nearby chair. Vaden was quiet for long moments just watching the man who watched the fire. His frown was intense and furrowed his brow deeply. He was lost in his thoughts, and she knew they were grim, for his jaw was clearly tensed. The room was still only lit by the fire, burning almost too violently, heating the room beyond comfortable. No light streamed in through the dusty windows, and Vaden surmised it was still very early morning. So deep in thought was Ransom Lake, in fact, he didn't see Vaden rise quietly from the sofa, and he did not turn to look at her when she quietly walked to stand behind the man.

Vaden's heart was heavy in her bosom with the

sympathy she felt for the man she loved. What tragic horror he had endured. It was no wonder to her he had withdrawn from the world, hidden himself away from any chance of being hurt again. Then her love for him, her profound and endless love for him, coupled with the anguish in her heart for his pain, overtook her prudence, and she moved forward, pressing her cheek to his back as her arms encircled his waist in a loving embrace. Immediately, she felt his body stiffen, and his hands covered her own linked one with the other at his waist.

"I'm so sorry, for you, Mr. Lake. For your pain. I'm sorry everything was taken from you so violently. I'm sorry for the scars it left in your heart and soul," she whispered to him. Vaden scolded herself inwardly, for she felt the fool then. Ransom Lake had confided his deepest secrets to her, and as she looked back on the conversation now, she was angry with herself, for her experience on Halloween paled so greatly to his. Further, he had blamed himself for her pain of that night. He had only placed further burdens on his already guilt-ridden mind. As her tears moistened the flesh of his back, she whispered once more, "I'm sorry."

"Thank you," he mumbled as he removed her hands from his waist and walked forward and out of her embrace. "Only I'm not certain if I did the right thing in tellin' you."

"Of course you did," she assured him, a bit embarrassed at acting so familiar with him. "A burden is not meant to be borne alone."

"But now I've taxed your mind with the horror of it. You'll never be free of the knowledge again." He paused, clearing his throat, yet he still mumbled when he continued. "It was wrong of me to deprive ya of your innocence in yet another area of life." He turned to face her, his eyes narrowed, his voice low and angry as he spoke. "I've corrupted you in a manner. Before I interfered, ya knew no difference between the touch of one man compared to another. Ya knew nothin' about the weakness of a man when his physical desires were taunted. Ya knew nothin' about such horrors as murder, mutilation, and guilt."

"You make me sound like quite the complete idiot, Mr. Lake," Vaden snapped at him. "Aren't all those things part of human existence? Just because I experienced them at your hand doesn't mean I am corrupted! I think what you really mean to say is in your eyes I'm marred somehow. Weak because I succumbed to your . . . to your . . ."

"To me," he prodded.

"Yes. Thank you."

"I meant no such thing, and ya know it," he argued then. "I only meant to say that . . . you've changed in the past weeks, and don't deny it is mostly on my head."

"I don't." Vaden softened her voice then.

311

"You've taught me much these past weeks. I've told you already what I've learned just this very night. And in the weeks past there have been many things of life I have learned at your hand. None of them, whether good or bad, pleasant or unpleasant, would I trade. For they are things that will help me in life, one way or the other, in my considerations, my decisions." Swallowing hard and straightening her back, she looked at him determinedly and added, "And now I will be bold and forthright in telling you that . . . that you're wrong not to tell your brother you're alive. Consider his pain and loss for a moment." She stopped talking when he raised his hand in a gesture indicating she silence herself and shook his head.

"Don't make me regret confidin' in ya any more than I already do, Vaden," he growled. He looked at the ceiling for a moment as if to gain control of his thoughts and then looked back to her, saying, "The storm stopped almost an hour ago. I figure the sun will be up in a few more hours. We'll leave for home at the first sign of it."

At his mention of their leaving this secluded place, this place where he had opened his heart to her, Vaden felt immense sorrow and fear. Never again would she have him wholly to herself, completely hold him so near to her . . . so solitarily near to her.

"Now, why don't ya try to rest some more?" he

mumbled, turning from her and back toward the fire.

"Quit treating me like a child!" she cried out, causing him to turn, surprise dominating his expression. "I don't want to rest anymore! Don't you see that? In a short time we'll leave here, and . . . and this won't ever happen again! You won't ever again confide in me as you have this night. You won't ever share such intimate conversation with me like you have tonight. We'll be back in town with every woman in the world groveling for your attentions, and I'll go back to being the irritating little girl at the mercantile who is forever and always an inconvenience to you. I'll go back to being your little friend instead of someone you confide in. Someone you choose to . . ." His eyes narrowed, and after inhaling deeply to try to calm herself, Vaden added, "I don't want to rest anymore. So please . . . please quit ordering me to do it as if I were—"

"I have not once treated ya like a child tonight, Vaden," he protested calmly. "You're hung up on thinkin' I have 'cause ya think everyone else treats ya like one. But it's not true. People who care for you are protective of ya. They like to handle ya with kid gloves, protect ya from agony and harm. That doesn't mean they consider you a child. I think my personal treatment of ya proves that I, for one, do not look upon you as a child, Vaden." He moved toward her, reaching out and taking her shoulders between his powerful hands. His eyes narrowed, and his voice lowered. "But if more . . . convincin' is necessary . . . then I for one am willin'."

"Why do you tease me so?" she asked, knowing full well he did indeed only tease her with his implications.

"It's in my nature to tease people I like," he answered, grinning. Then he lowered his voice as if he expected someone to enter the room and eavesdrop on their conversation. "You said it yourself. In a short time we'll go back to town, and everything will return to normal. No more bearin' our souls to each other, no more findin' comfort in each other's arms. And definitely no more tasty kisses." Vaden looked away shyly for a moment. "Things will be different than they are at this moment. No doubt I'll look back at this night and beat my brain to death for allowin' this to happen. No doubt you'll look back on me as the man who taught you too much about life. And you'll be relieved to be rid of me because of it." His hands encircled her neck, his thumbs caressing her throat lightly. "But," he whispered, "I suppose we can both live with our guilt and whatever method it chooses to torture us. Can't we? We can each live with it for one more taste of each other?"

Vaden's mouth began to water for want of his kiss, and a tear ran slowly down her face as she nodded, knowing this memory must live with her forever, for it would be the last of its kind.

"And I'll tell ya somethin', Vaden Valmont," he mumbled in the familiar provocative tone that was his. "Let go of your inhibitions toward me. Be the girl who fears nothin', cares nothin' for what anyone else thinks. Be yourself, Vaden, and I promise you . . ." He leaned forward, placing his cheek against her own as he whispered, "Ransom Lake is yours 'til sunrise. No matter what happens in the future. No matter who ya decide to live your life with, no matter who ends up in mine . . . right now I'm yours, just as I was that night in the wagon . . . and well you knew it, for you're too smart not to have known it. And you know my word is sincere now." He kissed her neck just below her earlobe tenderly, and ecstasy traveled over her. "You kiss me first, Vaden. Kiss me first. Prove to me the girl who found my soul, the one who drew me out of hidin' from beneath my whiskers, is still there inside you . . . and I'm yours until daybreak . . . if ya want me to be." He dropped his hands to his sides, stood erect, and stared at her with the gray intensity of his eyes.

Vaden found it almost impossible to breathe. Her breath, in fact, was unregulated as she looked at him standing before her. Weeks ago she would've been able to draw the courage to kiss him quickly; she would not have even paused perhaps in the same situation. But self-doubt and uncertainty, as well as heartache, had scarred her deeply, and now, with what she wanted and loved most in the world standing before her, hers if only she would reach out and take it, she paused, frightened and unsure of herself. She was unsure of his sincerity in his promise. What if he only laughed at her? What if he drew away from her, having only been teasing her? But deep within her soul she knew better. Ransom Lake would never behave so.

"You . . . you won't laugh at me?" she whispered all the same, her confidence still lacking, the demon of doubt still causing her mind to question.

Ransom Lake closed his eyes for a moment and sighed. "Vaden," he whispered and began to turn from her. Instantly, her hand shot out and clasped his. He paused, looking at her hand and then to her face questioningly. With the few shreds of courage left in her heart, she reached out and took his arm with her other hand, stepping closer to him. She focused her gaze on his hand she held as she tried to muster the bravery of her soul. In a moment, she released it, letting her palms caress the power in his arms and shoulders as her hands traveled up the muscular appendages to settle finally at the back of his neck.

She felt his hands clasp her waist, sending goose bumps erupting over her body, and it gave her the courage to look up at him then. His eyes were narrow, calm, and expectant as he gazed at her. He was so handsome. She loved him so desperately! Her mouth watered, her body quivered. How would she find the courage to take what he offered?

Trembling, she raised herself slightly on her toes and placed a lingering kiss on the cleft of his chin. Then she took his face gently between her small, trembling hands and tipped his head toward her, kissing him sweetly on the mouth. She was encouraged of his sincerity when he involved himself in that first tender kiss, as well as the more earnest one she administered next.

Instantly, she was in his arms, held firmly against his body as the now familiar, powerfully passionate kisses he could manipulate burned between them. His strength and pain, his need and sincerity at being her own, for that time, were all evident as the magical hours passed—hours finding Vaden in awe of what was happening— hours of shared affections now tender and soft, now demanding and passionate. Often he would separate their mouths and hold her to him tightly, whispering her name with something like regret evident in his voice. Once he lifted her swiftly into his arms, going to the small sofa and sitting down with her on his lap where they sat in continuance of their affections, he always the gentleman in every respect, for he never attempted anything beyond impassioned kisses— kisses moist with flavor and barely restrained desire, perhaps, but he was ever the gentleman. Vaden was comfortable, for she knew he would not force any improper attention or affection.

Vaden was breathless in his arms, so thirsty for his kiss it seemed no amount of time in drinking of it would quench her desire. His whiskers, rough against the tender flesh of her mouth, his hands so powerful—softly caressing her one moment, powerfully demanding her body meld with his the next—his mouth warm and moist, so familiar to hers, so passionately demanding. In those hours, Vaden knew absolute bliss.

All too soon, light broke through the dusty west window of the old house, flooding the room with sunlight, further enhanced by the brightness of the snow outside. With the illumination lighting the room, the fire dying in the hearth, the spell Ransom Lake had twined about them began to fade.

Taking her face in his hands and kissing her deeply, as if trying to satisfy a ravenous hunger one last time, he let his thumb trace her tender lips, scarlet from his attentions, and whispered, "Our moment is lost with the sunrise, Vaden. Time to leave the fairy tale and return ya to your uncle. Who," he added as he gently pushed her from his lap, "would strike me down dead if he knew what I've been doin' to ya while you were in my care."

Standing, he walked to the chair sitting across

the room and retrieved his shirt. Buttoning it quickly, and running his fingers through his tousled hair, he put on his hat and coat and pulled on his boots.

What have you done to me, Ransom Lake? Vaden thought. *In these few hours you've fulfilled my dreams of you and yet broken my heart!*

Picking up a bucket sitting near the front door, he exited the house, returning in a moment with the bucket full of snow. Vaden watched, relacing her boots slowly as he doused the fire in the hearth with the bucket of snow, causing steam and the odor of wet wood to rise in the room. Taking Vaden's coat from the chair over which it lay, Ransom held it for her as she slipped her arms through the sleeves. Then, turning her to face him, he grinned, rather regretfully, as he buttoned the coat's top button.

"It's freezin' out there . . . but at least the wind isn't blowin'. I put the horse back outside when the storm stopped, and she doesn't seem any worse for the weather." He opened the front door to the house and motioned for Vaden to precede him.

Vaden's eyes narrowed to a squint as the brightness of the sun's reflection on the new-fallen snow met her eyes, so long adjusted to the dark. All was perfectly quiet—no rustling of wind through tree branches, no snowbirds' songs or calls of wild geese. Not a sound. Vaden looked about for a moment, marveling at the endless horizon of undisturbed white powder and frost covering the earth. Her mesmerized wonderment was lost as Ransom Lake held his hand out to her to assist her into the cutter.

As the cutter slipped away toward home, Vaden gazed back at the lonely house standing midst the quiet of winter. It was a house whose beauty was in its quaintness of design. She smiled sadly. It would forever be a fixed vision in her memory.

Not one word was spoken between Ransom Lake and Vaden Valmont as the mare struggled to return them to town. Vaden found her silence was induced by sorrow and shyness at the memories of her intimate moments shared with Ransom Lake in the house.

Entwine thine arms about me, love. Protect me from the cold. Release me not for need of breath . . . nor fear of growing old. Keep safe our love with thine embrace. Keep warm my lips with thine. Let no one interfere this space that Heaven deemed is mine.

It was the first time since the dreadful Halloween night that Vaden's mind drew forth a favored verse from her memory. And though it was somewhat bittersweet, it seemed fitting. Vaden glanced at Ransom Lake several times and concluded his silence must be derived of the regret of letting what happened happen, for he wore a perpetual frown and did not once look at her.

CHAPTER ELEVEN

At long last, the cutter pulled to a stop before the mercantile. Vaden and Ransom Lake were immediately set upon by Myra, Yvonne, and Dan as all three came bounding out of the house and into the snow beside the cutter.

"Oh, my darling!" Myra cried out, taking Vaden in a tight embrace the second she had stepped down from the conveyance. "We were so worried for ya! Oh, my dearest!"

Yvonne was next, and Vaden noticed her puzzled frown as she hugged her sister, looking to Ransom Lake curiously, then back to Vaden. "We feared the worst, Vay," she said. Her relief at seeing her sister safely home was obvious and sincere. "The storm was so violent, and there was no way to find out if Mr. Lake had even made it to the Wimbers'."

"Thank ya, Ransom," Dan greeted him, putting a grateful hand to the man's shoulder. "I'd have been beside myself if anyone else but you had gone for her. Did ya weather it out at the Wimbers' then?"

"No, sir," the rescuer stated plainly. Vaden watched the color drain from Ransom's face as he removed his hat and looked her uncle squarely in the eyes to continue. "The storm moved in much faster than I anticipated, and the dark overcame us. So . . . we weathered the night at an old house out east on my property."

"Oh, how terrible for you!" Myra exclaimed. "And just look at your face, sweet pea!" Aunt Myra reached out and gently touched the reddened, chapped-looking area around Vaden's mouth. "Look how chapped your face is from the wind and such! Poor dear."

Vaden noticed Ransom Lake close his eyes for a moment at her aunt's referring to her damaged lips. He drew in a deep breath, and she knew he meant to confess to her aunt and uncle. She could feel his guilt radiating from him like the hot flames of a brush fire.

"Sir," he began, addressing Dan, "I want ya to know . . . that although the elements demanded my stoppin' with Miss Vaden to weather the storm . . . I did not act—"

"He saved our lives, Uncle Dan!" Vaden interrupted immediately. "For we would surely have been lost and frozen in the blizzard had Mr. Lake not had the foresight to stop in time." Vaden's eyes met Yvonne's, and her expression of suspicion mingled with delight.

"Of course! Of course, my boy!" Dan assured the man. "Like I told ya before, I wouldn't have sent anyone else for her, for I knew she would be safe in your hands." Dan smiled at the man who guiltily glanced at Vaden once more.

"Now let's get in the house and warm you two up."

"Oh, no, Dan. I really should check on the stock and—" Ransom began.

"Nonsense, Ransom. It's Thanksgiving Day! You've accepted an invitation to dinner, and there's no sense in goin' home when you're already here, now is there?" Dan was smiling and jolly as usual.

"Really, Dan. My stock. I'm bound to have cattle that didn't weather too well and—" Ransom Lake began, and Vaden sensed he wanted only escape from the situation—and her.

"Uncle Dan sent Marcus Donaldson out to your place this morning," Yvonne assured him. "Marcus offered last night to check on everyone out of town when morning came. He'll let us know if there has been any problem at your place."

"I'm . . . I'm not dressed for . . ." he began.

"Oh, now, Ransom Lake!" Myra scolded. "A body would think ya were trying to weasel your way out of spendin' the day with us. Is it my cookin' scarin' ya away?" she teased.

"Now, Myra, ya know there's no truth to that at all," Ransom Lake chuckled, finally grinning a bit.

"Good! Then go on in before ya all freeze out here. I'll take care of the horse." Dan took hold of the mare's reins and led her toward the back of the mercantile where the barn was. Ransom Lake glanced quickly at Vaden, shrugging his shoulders in defeat.

Myra took the man's arm and led him into the house, babbling unceasingly about the baking she'd been about while her mind was plagued with worry during the night. Yvonne took Vaden's arm and stayed her so Myra and Ransom Lake could not hear their conversation.

Lowering her voice to a whisper, Yvonne asked, "Well? Are you going to tell me what happened or not?"

"Nothing happened," Vaden lied.

"You're lying, Vay, and I'm not as stupid as you think I am! I know you, and I know how you feel about that man in there. So tell me . . . did you seduce him into kissing you?"

Vaden gasped and looked at her sister, eyes wide with indignation. "What a thing to say to me, Vonnie! I can't believe you would—"

"And I suppose your lips are berry-red and chapped from the windless drive home this morning." Yvonne giggled, and Vaden knew she was not being unkind, only playful.

"This is not the time nor the place to discuss the matter, Yvonne. Tonight. Tonight when things are quiet and Mr. Lake has gone home. Then maybe I'll talk with you about this. Maybe."

They entered the house, Yvonne giggling and Vaden smiling, though somewhat sadly, for it was at an end now. Her romantic adventure with Ransom Lake, the stuff of daydreams, the fairy tale . . . was over.

Thanksgiving Day had dawned bright and sunny, but as the morning wore on the sun hid behind dark clouds, and the snow began to fall heavily. Ransom Lake was nervous, pacing this way and that the entire morning as Dan conversed with him in the parlor. Finally, sometime after the noon hour, Marcus Donaldson arrived and reported all was well with Ransom Lake's stock. The windbreaks had sheltered the cattle, and the remaining stock was safe in the barn, fed, and watered.

Vaden watched as Ransom reached into his front pocket and offered the man a handful of paper money in exchange for his time.

Marcus shook his head and said, "Ransom, ya know we all look after each other out here. I'm sure there'll come a time when you'll be returnin' the favor. Everything'll be fine over to your place 'til mornin'. Ya go on ahead and enjoy your Thanksgiving with these fine folks." Marcus touched the brim of his hat to the ladies as he left.

"Ya see, my boy!" Dan exclaimed, slapping Ransom heartily on the back. "Nothin' at all to worry about."

"Still, this weather is turnin' severe again," the worried man mumbled. "I should get back before I get snowed in another night away from home."

Dan chuckled and lowered his voice. Vaden's ears were cocked and tightly tuned in. She heard his teasing remark to Ransom Lake. "Oh, I'm certain another night in the company of my niece won't do ya a bit of harm."

Vaden glanced up at Ransom Lake, whose face had gone as white as the snow outside.

"I, uh . . . I, uh, want to be sure ya understand that I meant no—" Ransom began in a lowered voice.

Dan's chuckling interrupted him. "Now, I understand perfectly, my boy. Don't you worry no more about it. I know she was safer with you than any other man on this green earth probably. A bit of sparkin' now and then never hurt nobody."

Vaden felt her face flush red and decided she must break her horrid habit of eavesdropping— as soon as Ransom Lake was no longer under the same roof as she was.

The turkey was splendid, the pie supreme, the conversation friendly and jolly. And the storm was monstrous. Just after dinner, Vaden heard Ransom ask her uncle for a lantern and an extra coat to borrow in order to make his way home. It occurred to her only then that the two of them had barely spoken a word to each other throughout the entire day. She chose that very moment to break her silence toward him.

"You can't go out in this!" she exclaimed,

horrified at the thought of him out in the snow. All eyes, including Ransom Lake's, were on her immediately.

"She's right, Ransom," her Aunt Myra agreed strongly. "Ya can't possibly be thinking of goin' out in this storm. You'll be lost and frozen for certain. Listen to that wind!"

"You're stayin' the night right here with us, Ransom. I'd be a crazy man to let ya go out in this weather," Dan boomed.

"You all are very generous . . . but I've stayed my welcome way past what I should've, and it's time for me to leave," he said.

"Nonsense," Myra sighed. She walked up to him and promptly removed his coat from where it had been slung over his arm. "You're staying right here. We've plenty of room, and I'll not have ya catchin' another cold . . . maybe the death of ya this time."

Ransom's eyes met Vaden's for a moment, and she immediately read their emotions. He wanted escape—escape from her. He'd been her own for one night, and she knew he had no wish to be in her company any longer. Indeed, she had played out her welcome in his presence.

"We've the spare bedroom, Mr. Lake," she offered quickly. "My aunt and uncle would be more than overjoyed to have holiday company. And don't worry. You won't be disturbed." His eyes narrowed as he looked at her, and Vaden was aware of Yvonne carefully studying both her sister and Ransom Lake. "In fact, I feel more than completely done in. It's been a very long day. I think I'll go to bed myself."

"But . . . but it's only just seven o'clock, sweet pea," Myra reminded her niece. "Are ya certain ya want to—"

Vaden nodded. "I'm tired. Very tired. I think I'll just go on to bed. Thank you again, Mr. Lake. For everything." Turning to her aunt, she added, "And thank you for the wonderful meal, Auntie. You've been so wonderful to us since we've come. I bid you all goodnight." Leaving everyone astounded at her early retirement, everyone except Ransom Lake, she went quietly to her room, readied for bed, and slipped beneath her covers as her tears moistened her pillowcase.

She'd had to leave him. In order for him to remain safely under her uncle's roof, she knew she could be no more bother to him. She thought of the boots hidden beneath her bed, but she would not look at them tonight. She would not touch them, for tonight the pain in her heart was too great, and she could not endure the sight of anything belonging to him.

Vaden was quite startled when she awoke some hours later to the darkness in her bedroom. Yvonne was in bed breathing quietly and rhythmically. The clock in the hall struck a quarter past some hour of the night. Had he stayed? she wondered. Had he been so tired of her that he had decided another night anywhere near her was unendurable and ventured out into the storm? She wanted to wake Yvonne and ask her, but she knew question after question would ensue, fired at her by her sister until she had heard of the previous night's antics and her curiosity had been quenched.

So she quietly stepped from her bed and tiptoed out into the hall. Even in the hall, she could hear the wind howling outside and knew the orange light emanating from the parlor was the fire in the hearth Dan had left burning to try to heat the house. It was terribly cold, and she wished she had taken the time to wrap herself in a blanket. The door to the spare room was closed. For fear Ransom Lake may indeed be asleep in the room beyond, she dared not open it. It would more than likely squeak open like every other door in the house. She placed her ear to the cold wood and listened, hearing nothing beyond. With a heavy, disappointed sigh, she made her way into the parlor to stand before the low flames of the fire. She closed her eyes for a moment, remembering the fire, the hearth, and the many warmths of the night before. The warm, provocative tone of Ransom Lake's voice echoed through her mind. His arms had been so strong, so capable, and warming when he held her, his face so handsome, his eyes so hypnotic. His kiss . . . his kiss had been ecstasy, perfectly embodied.

She startled, jumping nervously, as she heard a voice behind her whisper, "What're ya doin' up at all hours of the night?" Turning, Vaden found herself face-to-face with the very subject of her thoughts, standing dressed in only his trousers and holding a glass of water in one hand.

"I couldn't sleep, and I-I thought I might sit by the fire a moment," she stammered.

"You need your rest. You've been greatly deprived of it lately, I think," he muttered. Instead of returning to his room, however, he came to stand beside her.

"I suppose," she admitted. She looked about nervously, trying to find something other than the man on which to focus her attention. It was greatly unsettling to see him again only half clothed as he was. "I mean . . . do you have everything you need? Are you comfortable in your room, Mr. Lake?"

He grinned and held up the glass of water before saying, "Already got what I needed. And I'm snug as a bug in that room. But thank ya just the same, Miss Vaden." His eyes were stormy and mirthful, and she knew he knew she was uncomfortable.

She nodded nervously as her fingers fumbled with the bow at the throat of her nightdress. "I . . . uh . . . I need to say another thank you."

"For what?" he asked, taking a drink from the glass.

"For coming to get me last evening. I know it was no small task, and I wanted you to know I have an immense appreciation of your deed."

His grin broadened as his eyes traveled the length of her, resting at her bare feet. Vaden turned from him, going to stand nearer to the fire.

"I'm sincere in my thanks, Mr. Lake. I wish you wouldn't look at me with that amused look of doubt each time I find myself thanking you or apologizing to you."

"What amused look of doubt?" he asked in a whisper.

"That look. The one that is on your face just now," she said, turning toward him and pointing to his fine feature of face.

"Well, it does seem that you're always apologizin' to me for some sort of somethin', now doesn't it? Would ya like it better if I were grouchin' at ya every time? I swear I'd spend most of my time in town grouchin' if that were the case. And besides, maybe I'm the one who needs to be thankin' you for that warm evenin' last night."

Vaden blushed furiously, but she made no effort to defend herself, for she knew she would only succeed in making herself all the more uncomfortable. He remained standing beside her before the fire, and they were both silent for a moment. Then, an instant before she would've turned and left him for fear of verbally spilling her heartfelt love for him should she linger longer, he spoke two words.

"I'm sorry," he muttered quietly.

"What?" she asked, unable to believe what he'd said or to understand why he had said it.

"Now," he continued, "I see Jerome and Belva have stepped out of the room. So what say we have us a dance?"

"The proverbial water under the bridge, Mr. Lake," Vaden whispered, relieved he was only teasing her once more.

"Not to me." He looked at her, the firelight reflecting mischievously in his eyes. "I feel the need to make amends. And I promise I never make the same mistake twice." He set his glass of water down out of the way and put a hand at her waist, gesturing for her to place her hand in his outstretched one.

Vaden smiled at him and blushed slightly as he began to waltz with her. He kept his steps small, and she fancied he held her too closely, but she was entranced by him as they danced, the only music being the warm crackling of the fire. His steps weren't as smooth and fluid as Jerome's, and she was glad of it. He was heavier on his feet, and she knew Jerome would never contemplate holding her so closely. In fact, a few moments after they had begun, she cast her gaze downward and began to tremble slightly when she realized he held her close enough to his body that at every few steps she could feel the firm muscles of his upper chest brush against her chin or cheek—that every other turn she would feel the solid power of his thigh against her leg as he led her.

"You're cold," he muttered, misinterpreting her shivering. "You should get back to bed." He stopped their waltz and released her. Then, as she stood dazedly gazing up at him, he whispered, "And for Belva's benefit . . ." and he stooped, kissing her warmly on the forehead.

Vaden smiled even though she sensed tears wanting to rise to her eyes. How desperately she wished to relive the night before when he'd held and kissed her and almost lovingly whispered her name.

"But you see, Mr. Lake," she said quietly, "you've only just proven the other girls' point. I'm the kind of girl you want to take fishing. The kind you kiss on the forehead sweetly as you would a child. The kind you toy with in private once, when no one can see . . . but not the kind you make a habit of—"

Before she could finish her sentence, Ransom cupped Vaden's chin in his powerful hand and kissed her soft lips plainly and not so very quickly. Vaden felt the now familiar and instantaneous fire ignite within her as his mouth began to work a spell over her as it had the night before. She marveled at how instantly wonderful the feel of being in his arms was, how familiar the warmth and taste of his kiss was to her. But almost as quickly as he had begun to kiss her, he stopped, holding her away from him.

"I'm a guest in your uncle's house, Vaden. I won't take advantage of that by—" he explained.

She was suddenly humiliated, feeling as if she had again provoked him into faltering somehow. She felt a panicked desperation. He would leave her once more and truly never be close to her again, for she knew the past two days were never to be repeated. Never.

"But I . . . I . . ." she stammered, fighting to stop her mouth from saying what it had begun to confess to him.

"Don't say it, Vaden," he demanded, closing his eyes tightly as if to block out her words. "I'm not what ya need. I can't be what ya want. Ya only think that ya . . . it's because I was such a mystery to ya for so long. You have the curiosity of a fairy, Vaden. You'll find now that it's quenched . . . I won't seem as—"

"What on earth do you think I was going to say to you, Mr. Lake?" she exclaimed, though she knew full well she would have confessed her love for him that very moment had he not interrupted her.

"I know more surely than you can imagine

exactly what ya were about to say, Vaden. But it's only youth and admiration causin' ya to think . . . I've rescued ya twice now. I'm a man in your eyes . . . older than that flimsy Jerome Clayton. It's all just your . . . imagination. I'm not what ya think I am," he nearly growled.

"You may think you know what I was going to say to you, Mr. Lake," Vaden spat, "but don't flatter yourself. I was only going to say that you were not taking advantage of me; therefore, you were not taking advantage of my uncle's hospitality. I was not being lured blindly into your arms, Mr. Lake. I am not the idiot you continue to take me for."

She could tell by the narrowing of his eyes and the way he studied her face that he doubted . . . no, he knew she was lying. So she turned indignantly and began to walk away from him. She gasped aloud when next she felt him come from behind her and pick her up swiftly in his arms.

"Leave it to you to be wanderin' around in the middle of the night and completely ruin a man's chances of gettin' a good night's sleep. This is the second night in a row you've been the cause of my tired eyes and body, girl," he grumbled as he carried her toward the bedrooms. He paused before the door to the guest room in which he was staying the night. "You think you're too smart to be taken advantage of, do ya now?" he whispered. "Well, Miss Know-It-All Valmont . . . what if old man Ransom Lake was to take ya on into this room instead of on to your own? What would ya do then?"

She set her jaw squarely, and even though her body trembled with rapture at being held by him, she said firmly, "Scream for deliverance at the top of my lungs."

The awesomely handsome man glared at her. "Ya couldn't. My mouth would be exhaustin' yours, and ya wouldn't be able to scream." Then he lowered his voice even more, and as the beguiling gray storm in his eyes fixed on hers, he added, "And ya wouldn't want to anyway."

Her mouth gaped open in astonishment at his lewd remarks. "And you pride yourself as holding to high morals—in being a gentleman."

"I do, Miss Valmont." Then he turned and headed in the direction of Vaden's own room.

As he started to push the door open with his foot, she protested in a whisper, "No! Don't! You'll wake Yvonne, and she'll think—"

Ransom looked at her for a moment. "Not if ya keep that honeyed mouth shut for once, girl," he whispered as the door to Vaden's bedroom slowly swung open. Quietly he carried Vaden to her empty bed as she watched to be sure Yvonne did not stir. He laid her gently on it and then whispered, "You're lucky this night, Miss Vaden, that I chose not to stop at my own room."

Vaden sat up and spat in a whisper, "You would never have seriously considered it." She knew he was a gentleman and also a friend of her uncle's. He was only teasing her, and she knew it well.

"So sure, are ya?"

"Perfectly. Don't pretend to be the villain, Mr. Lake. I know better."

"Don't be so sure, girl," he whispered. As he leaned forward, his arms on either side of her body supporting his weight, she melted against him once more as he kissed her with a deep ferocity nearly causing her to faint from the rapturous intensity of it. His mouth was hot and demanding and left hers too soon. He exited the room quietly but with haste and anger, and Vaden wondered if she would ever sleep before morning.

"Am I dreaming, Vaden?" Yvonne whispered quietly from the other side of the room. "I could have sworn I just saw—"

"Yes, you must be dreaming, Vonnie. And so must I be."

Vaden was uncomfortable at breakfast the next morning. She could feel the blush rise to her face every time she looked at Ransom Lake and he caught her looking at him. He seemed to wear an eternal expression of knowing amusement, and it unnerved her greatly.

"Ya might as well stay through lunch, Ransom," Dan stated.

"No. I've got to get back. Hard tellin' what kind of shape I'll find things in," he explained.

"It'll take ya two hours to get home in this weather, boy! Ya better stay on." Dan shoveled another bite of eggs into his mouth.

"Nope. Can't. Found myself away from home long enough already, Dan. But I thank ya for your generosity. You too, Myra."

Ransom smiled at Myra, and she nodded and smiled back. "Any time, Ransom. You're a joy to have around, not to mention bein' Vaden's deliverer from tragedy."

Vaden looked to him, and as his eyes captured hers, his tongue moistened his lips slowly as he stared at her mouth, and her eyes widened indignantly. When she next looked to Yvonne, it was to see her sister's eyes practically bulging from her skull, for Yvonne had witnessed Ransom Lake's gesture. It delighted Vaden to know she had, for now Yvonne had seen his flirtatious nature firsthand.

As Vaden stood at the window watching Ransom Lake's mare struggling to carry him through the knee-deep snow, her depression and heartache continued. For nearly two days— definitely two nights—she had been in his company, and her heart ached for his arms about her. Her body ached to hear his mumbly, low-pitched voice whisper something, anything, in her ear. She wanted only to stare at him every moment of the day, to have him talk to her. Just one of their silly, argumentative conversations would've sufficed. She longed for his smile, his frown, the way he rubbed at the whiskers on his chin. Little things were what she longed for as well as the more obvious, such as his marvelous kiss.

As she watched him disappear around the corner toward his home, she knew her tale of companionship with the phenomenal man Ransom Lake was at an end. He would have all the more reason to avoid her now. She knew that for certain. It was mere common sense testifying to her that once someone had confided some deep-felt secret to another person, that person, having chosen in a weak moment to reveal himself, often felt uncomfortable around his confidant, wanting only to avoid them at all cost. And there was much more reason for Ransom Lake to avoid her when coupled with the fact she held knowledge of his pain, for not only was she forever and always tripping him up somehow, she also tempted him physically. This final fact she could admit to herself, for he had told her as much. She also knew it to be true, for she knew a man could not feign such passion. Even the best of players would've slipped up somehow. It was only another reason for him to want to avoid her as much as possible.

Vaden was in love with Ransom Lake, and she

would not let him suffer more than he already had, more than necessary. And it was not necessary. Perhaps he didn't want her. Perhaps she couldn't heal his pain or fill his lonely heart. But there was someone who could. She had promised not to repeat his secrets; she had promised, and she would keep her promise. But there was someone whom Ransom Lake needed—someone who needed Ransom Lake. And she would not let the man she loved suffer needlessly any further.

CHAPTER TWELVE

Vaden sent the telegram to Denver Lake only two days after Thanksgiving. It was a mere one week later, while she and Yvonne were tending to the store, when a tall, handsome stranger entered. Vaden's heart began to pound furiously, for his resemblance to Ransom Lake was undeniably obvious. He was perhaps even taller, and his own black hair was completely grayed at the temples. He wore the clothes of a man who had great wealth, and his eyes were the deepest of blues. He was not as striking to look at as was Ransom Lake but was very handsome all the same.

"He's here," Vaden whispered under her breath as, for a moment, she felt it difficult to stay conscious.

"He looks remarkably like . . ." Yvonne began, but the man removed his hat and approached the counter, and her words were lost.

"Pardon me, ladies," he began. His manner of speech was confident and well-enunciated. "I've come to town in answer to a . . . excuse me, but my explanation is rather complicated. I'm looking . . . rather, I'm told there may be living nearby a man whom I believe to be my brother."

Vaden held her breath, barely able to retain her balance and composure under the realization this was indeed Ransom Lake's brother—his only remnant of family. So it was Yvonne who answered.

"Well, pardon me for being so bold, sir," she began, "but I must tell you that you bear striking resemblance to our own Ransom Lake."

Vaden watched as the man's face immediately drained of all trace of color as he stared at Yvonne.

"Then . . . it's true . . . what the telegram said? My brother is living? Living here?" he asked.

Yvonne frowned, puzzled, and looked to Vaden questioningly. Vaden only took a step back from her, shaking her head, unable to believe what she had done and the result standing before her.

"Yes, sir. If your brother's name is Ransom Lake, it would seem to be certain, considering your resemblance to him, that it is one and the same man." Yvonne looked to the man, concerned immediately about his reaction as well as Vaden's. "Sir, do you need to sit down? You suddenly look quite unwell."

Vaden held her breath as the man's eyes concentrated on her. His eyes narrowed, and he held out a piece of paper to her, not to Yvonne, even though Yvonne had been the one to answer his questions. When Vaden shook her head and took another step backward, Yvonne reached out and took the paper, reading it aloud.

"*To Denver Lake, Leadville, Colorado. Sir, I believe it would be in your best interest, as well as that of another, to know a man believed to be your relation is living near our township. His last name is Lake, and he carries with him a pocketknife engraved with your name. Sincerely."*

Yvonne looked up to Denver Lake. "It was anonymous?" Vaden could feel Yvonne wanted to turn and look at her, but she also knew Yvonne would instantly understand why she mustn't.

"Can you tell me where I might find Ransom Lake?" the man asked.

He glanced again at Vaden, who stood paralyzed, unable to inwardly admit what her actions had caused to happen. Here he stood before her, the beloved brother of the man she loved—the brother whom Ransom Lake wanted to believe was alone in the world. And she had betrayed the man she loved in bringing him here. She felt that, from the depth of the pain and guilt in her heart, the organ must be ripping itself in two within her bosom.

"Certainly, Mr. Lake. He, um . . ." Yvonne looked again to the telegram, and Vaden knew the situation was almost as shocking to her sister as it was to herself. "He lives not but a mile north of town. And . . ." Yvonne's voice broke off. Vaden followed her sister's gaze to the front entrance as the color faded from Yvonne's face.

"Mornin', ladies," Ransom Lake greeted as he entered the store for the first time since he'd left them the day after Thanksgiving. "Is your Uncle

Dan around?" He approached the counter and stood directly next to his brother, completely unaware of the fact because his attention was directed to Vaden and Yvonne. "Are ya feelin' all right, Miss Vaden?" he asked as his gaze fell on her. "Ya don't look yourself. For that matter, neither do you, Miss Valmont. Is everything all right here?"

Vaden felt as if someone had plunged a knife into her chest as she watched Denver Lake lay a hand on his brother's shoulder. "Ransom? Ransom . . . it can't really be you," Denver muttered.

Someone twisted the invisible knife piercing Vaden's heart, Ransom Lake's eyes narrowing as he glared at her before turning to see standing next to him, for the first time in a decade, his elder brother.

"Denver," Ransom Lake mumbled as he looked back to Vaden. For a moment, his eyes filled with anger. Yvonne looked to Ransom Lake and then to Vaden and back, a frown of inability to comprehend the situation furrowing her brow.

"Ransom. Where have you been? I was told you had died with everyone else. Why didn't you contact me?" Denver asked, obviously awed by his brother's existence. The man was visibly battling to control the conflicting emotions of joy, pain, and anger simultaneously attacking his soul. Ransom Lake's attention was still on Vaden. She could no longer endure his abhorrent gaze.

Quickly she walked to the end of the counter and out from behind, meaning to flee past him and through the front door. He lunged forward, catching her arm and pulling her to him.

"How could ya do this to me, Vaden?" he growled. The storm in his eyes was seething—raging and violent! She had hurt him deeply, she knew. She could only stand before him, shaking her head. "How could ya betray me like this?" he shouted.

"Ransom," Denver scolded from behind him.

Ransom's eyes continued to glare at Vaden.

"How could ya tell him? After you promised me," he growled at the girl whose arm was held painfully tight in his grip.

"I told him nothing," Vaden managed to force from her lips in a whisper. "I told him nothing. I only . . . it was wrong of you, and you know it. You were wrong. It was selfish. I only . . ."

Ransom's chest rose and fell heavily with his angered breathing. "I trusted you," he mumbled.

"Ransom," Denver began, taking a step toward his brother. "Remember, Ransom. Remember what our father taught us. 'When a woman provokes you to anger and you're in doubt as to whether to strike her or kiss her . . .'"

Vaden tried to pull her arm free as Ransom Lake clenched his teeth and closed his eyes tightly shut for a moment, but his hold was too powerful.

Then he opened his eyes to her once more and

mumbled, "Our father told us, 'There is no consideration to be made, for the latter releases the frustration faster and more valiantly than the prior.'" He paused for a moment and, still glaring at Vaden, whose tears were profuse on her cheeks, said to his brother, though he still did not look at him, "I would never think to strike this girl, Denver."

Suddenly, he released her arm and cupped her chin firmly. "Quit meddlin' with my life, girl!" he whispered angrily. The next moment, the hot moisture of his mouth captured hers roughly, forcing a strong, deep, and very insistent kiss. The fierceness of the kiss softened but not the sheer, magnificent power of it. Vaden's body was weakened. Had it not been for his body before her and his powerful arms around her to hold her when her knees failed, she would've fallen to the floor. All the splendid sensations that had enveloped her the first time he kissed her, and every blissful time thereafter, did so again. In a mere moment, she was returning his kiss, and they were both lost in its passion.

"Oh, my! Vaden! Slap him, for Pete's sake!" Yvonne insisted, rushing from behind the counter to stand behind her sister. "Vaden! What if Auntie comes in here?" Yvonne hurried to stand between Ransom Lake and his brother, tapping Ransom Lake lightly on the shoulder. "Mr. Lake, please! Have some decorum."

Vaden heard Denver Lake chuckle and heard Yvonne protesting as he took hold of her arm, pulling her back from the embracing couple.

"If my brother kisses a woman anywhere nearly as perfectly as I do . . . then I think we must have something in common other than just our resemblance to our father, miss."

Yvonne's voice echoed through Vaden's mind, and she did indeed raise her hand to Ransom Lake's face. His kiss was overpowering, and instead of delivering a firm slap, she felt her hand tenderly caress his face for a moment.

His kiss intensified, and the passion of it frightened Vaden. She knew it was a passion of anger and frustration he must feel, yet to her it seemed to be something quite different. Her own passion for him frightened her, for she wanted nothing else in the world except to stay in that exact situation forever. Suddenly he broke their kiss, and Vaden drew in a deep breath, unaware until that moment the force of his kiss had made it difficult for her to breathe easily.

"Were ya sent on this earth solely to torment me, girl?" he barked, taking her by the shoulders and holding her away from his body. "My life is in shreds since ya came here. I have no privacy, no self-control, and no hair either, for that matter!"

"More likely she was sent here to save your soul, Ransom Lake! How dare you take such familiarities with my sister?" Yvonne scolded, wrenching her arm free of Denver's strong grip. Vaden knew Denver had willingly released her sister, for she knew Ransom Lake's strength and expected his brother's to be no less. Yvonne rushed to her sister. She raised her hand to slap Ransom Lake, but he easily caught her wrist.

"I would never harm your sister, and ya know it. And besides, it's not the first time we've tasted each other's affection, Miss Valmont." Ransom Lake released Yvonne's wrist rather violently and turned to look at his brother.

"There's time enough to scold your little pet, Ransom," Denver Lake spoke. "This moment is for you and me. We've far too many things to discuss."

"I'm not his pet!" Vaden was horrified the man would refer to her so, as if she was no more than a common, ordinary, uninteresting kitten.

"You melt in his arms easily enough, Vaden," Yvonne whispered scoldingly, and Vaden felt the stinging tears of humiliation rise to her eyes.

Ransom and Denver Lake still stood gravely facing each other.

"Why, Ransom?" Denver asked in a lowered voice, filled with pain in its intonation. "Why didn't you tell me?"

Ransom Lake looked to Vaden again; this time his eyes were sad and guilty—defeated. "Vaden," he mumbled, "why did ya do this?"

"I couldn't stand it," she whispered as the tears streamed down her face. "I couldn't stand by and watch you needlessly endure such misery and loneliness for the rest of your life. I couldn't watch you waste your life. It was wrong of you never to tell him you were alive, to sit feeling sorry for yourself all these years. You can hate me forever if you want, but I did it because I . . ."

His eyes narrowed as he stared at her, waiting for her to finish her sentence.

"Because you what?" he asked.

"Because . . . because somebody needed to, and I'm the only one who knew how," she finished. She scolded herself harshly for nearly letting the words of confessing love slip from her lips. "I didn't tell him. I only sent a telegram and told him there was a man named Lake living here. That's all. I swear it. I would never betray you. You know that."

"Go easy on the girl, Ransom. She did no more than right by you," Denver said calmly.

Ransom Lake hung his head in defeat for a moment before turning from Vaden to look at his brother. "There's so much ya need to know, Denver. Maybe when you've heard it all, you'll wish she hadn't sent ya that telegram after all."

"I've never been more grateful to receive a simple piece of paper in my life." Denver approached Vaden then. He brushed at the tears on her cheeks with one of his large, strong hands.

"I think you and I should have a reunion of our own one day, miss." His smile was sympathetic and grateful. Then, turning to Yvonne, he offered his hand. Yvonne took his hand, and he shook hers firmly. "Then you too, Miss . . . Miss . . ."

"Yvonne Valmont," Yvonne told him. Vaden was surprised to hear her sister introduce herself so, for she had never introduced herself as anything other than *Miss* Yvonne Valmont.

The gray eyes of Ransom Lake narrowed as he looked at Vaden one final time before leaving the mercantile with his brother. Vaden watched them disappear around the corner down the street. She accepted her fate where Ransom Lake was concerned. She had lost him finally now. Had she sensed a finality to his kiss? She was sure she had. Ransom Lake was lost to her, but he had found what he needed most—found his brother and found the beginnings of healing his heart.

"Never! Never in my life have I witnessed such a display, Vaden!" Yvonne scolded as she returned to her place behind the counter. "What do you mean letting the man maul you like that? For pity's sake, girl! How could you even breathe?"

"I . . . I couldn't care less if I ever drew another breath, Yvonne. And I'd appreciate it if you'd hold such jealousy in check." Vaden was irritated at her sister's sudden lack of sympathy.

"Jealousy? Jealousy?" Yvonne exclaimed. "What do you mean? I wouldn't want to be in your shoes for anything in the world, Vaden Valmont!"

"Yes, you would!" Vaden turned to face her sister, who was about to endure the brunt of Vaden's aching heart and need to scream. "You've never been kissed like that, Yvonne. Admit it! You're jealous!" Vaden spat. The consequence of what she had done—signed the death certificate on any chance she had at having Ransom Lake's heart—was making itself all the more painfully known.

"Ha! I meant I wouldn't be in your shoes for the mere fact you've just assured yourself of losing Ransom Lake for good! He told you in confidence, didn't he? He confided in you at some point—no doubt on that interesting night that you've kept silent about, that night you spent with him before Thanksgiving. He told you he had a brother. Ransom Lake didn't want his brother to know he was here, and you told him!"

Yvonne's tongue could be so sharp when she wanted it to be. Vaden brushed the tears from her face. "I broke no confidence, Yvonne. I told nothing that was Ransom's secret. I only . . . I only let Denver Lake know a man in town shared his name. Ransom never made me promise not to contact Denver. And you don't have to tell me I've lost him, Yvonne. I love him too much to let him live without his brother, whom I know he loves desperately. It's . . . it's much more important that he—"

"I am jealous, Vaden," Yvonne interrupted harshly. "I am jealous. You love him so completely, so unconditionally. You love him so much that nothing frightens you into not helping him, even the knowledge of losing what connection you do have with him. You still love him enough to take the chance to make him happy. I'm afraid to love anyone that way. I . . . I'm afraid to love someone that way and then have to endure life without them. I'm a coward, Vaden, and I admit it to you now. It's why I'm so proper and perfect in my manner. It keeps me hardened. It keeps me safe, Vaden." Yvonne wiped her own tears as she continued. "You're right. I've never been kissed like Ransom Lake kissed you. I know you're hurting, Vay. I know guilt is eating at you now as well. But the way he kissed you, Vay!" Yvonne paused, shaking her head in wonder at what she had seen pass between her sister and the man. "He . . . he wasn't just kissing you, Vay. The man was making love to you."

Vaden put her hands over her ears, shaking her head violently. "No! Don't say that, Vonnie! It's not true! He just . . . he just . . ."

"Even if I were to find a man I would desire affections from, I would not allow it because I would be too afraid to give into a love like the one you have for that unsettling Ransom Lake." Yvonne hugged her sister tightly. "Do you see now? Do you see what a coward I am? How selfish? Do you see how brave and selfless you are, Vay?"

"I'm as much a coward as you, Vonnie," Vaden sobbed, "for I know that you would at least have the courage to confess your feelings for such a man. But I've never . . . I've never been able to tell him what I feel, for I could not endure the rejection in his eyes."

"I'm sorry I pushed you toward Jerome Clayton so, Vay," Yvonne whispered as the sisters separated, dabbing at their cheeks with their aprons. "It was wrong. I just didn't want to see you hurt. But now I know. I know the old saying is true. I know that it is better to have loved and lost—"

"Than never to have loved at all," Vaden finished as she straightened her back, picked up a feather duster, and began sweeping the shelves behind the counter with it. She did not doubt the truth of it.

It was merely minutes later when Jerome Clayton entered the mercantile. Vaden's heart, which had been so overly taxed that day already, knew she must tell him, truthfully, finally, and so he would understand. She'd tried feeding him clues, little hints here and there, but he was ever persistent.

"Good mornin', ladies!" Jerome greeted cheerily. "Can ya get away for a walk today, Vaden?" he asked forthrightly.

Vaden looked to Yvonne, who nodded.

"Yes, Jerome. I . . . I believe it's time we had a talk." Vaden laid the feather duster on the counter once more. After putting on her coat, she left the mercantile with Jerome. She ignored him when he offered his arm to her. She knew he was not as unwitting as he pretended, for there was something in his eyes, the way he looked at her with a hint of suspicion. She shook off her uneasy feeling. It was her own guilt reading the suspicion in him— her own guilt over having let him hope for so long.

"We're almost a week into December, and ya still haven't given me any hints as to what you might want for Christmas, Vaden," Jerome stated. His voice was low and irritated. Vaden looked to him and felt he knew what she wanted to talk about.

"Jerome—" she began.

"He's poisoned your mind against me, Vaden," he interrupted. There was anger apparent in his voice. "He's a violent man, and women are often intrigued by his kind. I understand your infatuation with him, but he won't have ya, Vaden. He'll use ya, corrupt ya with his physical dominance, but he won't have ya, and this infatuation ya have will pass."

Vaden could only stand in the street next to him, staring up at him in disbelief. "What are you talking about, Jerome?" she asked. She could not believe what he had said—couldn't believe she had heard him correctly. It was completely uncharacteristic of the man to be so vehement and accusing.

Jerome's eyes narrowed, and he sneered repulsively for a moment. "Ransom Lake. I know you're infatuated with him. Do ya think I'm blind? Do ya think his threats to Nathaniel on Halloween kept Nathaniel from tellin' me, his best friend, what happened to ya at the hand of Ransom Lake that night?"

"Ransom Lake came for me when I was being tormented beyond your understanding, Jerome," Vaden stated firmly. "Your best friend, as you refer to him, was the cause of my torment! How dare you side with him?"

"I can wait. I want ya to know that I am a mature man, an understandin' man. I can wait. This infatuation with Ransom Lake will pass soon enough, and I'll be here to pick up the pieces when he breaks your heart."

Vaden shook her head, frowning at what was being communicated to her. He wouldn't listen to her if she tried to explain she could never be his. He had created a reason in his mind as to why she hadn't been his already—and as to why she would eventually belong to him.

"I know he won't ever have me, Jerome, that he'd never want me. But you must understand it makes no difference. You and I . . . we're too dissimilar. It won't work. You need someone who'll—" she began.

"I'll wait, Vaden. I'll wait until ya grow up enough to see what's before ya." Then he simply tipped his hat to her and walked away.

Vaden stood in the snow and mud of the street, simply staring after him in disbelief. He always seemed so secure, so sound, and well balanced. But to completely deny, to be so unwilling to accept what she was trying to tell him, it was not normal, and it worried her.

That day seemed longer than any other of her life. Vaden could not tear her mind and thoughts away from wondering over Ransom Lake and his brother. Would Denver be so angry, so hurt over Ransom not telling him he was still alive, that he would not want to see his brother again? Perhaps it would be worse for Ransom now, especially if Denver did not have compassion for his brother's reasoning. Vaden shook her head, knowing Denver seemed a good man. He was, after all, Ransom Lake's brother, and it only stood to reason he would have similar traits of personality, under-standing being one.

Vaden's mind was also greatly taxed over Jerome's reaction earlier in the day when she tried to confront him with the truth of her lack of feelings for him. It was so oddly calm, his denial. It somehow unsettled her nerves. So she tried to endure that day of wondering.

As night turned into another day, she busied herself with working frantically in the store, dusting and straightening, helping customers, and running errands for Myra and Dan. She found herself very fatigued when evening arrived, and the family retired from dinner to the parlor. They sat before the cozy fire listening to Myra and Dan talking about the townsfolk, their aching bones, and stories of when the girls were young. Vaden knew her aunt and uncle suspected something was bothering her, but she was all the more grateful they didn't ask her about it— didn't press her for explanations.

The frantic knock on the front door startled them all, and Dan went to see who could possibly be bothering them on such a cold night. When he returned, he held a small wooden box and smiled broadly.

"It's for you again, sweet pea," his deep voice announced as he handed the box to Vaden. "Seems like your secret admirer don't mind bravin' the elements." His eyes twinkled merrily, and Vaden smiled at him, suspicion foremost in her mind.

"Let's see," she began, winking at her uncle, "who could possibly know I've been having a rough couple of days?"

"It's a mystery," Dan chuckled, his eyes brighter than ever with delight.

Carefully, Vaden removed the lid from the small box and looked inside. There was a note, scrawled in somewhat illegible script, and she retrieved it, unfolding it gently and reading aloud, *"Remember, the hardened shell protects what's inside. I'm sorry."* Frowning, for it seemed an odd thing for Dan to write were he playing the part of secret admirer, Vaden then brushed aside the straw lying beneath the note concealing something deeper in the box. She was not surprised this time when she retrieved from the straw padding another rock. This rock was much larger than the one she had received previously. The crystal formations revealed inside when she turned it over were white and clear with tiny bits of something sparkling radiantly when the firelight caught them.

"It's beautiful!" Yvonne exclaimed. "Do you think Jerome is coming to his senses finally, Vay? Is it perhaps an apology for acting so insanely?"

"Oh, Vonnie!" Vaden exclaimed. "It's Uncle Dan who's doing this for me! It's as plain as the nose on his face." Vaden stood, went to her uncle, and kissed him sweetly on the cheek.

"I tell ya again, sweet pea . . . it's not me that's done this," Dan said.

He seemed in earnest. But it took the beauty of the gift away if she were to believe it was Jerome Clayton who left it. And it was completely inconceivable to think Ransom Lake would do such a thing. So Vaden determined it must be her uncle's way of trying to cheer her.

Still, as Vaden studied the beautiful marvel of

nature by candlelight just before she crawled into bed, her mind began to tax itself again wondering what was transpiring in Ransom Lake's life. She had trouble sleeping. When slumber did finally find her, her dreams were sad and tormenting.

Vaden's heart leapt in her bosom as Denver and Ransom Lake entered the mercantile very early the next morning. They were dressed in heavy clothing, and Vaden immediately noticed the expression of peace and joy obvious on both their faces. Her eyes brimmed with tears, for she sensed they had made their peace and were happy in each other. Myra and Dan had left at first light to go out to check on Mrs. Tilits. Vaden and Yvonne were tending the store alone.

"Good morning to you, lovely ladies," Denver Lake greeted.

Vaden looked away at once as Ransom Lake's intense gaze found her.

"Good morning, Mr. Lake," Yvonne replied. "What can we do for you this fine winter's morning?"

Vaden, nervous as she was under Ransom Lake's gaze, quickly looked to her sister, for her voice was all too pleasant sounding, all too delighted. She found Yvonne's face was blushing crimson as she looked at Denver.

"Well . . . I don't know about Ransom here," Denver said, lowering his voice and leaning on the counter in front of Yvonne, "but the best thing you could do for me today, Miss Valmont, would be to hop in the wagon and run down to the preacher's house with me." Vaden grinned as Yvonne's eyes widened with delight. Denver sighed heavily, as if a great disappointment were washing over him. "I suppose it's always the same story. All the girls around here, including the beautiful Miss Valmont, are probably so in love with ol' Handsome Ransom, as the girls back home used to call him, that you'll never see past him to my ugly mug. Is that right, Miss Valmont?"

Vaden's smile broadened, for it was delightful to see her perfectly proper, always-in-control sister completely undone by the man. Yvonne began to fiddle with the brooch at her collar, looking about as if something would need doing to save her discomfort.

"I-I . . . no, sir . . . I . . ." Yvonne stammered.

"So ya don't think I'm good-lookin' then, Miss Valmont?" Ransom inquired teasingly, still looking at Vaden. Vaden's eyes went to him once more, and his gaze mesmerized her. Had her sister and his brother not been standing just next to them, she could not have stopped herself from running to him and throwing herself into the power of his embrace.

"Oh! No! I think you're very handsome, Mr. Lake," Yvonne defended herself to the younger Mr. Lake.

"You see, brother. You've turned this one's head, and I'll never have a chance," Denver chuckled.

Immediately, Yvonne looked back at him. "Oh, no, Mr. Lake! I didn't mean that at all. You've all the chance in the world!" Vaden and Ransom both looked to Yvonne, shocked beyond speaking at her unwitting confession.

Denver raised an eyebrow and reached out, taking Yvonne's hand in his gloved one. "Well, that's very, very encouraging, Miss Valmont. Very encouraging."

"I mean," Yvonne stammered, pulling her hand from his grasp. "That is to say, I'm sure that when you find a woman you desire to—"

"Oh, but I've found her, Miss Valmont. I'm looking at her," Denver interrupted, winking at Yvonne.

Vaden was delighted. Yvonne was completely undone! It was obvious her thoughts were muddled and her heart aflutter.

"Leave the poor girl alone, Denver," Ransom chuckled. "We need to be headin' out."

"Heading out?" Vaden finally spoke, for his words frightened her. Was he leaving? Would he be returning to Leadville with his brother?

"We're . . . we're goin' out to visit our parents' graves, Miss Vaden," he explained. "We'll be gone two or three days, and I was wonderin' if you'd ask your Uncle Dan to check on my stock for me."

"You'll be back?" Vaden's question sounded more desperate than she meant to reveal.

"Of course we'll be back!" Denver answered, trying to capture Yvonne's hand once more. "We live here!"

"We?" Yvonne whispered.

"Yes. Denver's agreed to move out here with me. He says the silver's all gone in Leadville anyway." Ransom took several steps toward Vaden, and her heart began to beat ferociously as he approached. "You and I need to have a few words when I return," he told her in a lowered voice.

"I'm sorry, Mr. Lake. I'm . . . I thought it would be best for you, and I only meant to help." Vaden's defense of herself caused Ransom Lake to close his eyes for a moment and inhale deeply.

"I know it, Vaden." He reached out, brushing a strand of hair from her cheek with his gloved hand. His hand grasped her arm firmly, and his strength pulled her against his heavily coated body. "I'm sorry I reacted so bad at first," he mumbled into her hair.

"Mr. Lake!" Yvonne exclaimed, taking several steps toward them. "I cannot believe your boldness in taking liberties with my—" Her words were silenced, and Vaden heard Denver's amused chuckle.

"You've been a good and true friend to me,

Vaden Valmont. I'll never forget that," he said.

Vaden pushed herself from his arms and looked up at him indignantly. She meant to lash out at him, to tell him that once again he had hurt her deeply by telling her she was only his friend. But when she glanced over and saw Yvonne held tightly against Denver, her back flush with his chest, one of his powerful arms securing her waist and the other hand covering her mouth, she was so astounded she could not speak.

"So if you'd have your uncle do that for me, Vaden . . . I'd appreciate it greatly," Ransom Lake finished. "We'd best be off, Denver . . . before ya decide to drag that girl off to matrimony before ya have a chance to court her."

With a deep, amused chuckle escaping his lungs, Denver released Yvonne, who only turned and stood staring at him in awed silence.

"You'll be careful?" Vaden called to Ransom Lake as he turned to leave. "You'll be back?"

"If the weather gets bad . . . we'll just find an old house to shelter in," he answered, winking at her as he left the store.

"Miss Vaden," Denver said, tipping his hat to Vaden. "Mrs. Lake . . . er . . . I mean, Miss Valmont," he chuckled, tipping his hat to Yvonne, who gasped in astonishment.

Vaden felt a sense of panic and tragedy rising within her. She dashed out the door after her heart's desire.

"You'll come back, Ransom, won't you?" she called to him.

His head turned slowly toward her, and as his intense gray eyes looked at her, she saw him mouth, *Ransom?*

Realizing with horror that she had indeed called him by his first name for the very first time, Vaden began to correct herself.

"I'm sorry. I meant to say Mr.—"

But Ransom Lake was back up the stairs and on the porch before her, having taken her shoulders between his powerful hands before she could finish her apology.

"Ransom," he whispered as his eyes wove their bewitching spell about her. Vaden's body began to tremble from both the cold air in which she stood and from his touch. When he released her, violently removing his right glove an instant before his hand was at her throat, she thought she might not be able to stop herself from throwing her trembling body into his arms. "Ransom," he repeated again in a whisper as his now bare and very warm hand caressed her throat, his fingers dipping beneath the collar of her blouse. "Ransom," he whispered a moment before his hand slipped around to the back of her neck, pulling her toward him as his mouth was suddenly hot, moist, and demanding on her own. Vaden's body melted against his as his deepening, hunger-driven kiss commanded her to meet it. Though it was brief compared with the kisses they'd shared on previous occasions, it was powerful. It left Vaden breathless, weakened, and astonished. Almost as quickly as he had been upon her, he had climbed into the wagon next to Denver and slapped the lines at the backs of the team of horses.

"What did you say?" Yvonne asked, amazed at the display.

"I . . . I don't know. I only called him by his given name instead of—" Vaden began.

"Remind me to try that on Mr. *Denver* Lake when they return."

Vaden looked to Yvonne, unable to believe what she had heard her sister say.

"He's dashingly good-looking, isn't he, Vay? I noticed the first time he came into the mercantile he was far and away more of a man than anyone I've ever met," Yvonne confessed with a sigh.

Vaden still could only stare at her sister, stunned at what she was hearing pass from her lips.

"I wanted to kiss him, Vay. To reach out, take hold of his coat lapels, one in each hand, and kiss him soundly right on the mouth!" She looked to Vaden, her eyes sparkling, her smile resplendent. "I've lost my senses in that man, Vaden! Completely lost my senses!" Then, with a heavy sigh and continued radiance bursting from her countenance, Yvonne turned and went back into the mercantile.

Vaden watched the wagon carry Ransom away from her until it was far in the distance. Something told her he would be back. She knew this was a trip of healing for both men and that such a trip would be watched over by heaven.

"You let him paw at you like an animal."

Vaden startled at the voice and looked to see Jerome appear from the alley. "Jerome," she greeted him as a feeling of impending doom began to creep into her bones, "I tried to explain to you the other day that—"

Jerome mounted the stairs to stand before her. The hatred, the seething hatred, was frighteningly apparent in his eyes as he stood glaring down at her. "I don't want anyone else touchin' what's mine, Vaden," he growled.

Instantly, Vaden's hand stung from the hard slap she delivered to his face. "I don't want you," she spat at him. She was unnerved when he only smiled at her.

"Yes, ya do. He's left ya now. He won't be back. I can assure ya of that. You belong to me, Vaden, and I'll wait. I'll wait until ya finally come to your senses."

"I don't think you should come to the mercantile anymore, Jerome. You're not welcome here," Vaden warned him. Her voice was unstable, and she was truly frightened in that moment.

Jerome looked up at the overhang of the

porch and then looked casually back to Vaden. Suddenly his arms embraced her brutally, and his repulsive mouth was attacking hers ferociously. Vaden pushed at him, but he was too strong. Her struggling seemed in vain for a moment as his hands worked to restrain her until with all her strength she kicked him soundly in the shin. It was enough to cause him to release her.

"Don't you ever touch me again, Jerome Clayton. My uncle will hear of this, and believe me, you are no longer welcome in his home from this day forward!" Tears of frustration and disgust flooded Vaden's cheeks as she turned and fled into the mercantile.

"I'll wait, Vaden. I'm a patient man," Jerome called after her before descending the porch steps casually and walking away down the street while whistling a bright tune.

"What's the matter, Ransom?" Denver asked, having noticed the sudden frown owning his brother's brow.

Ransom paused. The feeling in his chest, the vision in his mind, had only been a flash, and now it was gone. Should they go back? he wondered. But the premonition had vanished, and so must his concern, he decided.

"Nothin'. Just . . . just . . . nothin'," he answered, though his frown lessened only slightly.

• • •

"He is not allowed to be let into this house or my business!" Dan shouted that night after Vaden told him of Jerome's behavior. "If he tries to set foot in the store . . . call the sheriff, Yvonne. Do ya understand that, Myra?"

Myra nodded and squeezed Vaden's hand reassuringly.

"It's one thing to spend some time sparkin' with a gentleman like Ransom Lake and another to have an idiot like Jerome Clayton forcin' things on ya, sweet pea."

Vaden's mouth dropped open at her uncle's reference to sparking with Ransom Lake. *However does he know?* she wondered.

"This worries me, Myra. This worries me somethin' awful. He seemed like such a nice boy all these years. How could he take us all in like that?"

Myra shook her head. "I don't know. I just can't believe we didn't see this before. You avoid him like the plague, Vaden. Like the plague!"

"You . . . you don't think he'd do her harm, do you, Uncle Dan?" Yvonne asked.

"I'm not gonna lie to ya, girls. The thought has crossed my mind."

Vaden lay in bed that night praying for Ransom Lake's return. He would protect her from Jerome's vile intentions. She knew he would. He did not love her perhaps, but he valued her friendship, and she knew he would keep Jerome from her somehow. Her anxiety was great, her fears founded, and so to soothe her nerves and enable her body to rest, she repeated his name over and over and over, "Ransom. Ransom. Ransom," until finally she was comforted and able to sleep.

Her dreams were vivid, emotionally charged, and intimate. She dreamt of Ransom—her love. She dreamt of his smile, his mumbling manner of speech. She dreamt of his standing before the fire in the abandoned house, shirtless and thoughtful. She dreamt the memory of his arms around her, his kiss heated on her mouth, the scent of shaving soap lingering on his face. And she awoke missing him. Desperately missing him!

"I've spoken with the Claytons," Dan announced at lunch the following day. "They deny their son could behave like he done. Of course. But ain't it just a real big coincidence he's gone up north to visit some relatives?" Dan shook his head and chuckled oddly. "Little weasel. We oughta just lump him in with them other boys pullin' that Halloween nonsense. He ain't no better . . . maybe worse."

CHAPTER THIRTEEN

It was in the late hours of the night on the third day since Ransom and Denver had left that Vaden awoke with a feeling of panic and her body awash with perspiration. It seemed in the days since he'd gone the sense of impending doom had increased by the hour in Vaden's soul. And now, something woke her. It was a feeling—a sensation of great bodily pain and suffering, of mental anguish. *He should've been back by now,* something told her. Ransom and Denver should've returned to town by that evening. She leapt from her bed, jumping to her feet as she seemed to hear him calling her name. The sound of his beloved voice echoed through her mind. She pushed against her ears with her hands, but it did not stop. Then, as if someone were whispering to her, she knew. She knew he was hurt, dying perhaps, and she must go to him.

Quickly and quietly, though tears streaked her face and panic wracked her trembling body, Vaden dressed.

"Yvonne," she spoke quietly, waking her sister. Yvonne rubbed at her eyes and frowned at Vaden, dazed with sleep. "Wake Uncle Dan, Yvonne. Something is wrong! I'm going out to look for Ransom."

"What?" Yvonne said, suddenly sitting up in bed.

"Something has happened to him, Vonnie. Go wake up Uncle Dan and tell him to drive out to Ransom's place and check it. Something is terribly wrong!" Yvonne leapt from her bed as Vaden left the room.

The snow that had fallen earlier in the evening lay quiet, its frosted icing sparkling in the moonlight. Even for her woolen mittens, scarf, hat, and coat, Vaden was cold. The temperature was frigid in the middle of the night, and the lantern burned warm near her face as she made her way down the snow-covered road of town.

It seemed an eternity before the familiar grove of elms loomed up before her. Vaden's feet were cold, but it mattered not to her. The closer she got to the grove of elms, the very grove that had held such terror for her weeks before, the more desperate she became to reach it.

The moonlight was blocked for a time as she entered the grove. In a moment it appeared again, and the sight it illuminated almost took the life's breath from Vaden's body. There before her was a large elm. Strapped tightly to its trunk, the ropes used to bind him causing his flesh to bleed, was Ransom Lake.

"Ransom!" she screamed as she ran to him. His head hung forward, his eyes closed. She feared he was dead. "Ransom!" she screamed again as tears clouded her vision. His chest rose and fell with feeble breath. She wiped at her tears as she tugged on the ropes to loosen them. "Oh, Ransom!" she cried as she lifted his head and saw the damage done his handsome face. His right eye was completely swollen shut. The color about it was so purple it was nearly black. His mouth bled from both corners, and a large wound brutally split his bottom lip. Dried blood was caked beneath his nose. At his forehead, his hair was matted with blood from a scalp wound.

He wore only his boots and trousers. Vaden had no way of telling how long he had been exposed to the elements. Even with the meager illumi-nation of the lantern and moon as her only light, she could see terrible bruising at his ribs. His bruised arms were bound against the tree at his sides, and his knuckles were so raw and bloodied it looked as though some animal had chewed them. The ropes binding him to the tree were tightly cinched, causing further bleeding to other parts of his body.

Vaden dropped to her knees. She prayed whoever had done this to the man she loved above all else had not found Denver's knife in his boot. She prayed quietly with relief when she felt the bulge in the calf of his boot. It was not easy to retrieve, however, and she cried out in anguished frustration several times before she was able pull it from its hiding place. Frantically, she sawed at the ropes with the knife, sobbing with frustration and fear. When she'd cut the last length of rope, Ransom's beaten, tortured body fell forward into the snow.

"Ransom? Ransom!" Vaden sobbed. It seemed his blood was everywhere. He did not move as she knelt in the snow beside him. She turned him on his back into her lap. "Ransom!" she cried as she hurriedly removed her mittens and placed a warm hand on his cheek. Quickly, she unbuttoned her own coat and covered him as she rocked back and forth, bitterly sobbing. How would she get him to safety? He was far too large and heavy for her to carry. Dragging him would no doubt kill him if he weren't already fatally wounded. She had to get him out of the snow first of all. Looking around as she sobbed, she noticed a patch beneath a nearby large elm free from snow. It took every ounce of her strength to drag his limp body, which had always been so strong, to the nearby elm, propping him against it. She retrieved her lantern, intent on using its flame to build a fire to warm him. She paused as she noticed a ways out from the grove stood a lone elm. It had died years before and would burn hot and bright. Taking her lantern, she ran through the snow to the old tree and endeavored to set it afire. The recent snow made it difficult to catch the flame to the tree. However, the wood was dried and brittle, and in awhile it did indeed take flame upon itself. Vaden rushed back to where Ransom sat beneath the elm. Carefully, she pulled him away from the tree and laid him in the warmth of her lap as the fire quickly engulfed the dead elm.

"Hang on, my love. Use your great strength and hang on," she whispered soothingly to the unconscious man. She again placed a soft, warm hand to his cold cheek, quietly humming a tune she didn't even recognize through her panic. The old elm burned fiercely, cracking and spitting like hell's own fire. It seemed an eternity before Vaden finally heard shouting and the approach of a wagon.

Relief flooded her body as she saw her Uncle Dan pull his team into the clearing. "Uncle Dan! Help me! Help me!" she cried. The man looked from the great blazing fire to his niece.

"Vaden!" he shouted as he ran to her. "Vaden! What's goin' on? I . . ." He paused, looking at the maimed and broken man lying in her lap. "Oh!" he groaned. "What happened, Vaden? Who's done this to them?"

"Them?" Vaden asked.

"Denver's back at the house. He came draggin' himself up the porch callin' for help just as I was leavin'. He passed out when we got him in. He's in a bad way . . . but nothin' the likes of this."

"He'll die if we don't hurry, Uncle Dan! Please! Help me!" Vaden cried.

As Dan hollered at the team, driving them on at a wild speed, Vaden cradled Ransom's head against her bosom, letting her tears fall on his bruised face. She knew who had done this to him. Somehow Jerome had been able to overpower her mighty champion and do him immeasurable harm. There was no other reason she should find him where she did. She sobbed, her body wracked with pain from the knowledge that his condition was on her head. She'd brought this on him.

Vaden was grateful Dan had possessed the foresight to toss several blankets into the bed of the wagon before he left home. She pulled them tightly around Ransom's shoulders and stroked his hair as she looked down into his face, so bruised and swollen. In that moment, the memory came to her of the time so many weeks and months before when he'd lain in her uncle's guest room, unconscious because of her. She thought of the thrill that had rushed through her body when she'd kissed him and hoped for a moment he would awaken. Carefully, as her tears fell excessively onto his battered cheeks, she kissed him lightly on his wounded mouth. As she looked at his face longingly, she heard a groan rise within his throat. In the next moment, the gray of his undamaged eye seemed to outshine the moonlight as it opened and looked at her.

"Vaden," he mumbled as her sobbing wracked

her body, "I-I'm not up to sparkin' ya just now, girl."

"Don't waste your breath teasing me," she whispered, relieved he was still able to speak at all. "We're almost home. We're almost home."

"They . . . they took Denver too," he choked anxiously. "I-I . . ." She could tell by the frown furrowing his brow he was worried for Denver.

"He's fine. He's already at our house. He's fine, Ransom." She tried to keep her voice calm and soothing, though she felt she might die of worry for his life.

"Denver," he mumbled, and he was unconscious again.

Myra fairly flew off the porch as the wagon pulled up to the house. "Vaden!" she cried out. "My goodness, child! Ya gave us such a fright and . . ." Her affectionate scolding ceased immediately upon glancing from Vaden's tear-stained face to the man who lay so maimed in her lap. "Ransom!" she exclaimed in a whisper. "Oh, Dan!" Myra looked to her husband as he jumped from the buckboard. "Oh! He looks far worse than his brother."

"Hurry! Let's get him inside. He's beat to a pulp, and its hard tellin' how long he's been out in this cold."

Carefully and as tenderly as was possible, Vaden helped her aunt and uncle carry the massive form of Ransom Lake into the warmth of the house.

"Just lay him right before the fire in the parlor," Dan ordered.

Tears fell profusely from Vaden's eyes as a deep and pain-stricken moan vibrated within Ransom as they laid him on the rug before the warm blaze.

"Oh, gracious providence!" Myra whispered as the light from the fire further illuminated Ransom's injuries. "I've already sent Yvonne for Doctor Sullivan because Denver was in such a bad way. But I can't believe . . . quickly, Dan. Hot water, cloths, towels!" Myra snapped her fingers at her husband and pointed to the kitchen.

"Jerome Clayton has done this, Auntie," Vaden whispered.

Myra paused for a moment, frowning at her niece. "Oh, don't be ridiculous, Vaden. Jerome may be an idiot, but surely he isn't capable of causin' damage to another man the like of this!" Myra ran her fingers over the terrible bruising on Ransom's ribcage. "These bruises are brutal. There must be broken ribs here. But," Myra pressed on the man's chest, stomach, and abdomen, "there's no swellin' elsewhere, so hopefully he's not bleedin' inside." Myra next inspected his hands and arms. "He gave a good accountin' of himself from the looks of these ragged knuckles. Same with Denver." She tried to lift the blackened and swollen eyelid. Vaden gasped and held her breath for a moment when she saw the brilliant gray of his eye against the completely blood-red white. "Poor man. Poor, poor man," Myra mumbled.

Returning with the water and cloths, Dan said, "Help me to sponge this blood away, Vaden, so we can see the damage."

"I'm telling you, Uncle Dan . . . someone we know has done this! If you won't believe it's Jerome Clayton, you must admit there is a reason I found him tied to a tree in that old elm grove." Vaden's eyes pled with her uncle for understanding.

Dan nodded and placed an arm about her shoulders. "Well, as bloodied as the knuckles are on these two boys, somebody will have a couple of black eyes and split lips, and that won't be easy to hide. I 'spect the light of mornin' will tell us a bit."

"This is my fault," Vaden cried, burying her face in her hands. "Somehow, I'm not certain yet how, but somehow I've caused this to happen. I refused Jerome's attentions, and now he . . . he . . ."

"That's nonsense, child!" Myra corrected, wringing the blood-saturated cloth into the bowl of water. "Nonsense."

Vaden could only sit beside the battered, mutilated body of Ransom Lake and cry her tears of pain and guilt. She knew somehow Jerome had had a hand in this beating—a hand in the near murder of Ransom Lake and his brother. And she knew it was her fault. The guilt she bore was unendurable, and she thought for a moment of the pain, of the guilt, Ransom had borne for so many years. But that had been quite different. He had not been responsible for the brutal murders of his family. He had been blameless. But she was the cause of this. She knew it. Jerome had done this to Ransom and all for the sake of mad jealousy.

Doctor Sullivan arrived soon and tended to Ransom's wounds. "He's in a bad way," he said. "But there doesn't seem to be any internal injuries. He'll recover, though he'll be sore and stiff for a while." After checking on Denver as well, the doctor left, and Myra forced the girls to bed.

"I've caused this, Yvonne," Vaden whispered as they lay in their beds. "Jerome did this. I'm telling you, he's mad. He's so completely different from what he appears."

"I'm afraid for them, Vay," Yvonne began. "They were nearly killed. What if whoever did this tries again? What if . . ."

Vaden could hear the fear in her sister's voice. Until that moment, Vaden had never considered that perhaps Ransom and Denver would again find themselves in danger. The horror of the evening had been too prominent, too vivid, for her to think beyond. But as she realized the truth in Yvonne's words, fear gripped her in its frigid vise grip, and she spent the remaining hours of early morning trembling with fear for Ransom's life.

The next morning, the scene that met Vaden as she entered the kitchen caused her knees to give way beneath her. She only escaped fainting to the floor by holding the counter's edge with a firm grip. Denver and Ransom sat at the table bandaged, bruised, and beaten beyond belief. Denver sipped broth from a cup. Ransom endeavored to do the same, though it was obvious the pain and stiffness in his mashed knuckles made it hard for him to hold the mug to his purple, bruised, and swollen lips.

"I've, uh . . . I've, uh . . . just been forcin' somethin' into these two boys, Vaden," Myra said.

Yvonne was already there sitting beside Denver, a look of grief and concern puckering her dainty brow.

Vaden looked to Ransom. When his one unswollen eye met hers, she felt the tears escape their restraint and flood her cheeks.

"Tell them who did this to you, Ransom," she whispered.

"Can't," he mumbled. "They were wearin' masks."

"You know who did this. I know who did this! Tell someone. They have to be punished! They can't get away with trying to murder you," she cried.

"We'll take care of this on our own, girl," Ransom growled.

"You can't! You can't possibly mean—"

"The wagon's hitched, boys," Dan announced as he entered through the kitchen door. "We'll go whenever you're ready."

"You're leaving?" Vaden shrieked. "You can't go! You . . . neither of you is in any condition to—"

Ransom slammed a visibly very sore fist on the table. Then, rising to his feet slowly and awkwardly, obviously still in pain, he pointed a damaged index finger at Vaden and mumbled, "I don't have the energy to argue with ya, Vaden. I'm goin' home to my own house and my own bed. I need some rest, and I don't think I can rest here. I couldn't possibly rest when I know—"

"But—" she began to argue.

He tipped his head and closed his eyes, trying to draw patience from within himself, and said flatly, "Not now, Vaden."

"We'll be fine at the house, Miss Vaden," Denver assured her as he stood and placed a reassuring hand on her shoulder.

"I'm sendin' the girls along with ya, Dan," Myra announced. Ransom started to protest, but Myra hurried on. "I want them to stay just long enough to see you two boys into bed and put somethin' to warm on the stove for ya."

"I haven't got the fight left in me," Ransom mumbled as he took the blanket she offered to him and wrapped it about his shoulders before leaving the house.

When they arrived at Ransom's house, Vaden was frightened once more as Dan insisted he go into the house first, armed with his rifle. How could she possibly leave Ransom, knowing the danger he was in—knowing he was too weak to defend himself if someone were to attack him in such a state?

"I'll be in my bed if you need me," Ransom mumbled. "Not that I'd be any good for anything anyhow," he chuckled.

"I'll put this pot of broth on, Mr. Lake," Yvonne said, lugging the large pot of chicken broth her aunt had sent with them into the kitchen.

"I feel like somebody chewed me up and spit me out," Denver groaned as he awkwardly laid himself on the sofa in the front room. "But it was obvious it was Ransom they intended to . . ." He broke off his words, glancing quickly and apologetically to Vaden.

"I'm gonna have the sheriff look into this," Dan stated. "Ain't nobody should get away with somethin' like this."

Vaden stood wringing her hands furiously. She'd removed her coat and mittens and now stood feeling helpless and panicked.

"Run on in there and check on him, will you,

Miss Vaden?" Denver asked. "Make sure he went into bed. You know what a hardhead he is. He probably snuck out the back door to check on the stock."

Vaden nodded, more than willing to check on Ransom. She entered the hallway and made her way past one room with a locked door to another room to her left. There on his bed, already sound asleep, lay Ransom Lake. He looked peaceful enough. Vaden watched him breathing for several moments to assure herself he did so. Then, as she was turning to leave him to his much-needed rest, a flash caught the corner of her eye, and she turned to look at the wall across from the foot of Ransom's bed.

What she saw there in the morning sunlight beaming in through the window amazed her. There were shelves on the wall starting from just a foot or so above the floor and rising to the ceiling. These shelves were heavily laden with all varieties of color and sizes of beautiful geodes! There were perhaps in excess of one hundred and fifty sets of them. A large geode, standing some two feet tall and bursting with amethyst crystals, sat in one corner. In awe, Vaden walked to the shelving and looked up and around at the many beautiful stones. On the shelf directly before her sat two stones, each singular, with no matching mates like the other stones owned. Reaching out, she took in her hands the two stones—the twins of the ones that had been left for her—the ones she thought her Uncle Dan had given her. All the time, it had been her one true love who had tried to cheer her heart, give her back her hope by bestowing Mother Nature's wonders upon her. Never had she seen, never had she imagined, such a collection of anything, let alone something so beautiful, unique, and marvelous as these rare stones.

Replacing the twins to her stones, she turned and looked at Ransom once more. Going to his bed, she knelt beside it and placed a hand on his head, letting her fingers bury themselves in the softness of his hair.

"In my dreams . . . I knew it was you," she whispered. He did not wake or move at all. She stared at him for some time before finally kissing him tenderly on the forehead and leaving the room.

"He's got quite a collection in there, hasn't he?" Denver mumbled from his place on the sofa as Vaden reentered the front room.

"Yes," Vaden agreed. "I've never imagined the like."

"Collection?" Yvonne asked, her brows meeting in a puzzled expression.

"Yes. The finest collection of geodes I've ever seen. He must have hundreds of rocks in that room of his," Denver added. His voice was becoming lower and somewhat slurred, making it obvious he too was near to a deep slumber.

Yvonne's eyes twinkled, and her bright smile comforted Vaden as she looked at her warmly and with understanding.

"I guess he's got to have something beautiful in his room . . . since he's kept himself from marrying a pretty girl all this time," Denver mumbled. Yvonne and Vaden quickly looked to Denver, surprised at his inference. He smiled at them wearily. "But he's got me here now. Maybe finding each other again will heal both our hearts, eh?" Denver winked at Yvonne with one of his bruised eyes, and she blushed profoundly.

"Let's get on home, girls," Dan said. "These boys need their rest, and we got a lot to do."

Leaving Ransom Lake at that moment was the hardest thing Vaden ever had to do. He was so weakened and vulnerable physically, and she feared another attack on him would be fatal.

As it went, Jerome had been out of town visiting an aunt and uncle up north when the incident with Ransom and Denver had occurred. Apparently he was innocent, Dan said. But the look in his eyes and Vaden's own instinct told her differently.

After a week or so, Denver and Ransom entered the store one morning looking quite healthy and robust. Their bruises were fading to a yellowish-green tinge, and both of Ransom's heavenly eyes were visible again. Vaden's heart swelled to near bursting when they entered, for she felt certain Ransom would be different toward her, more willing to show deeper feeling for her. But her elation was quickly squelched, for he simply smiled and nodded at her casually as he and Denver approached the counter.

"We've come to thank your family for delivering us from certain death," Denver told Yvonne, who immediately began blushing and smoothing her skirt. "We're quite strong and healthy once more, and we owe you all a great debt."

"Oh! Oh, that's a ridiculous thing to say, Mr. Lake," Yvonne stammered. It was the first time Vaden had heard her sister veer from propriety and argue a compliment or gratuitous remark. "And may I say that you do look very . . . quite healthy."

Vaden's eyes widened at her sister's awkwardness. As of yet, Yvonne had confided no tremendous confession as to her feelings for Denver. But it was all too obvious, and it delighted Vaden, yet at the same time breaking her heart, for Denver was completely attentive to Yvonne. He held nothing back. His regard for her, his admiration of her, and his profound interest in her were obvious. Vaden glanced to Ransom, but his eyes only narrowed intensely as he looked at her. For a moment, her gaze fell to his mouth, to his perfectly formed, delicious mouth, and she thought of his kiss, intensely longing for it. She'd tried to keep her dreams of him at bay—her dreams of being his completely, of his marrying her, raising their children with her, holding her in his arms every night of their lives. But it was impossible and excruciatingly painful. At that very moment, she winced at the pain piercing her heart.

"It was Jerome Clayton," she suddenly blurted out.

Denver and Yvonne both looked to her, and Ransom continued to almost glare at her.

"They were masked, and it was dark," Ransom mumbled. "There was no way to identify them. Besides, there were five. Not one."

"You may as well know, Vay," Yvonne began, "Uncle Dan questioned Nathaniel and Toby and the others. They truly know nothing, though they do admit to avoiding association with Jerome as of late."

Vaden indignantly looked from one person to the other, finally settling on Ransom. "Why are you so set on denying it? I think you know full well, just as I do, who tried to—"

"I think you want it to be Jerome, Vay," Yvonne accused. "But . . . he's too weak, too sneaky . . . a coward. Offending you alone is one thing, but two grown men who are much larger than he and—"

"He's a weasel," Denver finished. "At least . . .

from what I hear. He's too big a coward to attempt something like this. And those men who attacked us were strong. It wasn't a group of lilac-perfumed boys that beat us."

"Let's just drop this," Ransom mumbled, going to look at some boxes of work gloves lying at the end of the counter. "What's done is done. And it won't happen again."

Vaden wanted to scream. Why were they all so set on denying what her heart told her was the truth? Why didn't they want to confront the Claytons? Why did they all just want to go about their business and pretend the horror never happened?

At that moment, every drop of energy and every bit of the love of life in Vaden seemed to drain from her, and she promptly sat down on a chair. She looked up for a moment to where Ransom and Denver were looking through the boxes of gloves.

"Don't be angry with me, Vay," Yvonne said quietly as she came to stand beside her sister. "I . . . I just think maybe you're not thinking things through well enough."

"Were you robbed?" Vaden asked suddenly.

Denver and Ransom both looked to her inquisitively.

"Was anything stolen from you?"

"No," Denver answered plainly.

"Then . . . explain to me the reason these men

chose to ambush you and beat you . . . and tie Ransom to a tree in the very grove of elms where . . ." Vaden's voice faltered as Ransom's glare intensified.

"I think maybe we should come back for the things we need later, Denver," Ransom mumbled to his brother.

Vaden shook her head and fought to hold back her tears as she stood, saying, "No. No. You go ahead and get the things you need. I'll leave." She walked to the front door, took her coat from the coat rack, and wrapped her scarf snugly about her neck. "I'll be back later, Yvonne," she announced as she pulled on her mittens. "A walk will do me good."

The moment she left the store, her tears burst through her resolve and flooded her cheeks. As quickly as she could, she ran through the muddied street and turned down the road leading to Ransom's house. Wiping in irritation at her tear-saturated cheeks, she slowed her pace to a brisk walk as she looked off in the direction of her tree, of her brook, of her solace. But she doubted their power to calm her this day, for she did not understand. She did not understand everyone's need to deny what she knew to be true. She did not understand Ransom leaving her a tender note one moment, taking her passionately in his arms the next, and then nearly ignoring her.

Perhaps, she thought as she hurried along,

perhaps it was time for her to return home. She'd fallen in love, and her love did not return the feeling, it appeared. But when she felt his hand catch hold of her arm, she sighed with relief. He'd come for her. She paused before turning around and said, "Why are you so cold and indifferent sometimes?"

"I'm never cold and indifferent to you, Vaden." The sound of Jerome Clayton's voice answering her question instead of Ransom Lake's caused her to whirl about in horror, panic gripping her.

"Jerome?" she exclaimed.

He smiled at her pleasantly and innocently enough. "Glad to see me?" he asked. "I've been gone for some time. I had a nice visit, but . . . it's always best to be home, isn't it?"

Vaden wrenched her arm free of his grasp and stood staring at him in disbelief at his casual manner.

"And what have you been up to in my absence, Vaden?" he asked.

"I'm no idiot, Jerome." Vaden drew in a deep breath, trying to muster her courage. "I'm not as easily fooled as everyone else in this town seems to be."

"I know you're no fool, Vaden. At least, most of the time ya seem to have your wits about ya. But . . . lately I've noticed—"

"Leave me alone, Jerome. You know I don't want to talk to you, and my uncle—"

Suddenly, he reached out and gripped her chin firmly in one hand, tightly taking hold of her shoulder with the other. "Damn your uncle!" he growled as his face lowered to hers, his seething anger instantaneous.

"I know it was you, Jerome. Maybe you've got everyone else fooled, but not me. I've seen the true color of your soul, and it's blacker than night!" Vaden tried to glare bravely back at him. Her only chance was to outwit him, for she knew he was physically stronger than she.

"Ya have such a way of muffin' things up, Vaden. Actually . . . I suppose it's Ransom Lake who muffs it all . . . but you—"

"Get your hands off her, boy!"

Vaden felt relief flood her body at the sound of Ransom's voice coming from behind Jerome. Jerome sighed heavily and rolled his eyes in a gesture of extreme irritation. He shoved Vaden back as he released her and turned to face Ransom. Vaden saw then that Denver stood beside his brother, both men furious.

"Ransom Lake, you are so the proverbial thorn in my side." Jerome simply shook his head as if he were too uninterested to deal with the men. "What is the problem, after all?" he asked. "I'm certain your hands have ventured on much more familiar areas of the girl than mine have."

Ransom Lake's deadly fist was halted a moment before it collided with Jerome's jaw as

Denver reached out and stayed his powerful arm.

Jerome chuckled. "You be careful there, old man. I heard you're in no shape to be defendin' a woman's honor."

"You dirty son of a—" Ransom began.

"Get on home, boy!" Denver ordered. "You get yourself on home, unless you want to take on trouble all alone this time." He nodded at Ransom, who stood, eyes red with his seething. "You go on home, or I'll let him have at you."

Jerome angrily clenched his jaw and looked at Vaden. Then, glaring at Ransom Lake, he threatened, "This ain't over, old man. This is far from over." Denver had to further restrain Ransom as Jerome turned and walked away.

"Let the fool go, Ransom," Denver growled. After a moment, Ransom quit struggling to escape his brother's hold and inhaled deeply to calm himself. "Weasely as he is, you're not yourself yet."

"You do know it was him, don't you?" Vaden asked as she stared at Ransom, hurt he would have denied it so avidly.

"You keep out of his way until I'm better. Do ya understand me?" Ransom was angry and worried. Vaden could see the concern in his eyes.

"I didn't put myself in his way!" Vaden cried, her tears flowing once more. "And what do you care anyway? Who put you in charge of my well-being?"

Ransom inhaled a deep breath and closed his eyes for a moment. "I'm sorry. It's just that you've done so much for me. You've returned my brother to me. You've helped me find hope. You've nursed me back to health twice now and—"

"I've been the cause of your ill health both times," she reminded him.

Ransom sighed heavily. "I just . . . I just feel responsible for ya, Vaden. You've been such a kind and loyal friend, and I—"

"I think I'll head on back to the mercantile," Denver interrupted. "Hash it out with him, Miss Vaden. Hash it out. It's the only way you'll ever have your peace of mind."

Both Ransom and Vaden watched Denver walk away, and then the pain, the rising heartache, every emotion battling within Vaden broke the surface simultaneously.

"You just don't understand, do you?" she stated. She couldn't hide her feelings any longer or keep silent about them. Her strength was gone to resist confessing. "You really don't know what you've done to me."

Ransom turned slowly to face her. The air was frigid, and Vaden felt the cold begin to engulf her body and heart as the words poured from her lips. "I think of you every moment of every day! You dominate my dreams when I'm asleep. Every time I turn around, I'm devastated not to see you standing near me."

"Vaden," he began, holding up a hand to stop her.

"No," she said, closing her eyes and shaking her head. "I have to say this to you. If I say it all out loud, then at least it's been said, and I won't have to be haunted by my secrets anymore." Opening her eyes, she looked at him bravely. "Your voice rings in my ears and head constantly. The sound of it is sweeter than any other music of nature to me. Only to think of your smile, of your laugh warms my heart. Every time you touch me—in even the simplest, most unintended manner—my insides swell so warm and delighted that I wish I could take flight like a startled sparrow. Even just your looking at me. Just the sensation of those gray, stormy eyes of yours on me . . . it unsettles me beyond your comprehension." She turned her back to him, for she could no longer face his stare as she confessed. "And . . . and beyond that, you should be able to imagine. Do you know, Ransom Lake . . . do you know what power you have over me physically? Surely you've noticed how I've melted in your arms each time you've taken me in them. How completely I bask in the heavenly euphoria that envelops me when you . . . when you . . ."

"When we kiss," he finished for her.

Vaden winced at the sound of his voice and brushed the tears from her cheeks, only to feel them flood once more with the moisture from her eyes.

"There are times when—most of the time, to truly confess—my arms, my body ache to be held by you. To have you confide in me . . . simply speak to me. And because I know you're no fool, that you're very intelligent, I will admit to you now that . . . that I've loved you from the first day I arrived here and you drove your wagon past the mercantile. I suspect you know that all too well."

"Vaden," he began, and she heard him take a step toward her.

Immediately, however, she shook her head and hugged herself tightly, moving away from him. "Please. Please don't say anything to me just now. Please just walk away from me and let me be."

She couldn't look at him, couldn't let herself hear his voice. She feared were he to try to comfort her in any manner, she would completely lose control of herself and end up a sobbing, weakened mess, throwing herself into his arms and begging him to become hers to whatever extent he chose.

He did speak, however. Against her innermost wishes, he spoke, and Vaden struggled to keep herself from him.

"I'll leave ya to yourself if that's what ya want, Vaden. But it is maybe . . . no. It is definitely a very good thing ya chose to say these things to me here—in the cold, muddied winter of the outdoors . . . on a road well-traveled by the people of this town—instead of the night we were shelterin' in the old house before a warm fire . . . alone."

As her brow puckered in a puzzled expression, she heard his footsteps becoming fainter and fainter as he left her. She turned when she sensed he was too far for her to catch up with him, and her hand covered her mouth firmly as she tried to suppress her audible sobbing. Her stomach was wrenching with pain and anguish, and she feared for a moment she would collapse in the mud and die from the misery of her heartache. In fact, in the next moment her body did fail her, and she fell to her knees, sobbing over the grief and pain of what would never be hers. Several times her stomach began to heave, and she feared she would not be able to keep its contents inside. Though the sensation of extreme illness did not pass, she was able to gain control of herself enough to stand and stumble the rest of the way to her brook and her tree. But she found no solace there, only further pain, for it reminded her so of Ransom Lake.

Rather aimlessly she wandered for over an hour until she found herself in the grove of elms, the horrid scene of so much anguish for herself and for Ransom. The now charred and branchless yet still tall trunk of the old dead elm seemed a sentry for the place, an ominous reminder of the pain and terror endured there. Vaden wandered among the trees trying to clear her mind of any thoughts. How blessed it would be to have nothing but a void there—nothing to torment her further, no memory of Ransom Lake. No knowledge of him would perhaps be better than the pain with which she was stricken.

Then she came to the tree where she had been led, by whatever presence, to Ransom Lake. She realized somehow as she stared at the tree, the ropes that had bound Ransom still lying on the ground around its base, that she would rather endure a life of sadness, regret, sorrow, and pain. She would rather be miserable for the rest her life than never to have experienced the man. Reaching down, she picked up a length of the rope, studying the now brown stains made by the dried blood from Ransom's injuries. It was true. However horrible the pain of loss, the old cliché rang true to Vaden at that moment: it was far better to have loved the man and not been able to possess him than never to have known and loved him at all.

"Fancy meetin' you here."

The sound of Jerome's voice angered Vaden. Turning to face him, drained of defense and having only the strength to hate, she said, "Leave me alone. I have no feelings for you other than distaste at seeing your face. Leave me in the knowledge you were right. I am in love with Ransom Lake, and he returns nothing of it to me. You were right. But you're wrong if you still think I will turn to you to give me what he won't. I despise you, Jerome Clayton. So stop wasting your time, and leave me alone."

So drained of strength and emotion was Vaden that even the fiery red glint that jumped to Jerome's eyes did not intimidate her.

"I did so much for ya, Vaden. I tried so hard to prove that I was worthy of ya."

"You were very attentive and sweet, Mr. Clayton. Of course, we both know it was a facade." She began to walk away from him, but his next words stopped her.

"I had it all planned out so perfectly. And Ransom Lake had to mess it up for me. That day he was shot in the store, I had that all worked out so cleverly. And Halloween night. It would've been perfect."

"What? What are you talking about?" Vaden asked.

"It wasn't those kids playin' with a gun in the street, Vaden. Don't ya know that? I shot Ransom Lake. I meant to shoot near you to frighten ya, then rush to your side to be your comforter, your protector. But my aim must have been off because indeed my bullet would have hit ya if Ransom Lake hadn't stepped in front of ya. I was grateful to see he'd taken the bullet. I realized it was for the best because now ya would see how weak he was . . . how such a small injury could shake him. I knew you'd turn from him and back to me.

"And Halloween would've confirmed my worthiness to ya. I worked it out with Nathaniel and Toby and the others. I was gonna ride in there, your hero on a magnificent stallion. I was gonna save ya from that horrid trick. I had to pay those boys to do that to you . . . and even then they weren't sure. But when I told them it would surely win ya over for me, they were willin' enough. Then I followed the wagon home that night. It wasn't Nathaniel who told me what went on between you and Ransom Lake while he was drivin' the team home. I followed ya. I saw what he did to you. How ya let him do it.

"Of course, those friends of mine . . . they wouldn't help me anymore. They told me I was wrong. Nathaniel even said I was crazy to go after Ransom Lake and his brother. I could see how weak they were, so . . . I simply went up north and hired some real men to help me out. Ransom Lake would've died out here too if ya hadn't showed up to save his worthless hide."

Vaden could only stare at him with a brief inability to believe what he was telling her. "You shot Ransom when he was in the mercantile that day? You were the cause of that horrid event on Halloween? You intentionally had me drug out there and nailed into that box?" Vaden began shaking her head, unable to understand what would drive a man to do such things. Surely she could not be the cause of all Jerome's diabolical actions.

"It would've worked out wonderfully, Vaden. But that Ransom Lake . . . he's like a fly in the ointment at every turn."

Vaden could only stare at Jerome as her mind fought to understand the situation. Jerome hunkered down, picking up one of the lengths of rope lying at the tree's trunk.

"How did ya get him loose from here anyhow?" he mumbled.

Vaden's heart began to increase in its beating, and she drew in a worried breath as she saw Jerome pick up something from the ground.

"Well, look at that," he muttered as he held Ransom's knife, frowning as he studied it intently. "Hmmm. Did he have this on him?"

Vaden did not answer but took a tentative step backward. It was only then she realized the danger she was in. This man was mad! Capable of unimaginable things.

"I stripped him of his shirt, checked his pockets." Jerome frowned as he studied the knife. "He had it in his boot. Is that it, Vaden? And how would you know to look in his boot for a knife?"

"You sit there and puzzle on it for awhile," Vaden said calmly, taking another step back from him and indicating with one hand he should stay. "You'll figure it out, I'm certain. As smart as you are, it won't take you long."

Before she could turn and run, Jerome jumped to his feet and took hold of her wrist tightly. Vaden's instinct told her that to struggle would only serve to further agitate him, so she stood before him trying to appear calm.

"Where're ya goin'?" he asked.

"I do need to be getting back. Aunt Myra will be furious if I don't finish up my chores before—"

"You don't see yourself as men see ya, Vaden," he stated suddenly. "I know ya think everyone in this town is thinkin' your sister is the prettiest thing around—the most finished and refined of young ladies. I know that's what ya think. But ya don't understand men. There's something about you, something that makes a man start burnin' inside. Makes him want you above anything else."

Forcibly he pulled on her arm, causing her body to bump against his. Then he released her wrist and put his arms about her, holding her firmly against him. Immediately, Vaden began to struggle, to lose control of her sensible plan to not flee from him desperately.

"Now, come on, Vaden. Do ya think it was easy for me to stand by and watch Ransom Lake have his liberties with ya? That night I followed Nathaniel's wagon home . . . watching the two of you and the way you . . . believe me, I wanted to kill him long ago. To slit his throat open and watch him die, knowin' when he did you'd be in my arms."

Vaden ceased her struggling when she heard a click as Jerome revealed the blade of Ransom's knife and held it to her neck near the jugular vein. The blade was cold as death. Vaden could only close her eyes and swallow the lump in her throat, waiting.

"How do ya think Ransom Lake would feel knowin' it was his own knife that bled you dry? Hmm?"

Vaden tried to breathe evenly and keep her wits about her. She would be patient, waiting until Jerome's defenses dropped somehow. Then she would run. Run for her life!

"This coat of yours," he mumbled. Vaden could feel the heat of his breath on her face, and she winced at the sensation. "It's far too bulky. Let's just take it off, shall we?"

"It's cold out," Vaden stated calmly, looking him directly in the eyes. "You . . . you wouldn't want me to catch my death out here, would you?"

Jerome raised his eyebrows and chuckled. "Take it off. Or you will definitely catch your death."

Vaden paused, for the blade of the knife was firm against her flesh. Sighing with irritation,

Jerome, using his free hand, removed her mittens, scarf, and coat, letting them drop to the snow-covered ground at her feet. She was instantly cold. The breeze among the elms was icy, and frost had begun to fall from the sky.

"My, my," Jerome sighed as he placed a gloved finger in his mouth, tugging at it with his teeth until his glove was removed. Then his fingers began to toy with the lace at Vaden's collar. "What a lovely shirtwaist, Vaden. Did ya sew it yourself with your dainty little fingers?"

Vaden reached up, shoving his hand from her neck, but she stilled herself again as the blade of the knife bit slightly at her flesh.

"Hold still!" Jerome shouted. Then his voice was low and soft again as he whispered, "Ya know, not that I'm criticizing the seamstress who made this shirtwaist for ya—I'm sure she was talented with a needle, whoever she was. But . . . it seems to me this seam here . . . this one at your shoulder here . . ." Vaden felt the pressure from the knife at her neck disappear as Jerome moved it to her shoulder. "It . . . well, it just seems to me that there's a flaw in the stitchin'." Vaden gasped, and her body began to tremble as in one swift move Jerome inserted the knife into the fabric of her shirtwaist at the shoulder, ripping the seam from her shoulder to the base of her collar. "This side looks a bit . . . well, let's just . . ." he mumbled as he repeated the process on the other side of her body. "Hhmmm," he mused, wrinkling his brow and studying Vaden's shoulders a moment. "Well . . . must be the collar that's wrong."

Vaden held her breath as Jerome slipped the knife beneath her collar at her throat. The blade was facing away from her flesh, but one false move and it would be buried at the hollow of her throat. She felt her stomach wrench as Jerome used his free hand to tug at the torn fabric at her right shoulder. He then bent and placed a long, lingering, sickeningly moist kiss on her exposed flesh.

"Yes," he mumbled, "I do believe it's the collar."

With that, he pulled the knife forward, severing the fabric at Vaden's throat. Instinctively, Vaden's hand went to her throat to hold in place the fabric of her shirtwaist, for now the yoke of her shirtwaist threatened to slip down slightly, exposing her shoulders and clavicle. She felt the chilled bite of cold at her upper back, for the torn fabric of her garment gave her little protection, exposing her skin to the elements. Jerome grinned mischievously. Producing a match from his pocket, he struck it on the bottom of his boot. It fell to her coat, which immediately caught fire. Pulling her forward, his knife once more at her throat, he moved her away from the burning clothing as he chuckled.

"Now then," he whispered, putting his lips against her ear, "what is there to protect you, Vaden? What else is there to warm your body?" He glanced about him as if searching for something. Then, looking back to her, he raised his eyebrows and added, "I guess that leaves me."

The realization had been building, the knowledge trying to make itself known to Vaden all along. At that moment she knew, her mind accepted, what horror may be in store for her.

"Jerome," she began, addressing him by his given name in hopes it would serve to calm him, "please stop this. I—"

The words and her breath were knocked from her lungs as he turned her, slamming her back hard against the trunk of the elm.

"Didn't your mother teach ya that ya don't say anything unless ya can say somethin' nice?" he growled.

His hand went around her throat then, pushing her head painfully against the rough bark of the tree. From the corner of her eye, Vaden could see he still held the knife in his other hand, too close to her bosom to make a struggle safe. But at the repulsive feel of his mouth kissing her shoulders, the moist, abrasive sensation of his tongue grazing her flesh now and again, the danger of the knife he held seemed trivial. Vaden began to push against his chest, trying to maneuver her right foot so she could kick at him.

His hand squeezed her throat all the more violently, and he paused in his tasting of her skin long enough to cover each one of her feet with his own, standing on them and rendering her helpless. She felt as if life were being strangled from her. She ignored the horrid feel of his kiss on her cheeks and forehead, and her fingers clawed helplessly at the hand at her throat.

"I can't breathe!" she choked out. She thought, *He's killed me.*

She could not draw air into her body. His hand about her throat was suffocating her. She felt her arms and legs begin to tingle with an odd numbing sensation, and the strength left her hands as she felt her arms drop to her sides. She winced at the pain of not being able to breathe. As she felt her dying body slip to the snow-covered ground, a heavenly vision of Ransom Lake appeared for one last brief moment in her fading consciousness.

CHAPTER FOURTEEN

All was dark. There was no light and no sound. Then suddenly she felt the warmth of life-giving air fill her bosom. Vaden began to feel cold, to sense something tickling her face, to again feel the breath of life being forced into her lungs. Gasping painfully, Vaden drew her own breath and opened her eyes for a brief moment to see Ransom's perfect face near to her own, frowning with an expression of grief and deep concern.

"Take in the air, Vaden," his voice echoed in her mind. Then she saw Ransom turn and look over his shoulder—saw Jerome struggling to his feet just behind him, wiping blood from the corner of his mouth, his face twisted with fury. As he lunged toward them, Ransom sprang to his feet and shouted, "You're a dead man for this!"

There was an excruciating pain in Vaden's throat, and she closed her eyes again, unable to focus properly. She could hear the two men scuffling. She heard one of them fall to the ground, groaning in anguish. Then she knew her body was being lifted, and parts of her were warm again. She could hear the crunching of snow beneath feet bearing a heavy burden. She could hear the panting of a human being whose body was being pushed too hard considering it was still healing from its own trauma. Opening her eyes only a narrow slit, she saw Ransom's chin and jaw from where her head rested on his shoulder. Still, she was too weakened and disoriented to respond to him.

"Oh, please!" a familiar voice echoed through her mind. "Let me make it back! Drop me dead after if ya will . . . but please wait until I've made it back."

She wanted to ease the pain and worry she heard in Ransom's voice. She wanted to tell him she was all right, to shout out that he must not push himself to harm for her benefit. But Vaden could not speak the words. She could not even open her mouth without the searing, burning pain increasing in her throat. She seemed to have no control over the rest of her limp and nearly life-less body. She heard Ransom's pleadings with heaven as he carried her toward home. She felt the frost still falling, tickling her nose and lips. She felt her hands, arms, legs, feet, every part of her begin to grow colder and colder. She felt Ransom stumble and fall to his knees once, only to mumble some-thing under his breath, force himself to his feet once more, and move on. She heard his heavy boots as he climbed the stairs to the porch, and she heard his voice shouting as his feet carried him into her uncle's house.

"Vaden's hurt!" he shouted. "Hurry! Help me! She's hurt!"

Vaden was able to open her eyes slightly then.

But her throat felt dry and bitterly sore, and she still couldn't muster the strength to speak. She realized indeed the strength of Ransom's arms, for he'd carried her home from the elm grove.

"What in tarnation?" It was her Aunt Myra. Vaden peered through clouded vision to see the woman entering from the kitchen, drying her hands on her apron, only to find such a dreadful sight before her. "Ransom! What . . . take her to the bedroom," Myra cried.

Vaden felt herself gently placed on the familiar softness of the quilt covering her bed. All the time she watched Ransom through narrowed eyes, unable to focus completely. Ransom dropped to his knees beside the bed and shouted instructions to Myra over his shoulder.

"Go for the doctor, Myra! Now! Where is everyone? Go, Myra! She wasn't breathin' when I got to her and . . . go!"

"Ransom! What happened?" Myra cried hysterically, tears streaming down her face.

"Now, Myra!" he shouted back.

"What's goin' on?" Dan entered the room then, having heard the commotion, his attention going directly to Vaden. She tried to speak, to reassure them all of her well-being. However, she was still unable to utter a word, and she closed her eyes again for a moment, feeling completely exhausted.

"Myra!" Ransom shouted.

"Go for the doctor, Myra," Dan instructed

calmly. Vaden watched her aunt flee from the room, sobbing hysterically, as her Uncle Dan reached to the foot of her bed and pulled a warming quilt over her trembling body. "What happened, Ransom?"

"I found her in the elms. It was Jerome. I left him there bleedin' in the snow, but I don't think I got the job done. I didn't have time. I . . . she wasn't breathin' when I got there."

Panic dominated the intonation of Ransom's voice, and Vaden herself couldn't follow what he was trying to say. His features were stricken with anxiety and distress, and he panted hard from the taxing effort of carrying Vaden home from the elm grove.

"Why don't ya lay down for a minute, son?" Dan told Ransom. "Just come on over here and—"

"Don't touch me, Dan," Ransom growled, pushing Dan's hand from his shoulder.

"Ransom, you're not well yourself. Ya need to—"

"Leave me be. I'll sit right here until I'm sure she's—"

"Okay. Okay, son. I'm goin' for the sheriff. This has gone far enough—too far—and it's time the law did somethin' about it." Vaden watched her uncle hurry from the room, pausing to look back over his shoulder at her for a moment before leaving.

"Vaden," Ransom whispered.

She inhaled the comforting scent of his hair and

felt the warmth of his whisker-covered cheek against the chilled flesh of her shoulder as he laid his face against her neck. The bitter cold, the horrid lingering sensation of Jerome's touch began to disappear. She wanted to speak, to tell him how his touch healed her, but again her strength and voice failed her. Her arms felt as if they were weighted down with lead, and she could not move. Ransom laid an arm across her body just above her stomach, his hand coming to rest on the opposite shoulder, and she felt him place a tender but very fervent kiss on the hollow of her throat, another on the bareness of her shoulder. She closed her eyes for a moment. When she opened them again, a deep frown furrowed his brow as he caressed her throat and neck softly with his fingers. His fingers traveled carefully across her shoulder, and with an anguished moan escaping his throat, she felt his kiss caress her shoulder once more.

"Look at this," he muttered. "Look at the marks he's left here."

She coughed quietly, the only sound she could force from her throat, and he looked to her.

"Vaden?" he whispered. His eyes were filled with concern and the hint of restrained tears. "Vaden. I'm sorry. I shouldn't have left ya. But you were so insistent. Still . . . I'm sorry for this. I shouldn't have—"

"Stop. Please," she managed to whisper, though

411

her throat ached with pain. "This wasn't your—"

"I went to the elms, and there ya were. He had ya up against that tree, and I saw ya fall to the ground, and when I finally beat him enough that I could get to ya . . . I realized ya weren't breathin'!" He buried his face against her shoulder again, and she felt his kisses on her skin, at her shoulder and her upper arm, his fingers burying themselves in her hair. "My daddy used to blow into the mouths of calves that were born without breath, ya see . . . and I hoped the same thing would work on you. But I wasn't sure and . . ." He raised his head to look at her again, taking her face between his strong, trembling hands. "I thought you were dead! I should never have left ya!" Then, brushing a tear from her cheek, a tear that had managed to escape her exhausted eyes, Ransom Lake's stormy, guilt-ridden gaze searched her face for a moment. "What did he do to ya, Vaden?" he asked then. His voice was angry and deep.

"Just . . . just . . . he cut my shirtwaist and . . . his hands . . . his mouth was on my shoulders . . . my skin. I . . . I . . . ." It was still difficult to speak, and she couldn't tell him exactly anyway. It was too humiliating. She only wanted to forget it.

"Ssshhh," he breathed quietly. "Don't think on it again."

He brushed the hair from her forehead and

forced a smile, but she could plainly see the guilt consuming him. He wore the same expression of guilt, of feeling responsible, as he had the night he related the story of his family's slaughter to her.

"Don't look like that. Please, don't look like that," she whispered. She wanted to comfort him, help him understand he was in no way at fault for what had happened to her, but a great exhaustion overtook her, and she could no longer keep her eyes open.

It was shouting that woke her next. Vaden opened her eyes in time to see Ransom take hold of Doctor Sullivan's coat lapels and slam him violently against the wall.

"Watch what ya say!" Ransom growled into the man's face. "I'm not the one who did this!"

"Ransom. Calm yourself, son," Dan spoke calmly, placing a hand on Ransom's shoulder. "I'm sure Doctor Sullivan didn't mean to imply—"

"Of course not! Of course not, Ransom," Doctor Sullivan assured the infuriated man. "I merely asked who had done this to the girl. I only looked to you for an answer because you were the one to bring her home." Doctor Sullivan was obviously very rattled at having been so violently confronted.

"It was Jerome Clayton," Dan said bluntly.

Sheriff Howard approached the bed, but Vaden

still watched as Ransom hesitantly released the doctor.

"Miss Valmont," the sheriff began, "I know you're not feeling well . . . that you've been hurt. But I have to ask ya . . . was it really Jerome Clayton that did this to ya?"

"Yes," Vaden answered in a whisper.

"You see. One of your properly bred and raised local boys did this," Ransom nearly shouted.

"Calm yourself, Ransom Lake," Sheriff Howard warned, "or you'll find yourself in jail all the same." Then, putting a calming hand to Ransom's shoulder, he asked, "Do ya know where Jerome is now?"

"I hope he's burnin' in hell!" came his hateful answer. Ransom drew a deep breath, though his eyes were still the color of hurricane clouds. "I left him out at the old elm grove . . . and I left him out there to die."

"This ain't the first time he's tried to hurt my niece, Sheriff," Dan stated.

"What do ya mean by that?" Ransom shouted angrily, turning to Dan.

"He tried to force his attentions on her a while back, and we told him he wasn't welcome—" Dan began.

Ransom violently clutched Dan's shirt collar in one fist and demanded, "Why didn't ya tell me this before?"

Dan took Ransom by the shoulders calmly and answered, "I was afraid of what you'd do, Ransom. I never thought he'd do somethin' like this. I'd a shot him first myself if I'd known he would."

Ransom released his grip on Dan's shirt and closed his eyes for a moment. He inhaled deeply, trying to calm himself, and mumbled, "I'm sorry, Dan."

Dan touched his shoulder and reassured, "I understand, son."

"Vay!" Yvonne cried as she entered the room, pushing her way through the others to her sister. "Oh! Vay!" she cried. Quickly she dropped to her knees on the floor beside Vaden's bed and took one of her cold hands, stroking it affectionately. "Denver and I were out looking for you. I was so worried! I . . . oh, Vaden. What happened?"

Denver entered the room in time to restrain Ransom from assaulting the doctor once more when he said, "It's so hard to take in! That Clayton boy has always been such a fine young man."

With fists clenched and knuckles still bearing the remnants of healing scabs from his own beating, Ransom aggressed toward the man. "That Clayton boy isn't anything but a filthy—" Ransom shouted.

Denver took hold of his brother's shoulders, staying him. "Let it go, Ransom. Let him tend to the girl."

"I can't examine her with the entire township in the room," Doctor Sullivan grumbled. "Sheriff, clear everyone but her aunt out of here please."

"I'm not takin' a step out of this room while that idiot is anywhere near her!" Ransom shouted.

Vaden tried to speak, to calm him and reassure him that all would be well. He seemed completely out of his mind.

"Come on, boy," Dan said calmly. "We'll all wait together in the parlor."

Ransom began to argue the fact again, but when Denver nodded, confirming it to be the wisest choice, Ransom glanced worriedly to Vaden one last time before turning and storming out of the room.

"That man is a positive heathen," Vaden heard Doctor Sullivan mumble under his breath as he began to inspect her bruises.

"No," Vaden forced from her hurting throat. "I swear Jerome Clayton did this to me. He tried to kill Ransom and Denver. I—"

"Don't talk, sweet pea. Don't talk," Myra whispered in a soothing voice, forcing a smile onto her tear-streaked face and putting a cool glass of water to Vaden's lips.

Vaden sipped the refreshing, healing liquid for a moment before closing her eyes once more. Then she drifted once again into unconsciousness.

It was not until bright rays of sunlight drifted in through her window that Vaden woke. It was Yvonne's concerned expression she saw first as her eyes opened.

"Oh, Vay! I've been beside myself!" her sister exclaimed.

Vaden smiled and swallowed, noticing the incredible difference in the feel of her throat. "That must've been hard to endure, Yvonne, considering there is only one of you."

"Don't tease, Vay. I'm serious. We've all been so worried these past two days."

"Two days?" Vaden exclaimed, suddenly very alarmed. "Two days?"

"Yes. You've been sleeping for two days, Vay! And so much has happened. Ransom Lake was utterly a madman and went storming out of the house just after he brought you home and the doctor and everyone arrived. He went out determined to find Jerome, and . . . and I'm sure his intent was to cause a torturous fatality."

"Yvonne!" Vaden gasped, sitting up awkwardly in her bed. Her body was stiff and aching from lying down so long, but otherwise she suddenly felt quite recovered. "What happened? He . . . Ransom . . . he's all right, isn't he?"

"He's in jail, Vay! Imprisoned!"

Vaden shook her head, for her first thoughts were that Ransom had succeeded in ridding the world of Jerome Clayton. And now . . . would he hang for murder?

"Yvonne! He didn't . . ." Vaden began, fearful of the answer. "You're not trying to tell me that he—"

"No! Oh, no! Jerome—actually, Vay, it seems he wandered into the creek bed after . . . after Ransom found you. Vaughn Wimber found him there talking to himself and going on and on about how it was some voices or something . . . voices in his head telling him to do those things to you. Oh, he's quite mad, Vay. They've taken him up to an institution in Denver. He's quite mad. But Ransom is . . . well, he's an utter mess, Vay! He's been going on and on about how this was all his fault. How he should've known you were in danger. How he shouldn't have left you on the road that day. Oh, Vay! I fear he may eat away at his own mind and end up as mad as Jerome. We've all been waiting for you to wake up. The doctor says your body is fine, your injuries were minor, but that you were in a state of shock from the cold and the anguish of it all. It's why you slept so long. Oh, Vay! You've got to go to Ransom at once!"

Vaden threw back the covers and tried to stand. Her head went spinning at first, for it had been so long since she had been conscious. Taking Yvonne's arm for support, she went to her wardrobe.

"Of course, there's no way Auntie and Uncle Dan will let you leave the house, considering you must still be hurting and stunned. So we'll have to go out through the window."

Vaden paused in her dressing to turn and look at her sister inquisitively. "Yvonne? You are encouraging me to sneak out the window, and to the jail of all places, to visit a man—to visit a man unchaperoned, I might add—a man of whom you don't approve?"

"For pity's sake, Vay! Hurry up! We don't have time to think rationally!"

So, determined and knowing that no doubt much more than Yvonne had told her had transpired during her convalescence, Vaden did indeed dress hurriedly. She securely buttoned the coat Yvonne handed to her and climbed out through the bedroom window after her sister.

The bright morning sun tried in vain to warm the cold winter's day. Quickly she followed Yvonne toward the jail, thinking how cold it would be for Ransom in the confining building.

"Denver says they're just keeping him there because they think he'll follow the Claytons up to Denver after Jerome. But I'm sure that once you've talked to him, he'll be fine. Denver says Ransom is still blaming himself for what happened to the family," Yvonne babbled, barely pausing for breath.

"You know about the family?" Vaden asked,

stunned her sister should hold the knowledge.

"Yes. Denver told me all about it. How horrid for poor Ransom. And for dear Denver . . . to think his entire family was lost all those years, not knowing all that time he still had a brother to hold to."

Yvonne sighed heavily, and Vaden's brow wrinkled in wonderment. She could not believe the change in her sister. It was painfully obvious Yvonne and Denver had spent a great deal of time together for her to know such intimate details of the story.

When they at long last arrived at the jail, Vaden burst into the building behind Yvonne. Upon seeing Sheriff Howard sitting at his desk casually reading a book, her temper flared, and Vaden stormed over to him.

"You let Ransom Lake out of here this minute, Sheriff Howard!" she ordered.

Startled, the sheriff looked up, frowning. "Miss Valmont?" he mumbled. Then, clearing his throat, he closed his book and stood up, offering his hand to her. "It's good to see you're recovered from your—"

"You're holding him here, aren't you?" Vaden nearly shouted.

"Ransom Lake? Well, yes. I have him in—"

"You release him now! Do you understand me? He hasn't done anything to deserve being locked up in here!" Vaden felt hot tears of frustration filling her eyes, but she was determined to stand strong. Ransom was not the one who deserved to be confined.

"Now, settle yourself down, Miss Valmont. I've just had him in here for a couple of days until he could settle hisself down. When he left your place, he went out lookin' for Jerome. When he didn't find him in the elms, he took out to his family's home. He kicked their front door down, went chargin' through their house, shoutin' threats about how he was gonna make certain Jerome didn't live to see the light of another day. He scared the waddin' outta every one of them. And then he come stormin' in here, shoutin' at me to find that Clayton boy and string him up to a tree. And he was all fired up to go stormin' off to your aunt and uncle's house to make sure Doctor Sullivan did right by you, so I just figured it would be safer for Ransom and everybody else if he spent some time pinned up so he could think things out and we could find Jerome."

Vaden shook her head, astounded Ransom would react so irrationally. "Well then, now that the Claytons are out of town and I'm better . . . you will release him, won't you?" she asked.

"If you can go in there, Miss Vaden, and talk some sense into that man—get him to swear off revenge of any sort—then I'll let him go. He's calmed down otherwise now . . . near to despair it seems. But I want his word that he's got his temper under control," the sheriff said.

"You just take me to him. I still can't believe this was necessary." Vaden frowned at the man with disapproval, and the sheriff guiltily hung his head for a moment as she followed him to the back of the building. Denver sat on a chair just outside the bars that enclosed the jail cell. He stood up, an expression of profound relief overtaking his face as he looked to Vaden. Vaden was surprised when Yvonne rushed forward from behind her, throwing herself against Denver and into his strong embrace.

"Miss Vaden," Denver sighed with relief. "You're a sight for sore eyes, indeed you are."

Immediately, Ransom was on his feet, rushing to the bars as Vaden approached him. "Vaden!" he exclaimed, grasping the bars tightly as he gazed at her. "Are ya all right?" he asked anxiously.

Vaden felt a tear trickle down her cheek, for he looked so careworn, so thoroughly exhausted. The room was not comfortably warm even for the fire burning in the nearby hearth. Still, Ransom stood before her, his shirt unbuttoned and gaping open, his face unshaven, his hair disheveled, and the dark circles of great fatigue shading the area beneath his eyes.

"I'm . . . I'm fine," she managed to answer. Everything about her was so unfamiliar—a jail cell, Yvonne and Denver in each other's arms, Ransom looking tired and defeated. Tentatively, she reached out and placed a small hand over his cold, roughened one.

"Ya gonna behave if I let ya out of here now, Ransom?" Sheriff Howard asked.

Ransom looked up, glaring angrily at the man. "I suppose," he mumbled.

"I suppose ain't good enough," Sheriff Howard reminded him.

Ransom closed his eyes for a moment and drew in a deep, calming breath. "Yes."

"All right then."

Vaden stepped back from the cell as the sheriff unlocked it with a large key. Ransom stepped from the cell in one long stride, and instantly Vaden was in his arms, her face pressed firmly against the warm skin of his chest as he hugged her savagely. His hands clutched at the fabric of her coat and dress, squeezed her arms roughly, wound their fingers in her hair. He held her to him so tightly it was a difficult chore to draw breath. Vaden in return let her arms slide under his gaping shirt and around to his back, returning the fierce embrace. It was wonderful to be in his arms once more, to inhale the scent of his skin, to feel his powerful arms around her!

"I'm so sorry," he whispered, his lips brushing her ear briefly as he spoke. "I'm so sorry I failed ya, Vaden."

Vaden raised her head to meet his gaze, which was painfully filled with guilt. "You didn't fail me. As always, you saved me, Ransom Lake," she said.

He was so strong, so completely capable of overpowering anyone, anything that might try to break him. It unsettled Vaden that she would cause him such despair. And then, he slowly pushed her away from him. He stood staring down at her, the turbulence in his eyes disturbing her.

Vaden's heart began to pound violently as she saw, as she could actually perceive and read, the resolve forming in his mind. His eyes narrowed, his shoulders straightened, and his jaw tightened as he looked at her. The expression of concern and guilt left his face, and in its place was the look Vaden recognized. She'd seen it blatant on his handsome face several times before: the first time he'd kissed her, the day he'd awakened from his unconscious time in her aunt's spare bedroom, the night in the wagon after they'd shared the intensely passionate kisses, the night they'd spent together in the old house, on Thanksgiving, and even the day when Jerome had assaulted her—the day when, she only at that very moment remem-bered, she had confessed her love to him only to send him away, dooming herself to Jerome's will. Yes, she'd seen the expression many times before, but it was only at that moment—as they stood in the cold jail-house, the sheriff and Denver and Yvonne looking on—it was then that she recognized the expression as resolve—resolve to keep himself from taking her, resolve to deny himself of having her. Vaden was sure then that he did love her, that he did want her. But his past was still haunting him. He was still blaming himself, now perhaps more than ever. It frightened Vaden, broke her heart once more—violently broke her heart—and she stepped back from him.

"Don't do it, Ransom. Don't you dare do it," Denver growled, releasing Yvonne and going to stand ominously near his brother. Ransom's resolve only seemed to strengthen, and, unable to endure it any longer, Vaden turned and fled from him.

"Vaden!" she heard him call out. The tears had already escaped her eyes and were flooding her cheeks, and she clutched at her bosom, hoping to somehow lessen the pain in her heart. "Vaden!" he shouted again, and she knew he was at her heels as she fled. "Vaden," he breathed as he caught hold of her arm, stopping her escape.

"Don't do this to me!" she cried out, turning to face him and wrenching her arm free of his grasp. "Don't give me glimpses of my dreams of you coming true and then snatch them away because you're . . . because you're . . ."

"Scared," he finished for her, bluntly and admittedly. "You're thinkin' I'm weak, I know," he mumbled, holding her hand to his chest, clutching it tightly in his own.

"How could I ever think you were weak? It's just—" Vaden began, but Ransom interrupted her.

"I am. I admit it. I didn't have the courage . . . I didn't have the faith to pursue you. To tell ya what I feel for you. I . . . I didn't think it was conceivable that you could accept me when ya knew what I had . . . what I hadn't done for my family. I had gone cold inside. I thought I was incapable of feelin', of . . . of lovin' anyone ever again . . . any kind of love. And then ya conked me on the head with a pair of boots, and some remnant of who I was before flickered warm inside of me."

He sighed heavily, and his eyes caressed her face as he looked from her mouth to her cheeks to her hair and at last to her eyes once more. A slight grin spread across his face, and he chuckled a moment.

"You were so completely unspoiled, so completely in love with nature and ideas of romance, in love with life. And like everyone else ya touch . . . ya touched me, and I began to see there could be reasons to smile. I began to appreciate the simple beauties around me." Reaching down, he tucked a strand of hair behind her ear. "The grand beauty before me."

Vaden's soul began to rejoice, for the resolve to resist was gone from his countenance. Her throbbing pain began to leave her body as joy began to fill it. She glanced away shyly for a moment. As much as she had longed to hear him say these types of things, as often as she'd dreamt it, it was still difficult to believe, to accept in her mind, that it was true.

"And then . . . it got to where every time I saw ya, I wanted your touch, your smile . . . I wanted ya to be mine. Every time I'd come into the mercantile and find ya there weavin' a tale for those little ones, I'd think how wonderful it would be if they were our children . . . yours and mine. Children you'd borne of me."

It was as if she had to feel him saying these things, so taking his rugged face in her hands, she let her small, soft thumb caress his flawlessly contoured lips. How enticing his mouth was. *How perfect,* she thought. He closed his eyes for an instant, causing a tear to trickle down his cheek as he reached up, taking her hand from his cheek and pressing her palm firmly to his lips as he kissed her there.

"I'd think of you . . . in my arms . . . of our children . . . and," he continued as she could feel the guilt and resistance leaving his body, "it would scare me because I'd remember the pain of losin' my family. I'd imagine what my parents must have felt watchin' their children die, and I'd run from ya for a while. Then I'd smack my thumb with a hammer while I was puttin' up a fence or forget to feed the stock . . . because my mind would be on you all the time."

He took her face firmly in his hands then, and his eyes narrowed as he spoke through tightly clenched teeth. "If ya only had a shred of a notion what kind of fire ya spark in me, girl, you'd run from me like ya would the plague! There have been times I feared for your virtue at my own hand when I had ya in my arms because my desire for ya fought so furiously with what I knew to be right in my mind that I wasn't sure my honorable values could win out."

Vaden tried to look away from him, for the depth and meaning of what he was saying was truly exhilarating to hear but also very intimate. That he would say such things to her caused her to blush.

"You found me, Vaden," he mumbled in the sultry tone that sent her senses tingling. Releasing her face, obviously not wanting to force her to look at him, he added, "Ya looked and looked beneath the stone, the hard, cold stone until ya found me. Your smile melted that solid ice around my heart, and your kiss heated the flames of desire in me to a point that I am no longer able to bury them."

Vaden gasped and put her hand to his lips to silence his forthright words, but he only kissed her hand. She pulled it away quickly as the feel of his kiss unsettled her will to resist taking his mouth for her own. She glanced about them quickly to ensure they were not being watched. Chuckling lowly, he tugged on her arm, leading her into the space between the jailhouse and the barber's shop. Then, gently pushing her back against the wall, he continued, his gray, mesmerizing eyes weaving a spell about her, his voice low and alluring.

"Don't ya see, Vaden? I can say those things to ya now—all the things I've been thinkin' about ya since the moment I laid eyes on ya. I can speak them to ya now because of the faith . . . the confidence ya give me."

He took her face in his hands as he let his body lean fully against hers. As his thumb caressed her lips softly, he said, "I want ya in my arms every night—every night forever. I want to hold you, feel the warmth of your body in my arms, know that your soul is there with mine. Know that you're there every night for me to hold and love. Know that I can touch ya, kiss ya, and look at ya whenever I want to . . . whenever I need to."

It was too overwhelming to have him saying it all to her. Could she possibly believe she wasn't dreaming?

"I want my children to grow inside of you," he mumbled. "I want the Lake blood and the name of Lake to go on. I want ya to help me ensure it doesn't die away." He paused as he struggled to remove the ring on the smallest finger of his right hand. "This . . . was my mother's weddin' ring, Vaden. I know you've wondered about it. Her name was Darlina."

Vaden's mind fought to hold on to reality, to believe what was happening before her truly was real and not a dream from which she would wake. She watched as Ransom Lake took her left hand in his and placed his mother's ring on her ring finger.

"This was the ring my father put on my mother's finger when they were married. And I know . . ." He paused and grimaced painfully before continuing. "I know, Vaden, that even though my father and mother were killed—that perhaps one had to watch the other die—they would not have wanted to be anywhere but together. I want ya to know . . . ya need to| believe the truth of it . . . I love you like that." Vaden felt the tears burst from her eyes more readily even than they had before as he finally, after so long, told her that he loved her. "I would do anything for you. Go anywhere for you. I would endure a thousand times the death my father and mother did . . . for you. Because you are my life. My love . . . my heart and my soul. The reason I love living again. The reason I'm willin' now to endure whatever pain life may bring. I love you, Vaden."

He kissed her lips softly for a moment as if he were unsure she would accept him. But in an instant, she let go the need to resist him, and, taking his face between her hands, she encouraged him to take her mouth passionately, which he did, and she melted against his own. It was then her mind confirmed to her once more that no verse of poetry, no matter how cleverly written or labored over in pursuit of perfection, could describe the sheer ecstasy of this man's kiss. He was all she wanted in the world. The only touch, the only breath.

He broke their kiss for a moment, though his mouth lingered teasingly over hers as he studied her. Vaden was hypnotized by his gaze. The gray storm in his eyes was warm and inviting, and the true feelings in his soul were evident in them. He had forgiven himself at long last and, having done so, could give himself to her, finally. He was so handsome—so flawlessly attractive. Her mind still struggled to accept that a man so perfectly formed in body and spirit could truly mean what he had spoken to her.

"How can a man like you . . . how can you truly want me?" she whispered.

Laughing heartily, Ransom pulled her up from her brace against the wall, gathering her securely in his arms. She pushed at him slightly for a moment when one of the townsfolk walked by, raising an astonished eyebrow.

"It's not proper," she mumbled.

"Very little bodily contact between unmarried

lovers is, Vaden." His eyes twinkled impishly, the moisture of emotion still evident in them as he continued to smile. "That's why ya have to marry me, Vaden Valmont." He brushed an independent strand of hair from her cheek again as he gazed lovingly at her. "I can't believe how you've allowed the tables to turn, girl. In the beginnin', ya didn't care a whit for what ya had to do to have me. And now . . . I'm beginnin' to think you're a tease. You have me here in your arms, confessin' my undyin' love for ya—not to mention my physical desire for ya—and all of a sudden, you're shy and unconfident. Where's that girl who dug my old boots out of the trash barrel?"

Vaden gasped again, astonished he would know such a thing.

"Where's that girl who shaved my face so she could see if I was handsome or not under that mess of a beard?" Again, he took her face firmly between his hands. "Where's that woman who can make me doubt my own self-control when she gives me the taste of her kiss?" He kissed her softly once before continuing. "I've watched ya closely, Vaden. Watched ya go from havin' a kitten's curiosity about me to not knowin' what direction to take in life 'cause you had fallen in love with me. I've watched ya battle with doubt 'cause ya loved me so desperately and feared I could never be yours. I'm sorry it took me so long to find my way to forgivin' myself and confessin' to ya. And now . . . I have to tell ya my secret, asking your forgiveness and that ya not be too awful angry."

Vaden raised her eyebrows. What secret could he possibly hide that was more traumatic, more important than the one he'd already revealed to her?

"I knew what could be between us before ya ever got here to spend a year with your aunt and uncle," he confessed guiltily.

"What do you mean?" she asked, completely unprepared for such a remark.

"I woke up one night just a few days before ya arrived here," he began. "I woke because I'd seen ya in my mind. In a vision, I'd seen your beauty of soul and body. It's how I knew where ya were on Halloween and that the storm would put ya in danger if your Uncle Dan came instead of me on the night before Thanksgivin'. It's how I know you're hidin' my old boots under your bed, that ya put the apple seeds on a maple leaf from that tree ya like to sit in and sent it down the creek to me. I was a man plagued, or blessed, with visions. Since the day my family was killed, I've had them, but when you arrived, I started havin' them less often, and it seemed they only pertained to you. Now my premonitions —the visions of Ransom Lake, whether terrible or pleasin'—come less often. They started to fade the first time I let myself hold you . . . tasted your lips and the promise of love for me on them. They've been even fewer since the night I told ya of the great guilt I bore. And now that you're holdin' in your arms the thing you were so diligent and faithful in gettin', are ya gonna| tell me that ya don't want to have it?"

Vaden looked away for a moment trying to control her sniffling, which was fast turning into a sobbing borne of bliss. "When you've wanted something so badly . . . dreamt of it constantly . . . prayed for it every night . . . it's sometimes hard to believe you can simply reach out and take it all of a sudden," she whispered her confession.

Ransom kissed her neck lingeringly and then placed a short but enticing kiss on her mouth. "Reach out and have me. I'm yours, Vaden. Will ya take me?"

Standing before her ill-dressed for the weather in lacking a coat, his shirt still unbuttoned as it was, Vaden worried not for him, for he was strong, powerful, and apparently immune to fatal harm. His expression was alluring, tempting, and tantalizing. He was his confident, powerful self in that moment. He knew what her answer would be before she spoke it aloud, and his mind and body were already prepared to act upon her answer. Smiling, she slipped her hands beneath his shirt again, caressing the breadth of his strong shoulders.

"I've always been yours, Ransom Lake. You know how completely I am yours," she said.

Tentatively, she let the fingers of both her trembling hands be lost in the soft black of his hair, and when he closed his eyes for a moment, smiling triumphantly, she melted against him again, letting her head rest tenderly on one shoulder as her hands slid to his neck and down his powerful chest. Her arms rested lovingly about his waist for a moment. Then she let one hand caress the rugged smoothness of his unshaven face, and he kissed her fingertips as they lingered on his lips.

"Will you really . . . will you really . . ." she began in an uncertain whisper.

"Marry you?" he finished.

"Yes," she said, smiling at his familiar way of finishing her sentences when she was too shy to do so.

"The minute your parents step off the stage and see you're all right."

"What?" Vaden gasped, raising her head from his shoulder and looking at him.

"These past few days you've been recoverin' . . . I've been so angry! Angry with myself for not havin' protected ya . . . for not confessin' to ya, askin' ya sooner. Angry with myself for my own cowardice . . . my lack of self-confidence. It's why I sometimes wear that expression ya dread so much, and I'm sorry for it. Sorry for my weakness. I-I can feel it controllin' my face as my mind battles with my soul. My soul tells me you're mine . . . that all I have to do is reach out and take ya for my own. But all those years of guilt, of agony from the loss of my family . . . the visions of it flashin' through my brain like lightnin', and I . . . I hesitate. But ya have to understand that it's only an old wound causin' the fear in me, Vaden, and it passes. It leaves faster each time. And this time . . . this time it's gone for good. I've been so angry, and I actually drew strength, courage, and confidence from it somehow. So day before yesterday, before I could reconsider, I had Denver send a telegram to your daddy tellin' him what had happened with Jerome and . . . and . . . askin' him for his permission to take ya to my bed."

Vaden gasped. "You're lying!"

Ransom chuckled. "Yes. Actually, I told him I intended to marry ya the minute you were well once more. He sent a telegram back right away and said he and your mother would be here as soon as they could get here. And even though back at the jail I know ya thought I was resolvin' not to take ya . . . not to take your love into my life . . . but it's just that I realized I had sent that telegram and . . ." His face went solemn for a moment, and he asked, "Are ya mad at me for plannin' . . . for assumin' you'd accept me?"

Vaden smiled, joy bursting like radiant sunshine from her heart. "You know I'm not. I'm only glad that you didn't pause to reconsider. I don't know if I can wait even one more day to be . . ."

"In my bed?" he finished, chuckling and smiling mischievously.

Vaden giggled. "I don't know if I can wait one more day to be yours." Vaden slipped her arms beneath his shirt again and hugged him tightly around the waist. "Oh, how desperately and thoroughly I love you, Ransom Lake."

"I love you," he whispered. "And thank you."

Vaden gazed lovingly at the powerful, astoundingly attractive man as he took her hand and raised it to his lips, kissing it tenderly.

"No," she whispered. "Thank heaven. Thank heaven for giving me you."

And then, Vaden's soul reveled in the feel of Ransom's arms about her as his mouth rendered a kiss to hers so sublime it raised the vision of heaven on earth to come—that being the vision of Ransom Lake.

Author's Note

Believe it or not, when *The Visions of Ransom Lake* was first published in 2002, sales didn't leap as quickly as my first book, *The Heavenly Surrender*, had. I was worried about it. I decided it was probably the seasonal-style cover—you know, the pumpkin patch and overall orange tint to it. The book was released in early summer, and I decided maybe readers just weren't in the mood for pumpkins yet—though, knowing me as you do, I couldn't imagine why anyone couldn't be perpetually in the mood for pumpkins.

Anyway, slowly *The Visions of Ransom Lake* began to move up the ladder. As *Shackles of Honor* and *Dusty Britches* were released over the next two consecutive years, *The Visions of Ransom Lake* began to gain momentum. And before we knew it, ol' Ransom Lake had become a fan-favorite—and I'm not just talking about the book itself, though that is also true. I'm talking about the fact that Ransom Lake—the man, the legend, the hottie with a naughty body—was reigning neck and neck with Mason Carlisle as every reader's favorite hero back then.

Now, of course I *like* Ransom—for obvious reasons as well as reasons not so obvious. But I'd be an idiot if I didn't like him, right? After all, I like Vaden too; she's the most like me of any of my heroines. However, there's something about Ransom Lake that just seems to get into your very soul somehow. And I thought we'd investigate that a little bit today.

So, here's the question: what is it about Ransom Lake? Why are he and the book about the beginning of his romance with Vaden so very dear to our hearts? Is it simply because of the way he takes Vaden's hand and runs it over his washboard stomach in that one scene in the book? Or is it for much deeper reasons?

In striving for answers, let's begin with the obvious (his drop-dead gorgeousness), shall we? First, he's more than just traditionally tall, dark, and handsome. Ransom Lake is *legendarily* handsome! I mean, I could probably write a sequel book called *The Legend of Ransom* about Ransom and Vaden in their middle-aged years, and he'd be just as deliciously good-looking—a little salt and pepper in his sable soft hair, endearing, charming, attractive smile wrinkles at the corners of his eyes, etc. Yep, he's that good-looking! He's that alluring, charming, fascinating, comely, gorgeous, and just plain easy on the eyes.

But I know we're not all *that* shallow—you know, taken in with a tall drink of water just because he's luscious to look at. There's a whole lot more that makes Handsome Ransom a swooner. Tall, dark, and handsome—yes. But he's also strong, capable, and nearly invincible, not to mention protective, brooding, tortured, and lacking any ounce of vanity. Am I right?

And then there's his flirtatious manner—which is probably one of the things we like most about him. He's what I like to call a "good bad boy." Do you know what I mean? He'd never step over the line, but he'd back you right up against it and melt your knees with a moist, smoldering kiss! He'd beat the living daylights out of anybody who touched you but afterward hold you in his arms as if you were the most precious thing on earth. See? He's a good bad boy—the kind of guy we all gravitate to.

And let's just say it—we're all thinking it anyway. Let's just admit that the idea of slopping around in a smashed pumpkin with Ransom Lake is provocative! That being snowed in in an old house with nothing but a warm fire in the hearth and a soul-wrenching confession of harbored guilt from Ransom (followed by some dang serious kissing) would be life-altering! I mean, he *is* from Georgia, after all.

Yet even after our quick discussion on this, I'm still not sure we can put into words what it is about Ransom Lake that draws us in. At least not Ransom Lake the man.

As for Ransom Lake the book, I think it's a reader favorite (and mine) for more obvious reasons. First of all, there's Ransom Lake himself.

We've established that far more than just lightly. Second, I think I like *The Visions of Ransom Lake* for many other reasons as well, such as the fact that I identify with Vaden more than any other heroine I've ever written. I *totally* would've had to have shaved Ransom to see what he looked like! I love fairy tales, nature, pumpkins, autumn, and children. I love walks and climbing trees and picking apples and the scent of homemade bread. I love geodes, my uncles, pretty little snippets of poetry, pralines—and the list goes on and on. I also love, love, love the name Ransom Lake and the nickname Handsome Ransom.

Which that reminds me of something else I think I might just share with you—a true little story of my own Handsome Ransom and a kiss that was years and years in coming. I don't remember exactly when I wrote this thingy (for a blog), but I'll share it with you again (even though it makes me blush to think about it). It's entitled:

Handsome Ransom
(The story behind the name.)

Of all the heroes borne of my imagination, the overall popular one, the one I am questioned about most often, has to be Ransom Lake. Anytime I'm in a gathering of friends and readers, the majority of them confess to me that Ransom Lake is one of their favorites, if not favorite, hero. Truth be told, Ransom Lake is my favorite hero too, probably because he is nearly the personification of my husband Kevin in looks, sense of humor, and otherwise. When I envision Ransom, I see Kevin in my mind's eye, speaking in a rather Sam Elliott-ish voice. Yes, I would have to admit, Ransom Lake is definitely a kindred spirit with my husband. However, it is true the name Ransom Lake sprung from a vastly different venue—different perhaps, but romantic in its own right.

Although I have mentioned before what, or rather who, inspired the name, I've been so bombarded with so many questions about how I came up with it that I thought it might be time to tell the tale, anticlimactic though it may be. (But I hope it's not!) Yes, there was an actual person in my life who I often referred to as Handsome Ransom. Handsome Ransom was a nickname I coined as my own personal endearment to him. And yes, there was one delightful moment in time when we shared a kiss. Actually, shared might not be the right word, for as I remember the moment, I was rather stunned to the toe-seams in my pantyhose when it happened!

We begin in 1977 (this kiss was a *long* time coming). I was a shy, rather self-conscious adolescent, with the worst excuse for a Farrah Fawcett-knockoff hairstyle you could've ever imagined. Likewise I was a comic, sometimes intentionally so, sometimes unintentionally so, and I was just starting the big middle school scene as a seventh grader. Ah, yes, good ol' Taft Middle School in Albuquerque. This is where it all began—my renowned relationship with the (at the time) adorably cute, shall we call him, for anonymity's sake, "Tom" Ransom. One of the only blonde boys that ever managed to turn my head, Tom Ransom shared my sense of humor and, more often than not, my row in class. Yes, Marcia Reed and Tom Ransom, fellow class clowns almost always seated together in classes due to the alphabetical order of their last names. And let me tell you, we were quite a duo! We caused a fair amount of mischief in our day, specifically in typing class and language arts. To put it simply, we were kindred spirits, two peas in a pod, two inelegant seventh grade stand-up comedians who became fast friends. I dubbed him "Handsome Ransom," and we stayed good friends all through the seventh grade and the entirety of the eighth.

Still, teenagers are so often the victims of peer pressure, social circles, and not to mention acne. Tom and I left the eighth grade in May of 1979 as good friends, but when Valley High School became my future alma mater the next August, some things had changed.

Age fourteen and the onset of the ninth grade

found me having to make some difficult decisions. Not only had all the boys I'd known the year before grown six inches to a foot over the summer, many of the kids I'd counted as friends and hung out with in middle school were now the "party" people. Leaping into sports, adolescent arrogance, and the "party" mentality, my old friends, I found, were on the other side of the fence. My side of the fence was the green-growing pasture where crazy fun, music, church friends who attended other high schools, and no drugs or drinking was the grass for grazing. My friends now grazed in brown fields of rebellion, drugs, and drinking.

Back in Albuquerque in the early 1980s, you couldn't sit the fence—you were on one side or the other. Not that you couldn't be casual friends with everyone, but as far as good, solid relationships went, well, I was more than just sad to see my relationships with what had been such a good group of friends change to a more awkward, less comfortable type of existence.

Tom Ransom, though not the partier most of my friends had become, was still all "jock," a rebel, and a cliché bad boy (the rather heroic kind we girls all dream about—not the truly bad ones). He quickly became one of the most popular and handsome boys in school, the kind all the girls clamor for attention from. Still, even though his side of the fence had become different than mine, somehow we both managed to straddle it enough to have a good time together in classes. Another "R" name had been added to the list of kids slated to graduate in 1983, and that sort of busted up our capability of sitting right in front or in back of each other. Still, we managed, awkwardly talking over the new "R" kid's head or around her. Once in a while we got lucky and the seating arrangements would sit us parallel to one another, only an aisle separating us. This turned out to be the best seating arrangement, conducive to note passing, test questions and candy sharing, and, now that we were full-fledged teenagers, profuse flirtation! Yep, somewhere along the line, Tom and I had begun to mature into more than just fellow comedians; we were shameless flirts with each other. I blush to think of it now, but we did an aircraft carrier of flirting.

On we paddled through the first two years of high school and into the third, always passing notes, cutting up, and flirting like idiots. I remember how Tom used to suck on these round, flat lollipops in English and then reach over and stick them on my face. Inevitably I'd break out with a rash of tiny little pimples, which formed a perfectly round sucker-shape on my cheek each time. Fortunately, I had good skin and was able to recover fairly quickly from these incidents.

Through it all, Tom and I stayed close in a manner. Oh, we didn't hang out outside of school or anything, but at school and in any classes we shared, we always had a great time.

Junior year arrived, and Tom and I had only one class together—a zoology class taught by my very favorite teacher, Mr. Gunner. Zoology was awesome! We dissected sharks that year, and our hands stunk for days. It was great! But the best parts about that class were the people. I was a junior and already moving on in my mind, past senior year and onto college and life. While most others at my high school in 1982 seemed to pause, uncertain of what direction to take, I had become confident, seasoned, and ready to move on. I'd leapt over some fences and was sprinting head-long to whatever life held for me. This newfound confidence gave me wings to rise above feeling nervous or uncomfortable in the presence of those who had been good friends and no longer were. I found fear was vanquished in favor of determination and self-assurance. I had also been through a very dramatic romantic relationship and knew for certain what I did and did not want in that venue as well. Thus, I was able to completely be myself in zoology. (It helped that I was one of Mr. Gunner's pet students too. I think I could've gotten away with murder.)

Yep, for five years I had known old "Handsome

Ransom." For five years I'd secreted a sort of odd crush on him—sighing over him one moment and thinking he was far too skinny the next. Still, I knew I'd always adore him—knew likewise I'd always feel rather cheated at not having had any sort of romantic interlude with him.

No romantic interlude? Now there's naiveté for you! Looking back, it's so very obvious we spent our entire four years at high school waltzing around in our own kind of interlude of romance. For cryin' out loud! Neither one of us ever got anything done in the classes we had together. Both of us were constantly being reprimanded for talking or cutting up. As I was absolutely drowning in the romantic waltz, I couldn't see it for the water. I couldn't see it, that is, until one memorable day in Mr. Gunner's zoology class.

Let me set the scene of romance for you— Valley High School, one hot, Albuquerque day. Having recently finished up our work on molds and spores, Mr. Gunner was preparing our class for our fish test, as he liked to call it. Thus the room was lined with jars filled with formaldehyde and every kind of fish a person could imagine. (Mr. Gunner's room always smelled weird, by the way.) Anywho, I walked into Mr. Gunner's classroom one day, and another boy named Sean Hasten began slathering me with his rather monotonous flirtations. (At one point, I had actually sort of liked this other boy—until he turned out to be a lecherous jerk. But that's another story.) Mr. Gunner was in the back working on something for our fish test (most certainly a dead fish of some sort), and everyone was just sort of milling around out of their seats and goofing off. Irritated with the uncomfortable attentions of "lecherous jerk" Sean, I wandered toward the front of the room, out of his reach, to sharpen a pencil. (Back in the day, every classroom had a pencil sharpener mounted on the wall. Not sure they do that now with mechanical pencils so easily available.)

Now, in the interest of making this story as engaging as I can, I've chosen to write the following scene just as it happened. If it sounds like something you've read in one of my books, that's probably because it may very well be that you have.

Marcia inhaled deeply, attempting to calm her rather rattled nerves. *I can't believe I ever thought that guy was cute!* she whispered to herself. *What a jerk.* She was relieved Sean Hasten had given up on making any more advances toward her—at least for the time being.

Cranking the handle of the pencil sharpener, Marcia ground the writing utensil down much closer to its end than she needed to. She wanted to buy a few more moments—time enough for Sean Hasten to find another victim. But at last, and with a heavy sigh, Marcia turned around to head back to her desk.

"Hi," he said, stepping in her path. It was Tom Ransom now that stood before her, his brilliantly white teeth flashing a dazzling smile.

"Hi, Tom," Marcia greeted, relieved and rather delighted to find Handsome Ransom in her path. Tom Ransom, "Handsome Ransom," as she'd always called him, was such a way good-looking guy! Oh, sure, he was a bit on the skinny side, but what high school varsity basketball player wasn't? And anyway, he was way handsome, with his feathery blonde hair, dark brown eyes, and perfect smile. Yep! The boy had an awesome orthodontist, whoever he was.

"What're you doing?" Tom asked.

"Sharpening," Marcia responded. However, a puzzled frown puckered her brow when the handsome Tom Ransom stepped closer to her rather than moving out of her way.

"Oh," he said. Marcia took several steps back, but he only continued to advance upon her— like some lean, resolute lion progressing on his prey.

"Well . . . you know, Marcia," Tom began as Marcia's retreat was stopped cold when the wall behind her abruptly met with her back. "There's something I've always wanted to do."

"Really?" Marcia managed to gulp in a whisper. Her heart's pace had sped up. She sensed something was about to happen—though she didn't know what.

"Yeah," Tom whispered, his voice quiet and low, a rather seductive quality in its intonation.

"Wh-what's that?" Marcia asked. She couldn't believe what was happening! Surely she wasn't misreading the expression on his face—his rather intimate body language. But as he placed his hands against the wall at either side of her waist, pressing his body firmly against her own, Marcia was further assured of his intention.

Oh my heck! she thought. *He's going to kiss me!*

Tom grinned the famous "Handsome Ransom" roguish grin, which Marcia had come to know so well. It was the same grin he grinned each time before he'd stuck his suckers to her face in English class the year before. The same grin he grinned whenever he was flirting with her.

"I've always wanted to kiss you," he whispered. And in the next moment, Marcia thought her knees might give way beneath her, for the instant and delicious delirium washing over her as Handsome Ransom's lips met her own was dizzying! His kiss, though lingering, was not too roughly forced but wonderful in its consummating, blissful application. He meant to kiss her not because he was a teenage boy with hormones raging out of control nor because he was teasing. Marcia knew this kiss was sincere, taken and given for fulfillment's sake. She'd known all along—ever since she'd first met him in typing class five long years before—she'd always known that the tender crush she'd secreted for Tom Ransom was reciprocated. Oh, perhaps circumstance or differing social circles had caused that their mutual crush should forever remain secreted, but in those moments—in those blissful, satisfying moments when their lips were met in one mouth-wateringly consummate kiss—in that moment all bridled passions, all hidden secrets of the heart, were communicated.

As their lingering kiss ended, Tom smiled at Marcia a moment before his head descended toward hers again.

"Ransom! Get to back to your seat," Mr. Gunner bellowed as he lumbered toward the front of the room, a large jar housing an ugly fish clutched in his hands. "What are you doing up there?"

Pulling away and straightening his posture, Tom Ransom winked at Marcia as he turned and walked to his seat. On weakened knees—every nerve ending in her body jumping with excitement—Marcia walked to her seat as well. And as class began, Mr. Gunner threatening Fs to anyone who didn't get the name of the "surprise" in the back, Tom Ransom took a sucker from his pocket and popped it in his mouth. Sighing contentedly, he winked at Marcia, flashing another dazzling grin in her direction when she winked back at him. Looked.

"Rainbow trout," Mr. Gunner began, holding aloft the smelly jar filled with chemicals and a dead fish. "Can you tell me why?"

Yep. That's it. Too anticlimactic? I hope not, for it was an epoch in my high school experience—the culmination of five long years of mutual attraction. Yes, one kiss—that's all there ever was. And yet, it was enough to satisfy me. It was something like that painful longing for the first daffodil of the year to bloom—and when it finally does, cutting it from your garden and enjoying it in a vase on your windowsill until it withers and you are at last forced to give it back to the soil. Yet did you treasure it while it was there? Did you appreciate it forever? Of course you did!

Tom Ransom was definitely not for me, and I was never sad about that fact. I enjoyed him so much as a friend and fellow class disrupter that I am never regretful at only having the one legendary romantic moment with him. After all, what a great moment it was!

My senior year found Tom Ransom voted in as Class Clown, of course! I was voted (I shudder to think) Class Mouth—having never had trouble projecting my singing voice, silly jokes, or laughter. I went on to find the perfect man (*so* much more handsome than Ransom) and a wonderful life with countless fond memories of many people. I haven't seen ol' Handsome Ransom since graduation but did receive an e-mail from him a year or so ago. It was fun to find out he had married a girl who was my best little friend when we were both three years old and playing in kiddie pools in our backyards. They had a baby, and Tom? Well, he's a big real estate mogul in Albuquerque. Kind of fun, huh.

Tom Ransom earned a place in my memory—maybe for no giant, life-altering reason, but just because he was who he was. And because he owns a piece of my heart, his last name always stuck with me. It popped in and out of my brain over and over through the years until I found the perfect use for it—a legendary hero named Ransom Lake.

So there you have it—just a little something about the name Ransom and why I love it so much. It is a *cool* name, isn't it? Ah, good ol' Handsome Ransoms—I love them both!

After mulling it over in my mind for nearly ten years, I really can't tell you exactly why Ransom Lake is probably my most beloved hero. It's just who he is, I think—that he's our husbands, boyfriends, our romantic hero icon. He's mysterious and sexy—not to mention pumpkin-y somehow (or do I just think that because I love pumpkins so much and think of Vaden and

Ransom in the pumpkin patch every time I see the book?). He's so many things we girls love—handsome, shirt-less, scowling sometimes, and then when he smiles, *wow!*

In the end, we're just in love with Ransom Lake. In the end, we don't need a reason, right? In the end, I'm just so honored that readers have kept him in their hearts the way they have, that babies are named after him, that more people love pumpkins because of him. Ah, Ransom (heavy sigh). Thank you for loving Ransom with me.

~Marcia Lynn McClure

The Visions of Ransom Lake Trivia Snippets

Snippet #1—During the Christmas season the year I was fourteen, my dad opened the front door one morning to find a gift sitting on the porch and addressed to me. The note said, *To Marcia . . . From Your Secret Admirer.* I didn't recognize the handwriting, but I did recognize that it was a boy's handwriting—being that it was very straight-lined and nearly illegible. I opened the gift to find a beautiful silver bracelet, and I was stunned! I couldn't imagine who could have left the gift for me. But even so, it made my day and made me feel very special. The next morning there was another gift waiting on the front porch for me—a very pretty silver and turquoise necklace. I couldn't believe it! Another "from your secret admirer" note was with it, and I was overwhelmed with delight. Several more mornings, just before Christmas, found several more gifts for me on the front porch. I can't remember them all right now, but it was crazy—and wonderful! I knew that no one I actually liked at the time could've been doing it. The guy I liked most of the time was sort of off and on with his old girlfriend. So it couldn't have been him, right? Wrong! The last morning a gift was left on the front porch for me (I think it was Christmas Eve morning), my mom clapped her hands together and giggled as she saw what the gift was. "I knew it!" she exclaimed. "I knew it! It's Brandon Dailey." I asked her how she knew it was Brandon—because I did like Brandon, but he was so off and on with his old girlfriend that I couldn't imagine he really liked me, even though we hung out a lot and did a lot of stuff together. Mom laughed and pointed to the plate of perfectly made, delicious-looking pecan rolls. "Brandon's mother makes those. She's famous for them! Everyone knows she makes them." Yep, the last gift Brandon had left for me was a plate of the most delicious pecan rolls I've ever had in my entire life. I hurried to my room then and retrieved the school photo

Brandon had given to me months before. Turning it over to read the message on the back, I smiled; it was the same straight-lined, illegible printing that was on all the secret admirer notes. And, yes, this little story from my past is exactly where I got the idea for Ransom's leaving secret gifts (especially the pralines) on the Valmonts' front porch for Vaden. (This past winter I went to a matinee movie with my son Trent. As we got in the concessions line, the man in front of me ordered popcorn and a drink. At the sound of his voice, my head snapped up, nearly popping my head right off my shoulders! It was Brandon Dailey. I hadn't seen him in probably twenty years, but I would've known the sound of his voice anywhere. When he turned around, we hugged and exchanged happy greetings and catching ups. I smiled, having forgotten that he had a gold tooth (one of his lower ones) and suddenly remembering that it had been one of my favorite things about his appearance. I decided then and there that I need a hero with a gold tooth—don't you think?)

Snippet #2—Now, you already know that I *love* bacon. But do you know how long I've loved it— or how desperately? One day, when I was about two years old, my mom and dad noticed that my breath was not smelling baby-fresh. As they sniffed closer, they discovered the icky smell was coming from my nose. They whisked me off to the doctor, expecting to find that some horrible sinus infection or something had overcome me. But do you know what they found instead? That's right—bacon! I had secretly stuffed bacon up my nose a couple of days before. Gross—but funny! And from this story was borne the little incident of Vaden's stuffing beans up her Uncle Dan's nose.

Snippet #3—Did you know that the original orangeish cover of *The Visions of Ransom Lake* was designed using photos I had taken myself? The pumpkin patch in the foreground was a pumpkin patch where our little family used to go each fall to choose pumpkins for jack-o'-lanterns. The grassy meadow section with the big tree was actually taken at a cemetery in Ferndale, Washington. (The design artist removed the tombstones.) The creek and bridge were something the design artist added. You just never know with me, right?

Snippet #4—Snippet #3 leads us to Snippet #4 by asking the question, "Why is the new cover of *The Visions of Ransom Lake* so vastly different than the old one?" Well, the first reason is staying current. The old cover—the style of using land-scape and soft colors—was new and up to date when *The Visions of Ransom Lake* was first published. But I think readers also prejudged it, thinking it was something about a lake in the country that had psychic powers, you know? I love the pumpkins, but I decided it was time Ransom Lake got the attention he deserves! And I wanted the book cover to more readily reflect the fuller story of the book. I know we will all always cherish the first pumpkin-y cover of *The Visions of Ransom Lake*, but I do hope you'll embrace the proxy for Handsome Ransom on this new cover too. At least the handsome part (nose, chin, jaw, whisker stubble—gotta love it!). Snippet #5—Here's a trivia tidbit for you. In late 2002, *The Visions of Ransom Lake* was pulled from the shelves of one of the biggest bookstore chains in the United States. Why? Because it had one complaint lodged against its content. The scene where Ransom kisses Vaden in the ally? You know, when he pushes her up against the building and takes off her mittens? Well, one customer was absolutely appalled at the way Ransom unbuttoned Vaden's coat before he kissed her. Thus, she lodged a complaint to the bookstore chain, and the bookstore chain pulled *The Visions of Ransom Lake* from its shelves. Crazy, right?

Snippet #6—I've always been a Rock Hound. My mother was and is a Rock Hound, and one of her brothers is a Rock Hound. In fact, the only school club I ever belonged to was the Rock Hound club (fourth grade). There's nothing like a good rock, you know? Rocks intrigue me. I've always loved them. And with that goes the fact that I've always been mesmerized by geodes. They're so pretty; I just love them! I love to get one and hold it under the light or in the sunshine and just watch the crystals sparkle. Well, when I was a tweener (young teenager), one summer my friend Bobbie (she lived across the street) and I used to go into my driveway, search for rocks that held promise, and bust them open using a hammer and a small chisel. I don't know where in the world the rocks in our driveway were quarried from, but almost every rock we busted open that summer had a small hollowed space inside filled with tiny crystals. Why in the world we were dumb enough to bust rocks with a hammer I'll never know. We're lucky we didn't put an eye out. Still, we had so much fun searching for treasure (small geodes) in my driveway that year. I love geodes. Hmmm—you know who else loves geodes? Ransom Lake! What a coincidence.

Snippet #7—I thought I'd leave you with something kind of corny as the final snippet for today. It's Tom Ransom's signature in my 1981 yearbook—the year *before* our legendary consummate kiss. Here it is:

Dearest Marcia,
You have been the light of my life
ever since I met you!!!
During 3rd period you gave me chills up and
down my spine with your luscious body
and wonderful personality!!!
Good luck in whatever you do!
Love,
Tom Ransom

How sweet, huh? Yep, good old Handsome Ransom. You gotta love him.

My everlasting admiration, gratitude and love . . .
To my husband, Kevin . . .
My inspiration . . .
My heart's desire . . .
The man of my every dream!

ABOUT THE AUTHOR

Marcia Lynn McClure's intoxicating succession of novels, novellas, and e-books—including *The Visions of Ransom Lake*, *A Crimson Frost*, *The Rogue Knight*, and most recently *The Pirate Ruse*—has established her as one of the most favored and engaging authors of true romance. Her unprecedented forte in weaving captivating stories of western, medieval, regency, and contemporary amour void of brusque intimacy has earned her the title "The Queen of Kissing."

Marcia, who was born in Albuquerque, New Mexico, has spent her life intrigued with people, history, love, and romance. A wife, mother, grandmother, family historian, poet, and author, Marcia Lynn McClure spins her tales of splendor for the sake of offering respite through the beauty, mirth, and delight of a worthwhile and wonderful story.

Center Point Large Print
600 Brooks Road / PO Box 1
Thorndike, ME 04986-0001 USA

(207) 568-3717

US & Canada:
1 800 929-9108
www.centerpointlargeprint.com